ASCENSION

NOUMIN

ISBN 979-8-73664-910-5

Contents

Acknowledgements

This book wouldn't have been possible if it hadn't been for the influences of Alan Moore, Frank Miller & Stan Lee. Their writing and character designs are what stuck with shaping my view of what storytelling was. Daredevil & Batman in particular were the greatest of influencers. That led to my interest in books that had deeper themes. 1984, Moby Dick & Dune are my particular favourites. I hope to at least echo these great artists and masterpieces with my writing and provide the readers with the experience that I had watching the stories unfold.

While there were influences that led to the creation of this book, there were some that made it what it has become today. Family in particular are always helpful when you begin the start of a new journey. Mine was just as supportive as I wanted them to be. Especially my father learning about copyright law just to protect what was yet not finished. Someone in particular that had been actively helpful was my sister Shailee who designed the cover for the book. Her active inputs also helped shape the contents that are presented today. When it came to the actual storyline, a few people were influencing it more than they had known. My discussions on morality with Kaviraj, the constant fighting knowledge from Darshan, the humourous jabs from Harshil and the ever-present support from Parin were all that had shaped the characters, their behaviours and the storyline.

I thank all of you for helping me along this wonderful journey. Whatever may lie in the future, this book will always be your gift to me.

"*The misery that is now upon us is
but the passing of greed,
the bitterness of men
who fear the way of human progress.
The hate of men will pass,
and dictators die,
and the power they took from the people
will return to the people.
And so long as men die,
liberty will never perish.*"

- *Charlie Chaplin, The Great Dictator*

Prologue

Yaatnāh. It was Yashpal's dream to be the Mayor of the biggest city in the country. And he was right on the verge of achieving it. Just 28 days and he would be giving the test of his lifetime. According to the recent polls, Yashpal Vohra and his Union of National Citizens (UNC) were leading in 4 of the 9 sectors. Out of the remaining, 3 were favourable for the old Democratic People's Party (DPP) and 2 were favoured for the Communist Worker's Block (CWB). These were the only three parties representing the people of the city. While DPP CWB had always been a national front, it was UNC that was home-grown. Therefore, it had a connection with the people of the city. It was known throughout the city that Yashpal worked as a social activist for the past few years. He had formed the party after his unconstitutional arrest by the sitting Mayor Devendra Kasbekar and his DPP. UNC in its first month of establishment registered over 6 lakh members, an unbeaten record. The support for Yashpal and his party was overwhelming as people were tired of the corrupt administration of the ruling party. A successful campaign ran by UNC for over eight months had led to a shift in the status quo of the election. DPP's reign was challenged for the first time in 20 years. Despite the threat to their rule, no other steps regarding the campaign had been taken. DPP had even refused to appear on TV debate against Yashpal. Such has been his impact.

DPP's rule over Yaatnāh in the past 10 years had brought along more sorrow than infrastructure. The employment rate had dipped down, the growth of the economy was stagnant and the healthcare was non-existent. For this election cycle, there was a glimmer of hope. A ray of sunshine that the people of this city could cling to for escape. His belief to rid this system of nepotistic self-serving individuals that work with the corporations is what connected him to the people. However, some critics claimed that the cult of personality that Yashpal had formed would be very bad for the future of politics. His followers had transformed Yashpal's identity into that of a demagogue. Although Yashpal didn't mind the critics, his followers had formed the habit of painting the opposition's face with ink. It had boiled down to a war-like mentality that might not be a sight to observe in the near future.

Yashpal has claimed to be from Sector 9. It was where the city began; it was genesis. Yaatnāh grew larger due to the Port on its southern shores. Old kings started trading with the rest of the world from that very spot. As the city grew, so did the port. Only to a certain point though. The port at Sector 9 is where the Battle of Red River at the peak of the Kaalvasarah War was fought and won. The war had impacted the entire city's life. However, the effects of the were only visible only in the 9th. The rest of the city has recovered from it, visually at least but not this Sector. Here, the old buildings still stand like a story never to be forgotten. The Old Port located at the southernmost point of the city was a historical landmark for the city. It was one of the largest at the time of its opening famed for its architecture and advanced machinery. The Port, however, is what brought unwanted attention to the city during that war. The battles fought here for strategic advantage were brutal and legendary. Its people and the role it played during the war of Laksharuh raised its status on an international level. It always was a cultural capital for the country but the wartime legends gave it the honorary title of Stronghold. The city changed after the war. Especially when Kaalvasarah War reached its shores. The majesty of war looked great on television and glorious in speeches, but when reality hit them, it brought them all down like a pile of bricks. The old port is now used mainly by local fishermen and ship disassembling companies.

Another issue that has risen for the city was in the form of a masked vigilante, a hero or just a criminal. Whichever way one looks, the actions of the man had brought about change that had been appreciated by the citizens. The black mask has managed to wipe out three major gangs from the city and scared the rest into reducing their operations. His methods were simple; kill the criminal and the crime disappears. This method of crime-fighting although quite popular, still had its opposition. The argument boiled down to how people were processing their anger with the system. Those who supported violence were arguing that it had become a necessity, the ultimate solution to the city's rising crime problem. The death of violent offenders was celebrated. The flip side of this debate was that it wasn't a solution but rather a simple way out. In the long term, there would be a rise in crime due to the violent nature of society. The ruthlessness would not hold the civilization intact and bring everything tumbling down like a giant Jenga tower.

One of the oppositions to the vigilante was Senior Inspector A.H. Khan, 9th Sector, YCPD. He had tried his best to get on the job but the powers that may be denied it at every opportunity. He had his eye on the case and was hoping for a way to squeeze himself in to not only bring the criminal to justice but also to mend his tarnished past.

CHAPTER ONE

Another Day at Work

Crimson light, grey smoke and the sound of burning tobacco were occupying the complete attention of Khan. Each drag gave a subtle high that diverted his attention from the fact he was unable to sleep. Maybe it was a dream that woke him up or he never fell asleep. It didn't matter now. All that mattered was the pleasure of each puff. This felt sort of like a routine for Khan. On many occasions, he had found himself enjoying the government issued cigars. This box was gifted to him by a former subordinate a good while ago. They were his favourite, but very expensive. All of the legal highs were expensive due to government regulations and restrictions but cigars were at the top of the list. More tax was stamped on a box a cigar than a premium bottle of whiskey. Add to that the fact that no private business was authorized to manufacture cigars, and you get a tax for people with good taste as Khan called it. The ticking of the clock faded in every so often. It was faint but still audible. Curiosity got the best of him. It was 4 AM. Just 3 hours to his shift, yet he felt no more rested than he did hours ago. Tomorrow will be a stretch he thought. No point worrying about that now. So, he returned his attention to the flying ambers and the smoke of the cigar, taking each hit slowly.

The next drag however was also carrying a faint buzzing noise. For a moment Khan wondered whether he really had heard anything and halted his usually long drags. His suspicion was confirmed. It was a buzzing noise; his phone. He used to keep it with him always. It would rarely happen that Khan would be called in after his shift ended, though there was a particularly noteworthy incident when this occurred five years ago. A notorious serial killer was found alongside his latest victims with a kitchen knife in his throat. That's what Khan's mind went to every time his phone buzzed. Today was no exception. He answered without a glance at the screen and the voice on the other side spoke with a panic.

"I am sorry to disturb you, sir. But we need you. It looks like one of those killings." It was Deputy Senior Inspector Mahesh Talpade.

"Hmph" Khan replied indicating Talpade to go on. Khan knew that Talpade had handled important cases. He wouldn't have called Khan if there wasn't a real concern. By one of those killings Talpade was indicating at the Vigilante's Rampage; that's what the media had dubbed it to be. He swiftly stood up and walked towards his jacket that was on his other sofa.

Talpade familiar with his superior's conversational habits went on to explain more. "Shinde took Joshi out on patrol as a part of his training. They were near the Talegaonkar Theatre; the abandoned one when they spotted the 8 men dead in the compound. The forensics team is here along with Mishra and half the city's media." As he was explaining the situation, Khan had abandoned his cigar, put on his jacket, took his keys, wallet and walked out of his house. He rushed down the stairs as his elevator always caused network issues. By the time Talpade was at the end of his explanation, Khan had already reached his car. He replied, "Tell forensics to take multiple pictures and sweep the nearby area for evidence as well. Get Joshi to pull out the records and quickly get the identification of the dead." He continued, "We also need to check whether anyone saw what happened. Check with the residents of nearby buildings if there are any and get them to talk as much you can. Even check for the people sleeping nearby, there are always some around. But more importantly, be polite. You don't want them talking to media about us at all." Khan was worried that the residents might assume the questioning as interrogation and create a fuss in the middle of the important case. "You and Mishra get in contact with your informers. And most importantly no one talks to the media. No details of this case should get into their hands. I don't want them to declare another victory for that bastard."

"Okay, sir-" was all that Talpade could slip into the conversation before Khan hung up. Khan didn't even bother putting on the seatbelt as he got into the car. His standard-issue patrol SUV started with a slight delay. It usually did with cold weather. One of the drawbacks of diesel. He pulled out of his parking with a vigour he hadn't shown in a while. The Talegaonkar Theatre had been abandoned for the past 5 years. It went out of business due to financial issues and was scheduled to be resold. But in this case, the owner moved away and the theatre still hasn't been bought out by anyone. Once a piece of architectural marvel for the city, now ransacked by the druggies because of the available hiding spots. Patrolling around that area was in the regular schedule as it discouraged mass gatherings of addicts turning it into a squatters' hole. The theatre was located on the South-West section of Sector 7 near the tri-intersection borders. In this case Sectors 6, 7 & 8. On the way there, Khan was praying for it to not be another Vigilante's Rampage case as called by the media. This would be the 7th of these sort of killings and with every one media's & public's attitude to this blatant murder was disgusting Khan. Their disregard for law & order was shocking for him. Maybe it was his time in the army or maybe it was an innate desire for justice. He could no longer tell whether his disgust was natural or brought on by his experience. All that mattered now was to get away from that feeling. With years in the police force, Khan was getting numb to the idea of justice. It had been a long time since he saw it. Even with his last major case justice wasn't delivered. The killer was arrested but murdered on the way to the court. People of the city along with the media hailed it as the greatest example of Instant Justice. The truth couldn't have been further from that. Failure to catch the killer on time put Khan in the target sights due to which he was transferred to the quieter Sector 7. Where his biggest concern was a gang of weak heroin addicts.

Nearing the theatre, Khan spotted seven news vans with the dish antennas on the main road with a few even parked around the corner. They weren't usually hard to spot during day-time, however, at this time of night, they stood out like a high visibility jacket. The drive around that corner gave a glimpse of what would it be like on the morning news. Papers, tabloids, TV, Radio, all will be covering this news. The entrance to the theatre was the end of a street named after an insignificant politician. At least that's what Khan thought the honour would feel like. Insignificant. The journalists were being held off at the halfway point at the street by two parked police cars, the usual yellow tape surrounding them and three constables. Khan now preparing for the inevitable, drove towards the police cars. Parking on the left side of the street very close to one of the police cars, he was hoping to slip by. As soon as he went ahead to open the door, he knew this would push him right back to the wolves. Before he could even step out a reporter rushed to his car door followed by several others like sharks towards chum. Phasing them out, he waded through the reporters with the help of one of his subordinates and walked over to the scene. Talpade was ready to brief. But Khan raised his hand to halt Talpade in his steps. "Which moron talked?" were the first words that came out of Khan's mouth.

Talpade was expecting this question, just not put this way. He replied, "They reached here in hoards. It was like they knew about it already."

"Of course they came in hoards. Because a moron here or maybe at the HQ talked." Replied annoyed Khan. "At least wait till the crime scene has been examined." he continued as he reached the crime scene. The compound of the theatre was where the incident took place. The gates had a narrow driveway that could fit just about a medium-size van. The driveway was quite short in length opening up to the wide compound that served as an entrance to the theatre as well as the underground parking lot. The parking lot was straight ahead while the theatre entrance was to the start. There was a yellow tape starting from a large rusted dustbin that sat around the corner of the driveway to the wall opposite it. Behind the line were two forensic analysts that were examining the last body, someone photographing the bodies and two officers with a flashlight looking for scattered evidence. Eight bodies were lying in strategically defensive areas while the rest three were lying facing the opposite direction. As he and Talpade walked near the crime scene, something unusual occurred to Khan. The coordinated defence pattern was quite a usual one used to defend the area from the enemy. However, there were fewer bullets than one could have anticipated in such a situation.

This was what he was best at. Crime Scene Investigation. His experience of human behaviour was second only to his ability to concentrate on the moment. He had the ability to phase out every sound, person and distraction on the scene to focus only on the things that mattered. Using this ability, he quickly picked up things that would not seem so obvious to anyone else. As he carefully walks around a puddle of blood, most possibly from the first body, Talpade began his brief. But he was stopped by Khan. Cuts on the victim showed precise yet chaotic movements. There was skill but there was also madness and anger behind the attack. It seemed that the final cut was on the throat to finish off the victim.

Khan now clear of his thought indicated Talpade to start his brief. So, pointing at the victims he began, "Seven of these men are members of the Z0 tribe. The eighth member" - pointing to the furthest lying body, "seems to be a new initiate. There are two cases under his name or possible alias for chain snatching."

Khan interrupts, "Chain snatcher with the Z0?" without glancing towards Talpade.

Talpade replies trying to add possible justification for such an amateur decision, "Could be that he tagged along with one of his friends hoping to find a place in the gang." He pauses for Khan's reply but continues after a brief pause. "According to the forensics, all of them died around an hour ago either from their stabbing wounds or eventual blood loss. Three of them have straightforward cuts to their throats, the rest of them however have some form of secondary cuts. They will give their full report by tomorrow morning."

He moves over to the next two bodies that lie close by behind the massive steel dust bin. There were similar marks on the body. It was providence for Khan to stumble on such an important crime scene. There was only one other assault that had knife wounds involved. But it was considered to be such an outlier, there was no further thought given to it. For a second the thought of this not being the same perp did enter Khan's head but he dismissed it quickly. Partially because the victims were professional, hardened criminals and also because the cuts were too precise for any killer's skill. There were certain members of the community that could cut with such precision but usually, they had a medical license. The only other answer could have been a professional assassin hired to take members out. But then the question remained, who hired the professional? Khan now near the third victim was looking for any anomaly that would establish a connection to the man in the black. But as usual, there wasn't any.

Talpade pauses and looks at his superior who was now too close to the fourth victim. Khan was lifting the victim's left arm with his own thumb. Examining it carefully he dropped it as soon as he was done. Talpade was curious to find the motive behind Khan's action. But he knew there wasn't going to be an ex planation until later. Despite that, he waited for a moment but after no response from Khan, he continued, "There are no functional vehicles around but we did find some tyre marks in the underground looking for an

SUV or a large sedan with some sort of illegal substance or cash. Other stations have been informed and asked to search every car matching that description."

"That might just be a waste of time. The victims were dead an hour ago and it takes a human approximately five minutes to die from blood loss giving our perps 50 good, calm, panic-free minutes to switch vehicles." Khan replied as he stood up and walked straight to the final victim whose body was in a left-leaning sitting position with his back against the wall. There were blood splatter stains on the wall with droplets and marks all the way down to his body.

Talpade was following Khan and responded to his remark, "Perps?". This line of inquiry was to confirm that his superior suspected that more than one aggressor was involved with the crime.

"Probably." Khan dismissed his query without further information. Talpade not sure whether to poke this certain topic continued with his brief. "This is the chain snatcher. He only had a single cut across the throat. No visible bruises or initial signs of struggle."

"Two oddballs, no three oddballs in one go. There is no doubt that this was the man in black but why change his tactics? It is almost as if he was mocking them by showing off his skills. Putting these otherwise scary criminals into a frenzy." Khan now almost excited at what this case would entail started walking around to the underground parking entrance. Talpade, caught off-guard rushed to follow Khan and continued, "We have swept the underground as well. There were tyre marks near the parking spot and another near the turning point. They seem to be either from a small van or an SUV. We have put out an ATL." Talpade heisting, murmured "He has never stolen from a scene. Maybe it is someone else."

Khan with a slight surprise replied, "So the murders were fine. But the theft-." Khan now piqued with his subordinate's behaviour continued, "You as a policeman are bound by a duty to uphold the law. Don't you dare take sides?" Talpade wasn't taking any sides but the remark had ticked off Khan. He continued, "Especially of someone who has possibly murdered eighteen people. Murdered! Have some conscience." Khan with his head shaking spotted one of the juniors walked towards Talpade with his walkie at chest level, drawing attention to it. "Sir, Sector 4 found a van. They think it's the one we are looking for." Talpade and Khan shared a surprised glance before Talpade took the walkie and raised its volume. "DSI Talpade here, where did you find the van? Over."

"Outside our police station. Over."

"Can you confirm it is the one we are looking for? Over." "Yes. There is a body and two bags of Substance 99. Over"

"We are sending the forensics, have them check for any evidence. Did anyone get a look at the driver?"

"No. Someone must have snuck it in while we were scrambling to get the roadblock in our sector."

Khan still staring at the body under his breath mutters, "They'll never find any evidence."

Khan now sure there was something bigger at play, decides the only way to be sure was to catch the man in black. First things first though. The media and people of the city needed answers. As he prepared himself, Khan realised that the last time he appeared in front of the entire media platoon was during the Black Sunday Killings and that didn't go well. But after 6 years, he has been preparing himself so as to not create another debacle. Approaching the gathered media circus, he prepares himself by counting down from 10. His usual technique to calm himself. He raises both of his arms and waves to the journalists to quieten down and proceeds to take control of the situation by saying, "Silence, please. I will answer all of your questions. Please ask politely and one at a time." And indicates to the lady nearest to him.

"Sir, is this another incident of the Vigilante's Rampage? Was the masked man involved in this case?" she asked as soon as she saw

the finger.

"First of all," now counting down from 10 again in his mind he continued, "there is no proof or any witness to suggest that this was the masked man. Please do not promote vigilant-"

"What else could it be?" he interrupted knowing full well that it was very much a gang killing like the other. "If it was another gang that was wiped out and justice severed, then isn't it good for the public to find out?"

"Are you a journalist or a fan? This man has been killing people left and right and you think this is justice served?" realising what he had stepped into, Khan stopped himself. But not soon enough.

The man next to her jumped at the chance and asked, "So it was the man in black. What gang members did he serve justice to this time?"

"You didn't answer which gang was involved." Interrupted the journalist.

With an inaudible but visible sigh, Khan replied, "The gang involved was Z0. But I repeat again, there is no evidence he-"

Interrupted again by another journalist, "Z0 operates usually near the new docks. Why was the gang here? And how many were involved?"

Khan now realising that this conversation was no longer in his hands tried to keep it on track by a thread. "8 members of the gang were involved in what currently appears to be a drug deal gone wrong."

Without missing a beat, the lady at the front went, "Did you find the drugs or cash to be used in the deal?"

To which Khan replied, "Yes we have found the evidence that suggests a drug-"

Again, there was an interruption, "Will officers Panditya & Shah

take over the case or does this fall under your jurisdiction?"

"We will." Replied a voice from the back of the assembled journalists and reporters. Unknown to either Khan or the assembled media standing over there, Detective Panditya Suri & Rishabh Shah had been at the scene for a few minutes. Their reply turned the reporters' attention along with their cameras towards the two detectives.

Shah continued, "This case has been handed to us personally by our Honorable Mayor Mr Devendra Kasbekar. And with all of his confidence along with the people of this city, we will solve this case and make sure that the guilty parties are convicted and tried in a fair and unbiased trial."

Sristi Pai, a prominent ground reporter went, "What about the fact that this man in black is helping the police clean up the city? Will you take that into consideration while working on this case."

The other detective replied, "I understand that the people believe in this man cleaning up the streets and doing good for the society, but I can assure you we are agents of the law. We will be unbiased in his treatment. If the motives and intentions are clean and worth the high praise that he is receiving, then not only will he be recognised as the same in the eyes of the law but will also be free of any prosecution. Thank You all for your time. I hope the next time we see you is when we have caught the guilty party." With that, the detectives left the scene.

Khan during all of this had moved towards his car and got in. He sat there trying to move away from the circus. The end of the detective's interview freed other constable's attention and they started to help Khan's car pull out of the street. As he turned around to join the main road, his phone rang. CG Azad was on the caller id. It took a while to prepare himself but he answered the call eventually.

"You still haven't learned, have you?" a stern and tenor voice stated

on the other side of the line. It was Laxmi Singh Azad, Commissioner General of Police, Yaatnāh. As Khan's former subordinate officer, Laxmi had known him for the better part of twenty years. Since Khan's dismissal from the army, they had lost contact and only came back when Laxmi joined the force six years ago. Their working relationship had been deteriorating slowly and with every passing year, came the realization that they no longer shared the bond that was in those army days. The relationship was now respectful but distant. Laxmi sometimes used to lean for a playful conversation but Khan never budged.

"I have my weaknesses. If I knew or wanted to get in bed with the media, then I would have taken your seat" replied Khan.

Laxmi was interrupted by Khan, "Dream On. Having media on your side has its perks. You can-"

"Cover up your laziness and get more time on cases?" Khan spoke with a snide tone. Laxmi still willing to poke went on, "Or you can even hide your incompetency in catching a criminal that lived under your nose."

This was a jab at Khan's failure that lead to his transfer. He wasn't impressed with the joke and replied, "How can I help you Commissioner Madam?"

Realizing that Khan wasn't playing even today, Laxmi went on, "How is it looking so far? Any clues to identify the bastard?"

Khan was glad to be sharing the same feeling on this case. He said, "Nothing more than further evidence proving he is not a hero for the people." He continued, "We found the van but there was just the 99 in it. No money. Chances are the bastard took it and then parked the car at the station to look like a hero. The victims were killed with a knife, that's the only curious thing."

"That anomaly you insisted should be looked into?"

"Yeah, this however is not a good sign."

"Because he has multiple skills as well?"

"Maybe, but it could also hint at either a copy-cat or a partner."

Laxmi replied, "The dynamic duo won't like the idea." After a pause, she continued, "How did he manage to kill gun-carrying criminals with a knife?"

Khan explained, "Probably fear. If you create the idea that bullets don't hurt you then they won't even try. Quite simple."

Laxmi with a sigh said, "I am sorry that I couldn't hand this case over to you." There was no reply on the other end. So, she continued. "The order came directly from the mayor. And he doesn't listen to anyone except his yes-men anymore. You were my first choice but trust me Panditya & Shah will do just fine."

"Yes, they were quite good talking to the press earlier," he commented.

"You know, after all these years I thought I would be used to all of this. But no. It still surprises me that people care more about what people think of them rather than just doing their job."

"Welcome to the world Inspector Khan."

Khan didn't appreciate the sarcasm, "Thank You."

Laxmi continued, "But you have to understand that there are other people who do their job. Maybe not to the extent or the way you. But most of them will finish the job. And in this case, they will do their job and catch the criminal."

"Some of the cops here already hail him as a hero. They won't work to catch the guy but rather help him. I will handle the case myself, under the radar."

"I cannot authorise that."

Khan paused but continued after a while, "Then don't. This conversation never happened."

"What if someone discovers your little plan?" "We will cross that bridge when we get there."

Laxmi wanted to argue her point. She wanted Khan to stay away from another high profile case, but she also knew that it was impossible to keep him. He would have just gone around her as well to finish the job. So she accepted Khan's decision and proceeded to help him with the rule being that she would get regular updates this way. She had thought of something else, "No point assigning you a partner is there?"

"No."

"Fine then. But you have to keep up the appearances and work on your administrative duties. Also, update me regularly."

"Sure, not an issue."

Laxmi was happy that Khan agreed with the last part. Even though he was difficult to work with sometimes, there was no denying the extent of his skills. She had seen it firsthand working under him. His obsession with the work drove him away from people most of the times but it didn't matter to Khan. Laxmi then asked something else that Khan had ignored, "Why haven't you visited him? You know he can help."

"Who?" after a short pause, "Oh! Him. He's a politician, not a detective. What can he do? Make a speech to motivate me?"

"That's not what I was talking about. Your public perception matters. It seems people associated with him also get that respect from the media and the public. It will help you work with ease." "Is that an officer's top priority? To have a good public image?"

"No. But-"

"Look you may give a shit about what people have to say about you and your work. I only need to know what I do is right."

"Whatever. I rather not fight with you on that topic. Tell me about

the crime scene. You should already have a profile sketched out. Wouldn't you?"

"No, not as much as I would like." "I don't believe that for a second."

"This one is trickier than I thought of before." "How so?"

"First, these murders are too precise and well planned for a vigilante or a wannabe hero. There seems to be an extensive understanding of the location and the situation. That requires skills. Secondly, this one is far different from the other ones. Not just in terms of weapons, there are also things missing and clues left behind. Previous cases as far as I read had no clues and were committed with a gun. My theory from what I saw today is that there are two of them. Both are equally trained in close-quarter combat and weapons by an expert. Possibly military. One of them prefers guns and the other knife. And that one of them appears to be sloppy."

"Sloppy? How?"

"Tyre marks in the underground parking lot." "But that doesn't mean anything."

"Any other criminal I would say the same. But this guy has been cleaning up everything, right up to boot prints. Why would he drive like an idiot and leave track marks?"

"I would say they were incidental. They did leave the car outside a police station. Marks wouldn't have mattered."

"I get what you are trying to say but hear me out. This clean and precise working pattern is like any other type of habit. You have to train yourself to do the same. One of these guys has the habit of clean up and precise action. The other does not."

"But it didn't matter in the end though."

"I know. But that also adds to the theory that there are two guys

with some doubt. They might not be associated altogether but I would like to believe that they are. And a sloppier one is easy to find rather than the clean one."

"And how would you find the sloppier one?"

"Chances are that they have been committing these crimes as a pair. And just this once, the second one got involved in the action. It's-"

"That's a long shot."

"I know but that's all we have right now. How else are we going to find these guys?"

"Other than waiting for another crime, I have no idea. There aren't even any patterns other than their targets."

"They have inside knowledge of the deals happening in these gangs and have an ulterior motive that is yet to be discovered. There is no pattern to their attack or at least no one that I could find. The possible goal could be to eliminate all gangs to establish themselves as superior but that seems too simple."

"I know where this is going. You are going to revisit previous files and crime scenes. When-"

"I know how to be careful. After all-"

"No, you don't. You won't be given access to those files. Not just because Panditya and Shah have them, but the copies will be stored in the records room for my eyes only. You will need my help to get in there.

"Okay. You know even after all these years, it is still bizarre for me to be taking orders from you."

"And also, advice. Advice on social skills that is."

"Alright. Thanks. I will try and update you as and when I can." "Yes, and if you don't I will transfer you to the east."

And that was the end of their conversation. While driving to his police station, a thought occurred to him. This was the longest conversation he had with Laxmi in over a decade. He thought about how they had changed over the years. Some for good, others not so much. But that's how it goes. Khan had his eyes set on the goal and had already started calculating the killer's next move. His only concern now was to prove to the people around that this guy was not as helpful as he appeared. And in the eyes of the law and Khan, he was a murderer and so were the people helping him. The mystery though still surrounded his ultimate movies. As he pulled into the station compound and parked his car, a rare feeling emerged through his spine. Something he hadn't felt in a long time. It was excitement but encased with a thick layer of nervousness. While this case was about justice for the people, it was also a way he could do something about things that mattered in the world again. Not turning into just another paper-pushing sign-off.

Meanwhile, on the other side of the city, in Sector 9 Saint's Refuge was woken up by loud and violent banging on its door.

CHAPTER TWO

DUTY &
MISTAKES

In the Eastern section of the study room, under the dim amber light, sits an open white book with old cream leaves. A raspy tenor voice with a soft whisper reads "Were there always these vistas of rotting nineteenth-century houses, their sides shored up -". Chirag had taken up the hobby of reading books he often heard of in college. However, between his 9-hour shift working at the Relifx Infotech as a programmer and volunteering at Saint's Refuge, he rarely had the chance to take up any hobby. But with some time management, he learnt from a colleague he had taken up reading at his pace. His current target was to read 4 pages every day which started from 1 page a day. Volunteering was something that came by association with Purav. Purav grew up in Saint's Refuge and came to give something back like many others. Chirag got into the habit of helping at the shelter through his school buddy. The school friends went on to college together but were separated by their jobs. Their close friendship stayed so until Purav's accident. Volunteering now also became a way to keep Purav's memory alive at Saint's Refuge. Opened up by an industrial tycoon some of 40 years ago as an orphanage, it was a landmark back in the day. People were praising the advances and generosity of the city to start such a project. Kids from around the villages who has lost their parents were housed here and given every comfort possible to turn into a nice human being. It hosted the largest annual fundraiser for charity in the country. Sadly, like always the world moved on. The donations began dropping every year. The final blow was dealt with the arrival of the Kaalvasarah War. The place became a safe haven for the army rather than the kids. All of them were moved to other safer refuges in the city for safety. After the war, most of the kids didn't return. Neither did most of the charitable compatriots. The refuge then ran only on the support of local residents that had a connection to the place and its people. Since then, even the kids that grew up and moved out of the house have returned favours to the refuge in some way or the other.

As Chirag progressed onto his goal for the day, "He had set his features into the expression of quiet optimism which it was advisable to wear when -", a hard but muffled bang distracted him. It alarmed him, but also mind took a few seconds to process the sound as it was so strange. The second bang, however, was louder. So much louder that he turned around and sprung up, rushed to check on the noise without realizing. Reaching his office door, as soon as he turned the knob, it swung open and standing there were 3 men. The first, gigantic specimen of a man had what looked like a bat. The two right behind him were also carrying some sort of melee weapon. They appeared to be large bulky and well built, like terminators. At least the first person was. But by the time he could register any other detail, the man standing nearest to him raised his arm along with the weapon and hit him on his head. As soon as Chirag was hit, his legs buckled up and he fell to the ground. The pain took a while to register but as soon as it came, it was like a Tsunami. It washed over every other sensation or feeling. No matter how much Chirag pressed his head with his arms, the pain was the only thing he felt. Not even the feeling of wet arms or the trail of red liquid running down his eye mattered to him. He was washed down with the worst emotion of the human mind. And then came the thought that all of us dread. 'Is this it?' His brain couldn't keep up anymore and with that, Chirag lost consciousness. The next image that his eyes and mind were presented with were at the very least comforting. Lying on the stretcher being carried by two paramedics, Chirag felt his hand being held tightly by Acharya.

Even though he saw Acharya's lips move, he couldn't hear anything. He tried to speak but before he could form a sentence, that dreadful wave of pain came rushing back. He saw red and blue lights through his peripheral and heard at least what he thought was, "You will be alright." His hearing came back, though muffled. With that, he was in a silver room which he soon realized was an ambulance. As it started moving, one of the paramedics reached near him and gave him an injection of what he later would realize was a painkiller. With that, the wave of pain started fading away slowly along with the sensations in his body. His last thoughts before passing out were trying to remember what had happened. All his mind flashed was the image of Acharya with a bleeding forehead.

Acharya was Chirag's official senior but he preferred to call himself a fellowman. Acharya was one of the people who had raised Purav. Chirag knew of Acharya but became familiar and familial to him after his volunteering duties for Saint's Refuge. Acharya was the senior-most official and the longest-reigning head of this Organization. His role while limited, was still of the utmost importance. Although not many knew of how Acharya came about working in this place, it was known around the Sector that he along with his wife served as medics during the 2nd War where he lost her to a rogue bomb attack. His refusal to talk any more than this to anyone is what has kept his personal life a complete mystery to everyone.

As soon as the door of the ambulance were shut, Acharya was called back by the two policemen who were interrogating him regarding the incident. They restarted their line of inquiry, "So, as soon as you opened the door, you saw uh-" looking at his notes he continued, "Chirag getting hit on his head. What happened next?" Acharya still a little distracted by Chirag's injuries was snapped back to attention by the policeman. He went on about the incident, "Yes. I am sorry. Two of those guys shifted their attention to me and rushed to attack me while one of them locked the door of the study room trapping in Chirag. As the two of them came towards me I prepared myself to defend. I blocked a straight swing from one of the guys -" This line had one of the officers smirking in disbelief and interrupt, "You blocked a swing? From what you described as well- built guys around

6 and a half feet in height?" The second officer realising the uncomfortable nature of the situation poked his colleague with his elbow gesturing him into quietening down. Looking at Acharya with an apologetic face he said, "Please go on."

Still shocked that this was what the officer had a problem believing, Acharya swiftly moved on to the incident and continued, "Yes, as I dodged his swing, I tried to get both of them to the ground but failed." Wanting to move this conversation to the real issue, he decided to skip on ahead to him getting knocked down. But in reality, as both the attacker had moved in to attack. The other one had raised his arms half expecting not to go through with it. Achara's dodge caught him off guard and he managed to throw in a punch to his liver, shocking his body from pain. After which turned around to catch the first attacker in a sleeper chock hold hoping to swing him around to face the third person. However, his age and the weakness that came with it had escaped Acharya's mind. He was unable to move the first attacker around which gave an opportunity to the third attacker who was done trapping Chirag to rush towards Acharya and attack him. Instincts telling him that this was a vulnerable position, Acharya started to loosen the grip which led to him being thrown back by the first attacker. Now the attack from the third attacker landed on his shoulder rather than his head. Even though this swing was painful, it wouldn't have been as painful as it would have felt on his head or neck. Having attacked Acharya on his shoulder, the third attacker had now started to kick and punch now staggering old man assisted by his thug colleague. After taking on two muscled men, with only one arm, Acharya was no longer on the front foot. His defence was using the bruised arm to take in all of the possible blows and save the other for any other opportunity to attack. As he had laid down from the storm of kicks, he noticed that two other men had entered the room and had started walking towards the stairs.

Acharya continued, "At that point, I saw two other men walk through the door while the others were beating me. I presumed that it was their boss that had hit me on the head and tied up. The other volunteers were locked up in the living quarters before they could do anything."

At this point the compassionate officer raised his pen and asked Acharya, "You said that one of them ordered the others, correct?"

Quickly realising what the officer was getting at, Acharya responded, "Yes, he spoke English but at the end of the sentence, he spoke a strange language. I am guessing, Ghusedi"

Officer continued this line of inquiry, "What was the word?

Maybe we can get it confirmed." "Zhǎodào háizi"

The officer noted down the word but also looked towards his colleague hoping to ask him about it. However, at this point, he had turned around was completely disinterested. Not wanting to stretch this any further, the compassionate officer asked the old man to continue.

"Two of them stood right above me pointing their guns while the other 3 went upstairs and started going through the kids' room. One of the fellows standing above me joined the others upstairs after being called and stayed there for a few minutes. That's when I started hearing screams from the kids. After a while, they came down with two kids each and took them outside. They continued the process again. I tried-"

Hearing the desperation in Acharya's voice, the officer tried to console him by placing a hand on his shoulder.

Acharya continued, "They took 16 kids; 7 boys and 9 girls. All of us were left helpless."

"I am sorry you had to go through that. We will try our best and get those kids back."

"Please hurry, before they hurt them. We think they took them to the docks" chimed in Arjun. His information wasn't off but it was still unsubstantiated.

"How the hell do you know that?" interrupted the rude officer. He continued with anger towards Arjun "You weren't even supposed to be here during the incident. Is there something that you are hiding from us?" with every word he had started pointing and moving towards Arjun. By the end of his sentence, he had to be held back by his partner.

Now worried that the officer might create a real problem, he pulled the rude officer away from a scared and shocked Arjun. He had some insider knowledge due to some of his shady dealings, but the officer's unwarranted behaviour had him shaken to the core.

Taking control of the situation, the nice officer handed the carbon copy of FIR to Acharya and again assured him that they would do everything possible to get those kids back. With that, all but two cops remained for protection. Arjun still not sure of the cop's competency started to think of alternates. While he could take a few of his friends, they would not be enough to take down the gang. Moreover, Acharya wouldn't approve of this action. He eventually did prepare himself for Acharya's reactionary, disciplinary actions but the question of how to get the kids out still remained. Finally confronting the elephant in the room, he realised that Vasu was his best hope. Knowing of Vasu's skill set and training with Acharya, Arjun decided to recruit him on this mission. He had thought up a plan and exit strategy. All that remained was convincing Vasu that this was a good idea. Taking his phone out, he still hesitated at what he was about to do. At this point, Arjun desperate to get the kids back safely, decided to make a phone call. As he opened his phonebook, scrolling down, he clicked the call button on the name Vasu. As the phone call rang, his desperation caused him to lash out. His anger raised with every ring. By the end of the call ringing, Arjun was almost screaming at the phone. This anger wasn't justified but in Arjun's mind, it was. Vasu and Arjun grew up in the

same neighbourhood and went to the same school. They had a great friendship, nearly inseparable. However, college life and Vasu leaving the sector changed both of them. Tensions grew after a particularly heated argument and resulted in a fight.

Separated by Acharya, Vasu after that stopped visiting. However, a few months ago, to everyone's surprise, even Arjun's, Vasu started visiting again. Still bitter towards each other Vasu and Arjun didn't acknowledge each other. This deep resentment caused a surge of anger in Arjun.

Meanwhile, at Sector 4's southern-most tip, in a small apartment was a phone vibrating. Vasu had a habit of sleeping with his phone keeping it on his pillow. Instead of a clock, Vasu liked the alarm app on the phone as the vibration was more effective in waking him up. Often his phone would find a way under a pillow by the morning and get him late for his college. Today was one such time where the phone was under the pillow and he was sound asleep above him. Twice had the phone completed its ringtone but Vasu's sleep didn't allow him to move. On the third occasion, however, his mind sensed something out of ordinary and Vasu woke still not completely out of his dream or the blanket of sleep that it was covered in. After a delayed realisation, he searched for his phone under the pillow with one eye closed and the other half eye open looked at the screen. It was Arjun. Not feeling like answering the call, he put the phone back under his pillow and tried to go back to sleep. But his thoughts now were also waking up. He realized that there must be either a very important reason for Arjun' call or a stupid prank. Arjun was not a drinker reducing the chances of a late-night prank call. So the thought of an issue so important that Arjun would call him took hold of Vasu's mind. Not the one to like suspense, he removed his phone and answered right before the ring ended. There was no answer on the other line. He concluded it to be a prank call crept back in. After a few of the low and raspy 'Hellos,' there finally was an answer at the other end.

"Uhh, there is a problem," replied Arjun

"With you or Saint's Refuge?" responded Vasu with a snide tone. "With Saint's Refuge of course." With a loud sigh, Arjun continued, "There was an incident and the cops were here. Get down here and I will explain everything."

"Dude, if cops came by then why do you need me? They'll take care of it." now upright and woken up Vasu replied.

Arjun now angry at his lack of understanding said, "Goddammit, get down here. Can't you for once just do as I say."

Vasu just as irked replied, "Go fuck yourself." And with that, he hung up. But guilt started creeping in immediately. He realized that situation had to be quite grim for Arjun to call him. So, with hesitance, he dialled back. Arjun answered with the first ring however there was silence from both sides for a few seconds. "I will be there in a few minutes" spoke Vasu.

"Alright." Replied Arjun. With that, both of them hung up.

Vasu had now committed to getting to Sector 9, however, it was not that easy. He lived with his mother who was unapproving of his visits to Saint's Refuge. Their feelings about the area hadn't changed since the tragedy. Vasu's father was shot down during a burglary gone wrong. The criminal was prosecuted and sentenced to life in prison. Now Vasu was in a real dilemma. He had no choice but to sneak out. As he got up from his bed it made the usual wooden squeak. However, now in the middle of the night that the usual sound was as loud as a gunshot. Now alert and vigilant of the noises that he could potentially make, he tried to find his keys in total darkness. He thought that they were atop his bag sitting on top of the chair. But it wasn't there. His wallet and bike's helmet were outside. He didn't have time to clean his eyes, the ride to Sector 9 would wake him up. Opening the door carefully trying to avoid the creak, he stepped out. The lights to his mom's room were off. So he was successful up till now. Now his helmet was visible but the keys were hanging on the main door along with other random keys. Carefully moving and lifting his helmet, the keys

silence. Closing the door was what crossed his mind next. Easy he thought. He would turn the lock and ensure that there will be no clicking or hitting sound when it closed. Phew! His eyes were now open. Taking the stairs, the 4 floors down were sure to give his body the stretch it needed.

Still apprehensive of his escape, Vasu elected to push his bike out of the building rather than start it. As he pushed it out, the bike started to roll along gaining speed. Vasu, feeling its momentum, mounted the bike and started it by putting it in the first gear and jerking open the clutch lever. Against his instincts, he didn't rev the bike high and rode out of his street with utter resilience. The first signal on his path was an indication of his freedom. That's when he let it all go and pushed the bike to its limits. Now, in this moment, there were no thoughts of worry. No fear or any sorrow. Now on this bike with this push he had all the concentration that one would require and more. His goal was set and he was determined to achieve it on time if not sooner. As he cut through the minimal traffic present at this hour, he was already on the highway. The last remnants of the old highway system remained between Sectors 4, 5 & 9. Although the fastest way to get through on a personal vehicle in its time, the environmental impact it had on the surroundings led to Sector 6's protest and its eventual expulsion from the road networks. Other Sectors followed suit and soon the old world came tumbling and in its place were long flyovers and bridges that seemingly would reduce the city's atmosphere and smooth out the city's traffic flow. And today Vasu had found it to be a boon as his bike ate up the distance like Pacman. It was a mutual capability. The bike's ability to stay more or less stable at 100 km/h and Vasu's nerve to be calm at that speed. It was not just the speed but the location that aided the speed. Since Sector 5 was mostly an administrative centre for the city, there wasn't much traffic to be seen there after 7, let alone past midnight. In eight minutes he was in Sector 9. The modern section of roads in Sector 9 ended right after its Police Station. That usually was Vasu's marker for the exit. The exit off the highway that led to the old system wasn't unusual, but deceptive. It was an accident-prone area because of a later than usual marker indicating the end of the new road. Most of the 9th was used to it. But anyone arriving in blind was in for a surprise. Reaching the exit, he slowed down to a more manageable 70 and continued along the way. His speed fluctuated due to the conditions of the road. Some bumps became invisible in the dimly lit streetlight and could cause suspension failure or even a severe incident. Even though he was familiar with the road, Vasu still drove with caution. As he reached outside Saint's Refuge, he called Arjun. The call was not answered. The thoughts of it being a tasteless prank swiftly entered Vasu's head. The second call was picked up by Arjun and a flustered and annoyed Vasu spoke, "Where the hell are you?"

"I am near the medical store. The one on the corner" replied Arjun.

The medical store that Arjun mentioned was just a block away and was quite popular among the residents. Operated by an old couple, this shop was as old as their marriage; 35 years. Vasu drove to that shop where he saw Arjun standing right near the glass windows, holding a hockey stick. This confused Vasu even more. Before he could ask Arjun anything, he was handed the hockey stick without any explanation. With a dumbfounded look, Vasu said, "What is this?"

"A hockey stick. Fo-" Arjun was cut-off before he could continue.

"Fucker, I know that. What the fuck is it for? And what happened here?" with that returning rage Vasu replied. He had detected a condescending tone in Arjun's answer and was unwilling to let that slide by.

"Relax! You didn't let me finish. The hockey stick is for helping you beat those guys up."

"What guys?"

"So.." with that Arjun explained the situation and with every sentence of the story, Vasu started to fume. This was unacceptable. Looting the house was one thing but people entering and taking

away the kids was just reprehensible. For once in what felt like a lifetime, Vasu agreed with Arjun. Willing to do anything to get the kids back, he was ready for whatever was in store.

"So, what is your plan?" asked Vasu.

"We sneak in the port. Find the warehouse and get those kids out."

"You mean I sneak in the port and get those kids out."

"No, we do. I will wait in the car outside. While you go in. It will be a joint effort." Arjun tried to alleviate the tension.

"You'll need a bus or a van" replied ignoring all of Arjun's attempt at humour.

"Where are we going to find a van now?" Arjun paused hoping for a cohesive answer from Vasu. But there was none so he suggested something, "I mean we can always boost one."

"No. We are not going to steal a van." Vasu was stern with his reply.

"Think of the kids."

This was a cheap trick from Arjun. Using the emotional angle to get his way. "Fuck!" He turned around frustrated at the circumstances. But with no other option, he replied, "If we get in trouble, I am going to kill you before the cops do."

"We won't get caught." Arjun was confident in his reply.

They start riding around on Vasu's bike looking for a van. It was not as easy as it seemed. The idea although simple on page had many nuances. Finding a van was the biggest one. Riding around the 9th close to the Saint's Refuge for a good 15 minutes, there was no van parked. They elected to go east hoping to find one near the industrial sector. And right they were about the assumption. About two kilometres east, they found a grey van with a chemical company's name neither had ever heard of. It seemed that luck was on their side as the model of the van was something Arjun was familiar with. Mounting off the bike, he started looking for something around. Few seconds was all it took to get Vasu curious. But his query was interrupted by the surge of memory that washed him down. This was not the first time Vasu was pulled along by Arjun for such an adventure. He had been partnered enough to know of Arjun's methods. Older cars didn't have alarms and could be opened with a long thin wire. All one had to do was push it down hard between the driver's window and the panel. And voila, you now had access to the vehicle. The only obstacle remaining was to start the car. It was not easy to find such a piece of metal. And realizing that time was of the essence, Vasu got down from his bike and started to help look around. Vasu decided to look around the corner of the street while Arjun elected to go around the back of the building. As he walked towards the street lamp hoping it would assist in his search, the realization of Arjun's plan set in. His mind was now solely focused on the fact that he had to sneak into a gang's territory and get people out, children out. And that too without being detected or killed. The daunting task was not helped by the fact that the Port was unfamiliar territory, and Vasu hadn't practised his combat for over a year. As good as he may have been then, today his prime skill just nervousness. He started to reason with himself on how this was a good and noble thing. However, on the other side of the argument was the fiercest enemy of doing the right thing; survival.

Just as he was about to begin this crucial debate, there was a tap on his shoulder. With a defensive stance, Vasu turned around to find a startled Arjun staring at him with his arms raised and a long strip of rusted wire. Vasu returned back to his normal self and signalled Arjun to open the car. With a little to prying, pushing and jerking at the wire, the van door opened. As soon as they were in, Vasu saw a problem. How will they start the van? They didn't have the kit to hotwire and it would be highly unlikely that there was one in the back of the van. He stepped outside again to look for a sharp object that might be of aid. His train of thought arrived at this station a little late as the van spurted into life. Vasu rushed and opened the door to find Arjun putting his tools back into the pouch. In a fit of rage, Vasu snatched the tool bag from Arjun and started to examine it. He confirmed its authenticity. It was Arjun's dark blue tool bag. Then it dawned on Vasu, this was a part of the plan. Before he could scream at Arjun about the deception, Vasu remembered the reason for this crime. It was now necessary to go through with it and fight the morals later. Time was of the essence here. He threw the kit back at Arjun and with a disappointing tone informed him that he will follow back on the bike.

As they drove towards the Port, Vasu realized that this was the least enjoyable ride he could remember. Every moment of this ride was a chore. But now, his body was no longer in control. His actions were mere puppets of his words. His mind was now on autopilot and did things that he didn't even know were required like switching the lights to high-beam. The port was on the 'dog tail' as it was called; the southernmost point of the city. It looked like a short tail of a dog or a puppy. The docks were usually guarded in the morning and never at night. That was officially. However, in reality, it was always guarded by the gang around. Today was no exception. A kilometre away from the docks, Arjun stopped on the side of the road. And Vasu followed suit. Arjun started explaining that since it was late at night, the noise of the cars can be heard from far away and advised Vasu to turn off his engine 500 meters from the docks' entrance. He agreed and they carried on. Vasu waiting for Arjun's cue turned off his engine and relied on the momentum to get him towards their desired spot. The layout of the area was such that they couldn't park the car less than 200 meters from the entrance after which there was a sweeping turn that led them straight to the entrance.

Parking their cars, both of them started to go over the plan again. "Okay so, I will stand behind that water tank in the bushes. As soon I see you coming out with the kids, I will start the car and the bike for you. Nothing left to chance." Arjun was referring to one of the large water tanks that stood opposite them. They were 5 lines with thick bushed covering their pillars. It was a good hiding spot

in the dark of the night.

Vasu was not visibly nervous but tried his best to hide it. Surveying the road up ahead, he had decided on climbing the fence near the entrance. It looked just as dark as the streets here and would serve as a perfect blanket on his sneak entrance. He replied Arjun with this plan. "I will sneak along the side and then climb that fence near the entrance."

Just as he spoke these words, Arjun came back with, "What about the barbed wire?"

"What?"

"You didn't see those wires? They are right above the fence. Can you get over them?"

Not wanting to bow down from his ego Vasu replied with, "Yes of course I can climb them. You doubt me?"

"No, no I just thought that without protection you might get hurt."

"I will be just fine. You just focus on the escape plan. Be ready for me."

"I will be. Don't worry."

With that Vasu started walking towards the entrance. Realizing that it could come in handy, Vasu turned around and took Arjun's kit to his dismay. However, today there were no protests. Just an agreement to get this task done. A few seconds of walking later, he glanced behind him and couldn't see Arjun. Nor could he differentiate between darkness and the bushes. This comforted him. Knowing that the darkness to some extent will protect him. Now it was time to focus on getting over the barbed fence. He realized that his ego had got him in this problem. But there was no turning back. Looking ahead, he could see some lights illuminating the street. The light meant that Vasu could clearly make out where the concrete wall had ended and the steel fence had begun. He could also see a guard standing right outside the gate, while another in the inside perimeter. Both of them seemed unarmed but Vasu knew better. They were carrying at least a handgun if not anything else. If he was to be spotted, death's arrival was imminent. The fence, as Arjun had mentioned was quite high and had a large barbed wire running over it. There was a section of fence which was not properly wired and dimly lit. That could provide an advantage. However, on closer examination, Vasu found that there would not be enough grip to get over it. Plus, the noise of the fence will indefinitely give away Vasu's position. Now on the edge of the darkness, he stood waiting for an opening that could help him sneak through the entrance. That was his only way in. The patrolling guards were always moving in opposite directions, meeting at the centre and sometimes chatting for a few seconds. The sight of the guards standing around to chat gave him a stupid idea. He could see no one else in sight. Taking both of them out would mean an easy entry as well as an easy exit. The only thing lacking in this plan was his confidence. For the next three minutes which seemed like three seconds to Vasu, he kept playing the scenario in his head. How could he take both of them out with minimal damage? As with every fighting plan, he laid out the strategy based on his priorities. Estimating that there were more than twenty feet between him and the guards, he decided to distract them with the fence noise. That would bring them out and near the edge. Then it would be easy to put down one with a groin kick and the other by a punch to the throat. His thinking with the throat punch was that if a direct wasn't possible at least a chin blow would be enough to get him down. But then a small pain in his right arm caught his attention. There was a toolkit that he was gripping tightly he could use. Opening it slowly without any noise, he found a small plier with wire strippers, two screwdrivers; a flathead and a Philips, a set of gloves and a small roll of electrical tape. This was a genius move from his subconscious. The tools would be helpful no doubt. Although, all this was just a presumption. The moment was here though. The guards again had convened at the entrance and were chatting. Vasu prepared himself and stood up. With a deep breath, he stepped out of the shadows, hit the fence as hard as he could and stepped back a few steps. The blow was hard enough to cause tingling in his arm. The guards drew the gun like lightning and started to move towards the noise. Both of them were pointing their guns in the darkness, however, they were yet unaware of Vasu's presence. They tried adjusting their visions before actually reaching the spot of the noise. The one patrolling outside told the other to walk towards the shadow and look for anyone there. While they were doing that, Vasu had readied himself in the attacking position and was waiting for the moment to strike. As they reached the spot, one of the guards touched the fence with his arm while the other kept his gun firm. The guard's eyes met Vasu and he knew which one was to be hit in the groin. The one standing firm. Before the guard could even process what he saw, he was struck down by a sharp and spreading pain. The second looked towards his partner to check but was hit on his chin which staggered him. Vasu realizing that his punch was not as accurate or as powerful as he anticipated, hit again. But not at the throat. This punch was at the guard's cheek. It landed as intended and knocked his lights out. The guard lying on the ground started groaning. However, now overcome with a wave of confidence, Vasu knocked him out with a similar punch. His final part was to drag the knocked-out guards enough into the darkness so as to not draw attention. With the few minutes he bought himself, Vasu checked the guards and used electric tape to their hands together. While using the shirt from one of them, he tied their faces together through their mouths.

He then put on the gloves over his bruised, paining hands and rushed towards the gate to quickly hide behind the first big object that was visible. Filled with adrenaline, Vasu now found himself behind a container in the old port trying to rescue kids from a gang. He still hadn't come to terms with the fact that he could potentially be walking towards his death. As it has been going on today, the thought was gaining momentum when he noticed something move in his peripheral vision. He quietly but quickly moved to the other side of the container and started looking around for the movement again. There was no movement on the ground. However, on top of one of the containers facing the entrance, sat a man in a garden chair with a shut spotlight. The light was facing the entrance; however, the guard was not. This coupled with the fact that the guard had headphones on proved to be lucky for Vasu. Heeding Arjun's advice, Vasu moved towards the docks to check on the warehouses. They were usually closed and unlit. This required checking each of them by either entering or by using one of the windows. Moving towards the docks, Vasu saw movement up ahead. He could see one of the guards walking with a leashed dog. His heart sank. There was no way he could sneak around with a dog guarding the perimeter. His instincts pulled him towards the stacked containers that went towards the crane. Although it seemed unreachable, his legs disagreed. They were moving before he could command them. So, realizing that his subconscious was more proficient at this than him, he let go of his fears and fell at the mercy of his instincts.

Climbing the containers, he tried his best to be silent. Standing on the first container gave him a good look at the path that laid ahead. There were a couple of larger gaps but most of them were short. Shoes! He realized. They would make noise while jumping. So, removing both of them, he tied both of them together by its lace and hung them by his right shoulder. First, second, third, jumping all over then, he kept moving ahead until he reached the crane. It had a ladder but on the far end of the crane. Optimistic about his chances, he readied himself for the jump. But a moment before the take-off, Shoes! He thought again. Putting them on would be better. The impact on the thin metal ladder would not hurt his feet if boots were covering them. And so, he laced them on. The leap was miscalculated and he fell a few bars below, barely catching it. With a louder groan than he wanted, he climbed back on looking down and around for any movements below. The groan may have been loud to his ears but the guards seem unbothered.

Reaching the top, he could see that there was no easy way to get on the crane hand. Climbing the cab, he got below the crane hand and hung 30 meters above human comfort. Now the gap between the cranes seemed larger, and death imminent. But yet again, he gave up the control. This time there was no error. He jumped just right and reached enough distance to hold on to the other crane. With great difficulty and pain, he pulled himself on top. As he was lying on top of the crane, he could feel the breeze and the blood pumping. Wanting to take full advantage of this rush, Vasu got up and ran towards one of the godowns. That is where the kids could be. But there is no guarantee. The jump down was 10-15 meters. Vasu couldn't tell anymore due to the lack of light. It was a no brainer jumping down. The ladders were on the other side and going there would make all of his effort for nothing. He was nervous. Who wouldn't be? Most people can't even imagine a 15-meter jump let alone do it. No one would blame Vasu for not going through. However, to go back, he would have to jump on the cranes as well. That was now a 20-meter drop. Here or there, it was just a matter of location. He stood up and sat down nervously, the idea of jump turned into a fall down. It would put a strain on his arms but will also be quieter and safer.

No brainer thought Vasu and began his climb down. Holding his arms and legs around the beam with a tight grip, he pushed his body like he was climbing down a ladder. It was a dangerous ordeal. Even a hint of loose grip and it would be rock bottom. Or in this case concrete bottom. That thought of cracking everything rushed past Vasu and he shuddered. As he reached his desired jumping off point, Vasu looked as limited as he could, towards the godown to confirm. He prepared himself by tightening his grip and climbing up a little and positioning himself in the way an Olympic sprinter would before a start. This was a time-constrained manoeuvre. By wasting time, he would lose his grip. So, with the last deep breath of his life, or as he thought at that moment, he pushed his legs will all the power his body could muster and flipped like a moonsault. For a split second his eyes were closed. But as soon as he opened them, he could see the edge of the godown and the steel steps leading to the roof. There was a noise, but not as loud. His impact was mainly absorbed by the concrete floor of the steps but the little noise made was due to his impact with the steel piped wall. He froze in the moment. Another false instance of him thinking it was over. He was caught. But no. All that he was caught in was a dangerous situation he chose, to avoid an embarrassing one. Now he was on top of the godown roof. But there was no way to get in from here. So he went down a few steps and saw the windows looking into the building.

The glass was old and stained. The darkness of the night didn't help either. Tired of the stress and the situation, Vasu rested his head on the glass window. But now, he could hear footsteps on the other side along with some whimpering voices. This could be it. This could be the spot with the kids. Vasu decided to wait and listen. Maybe get some insight as to how many people were there inside. After a few seconds, Vasu got impatient. The thought of getting caught from the back kept him on his toes. As soon as he moved along to check on the other side, Vasu heard another whisper followed by laughter. This was a great insight. There were up to three people inside he presumed. Two were sitting or standing near the kids while one was walking around the door. However, this was just speculation. There could be a whole group of them covering the kids. Short of breaking the glass and alerting the gang, there was nothing at the window that could help him. So, he sat down and looked around this time with the hope that he wouldn't have to take any desperate measures. Realizing that he still had the pliers from the toolkit, Vasu came up with the idea to throw them and distract the guards. He was hoping that the checking will be minimal. Ridiculous is what he thought his idea was eventually. And many would agree, even Acharya. They usually would butt heads over strategies and Acharya would always win, no matter what the game. He therefore would exclaim in each situation, what would Acharya do? The answer would usually turn out to be a simple straightforward rectification. However today, Vasu was dreading to ask himself that question. Deep down he knew the answer. Even as he avoided confrontation now, Vasu knew that there was no other way. So, as he threw the plier towards the crane, he let out an audible fuck.

The plier didn't hit where he wanted. It landed at an awkward angle and did more than intended. The pliers hit the leg of the crane and crashed between the edge as it fell down. It was loud. Loud enough to get the dogs barking and the torches lit. This cued Vasu in and he walked towards the front gate. As two of the guards got out of the godown to check on the noise, Vasu quietly but quickly went to another side of the roof. The guards gave him more than enough time before pointing their torch at the godown's roof. Now Vasu had anticipated them getting on the roof, but he didn't realize that the floodlight at the entrance could light up that section. The light was on before he could get down and hide. It was so bright for a brief moment that it would embarrass the sun. And Vasu was seen in it. At least that what he thought happened. He sat down covering behind as best as he could and prayed that this would end. As he readied himself to face the flood of bullets coming his way, to his surprise no one was on his side. All of the lights, guards and guard dog were focused on the other side of the roof. An opportunity was knocking at his door. And luck was on his side oddly. There was a half-broken window on this side of the roof. He took advantage of this commotion and decided to sneak in via the front unguarded gate. Risky, but not as much as staying there finding the latch to the window and missing on this opportunity. As he stepped and rushed into the godown, he noticed that it was dimly lit. There was just a single row of incandescent light bulbs. They were old judging from their brightness. Vasu was aware of the time crunch he was in. They would look around for a few seconds and would eventually either find him or give up. So, he moved ahead until eventually, he found a man with what seemed like a machine gun watching over the kids. There were more than what he was told. As he slowly moved forward watching his step. he gestured towards the kids with his finger on his lips. He moved in slowly and decide to disarm the man first hoping that he would be quiet enough going down to not alert his friends. The easiest technique would be to block his trigger finger with one arm and knock him out with the other. Possibly a chokehold. There were a few problems there. One, due to the low light he couldn't make out the position of the gun; and second, he was strong enough to resist his one arm chokehold. So, the next approach came in form of an elbow hit to the head. This possessed enough force to knock out the person unconscious without permanent damage. The angle, power, and precision had to be perfect here. A single mistake and it was game over for him. Stepping in to hit, Vasu raised his arm, tilted it backwards and brought it down with a force not even known to him. And the guard came flopping down like a water balloon. He was laying down while the kids watched in shock and horror.

He quickly dismissed any reactions that the kids would have by putting his finger on the lips again. Now, there were 40 kids in a godown surrounded by a dangerous gang in the middle of the old port. The right thing to do was to take all of them and risk getting caught outside. But the safe bet was to take half and come back for the rest. It wasn't easy for Vasu to convince himself, even harder to convince the kids but he tried his best. He explained that there was a van outside waiting to take them but it wasn't big enough for all of them. So, he would take half of them and come back for the rest. He would also bring back the cops and their parents. This seemed to convince them enough to cooperate. Their reluctance was justified but the situation wasn't ideal of anyone involved. So he chose twenty, including sixteen from his refuge and moved to get them outside the godown. He had also picked up the guard's gun for safety.

Guiding the kids upstairs, each of the kids started to repeat the same thing; this was the wrong way. However, rather than explaining to them why, he focused on keeping the noise down to a minimum level. They approached the broken window. Pushing it open turned out to be difficult. It could be the rust from sea wind or just that the glass was that heavy. So, he told all of them to push the window gently but firmly. He stood near the broken part of the window while the others were next to him. Their collective force pried it open. Realizing it wouldn't stay there forever, Vasu put the gun length-way between the window and the wall. Rushing the kids out of the window, he stepped out last, standing as a lookout.

Now they went up till the roof while Vasu explained then with a whisper about the guards. The security dog scared most of the kids while the rest listened with intent. The kids stood on the last staircase to the roof while Vasu sat waiting for the lights to turn off. And it did after a while. Signalling them, Vasu led the way towards the other side of the roof with a lookout for any guards around. None as it turned out. They reached the other side of the stairs and slowly stepped down. Now pointing towards the stack of containers, Vasu took them near it while staying at the back looking around in fear. All of them stood bunched up against the container looking at Vasu to lead the way.

Going around the containers towards the entrance, Vasu realized that the floodlight guard would be now alert and sneaking past would no longer be possible. So, while thinking of another way out, he catches a glimpse of the guard with the dog and snaps back towards the container, followed by 20 little people. This was impossible. Even if there was a chance of getting past jumping on the containers, there was no way the kids could sneak by like him. They would need another way out. Any other way. The sea was out of the question. At the other end of the port was an abandoned shipyard, which would be a completely unknown territory even for him. Getting 20 kids through such an environment was madness. So, at the limit of his own strategic imagination, he asked himself the dreaded question. What would

Acharya do? The answer was as clear as day. Distract the guards and sacrifice himself for the kids' escape. That is what any good person would do. And Vasu wanted to be good. He desperately wanted to be a good person. Maybe his reasons to be a good man were wrong, but today his action was about to speak louder. He instructs kids to keep hiding behind the containers till there is an opportunity. Then run towards Arjun waiting for them in a van. They agreed, although reluctantly. Now with a deep breath, he walked towards the edge of the container. There standing with a vibrating leg, he looked for a way to keep them distracted while the kids ran. Getting back on the crane was easy, but then there would be no way out for him. Getting on the roof would have similar consequences. The other side of the port. He thought that there will be a way for him to get out and make his own escape.

So he stepped outside and screamed his lungs out. That got the dog barking and then the lights on him. Now he ran. He ran towards the shipyard. But right away he saw 2 guards with guns pointing at him. Moments before they could shoot, he ran towards the crane. Hoping that the pillars, containers and his speed would provide enough shield to avoid any bullets. There was still a worry of the kids getting caught. So he ran around the crane, sat down and quickly ran back. Into the thick of the containers, he decided that hiding for a while would buy some time and they wouldn't just run in the container stack to find him. So slowly, he started to move out and avoided every opportunity to make noise. But the dog came towards him like a bullet. It bit his arm and had Vasu dropped to the ground. The adrenaline and the recovered strength gave him enough power to punch the dog away and drop his arm. The dog, having recovered quickly stepped back to pounce but this time Vasu was ready and bent down to uppercut the dog. The punch landed and demoralized the dog for another attack. But it still stood there barking, which would give away Vasu's position. Scaring the dog away but stepping ahead, Vasu ran through the containers and caught the guards by surprise. They were looking for him just a few sections behind where he was. With that advantage, Vasu got ahead enough to not get shot or caught. But he still was chased by men and bullets, out of the port and onto the street. None of them got closer. At the end of the street, he didn't see the Van, which was a relief but not one he could cherish for long. There they were, the goons and their guns. His bike now was pointing towards the road for his escape and running. Vasu, without another thought, got on and twisted the accelerator with all of the strength of his arm. Pulling away from that place gave him a wave of relief he wasn't ready for. As he drove without paying attention to his route, all he could think of was his luck. What a stroke of luck! Maybe this wasn't a bad plan after all. The light reflecting from his rear view mirror distracted this train of thought. He couldn't see through the mirror who it was. But a moment later, even before he turned around to look, his doubts were cleared by a bullet hitting the mirror. It wasn't over. So he pushed the bike even more. Now looking around to find escape routes, he realized that the locality was unfamiliar. Knowing that the way back was his best bet to get on the right route, he took a series of lefts and leaned down to avoid any hits. With the last turn, he was right where he wanted. Going back. The bullets had stopped but the car behind hadn't. Maybe they ran out or were conserving. None of his concern thought Vasu and drove on weaving actively through whatever traffic was around. After the fourth junction he recognized the area. And so armed with the information, he made his way towards Saint's Refuge. However, taking these men may not be the best idea. Or it could be. Vasu remembered the officers outside Saint's Refuge. And more importantly, Arjun would have reached Saint's Refuge before him and called the police. So not bothered about the men following, Vasu rode on. After a left turn on a junction which caused Vasu to slow down, he felt a push from the back causing him to nearly lose control of his bike. This dismissed the theory that they were following him. They were rather trying to take him out. He got back on the power and pushed the bike to its limits, or his limits. It wasn't clear. Vasu was losing them with every corner, with every close-cut through the traffic. The road was all that he saw. He had completely blocked out his peripheral vision and was focused, determined. That may have not been a good idea as he didn't have the time to observe the car coming towards him after another turn. He panicked and lost control falling face down from his bike. Now, this incident might not have happened at slower speeds. Not because Vasu couldn't ride fast but the action of leaning to turn might create certain unwanted limitations. Chief among them were manoeuvrability and visibility. So here he was, kissing the tarmac, breathing in the dirt while his body felt like jelly. His eyes met the bruised up state of his bike. It was tragic for him to look at it. His prayers were answered soon though. But not as he was expecting it to be. Blocking the line of sight to his broken bike was a pair of heavy-duty boots. They got close and his body felt the pressure. He was lifted upright. One of the goons who Vasu recognized from the godown was facing him. He was not of this country. A thick beard and a pair of glasses were all he could make out before he was dragged towards the car.

Now the senses had kicked in. He will be tortured, made to get the kids or even be killed in a horrendous manner. His mind was ready but his body wasn't. As they opened the white SUV's door, one of the goons let go of his hand so the other can push him in. Chance here to escape was worth the risk. His body may have not been ready but it had to be. Realizing that all of them were a bit relaxed, he balled up his right fist and swung it at the goon holding him. It landed just below the jaw, hitting it hard enough to surprise him. He let go, and with a stumble, Vasu was on his feet. Now he had enough energy for a punch. He had a choice, either the stumped man or the distracted man. He chose the distracted one. His left arm swung hard enough to knock the man out. At this point, Vasu's knuckles were bruised enough to start bleeding and cause him more than mild discomfort. But the pain wasn't harsh enough to distract him from the incoming punch. It came from the left. Putting his right foot back and turning right, he dodged the punch. Quickly looking for a weapon, he was distracted enough to miss the elbow that returned after the punch. He fell stumbling from the impact about 4 feet away right next to his knockout. Now lying on the ground. His blurred vision didn't help him focus on the standing men but it did show him the belt of the lying goon. Long and a short-range weapon if used correctly. He could also see the gun tucked but Vasu wasn't keen on it. Not willing to debate his survival self on the topic, he pulled out the gun and pointed it quickly at one of the goons. They too had their guns out and pointing at Vasu now. As he slowly got up, he started to remove the belt with his left hand while still focusing his gun towards the standing men with his right hand. The belt, with a little effort, was out. Even without the strength to get up, Vasu willed and ordered his body up while holding a handgun in his right hand and a belt by its buckle in the left.

He slowly started to move back and towards his bike. Each step was alternating. One was back and the other was toward his bike. After about ten steps he realized that he had no way of riding away without both of his arms. And that would be the moment when he would be captured. So he started working out ways he could get on the bike without handing control of the situation. However, doing this put him in an even dangerous position. Having moved towards the bike with every other step, he was now in a position where he couldn't see the bike without turning his head. Now, it was between risking taking eyes of people trying to kill him and stumbling and falling over on his ass. Turning his head was less risky. At least that's what he thought would be. Because as soon as he took his eyes off the men, one standing closest to him nearly leapt trying to take the gun away. However, the peripheral vision of Vasu caught the leap and he swung the belt with all of his might. A few inches of it landed light on the attacking man's temple. The hit was good enough to stump him. With that Vasu used the base of the gun to land a hit on the man's head. And prepared himself for a shower of bullets. But there were none. They all were out of bullets. They used up while trying to chase Vasu down. Relieved at this, he moved forward to face the other two running towards him trying to attack. Vasu prepared himself for pain. He decided to take one of the guys out while the other attacked. This way, he at least would manage to halve the danger. Vasu raised his arm to hit the guy on his left with the base of the gun. He had calculated the position correctly causing the man to stumble back and fall down holding his head. It was bleeding. The other one meanwhile had managed to rush near Vasu and began assaulting his abdomen. It worked and Vasu stepped back to dodge some of the punches. They were too painful to bear at this moment. But he had to persevere. As he whipped the belt, the guard dodge with his right giving Vasu an opening to kick him in the groin. The attack was miscalculated to the horror of the man. Instead of Vasu's shin hitting the eggs, it was his knee. The impact was felt by both men along with the horror.

However, the complete share of the pain fell on the man's groin. He slowly bent down, then on his knees and eventually settling on his face. Vasu was not proud of the attack but was happy with the outcome.

Exhausted, all he could now think of was his warm, soft bed. The night, sleeplessness, fights, all had taken their toll. Walking towards his bike, he remembered the accident and had started to calculate the repairs it could cost. By lifting his bike up, he confirmed most of what he anticipated. The petrol tank had a huge dent, almost 25% had caved in. The footrest for the gears was broken off. The crash guard was dented and scratched but was mostly fine. Left front and back indicators, mirrors and the front mudguard were all part of the casualty risks. The most important thing right now was to get the bike started. With great trouble, he got on. First ignition, nothing. Second ignition, a splutter. At the third ignition, it stared for a split second. Fourth time was the charm. It started but keeping it working required a lot of acceleration input. Not risking another shutdown, Vasu drove with his bike screaming and losing power. As he got on the road, his arms were aching. The pain in his left leg was not helped by the fact that it had no support and his face was now burning. The journey to Saint's Refuge felt like a decade. It felt like a fever dream when he saw the van standing outside. As he parked near it, he got off and nearly fell down. His foot wasn't ready for the journey. Arjun who had been standing at the window of Saint's Refuge, rushed out to help Vasu. He was followed by Acharya. They both put Vasu's hand over their shoulder and lifted him to walk him in Saint's Refuge. Acharya held the door open and gestured Arjun to put Vasu in the staff's living quarters. After placing Vasu on one of the beds, Acharya requested Arjun to get the first-aid kit along with warm water. Acharya pushed one of the chair's next to Vasu's bed and sat down looking intently. They didn't speak for a minute. He had anticipated Vasu's attempt at explanation while Vasu had expected a scolding.

But eventually, Vasu's patience ran out. With a hint of surprise, he began, "Are you not going to scold me?" There was also a flicker

of hope with that sentence. Maybe he was spared today.

"There will be time for that" replied Acharya. With that Vasu's hope and surprise vanished. He knew what would be asked next. And the query came in the form of an order. "Tell me everything."

Vasu hesitantly began the story with some variations to spare himself and Arjun from as much trouble as possible. During his recanting, Arjun arrived with the warm water and the first aid. Acharya began treating Vasu while Arjun went to check on the kids again. After listening to everything patiently, Acharya still had a neutral expression. He asked, "Why didn't you say no? To Arjun"

"Well… I wanted to help the kids." Replied Vasu. "And get fame?"

"No, of course not."

"Good. Because the cops don't' know that it was you." "Then who did you tell it was?"

"The masked guy. Besides, you would have been arrested for that."

"I am happy with that. It also means they would be scared to retaliate back at us."

"Hmmm"

Vasu was now washed over with the thoughts of the remaining kids. With never felt before sense of worry he asked Acharya, "What about the other kids?"

"Arjun said that there were other kids. We informed the cops about that and the SI promised a raid on the port tonight."

Still not convinced of the kids' safety, "They might be too late for that. We should go back and help them."

"You have done enough for today. You will only get in your own way. Besides, other people are doing or at least trying to do good. Let them do their job. Let them do the right thing."

"I made a mistake. Let me amend it. Others shouldn't suffer

because of me,"

"Patience. Think before you act next time. Going out like this, without any foresight? Won't you make the same mistakes?"

"Maybe. But if there is a chance that I could help them today wouldn't you want me to? I have learned from my mistakes."

"Clearly you haven't. You went in there unprepared and were overwhelmed. I am not saying don't do it again. Do it with some planning?"

Vasu knew this wasn't right. He was convinced it was his fault that the kids were in trouble and Acharya was right, he needed a plan and a lot of patience. But tonight, there was nothing he could do to help him. That was eating him away. The inability to do the right thing.

CHAPTER THREE

IN THE NAME OF JUSTICE

Dangerous cases like these were Khan's métier. His time in the military and his service during the war was evidence of one singular fact; he was an effective investigator. However, his cases were involving certain niche; either espionage or war crimes and both of them had a certain amount of black tape around them. Not many outside the unit were aware of the cases and that's how Khan liked to work no interference. This peace with work was taken away from him here, working in the police force. All of the inactions and mistakes were exposed by the media. That might not have been a problem, but the fact that important details were also being exposed along with that would be a hindrance. At first, his naïve belief in the media's function was what kept him feeding information to them. But as soon as he became aware of the impact they had on public opinion, his habits changed. Khan hoped that the media would present the facts as they were, informing people of the work being done for them. However, certain loud-mouth elements who wore the garb of nationalism and nation first had created chaos that was hard to hold back. Their criticism was far more damaging than it was constructive. There may have been a point or two where the questions were warranted, but the way such elements had created a negative atmosphere in the public had long term effects. The belief in the justice system was reduced to a husk. The judges, the lawyers and the police officers, all were corrupt. And if there was justice to be delivered, only the hands of the politician they supported were clean for it. And they had favourites.

Usually the one in power. Right now it was DPP all the way. Khan's reputation was taken down by such a screaming troll on television that would question everyone but his dear leader. After the incident, all that remained were his self-worth and his work ethic. They would also have been sodomized had it not been for a friend that paved the way to safety. His pull-down into paper- pushing jobs and multiple transfers were the reason for his escape from the limelight. Yesterday reminded him of the light and the burns they had caused. Had this case not been given to him under the table, his remaining ideological wealth would have been looted by the so-called 'media'.

Completing the report for yesterday's incident, he thought that instead of asking for access to files, making copies of them would be more efficient. He wasn't sure why he didn't think of that before. Checking for any other meeting in the schedule, he texted Laxmi of his intentions. By the time there was a response he was already packing, ready to visit the Records Room. "Talpade" he called at the top of his voice. There was no answer. "Talpade" he called even louder to which a voice called, "Sir". As the owner of the voice walked in Khan realised it wasn't Talpade but one of the juniors; Rishabh.

Before Khan could enquire further Rishabh spoke, "Talpade sir has gone out. He was called by the Headquarters."

"When?" asked Khan with a tone of surprise and a smirk on his face.

"Before you came in. He ordered me to inform you but I forgot.

I am sorry sir."

"Fine. Is Ashfaq in?" he asked dismissive of the previous remark. "Yes sir."

"Ask him in."

"Yes sir. And I am sorry for the earlier-" he spoke worrying about a

disciplinary remark but was interrupted by Khan.

"It's not the end of the world. Just note things down next time and you will be fine." With that Khan put Rishabh at ease. He stepped out to call on Ashfaq.

Ashfaq was Deputy Senior Inspector for the 2nd shift. His duties were the same as Talpade's but at a nocturnal time. Ashfaq and Khan hadn't interacted that often. Since Khan usually was at the station in the day, their conversations were limited and strictly business. Although there was some mutual respect, it never amounted to a comradery similar to what Khan had with Talpade.

Two knocks on the door indicated the arrival of Ashfaq. He was not dressed for duty. Clearly at the station in an informal capacity. His un-ironed white shirt and khaki pants did not match the clean- shaven but fuzzy-haired Ashfaq.

"Good Morning Sir." He greeted Khan with a formal unenthusiastic sentence that would make even a dead-end corporate job employee seem gay and friendly.

"Good Morning. Please sit." Replied Khan with a similar tone. Both took their chairs and sat. Khan continued, "Talpade called you in?"

"Yes, he called me to cover his shift for an hour." Repled Ashfaq. "Okay. Like Talpade, even I would like to ask for a favour from you?"

"Of course sir. What's the order?"

"No. Not order but a favour. I need you to stay in command until I come back."

"Of course, but where are you going if someone were to ask?"

"I am going to Headquarters. CG called me in. Cover me until I get back and I will cover your rest of the night. In fact, I will cover any other night you want as well."

"Sir, I will help in every capacity. You don't have to ask for favours. I will be here until you back."

"Thank You, Ashfaq. I will owe you one."

With that Khan left the station. The Central office was on the north corridor of Sector 5. It was closer to Sector 9's station than to Sector 7's station. Driving to the Central office was a chore as it was in the Capitol District. At least that's what the area was known as. The Court of High Justice and the Municipal building which served as Mayor's office all were located in Sector 5. The distance was such that most of the area felt like a different time zone. Even on good days, the drive took over an hour. But on a weekday, you could spend up to two hours on the road. So Khan buckled up and began his journey. The obvious route to take was to go through Sector 6 going straight into Sector 5. However, his contact with the 'Forest Territorial Protection' meant that he could take a more direct route through Gaura Devi Reserve saving a chunk of time. The road was small providing a path for a single car. This route meant that the entire Sector 6 was just woods, a forest and a river. Khan had a soft spot for this road. Especially the bridge over Neer River. He had used that spot to clear his mind a few times. It was one of the few places where he could find peace. Today there was no time to ponder. As he rushed through the GDR, there was always the musical soundtrack of birds with the occasional glimpse of the odd deer and elephant. Time flew by as he cut through the reserve. In time, as expected came the border and Sector 5. The ring road and a few well-placed short-cuts were in line. The traffic, noise and a suffocating feeling rushed in like a stampede. Suffocation was maybe due to the people or maybe it was just the atmosphere shift from the changing sectors. It felt disconcerting. But not even a per cent of the feeling could be seen on Khan's face.

The ring road was easily accessible from the route Khan went on. However, the traffic on the road was murderous. His average speed went from 60 down to just 20. With great struggle and patience, he was able to get near his exit. The next task was to solve the puzzle that was the Capitol District. Any newbie would easily be lost as there were no two-way streets. You had to follow a pre-mapped out route to get to your destination. This, the officials claimed reduced traffic. There was no evidence that Khan could find on the road. But that's the government for you. Their data always defied reality. And the anecdotes were just that. But most people spend their lives in an anecdote. So, with his memory serving as a map, Khan weaved through the traffic like a fish in the river. His car achieved speeds unheard of in the Capitol District; 30 km/h. His route went through the smaller governing units, the employee's quarters and the postal unit's headquarters. At the centre of the Capitol was the City Court and right next to the city court was the Headquarters.

Yaatnāh Police Headquarters was a compound of 7 buildings. The Administration Office, the Records Room, the Bunker, the Armoury, Forensics Lab, Riot Guard and the Public Service building formed the central office. With each serving its purpose, the administration office was for the officers and an operating headquarter for all of the sectors. All of the sectors' chiefs reported to the CG who worked in this building. The bunker was the training building for the applicants of the police force. It was an all-purpose building, even containing a complete state of the art weapons training course. Its sister building was the armoury that was a conjoined twin. Although self-explanatory, the armoury was also a housing unit for all the police vehicles and their mechanics. Forensics Lab was the newest addition that replaced the former housing unit for the trainees. The building was still upgrading and had a dedicated travel team working for all the sectors. Riot Guard was the quietest among all of the buildings also on the furthest side of the compound along with the Forensics Lab. Rarely being used, its members were still held in the highest regard among the policing community. Their building was one of the few Khan hadn't visited along with the Forensics Lab. The public service building was the frontmost and easily accessible for the citizens providing services that would benefit the police- citizen relations. Finally, the records room. It shared the front section along with the Public Service building. Used just as a storeroom for the records and evidence on pending cases, this building was a small construct of 4 floors. But that was just for show. In reality, this building also had an underground records room for the old completed cases. This area was rarely visited even by the officers due to the restrictions. There were a few documents that needed to be produced for any access to this place. In case of an urgent requirement, one of 5 employees would produce the records which could be viewed in the presence of the said employee and nothing further. That would also require documents but not in the quantity of the former instance.

Posing a dilemma for Khan, the records would create a paper trail that could lead to his dismissal due to interference in the case. This required a quiet and discreet approach that would leave someone investigating with just the words of the employees thus dismissing any grounds for suspension. Here, not only Khan's but Laxmi's position could be jeopardized. And according to their long- standing agreement, Laxmi would disavow Khan in case of such a situation. Hoping that just a phone call from the CG would be enough to gain access, Khan entered the Records Room. The building was old and had a faint olive colour. The entrance looked like any other public office with a large waiting hall and a giant desk that had a disinterested employee at the helm. Approaching the desk with the authority that he didn't possess here, Khan asked for the senior officer in the office. There was only one. The one man- in-charge policy was introduced after there was a theft of evidence and finding the responsible party became a challenge. The current Superintendent of Archives was Kiran Parthi. Her appointment was a noteworthy event due to her being the first female S/A of the records room that culminated with her being the longest- serving as well. 8 years and oddly Khan and Parthi were both never introduced. Khan had already dialled for Laxmi and was on the phone private conversation. Rejected at first, Parthi did warm to the idea when informed of the individual arriving on the phone call. Parthi led Khan to her office on the second floor. There were no lifts

only old exposed stairs that spoke to the age of the building. His first impressions were being solidified with every step. She spoke with an authority that Khan had only seen in a few officers like Laxmi. Her physical presence only added to that authority.

Now in Parthi's room, Khan noticed the simplistic and minimalist furniture. They sat at the desk which was one of five pieces of furniture in the room. She raised her arm in a motion indicating Khan to start explaining himself.

"I want access to the records room." Khan put forth his request in a succinct way. This was influenced by his phone call with Laxmi. "Why?" replied Parthi to the question. This was in line with what Khan was expecting.

"Because of an undercover case I am appointed to by the CG, I require to study old material." Again, Khan was using limited words to explain himself.

"Call her." Parthi requested.

Although it was a request, the sentence came off as an order. Obeying the request, Khan pressed the redial button and passed the phone to Parthi. Her conversation was short with Parthi only using affirmative words. The conversation resulted in Parthi getting up and instructing Khan to follow; which he did. Now they walked down to the main hall and went into one of the rooms behind the desk. The room had a small desk, a plant pot, and two cabinets. One steel and the other wooden that seemed to be attached to the wall. She opened the wooden cabinet that was empty and pushed at what turned out to be a button on the top right corner. This made a heavy but low metallic noise which was followed by the back of the wooden cabinet pushing back and opening inward. It was an old technique Khan was familiar with. He just didn't expect it to be here. This seemed like a fuss at first to Khan. As they entered the room, Khan noticed the cold atmosphere and wide path that led to a corner turning right. Around the corner were 3 sets of stairs. It was followed by another door guarded by an employee holding an SMG. It still didn't make sense. Why go through such a fuss to protect records? Hoping that he would ask Parthi given the chance, Khan followed quietly. The guard knocked in a rhythm, which resulted in the door opening to another guard holding his SMG. Now they were in another waiting room that had large twin doors. The waiting room was quite short in length but just as wide as the corridor. Opening the doors, Parthi led Khan in the records room. The room was lined with 8 feet high, steel cabinets arranged side-ways. Khan, from the entrance, could only see the side panels of the cabinets. The room had only a few cabinets on his left and a seemingly endless number of cabinets to his right. The end of the room straight ahead was barely visible, but from his experience Khan assumed it to be approximately 50 meters. His sense of direction indicated the left side was the entrance to the compound hence the shorter end while the right and the straight sides were in the compound property. While Khan had been wondering and observing the records room, Parthi had whispered to the old man regarding Khan's purpose. The old man sat at the desk that was on his left towards the end of the room. Khan had somehow missed the man and his desk.

Watching Parthi leave, Khan decided to gamble at the chance and presented the question itching away at him, "Why all the fuss for old records." There was no answer, just an inexpressive stare that indicated to Khan, he had asked the wrong question. Parthi stepped out of the room closing the doors behind her. Now, Khan had reached his goal. The records of the old case were here. He could access them without anyone's interference or questioning. But the cabinets were a maze with no identifying system. So, he approached the desk and asked the old man. "Hi, how can I find the files that I am looking for?"

"You can't" replied the man in a raspy low voice. "Only I can." Khan, now aware that the old man had the key to the puzzle that was the records room. So Khan waited for him to continue.

"What sort of records are you looking for?" "Unidentified suspects and gang members' profile." "There is no computer to sort that out you know, right?"

"I am aware. But I was hoping that there was a general section for murders and gang crimes and I could find the cases myself."

"What do you think we are? Stupid? But of course, there's a system for storing. How else do you think I find things?" With that, he pulls out a register from his desk and hands it over to Khan.

"Here, this will help you." The register contained a key to identify all of the files. The rows were divided based on sectors. And the stack of each cabinet had an alphabet. Each indicating a set of crime. 'A' would be for the robberies. 'B' for the kidnappings, so on and so forth. Preparing for the inevitable long haul, Khan began going through the first row which was for Sector 5.

Recovering from the accident, or so he claimed, Vasu was now bed-ridden. He stuck to a story that would hurt his mother's psyche the least. Ganga's life as a single mother revolved around Vasu. And her greatest fears due to the trauma were the reason for her restrictions. Vasu understood that and was the only reason he was afraid for her mother. Vasu, as he entered his house assisted by Arjun had claimed that he went on an early morning joy-ride ending in an accident. His injuries were treated in a manner as to appear minor. Although a giant shock at first, Ganga's examination of the injuries kept her worries and fear at bay. Arjun explained the incident as a drunk driver's fault that led to his arrest and Vasu's bike being put in a garage for repair. Apprehensive of the story due to their tension, Ganga felt relieved at the fact that the man was put to jail and her son had escaped with minor injuries. Ganga thanked Arjun and he left Vasu without another word to him. Among all of this, the sneak out didn't go unnoticed. Ganga ruled Vasu guilty and sentenced him to a curfew past 10 and the bike to be sold off for scraps. Had it not been smashed and left at the refuge, Vasu would have felt more hurt than he did today. Vasu had realized that the money for repairs wasn't arriving anytime soon. So, the Riddance

of the bike today was a mutual conclusion for both mother and son. Ganga feeling guilty of having to leave his son unattended, made him breakfast and lunch before leaving for work. She had no choice as her job was the only source of income currently running their life. Vasu's start-up was just a one-man mission and didn't have a scope of income for the foreseeable future. Vasu's thoughts were concerned with none of these issues today though. His eyes only saw the teary kids; in light or dark.

He had enough of the thoughts and decided to take up Acharya's parting advice and focused on his tech idea. His goal was to create a fully functioning marketplace for the local grocers. His idea not only required a coding expert but also a silver-tongue to convince the local shop-keepers to get involved. Now, the coding issue was solved by one of his college buddies who was returning the favour. He now had to find the man to convince the sellers. His experience visiting the sellers made one thing clear, he could not do the job himself. Someone like Arjun but with a better track record was required. His mind was revolving around one person, but she was out of the equation. Her internship at a law firm made her goal obvious to everyone. But Vasu always felt that she could have sold a sack of dirt to a jeweller. The girl in question was Shreya. One of the former locals like Vasu and his secret childhood crush. The secret was what Vasu believed it to be. Everyone apart from Shreya knew. Their relationship was similar to his with Arjun but without bitterness towards Vasu. She wanted to make it big and worked hard towards her goal. The lawyer dream came in through a childhood TV show. But everyone also knew of her silver-tongue. In fact, many fell victim to that superpower. It also gave her a chance at one of the most prestigious law firms, outbidding some of the best graduates in the city. Vasu was convinced that Shreya could do better and thus supported her move to Sector 3. That may have been the reason for the lack of bitterness with Vasu but indifference was still there.

Vasu snapped himself away from his dead-end train of thought and tried to focus on the job at hand. Unknowingly, with every passing minute, Vasu was checking his body one part at a time for mobility. He twisted, stretched and massaged them in every way possible to get them to the desired condition. Pain caused by swinging his shoulder brought his actions to the forefront. Now aware and accepting of what he was doing, Vasu got up and actively started to check his body. The shoulder and the knee was the only thing that was of concern to him. However, why was he even doing this? Acharya had strictly told him to not interfere in the matter. The cops were now involved and the risks of getting shot had gone up through the roof. But, Vasu was still carrying the weight of guilt on his chest. Hoping this would get the pressure and the uncomfortable feeling off, he picked up his phone. Pacing nervously, he argued the merits of getting involved again. On one hand, the kids could be saved and his guilt could be pulled off. On the other hand, he could get shot, tortured or killed. On the one hand, there were 20 kids or more, on the other hand, was his mother. The phone was the representation of his dilemma as he dialled and cut-off the call to Arjun before it could connect. Indecisive on his choice regarding who to hurt, Vasu decide to toss. That would provide the answer, right? Maybe. But it was still worth a shot. He could arrive at a conclusion this way even though he will not like either of the choices. Taking a coin out of his wallet, he assigned a decision to each side. Heads and he would try to save the kids. Tails and he would forget all of it and walk away. With a deep breath, he flipped the coin and shut off his eyes. The coin made its usual clanging noise as it hit the uncarpeted floor a few times before settling down. Vasu opened his eyes but hesitated to look down. The choice was made for him. The only thing left for him to do was look at it and follow it through.

Looking down at the coin, his heart sank. It was tails. He stared at the coin trying to justify the decision. Maybe the universe wants him to stay out. This for the best. Taking care of mom and giving her a better life is what he wants. All good excuses. All of them acceptable. But he still wasn't convinced. To solidify his decision, Vasu picked up the phone and called Arjun. As the phone rang, he practised the things that he wanted to say. Things like 'Please don't call me again. I don't want to get involved.' 'For my mother's sake, I cannot help you anymore.' Even the odd 'I want to live my life my way' was considered before Arjun picked up the call. Convinced that one of those would be enough, Vasu prepared himself to receive any form of judgement, argument or convincing Arjun could throw his way and spoke his mind. "Will you help me?" That's what was uttered. It shocked both of them. The line remained quiet for what seemed like ages. The silence was broken by Arjun who was able to only ask "What?" That was enough though. That single word was responsible for a series of questions and thoughts that would form Vasu's next sentence. This time, Vasu was convinced that this is what he wanted. His conscience was speaking on his behalf and questioning it today would not be wise. "I want to get those kids out. Will you help me?" That was all it took to convince Arjun. He replied with "Yes." Both were relieved. This was the elephant in the room sitting on Vasu's chest. Agreeing to gather supplies for the rescue, Arjun asked Vasu to meet him in the evening rather than at night. They had to formulate a plan that would work and not result in anyone's death.

Relieved at the idea, Vasu started to warm up his body for the extensive strain it would face tonight. There was no doubt that he got off easy the last time, but now they would be prepared. He had to be in the shape of his life in a few hours. Impossible to achieve, but getting it as close as possible would also work. His left shoulder, left part of the ribcage and both of his knees were hurt in the accident. Apart from that, there was also internal damage due to the strain he faced while jumping and climbing around like a spider or a bat. Those injuries amplified the pain of the accident. Resting was the best way to get those things in shape. However, a painkiller would have also helped. There was no way to get them right now. And no doctor would prescribe it to him based on his relatively mild injuries. He had to acquire them illegally. Not convinced that this was the right thing to do, Vasu focused and tried to remember his training with Acharya. So resting down, he focused on all of the

aspects of Acharya's training. He was a part of one of the few batches that had received defensive training from Acharya. This program was developed to counter the gang culture that tried to infiltrate the neighbourhood. It lasted all of 8 months before Acharya fell ill with TB. Deteriorating health meant that he could only work in a limited capacity. Vasu, by that time, had grown close to Acharya. His training was a major reason for strengthening their relationship. Acharya was an anchor in the storm that hit Vasu. Maybe things could have gone better but not much more than they could have in this situation. They made the best of it. Their training sessions were at first just him instructing Vasu on strengthening the core. That was during Acharya's hospitalization. It progressed further developing Vasu's skills and their relationship. Their bonding was such that Vasu visited the Home despite his mother's protests.

Now the basics of Acharya's training dictated patience, perseverance and protection. Patience rewards with better insight, Perseverance rewards with victory even after defeat and always protect your body. These basics were to be trained intensely. Enough for it to become an instinct rather than a calculated response. Eight months that were invested in basics paid off enough that Vasu no longer had to think about defending. His arms protected him before there was even a thought processed. Then there was perseverance. The ability to get up even after the worst possible defeat required a mental strength that would be unparalleled. To learn about perseverance, Vasu was given the task of practising punching a tree every day. His ultimate goal would be to lay down enough punches that the tree would break. Finally, Vasu's greatest enemy was patience. His training was a form of torture but was formally never completed He had to sit below a bucket of water while it dripped down one drop at a time. This was the greatest test of patience. Acharya knew that this was against Vasu's basic mental structure. But all he could offer Vasu was training and guidance. The steps towards it should be taken by Vasu.

Thoughts that came to him were distracting enough for Vasu to lose track of time. By the time he looked at the clock above his door, it was in the middle of the afternoon. Now he had fewer hours than he desired to use in the first place. So to begin with the basics, he got up and started searching for a rope. The kitchen didn't have it or even the living room. He remembered that there still was that skipping rope that he used to work out with. That should have been in his room, and it was. With the rope tying his legs a foot apart, he started the basic footwork and balancing exercise.

With every step forward, he attacked. The attacking moves were anything ranging from an uppercut to a simple jab. He even ducked on occasions. Reaching the far end of his living room, he would then start stepping back. With the backsteps, he would try out all of his defensive moves. This activity continued for an hour straight. By the time it was done, he was left with a painful shoulder and aching ankles. On multiple occasions, he nearly fell on the glass coffee table he had to move to make space in the living room. With the exercise complete, he fell right down on his couch. But remembered that sleeping on the floor facing up would benefit his posture more, so he rolled down. Now, in the middle of the living room on the colourful rug, he was facing towards the roof staring right at the fan. The blades served as the perfect distracting segway from his pain. His thoughts again turned to the kids, the condition that he left them in. His feelings for them were amplified when the thought of the kids led to him remembering his father's funeral. He hadn't cried up till his father was on the funeral pyre. Lighting the flame brought him to the realization that the man lying there was his father. All of the moments of fun, enjoyment, love and affection were all now just that; moments. And of the ways he felt that day, the feeling of fleeting hope is what Vasu thought those kids felt when he left them at the port. There was no way, he was going to let anyone go through even a remotely similar experience. But again, lost in his thoughts, Vasu realized looking at the clock that another half an hour had passed. No matter how much he tried to focus, any idle time, and his thoughts would always take over him.

He had no time to give to his imagination today. So to keep himself focused, Vasu decided to set an alarm. As he started working on his moves, he decided to spend the remaining time equally between the upper body moves, which he was best at and the lower body moves. And finally before leaving dedicating an hour to perfecting combos and holds a part of the last-minute preparation that he always did even outside of combat training.

Khan, now glanced over his notes to check if he had noted down everything of interest or at least curtailing to gangs. It was 15 pages. That number of pages might not seem much but that is what he found curious from the files that he looked at; 127 to be exact. There was no way that he could take a copy of the photos let alone the original so for them, he had to rely on his memory. He started to associate every important photo with the related line in his notes. There were multiples sometimes but Khan today had to make do. There was no other way. Even getting back here was no longer an option. So he went through all of the anomalies again. First was a kidnapping in Sector 1. It was rare and there were no suspects. There wasn't even a ransom note. He started to eliminate the cases with anomalies by reading all of them over again and again. Each time there would be either a kidnapping or a shootout or a simple robbery that would be eliminated because it didn't fit the pattern. The pattern was simple. One of 3 things had to be involved, one or two unidentified criminals, killings with precisive actions or shots or a complete wipeout of the gang. What felt odd to him each time reading was multiple of those cases had the first two criteria but not the third. Instead of his original plan to eliminate the cases without all of the three, he decided to entertain his instinct and keep in the ones with the first two as well. By the end of the 5th round, there were only cases with at least two of the criteria that remained unstruck. Alarmingly that remaining number was 17. It was unusual that such a large amount of crimes could go unnoticed. So he went through those files again. The cases were only filled with kidnappings and murders. In 2 of the 6 kidnapping cases, there was no cash exchanged and the victims were returned unharmed. One

unsolved while the other 3 had the usual sum of money involved. Of the remaining 11 cases, murders, they had 7 gangs related violence. So these 7 were the obvious cases to look at. The rest 4 were even more curious than the kidnappings. The victims' had been killed with knives with similar precision to what he witnessed last night. But all of them were in one way or the other, involved with the government. Subodh Mishra was a Sector 5 bureaucrat part of the communication department, Vandana Singh was an activist fighting against the ineffective municipal functionings, Zakir Khan was a senior officer at the GD Reserve and Sugandu Das was a real estate agent mainly involved in government occupied land.

Now Khan was sure that he was on the right track. First, he got a confirmation from the method of killings that there were 2 people involved and second, as he suspected this was more than simple killings of gang members. Now all he had to find was the reason for each of their murders and he eventually finds the man benefitting from it all. In two of the above-mentioned cases, Vandana Singh and Zakir Khan, there was a feasible motive of clearing the way for new government rules. Only the current Mayor would have benefitted from these killings. But even he wasn't that stupid to have these crimes associated with him directly. So he decided to dig deep. Maybe there was more than what appeared on the surface. There could be a link between all of these people, and that link could be the rope to hang the criminals involved. He decided to draw out a report of all of the seventeen cases to make it easy for him on the investigation front. Completing the last line of the report, Khan was tapped on his shoulder by the old man.

"How long will you be?"

"Umm, just a few minutes I think I have noted down everything I need. Is there any problem?"

"Yes. My shift ends in 5 minutes. And that is how much I am going to give you." He said point at his wristwatch.

"Alright. I will finish up soon." "5 minutes."

"Yeah. 5 minutes."

So Khan did what he had to do and made sure that he was satisfied before getting up and putting each file in their designated space. He called out to the old man to get things done fast. They got on the job and finished just 2 minutes after the old man's duty time. And just like that, Khan began his long tedious journey back home like every other working sheep in the capitol. Well, in his case back to the police station has he promised Ashfaq he would. He also decided to drop a simple text explaining to Laxmi of his progress. This time around, Khan had noticed the number of posters promoting Yashpal's campaign. It was as if he had handed over the reins of his PR to some international relations firm. The slogans, the design and even the look of it all were such that it would put most multi-national companies to shame. He wasn't bothered about it all that much. All he knew was that the marketing campaign wouldn't sway his opinion or his ideologies. So, he tried to shift his attention to something more appealing, like murder and death. In most instances, most cops would think about cases on their journeys but Khan didn't. His mind usually was so full of thoughts that the journey time was one of the few instances of him being clear of thoughts. The clutter, tense and sometimes graphics thoughts could at least be replaced with thoughts of the route, traffic and road ahead. That was completely fine with Khan. He had come a long way from constantly focusing on his cases all the time in his army days to 'letting things go'. That phrase was from Laxmi. She was a major reason for Khan's recent changes. Their history became less of what brought them together and more of a reason for not parting ways.

The late-night traffic had grown more and more on Khan each day. It became his favourite pastime of observing people at their worst. There may have not been any other place where people showed their basic animalistic, hounding instinct. Trying to get ahead of others wasn't a necessity here, but a desire, an obsession. So much was that obsession, that people were willing to slip down their mask of civility and their 'culture' to have it out and get their own way. Every day looked like a new fight. Khan's favourite was watching a quiet, respectable man exploding in a fit of anger at a fellow colleague when just a few hours ago he would have even respectfully repositioned a mosquito biting him. Such was the nature of traffic. The traffic of Capitol was atrocious, keeping him occupied for almost an hour this time. And the news going back wasn't better either. The route through the animal reserve was not an option this time. Even his contacts wouldn't let him go through that place at night. There was a different breeze at night. The predators had a habit of climbing fence to walk on the road. There had been instances when people had wandered through that place that night. Breaking the law in such instances carried punishments worse than what the government could hand out. So, there were two options, through Sector 6 and into the slow-moving, speed limit following traffic or through Sector 4 into the long haul. And honestly, both were equally tiring. On the one hand, you had a direct route that would cause a delay due to the people and on the other hand, you had a clear line away from traffic and an open road that was so long that it would not make any difference. Flipping a coin would be a viable choice in either of these cases. So, Khan decided to risk going the direct route hoping that he would get a clearer run. But he didn't. For all that it was worth, Sector 6 had better roads than Sector 4 making the journey at least comfortable. By the time he reached the station, it was already into Ashfaq's night shift. Night shift demanded that there be at least one senior representative of each section and so for every night, every police station would house only ten people. Mind you this was supposed to be a major station responsible for the entire sector. However, the rules were set and not many policemen were in favour of turning them around. Entering the station, Khan saw an empty desk. It was odd to find an empty desk at that time of the hour. Maybe they were having dinner, Khan thought. He was hoping that the junior at the desk could get him some food. He moved inside and found multiple desks empty. Desks where there should be at least one officer. So, he rushed to Ashfaq's desk to find out the issue. Khan's and Ashfaq's offices were near to each other. He knocked twice in anticipation of an answer, however, there was no reply. So, he tried to open the door but it was locked. This was unnerving. An empty police station in the middle of the night? Khan took out his phone to call Ashfaq but was interrupted by a voice from the entrance of the station. It was one of the juniors. Rishabh. "Where is everyone?"

"Sir, they were ordered by the HQ to create checkpoints in the sector."

"The HQ directly called?"

"Yes sir, DSI Ashfaq then ordered everyone to team up and set checkpoint at designated positions. He ordered me to stay back here."

"Okay. Get me a walkie." Khan thought about it a second and stopped his junior. "On second thought don't. Could you just get me some food? Whatever is available will be fine."

"Of course sir. Anything else?"

"No, just tell Ashfaq to visit me once he arrives back." "Yes sir."

The notes were on the table and the food was on its way. There was time now to glance over them. Sure that he was right about the man in the mask, he decided to talk to victims' families but with discretion and a false identity. That might help him get to where he wanted. This evening seemed bleak to Vasu. It was unnervingly quiet. The traffic was usual in Sector 5 but Vasu never had a problem with traffic while on his bike. But today, he didn't want to take any risks. So, he got to his nearest station, South Garden. There he could get on a train and reach Sector 9 in 45 minutes. Before leaving, he had updated Arjun of this plan and asked him to bring along a large van for the operation. Vasu meanwhile had packed his black sweatshirt, a pair of dark grey track pants and a black full-face

mask. Now, the fast train could get Vasu to Sector 9 in 30 minutes with the required change. But at this hour, that task would be impossible. The trains would be packed with people trying to get home and on top of that, the train would go through Capitol. That was the biggest and busiest station in the city. At rush hour, that station could pack up to 20,000 people at once. That includes the national line as well as the local line. With approximately 30 platforms, it would be hard to navigate if there was a train change needed. Most locals knew what they were doing, however, there used to be the usual herds of immigrants and tourists that could increase stagnant crowd due to confusion. Vasu was familiar as he had visited Capitol on multiple occasions for his startup. Now more than ever that experience was required. The train arrived just a minute after he landed on the South Garden station. There was the usual crowd and the unusual rush to get in. Having missed the train, Vasu confirmed his suspicion that it was a fast train. No way in hell he could have got on that. The next might be easy to get in. However, 7 minutes of waiting at the station didn't bring him any good news. In fact, it was no news at all as the train was just as packed as the last one. With a deep breath, Vasu got on the train pushing and shoving like he was a regular. He, like many others, got on and now was stuffed in a hot, sweaty metal box for the next 15-20 minutes. Vasu knew that this was not how the train connection was supposed to function. There was a proposed multi-line approach that didn't pass through the legislation, condemning people of public transport to horror and discomfort. Instead of multiple stations connecting each other just like any other major city would, this beacon of economic prosperity had just nine connections. Yes, nine connections for the nine sectors. So if you had to go from one sector to another via train, you had to go to the sector's head station and then catch the train there.

These trains had also been decked up with audio advertisements. This was a radical idea but with the benefit of targeting ease. Today's ads were for some travel agency, housing loans and the political campaign of Yashpal Yadav. Vasu liked Yashpal, though this form of advertisements he didn't approve of. He still had time to listen to other ads and wonder about their irony. Thinking about these issues did wonder, Vasu's struggle was almost at an end. He was at the foot of the Capitol station. This was one of the largest stations in the country. Designed almost 100 years ago, this was the humble station that shipped the liberation army around the country. Its almost gothic structure was now due for renovation. There were multiple proposals and tenders pending. The current government is although hesitant to change. According to them, people still want to look at the beautiful architecture of this station. So those proposals were in a purgatory of neither approval nor rejection. Vasu had been deposited on the 11th platform of the station and the information panel up above the main hall showed that the trains for Sector 9 would depart from platform 23rd. Platform 23 was easy to navigate, at least in Vasu's mind. The station was designed like most stations with platforms next to each other. That was for 20 platforms. The other platforms were up ahead in an expanding design after the others. They were stacked like KitKat bars but after the first 20 there would be 4, then after the first stack another 4 and lastly 2. With 2 on either side for the former and one on either side for the latter. Vasu didn't realize how deep crap he was in. The train leaving was in 4 minutes and he had to find the platform that was approximately half a kilometre away. And on this of all days, Vasu had forgotten on which side. Asking someone might help. So he asked around, and a group of distracted people rushing for their trains, point towards the platforms. Whether that was the right side or the left side, Vasu was unsure. Realizing that he was wasting his precious time and energy, he decided to gamble and go right. With every step crossing the platform, Vasu's heart grew nervous. Not only would he be late, but he had to go across the entire station again to reach the train. And that nervousness did not vanish even after seeing a train. He had to cross another four cars to finally find a plaque informing him of the platform number. It was 23. But the train was full now. He could either push in or risk waiting for another. Most people would have pushed in, even Vasu did earlier. But his disgust at the thought of sweaty armpits and the discomfort of people stuffing in a can was ever present. Today it was even visually displayed. But swallowing his spit along with the vomit that could be following, he took a deep breath like it was his last and dove in. People aren't grateful when you push them around for space and today was no exception. With abuses being heard from all eight directions, Vasu had to swallow his pride as well to get to his destination.

Excruciating 25 minutes of slow travelling, stopping at everything from signals to stations, the journey had finally come to an end. This however was the first time Vasu had seen Sector 9's Head Station. Portmouth. Named by the community as a joke, this station now serves as a symbol of pride of the bygone era. The people who have such pride are just here for financial reasons. Vasu's experience had taught him that anyone living here would fly out to any of the other sectors in a heartbeat given enough money. Their loud mouth was now just a part of their personality. He didn't mind that, he was one of them. Not on the pride front but on the getting out of the here front. The annoying part was when one of them would find out, they would cry fake outrage about their patriotic dedication to the area. That felt nauseating. Portmouth like Capitol had its gothic designer building standing tall. The difference however being, Capitol maintained its building while Sector 9 didn't. There was blackening of the stones along with major sections being broken and even falling off on occasions. Promises were made for their repair and restoration but they were just that; promises. Again, Vasu's journey outside of Portmouth was entertained by these thoughts. There was Arjun, standing on the footpath leaning on the brown Van which was probably stolen. Vasu however, decided not to ask regarding the Van but decided to focus on the plan that he had thought of. Knowing that keeping the kids in the port would be a risk, they would have shifted them but nearby. Additionally, there was a chance that they could be going out to get more kids to complete the consignment. At least that's what Arjun stated when they were travelling back to Vasu's home from the hospital. Arjun had been informed by the officer regarding this gang's activities and this had confirmed his long- held suspicions. The problem was that the cops didn't have enough evidence to convict those criminals. Even for any checking, they needed a warrant. With the FIR taken from Acharaya, the cops had raided the compound.

"Any news from the cops?" Vasu asked Arjun as he climbed into the passenger seat of the van. Their destination was now the outskirts of the Porting area. The Van was basic in performance but its enormity meant there was enough space to get 40 kids if required in the cargo hold. And its ability to do the job was what mattered to Vasu.

"Yes, they searched the same compound but were unable to find any other kids" replied Arjun.

"That's what we expected," said Vasu shaking his head in disappointment.

"Yeah, but that makes our job tough now."

Vasu looked at Arjun and confirmed, "You mean security?" "Yeah," Arjun was nodding his head.

Vasu had to correct him, "No, the problem will be locating the place where they kept the kids."

"I mean where else could they be?" He had raised his hand gesturing the question and continued. "They will be in the port, right?"

"No, they could be in one of the abandoned buildings nearby.

Like one of those plants, or even the lighthouse."

"Well, fuck me. How are we going to find them then?"

"I think instead of jumping in right away, we should keep watching them. Maybe their movements tell us the location of the kids."

"Maybe, but what if they moved them back to the port? Those kids

could be out of the country before we even figure out their plan."

"That's why we are splitting up. You will watch the lighthouse. If there is no movement there, then we will only focus on the port."

"That is stupid. What if they find me? I cannot kung-fu out of there like you."

Vasu chuckled at this reply and cleared Arjun's doubt. "No, but you can drive out."

"The reason I will be at the port is so that in case we are wrong, I can at least fight them long enough to get those kids out."

Vasu had a point. But Arjun also had a concern on that part of the plan, "You know they will shoot this time."

"They did last time. But here I am." Vasu was trying to be or at least sound confident.

He had failed, "That's overconfidence. Keep it out of this van please."

"Relax. We will be just fine."

"There is another issue. There will be more guards. How will you be able to fight them all off? Have you got any weapons?"

"No, I don't have any. And I don't think I will need either." "Tone it down a bit. And here take these," Arjun said while handing Vasu a black cloth bag. It was surprisingly light. Putting his hand inside, Vasu first pulled out what felt like a small metal rod. But it was lighter than it looked. Vasu knew in an instant what it was. Acharya's expanding titanium baton This weapon was designed to be light and effective. Unlike a regular baton, its expansion was from the middle. Rather than an antenna expanding, this baton would split in the middle. Additionally, it could be locked to restrict any movements. The split also meant that there was proper weight distribution. The second time Vasu's hand went in, they brought out heavy-duty pair of ordinary glasses. All he remembers

of these was that there were 2 colours. Red and Green. Vasu wasn't given any other details about these though. Now, finding these in Arjun's possession, Vasu had a déjà vu.

"How did you get them?"

"Same way I did the last time. Acharya didn't even suspect." Arjun was referring to an incident from their teens. After Vasu was shown these items by Acharya, he desired to use them. With the help of Arjun, Vasu kept Acharya busy while Arjun snuck both of the items out.

"You bastard. You know what these mean to him." "That's not how you say thank you."

"No, that's a polite way of saying you're fucked."

"Fine then. Give them back." Arjun said that gesturing at Vasu to hand them over.

Vasu turned to show his denial, "Since you have brought them here, I will use them and then you will return them."

"I am still waiting for the thank you."

"Here, this will help." Vasu's finger was raised. The middle one.

They were already in the southern section of the Sector by that time. This was Portland and everyone here was a suspect. Vasu & Arjun had to act as if they belonged, to avoid anyone spotting them. This area was teeming with abandoned factories and plants. There were a couple around functioning but most of them had been shut off. It was your standard industrial sector, only more ghostly and empty. The area was well planned and instead of giving companies free rein, the government of the time had allocated limits to the land's utilization. Like a well-made waffle, there were lines around the boxes. Here, however, the lines were replaced with roads and the boxes were the land available to companies. This led to innovative planning from the industrialists. Smaller companies decided to join together and use one large piece of land, whereas larger companies who weren't satisfied with limitations, split their architecture to accommodate their entire factory. This meant that utilities like waste, water and parking became a communal service that created unparalleled opportunities for the workforce. The community prospered and the industries grew until they were too big to fit here. That's when they transferred to Sector 8 and abandoned this place eventually. Today the structures stand without an audience. There are just two industries functioning, a small Paint manufacturer and a shipwreck waste management company. Both are closer to the sea, just on the opposite ends. The coast guard that was once prominent in their presence here, would barely visit now. Even the lighthouse was now a relic of the past. It looked like an ancient technology like it was built during the whaling era. And it was at first, but since then, it had been used by port authorities to maintain the flow in the harbour. Even that era had passed. It had been forsaken like an unwanted pet that you love but don't want to clean up anymore. Disused and beyond restoring, it stood waiting for its eventual dawn.

There were three compounds facing the entrance of the port. Ideally, Vasu and Arjun wanted the same spot as before but that was no longer the option. The spotlight at the top of the watchtower was now watching over like the eye of Sauron. So, the compounds on either side then? Not a chance in hell. The further away compound was the one they were supposed to check for movement while the one nearest was unfortunately inaccessible without alerting the guards. So, finding a vantage point for the overlook had just got difficult. Vasu spotted a glassed factory that had a view of the port but it was at a distance. Almost 200 meters away. With hesitance, Arjun and Vasu agreed to make that into a watchtower. Hoping that it would also provide a good enough view of the suspected compound, they drove their car out from their old getaway spot towards their new one. The factory was hollow with only a single standing structure. It was rusty, damp and smelled like a sewer. The structure looked like a church but with metal, glass and without a tower on top. They parked the van facing the exit and made their way into the tower. Not one to mention it, but Arjun felt safe going in due to Vasu's presence. He was confident of Vasu's skills and took pride in them. Especially after last night's incident. They had to climb the metal steps to reach the top. And Vasu who was now aware of how loud even the minute noise could be warned Arjun to be light on his feet. There were officially only three storeys, but each of the steps was higher and further away than in any other building they had step foot in. Arjun and Vasu both tripped the first time up. And despite Arjun's protests, Vasu refused to let him light up his torch. He had a torch among other tools and potential weapons he brought along this time. There was also a medium-size bolt cutter but Vasu had vetoed that out. So, it sat in the van. At the top of the steps, there was a walkway that circled the building 2 feet away from the glass windows. The broken windows were knocked enough to provide Arjun with a view of the port, at least in one direction. A pair of binoculars would have helped but those were not potential weapons, so Arjun didn't have them. As a method of communication, Arjun was supposed to light up the flashlight to communicate things. Quick strobes meant that Vasu was in danger of getting caught and needed to escape. Slower dips meant that there was activity in the port and permanently switched on meant that Arjun was in danger and had abandoned the position to escape. Vasu reiterated the point of the mission, as soon as the kids were with him, Arjun had to leave. The kids were the first priority.

With the watchtower installed, Vasu moved out of the building and started to make way towards the suspected compound. There was one entrance that had potentially multiple guards, so he had only one way to get in, through the roof. Not as simple as he thought it would be. Knowing that there was no way to get in the compound near him, the walls were too high and too smooth to climb, he knew that there was either the way from the other side of the compounds or risking it through the floodlights. Vasu decided to try the easy way and snuck to the other side of the compounds. The road was empty and had only a couple of lights. His black outfit did the rest.

He was like a ninja, in fact, in his mind he was one. Sticking to the wall, he kept glasses switched off as they gave out a mildly visible glow, red or green. He decided to use it only in required situations. Annoyingly, this was one of them. Potentially this could get him caught, so he had to get a swift look. And he did. It was not possible to climb up this way. Not amused at the prospect of sneaking through the light of doom, Vasu decides to use the glasses to examine the other buildings in the hope that they could contain a way up. There was no potential on any of them. However, the building across the road from the compound had potential. It was similar to the middle but an inaccessible backside. Looking around, he found that there were grooves big enough for Vasu to climb. This was dangerous. But so was sneaking the other way. And there was no guarantee of a possible way up from that side either.

The road between the buildings was only a single lane. That meant more visibility for Vasu and for the guards as well. But risking it was the norm today, so he thought what the hell. The first hole was big enough to get a practice start. It was approximately 8 feet high but that was reachable with a run-up. So, he got one and on the first try, he rushed towards the building, stepped twice on the smooth paint and the green algae and grabbed at the brick that was exposed. He did it. He was now on his way to the top. But just 2 seconds later that feeling vanished as his hand slipped and he was back on his feet. Resting his head on the wall, Vasu was already annoyed with himself. Again! He screamed to himself, in his mind. This time his hand didn't slip because his other hand was supporting it by grabbing another brick in another hole nearby. Now it was just repeating steps 3 and 4 till he reached the top of the building. On his way up there were two betrayals, one from the bricks and another from his right hand. By the time he reached the top, the memories of a floodlight and potential guard came back. And there they were waiting for him to reach up. But with patience and luck, he climbed on the roof before either could look at him. On the roof, he realized that the glow of the floodlights at this distance was so low that he could not be seen by them, but the guards were a real threat. That threat became even more real when he moved around the building to get a better look at the compound. The presence of the guards was minimal. So with all of the efforts, the question still remained whether there was any chance of kids being kept there.

He climbed down and returned to Arjun who had news to share. Despite his limited vision, he had spotted movements in the lighthouse. He verified this discovery by standing over the gap and sticking his head through one of the broken windows. In fact, that was the position Vasu found Arjun in when he got back. Confused at the arrangement, they decided to function as if there were kids at all of the suspected places. Nothing could have been left to chance. The easiest thing would have been to go in shooting with a gun. But Arjun was aware of Vasu's reservations with shooting guns. So the obvious choice was, just like last night, sneak in and sneak out the kids. Going in the lighthouse first would be better, so if required, Vasu can catch them from the back to attack while returning towards the godown. And to make sure that the kids were safe before Vasu could get them out, he had to take out all of the guards. There was no option of running away left today. There was also the question of sneaking in. The mini star they had fitted was on today and lighting up the whole road. Suddenly Vasu had a brain wave.

"Can we steal a car?"

"Why? We have a van."

"No, we could use the car as a distraction." "How?"

"We could drive the car near the wall, and mount off at the corner near the entrance. That way, their entire focus and attack shifts on the car and I can sneak in without getting caught."

"Okay. So how will you get in? I mean, if the car will be near the entrance, how will you get around that. They will be firing to kill this time."

"I know." Vasu thought about it for a while and came back with a

potential answer. "The wall. You will drive the car, while I stand on it. I will get off before you do and with a boost up, I can climb the wall."

"This is dangerous."

"I know. I am asking you to risk your life as well but-"

"Okay, I will get the car." Surprised at how easily Arjun was ready to put his life on the line, Vasu was proud of his friend. A few minutes after that exchange, Vasu came back with an old sedan. Without asking many questions to save time. Vasu got on the car and both of them prepared for a bang.

The noise of the car should have been enough to alert the guards, thought Vasu. As he reached ground zero, Vasu prepared for his leap. Before the big turn, Vasu jumped off right at the boundary of the port. This section for Vasu was unexplored. As he sat on top of the 8-foot wall, he saw Arjun execute the plan as intended. Arjun escaped with basic injuries and was quickly up on his feet running towards the safe point. Vasu sure of his friend's safety was now on the right side of the port wall. His feet hadn't even touched the ground before the airways were hazed with screaming men followed but bullets. There was just one gun firing at first. An automatic gun. But just a few seconds later that sound was multiplied. There were enough guns firing that sound alone could bring a man to the ground. However, as Vasu suspected, this was the ultimate opportunity. All eyes were on the car, all guns were in use and the dogs that were deployed ran around confused and scared.

Vasu rushed through this new side of port towards the lighthouse ready for something unexpected. There wasn't anything. No guards were on his path, neither were any dogs. By the time he had crossed the first set of containers, all of them were near the entrance. The 2nd and 3rd set of containers felt like a breeze before he got near the tall obsolete tower. His night vision glasses were on with lights at red for maximum concentration. He ran like he did running from

the dogs last night. Only this time there were no guards following him, men or dogs. The door to the lighthouse was unguarded. It was odd for a well-organized gang to have a hostage room unguarded. But Vasu then remembered, there was a chance that this place was empty. Just another shitting room for the degenerates.

The tower was round, faded yellow base and a dull red at the top that stood approximately 3 storeys high. The paint was failing to hide the now exposed brick design. There were windows at a set distance on the outside that imitated the steps leading to the top. Despite reason and logic, Vasu refused to lower his guard. He acted as if there were kids inside this building and there was a guard pointing a gun at the entrance ready to shoot him. Instead of going through the entrance, Vasu decided to climb up and attack him from the other side. The way those windows were placed, someone capable, who had earlier tried out his climbing skills on a broken building could climb it with moderate effort. The bricked design of the building was an additional bonus. The only potential concern was noise even that was eliminated by the ruckus down a few meters away. Vasu began climbing using the archway as the first step and reaching out to the window a few feet above him. He knew that this exercise would eventually make him weak and exhausted but today that was of no concern. The baton was here. Any lack of power would be taken care of by the baton. Climbing on to the third window, he was on the other side of the lighthouse. A slip could introduce him to the sharp edge and the rocks of the old port. Fortunately, Vasu was too busy to look down and ponder on his potential fate. His focus and agility were enough to get him to the top in a few minutes. The top of the lighthouse was surrounded by a metal rail and luckily on this occasion, a switched off high powered light. Climbing the rails, Vasu sat down to catch his breath. A few seconds were enough for now. The steps were concrete which meant that the chances of the guard hearing went down sharply. As he reached the gates below, all of the speculations about the guards pointing the gun at the door and kids

being inside the lighthouse proved right. Instincts saved Vasu from getting shotgunned in the chest today. The guard's gun was not as high as it should have been. Maybe he was tired of waiting for someone to burst through. The steps ended on the other side of the door where the guard stood. Between the step and the guards were approximately 10 kids. Damn! Thought Vasu. He was almost relieved when he saw the kids. Now he was in the same dilemma as last night. But today leaving the other kids was not an option. Standing a few step above the end, Vasu stepped his right foot on the rail and leapt with his baton. It opened with a swift motion ready to hit. And the hit landed right on target. Between the neck and the head. The blow was so effective that the guard fell with Vasu.

Vasu got up to confirm the number of kids, 12. The rest had to be elsewhere. Surprised at the kids running away from him scared, he realized it was the outfit he was wearing. Turning his glasses off, Vasu took off his mask and revealed himself. The kids recognized and embraced him. Touched at the gesture, Vasu again had to deliver heart-breaking news. They had to wait. The eldest, who was 12 was given the task to lead all of the others halfway up the tower, while Vasu stripped the guard of his gun and dragged him upstairs ahead of the kids. Not having any rope this time. He locked the guard out on the roof of the tower and promised the kids that he will be back in a few minutes to get them. He also took the opportunity to ask them about the others' potential location but none of them could confirm. So, before making his exit from the front door, Vasu rested his ear on the door to listen for the commotion. As it turned out, while they were in here dealing with their problem. People on the outside had stopped reacting to it audibly. There was no longer any sound that could be heard inside. That was a problem. There could be people watching for him, watching the tower. So he decided to walk up the stairs to the window that had a view of the watchtower. The building wasn't fully visible but he did have a decent view of the window where Arjun was supposed to be. There was no flashlight. But here, at this moment, Vasu encountered a massive flaw in his communication strategy. There was no way of knowing whether the coast was clear or if Arjun wasn't at the building. Risks are the norm of today. He walked up the stairs and decided to take a look, out from the top. He opened the door half expecting the guard to attack him, but he was still unconscious. There was no light on the tower, and there seemed to be no eye on either. There were two groups visible, one inside the building opposite the port and the other near their watchtower. There was hope yet. Something occurred to him, he had to confirm there were kids in the godown, if not find their location in one fell swoop. There would be no better opportunity than this. An isolated guard that he could interrogate in peace. All he had to ensure that the guard would be too scared to scream and alert the others. Vasu dragged the guard back near the stairs and shut the door to the top. How to wake him up? He asked the kids for water. Even though there wasn't any, ne of the kids volunteered to look for it downstairs. Before he could o come back, one of the kids remembered that the guy had a small bottle on him. Flask! Vasu realized. That's what the kid meant. Searching for it, Vasu found the flask in one of the back pockets. It was light, but there was a swashing sound when shaken. Hopeful, that the contents would be enough to wake the man up, Vasu tilted the flask and waited for some liquid. There was just enough for a mouthful. The dripping liquid, some sort of alcohol, was then splashed on the guard's face. This didn't have an effect at first. But a couple of seconds later, there was movement. The guard was licking the liquid that made its way on his lips. His eyes opened. The sight of a masked man with red eyes terrified him enough to push Vasu away and rush towards the door. No escape though. Vasu had already whipped out his baton, and with all the grunt and base he could manage, Vasu warned, "Don't even think about it." His hand was raised and the guard still disoriented, turned around whimpering. The voice did the trick. But it was the fear of the black mask that was evident here. The guard with this shaking sweating hand joined, begged Vasu, "Don't kill me, please." There was a real sense of fear in him that startled Vasu. A grown man that could potentially kill everyone here, was whimpering, begging and now even on his knees. Vasu had never felt this kind of power. There was a wave of confidence in him.

With that approaching sense of power and authority, Vasu commanded the guard, "Where are the other kids?"

Complacent to save his life, the guard stammered out, "In th-the godown. I am sorry. P-Please let me go. Please."

Still unsure that this was the gang's ultimate plan, "Why would I believe you? Tell me the truth. Where are the kids? or I swear the next swing will kill you." The line gave Vasu goosebumps. Where did the poison come from? Now was not the time to ponder over ethics.

"I swear, I-I swear the kids are in the godown." The helpless man could be telling truth. But Vasu had no way of knowing besides looking for himself. Vasu was prepared to accept whatever his fate will be now.

Even with all of that, Vasu was now in a dilemma, thought for a second, knocking him out would be the best thing. But how. The way the guard had been sitting down, there was no way to get in a knockout punch. So give himself a chance and catch the guard by surprise, "Get up, you will stay on the rooftop. If you alert the others, I will kill them first and come back for you."

He rushed down, closing the door, not wanting to miss the window given, and stepped out the entrance. His mask and glasses were on, the scene he viewed at the top was still the same here. No one to observe the tower. So he ran, without a worry about sound from his sneakers or the possibility one someone spotting. In what felt like forever, Vasu made it to the stack of containers he was previously hiding behind. Standing here, he had a choice, go in the compound sneaking around or go through the entire gang, clearing the way for all of the kids to escape. The latter would not be an option, but there was still time to cross that bridge. The man with the big light was a problem. He could easily hear and spot Vasu sneaking through. Even knocking him out would raise attention towards his location. Sneaking was the only way. However, the question still annoyed him. Wouldn't taking out all of the gang members ease the escape. There would not be any danger for the kids and the fear of the black mask help Vasu by scaring off a few members as well. Here he was at the crossroads, repeat yesterday's plan or capitalize on the new information. He was prepared for a fight, there was now a weapon that he could use and he had the greatest ally one could ask for. So, deep breath and the attack began. The first target, light man. He was alone on the top but armed. His focus at the gate meant that sneaking up on him would be easy. But rushing would also alert him. Speed was the answer. Rushing towards the container, Vasu's steps weren't loud. His swift movements got him close to the containers without alerting the guard. His momentum meant that Vasu could use the container as a stepping point to get on the stacked container tower. The same way he climbed the building, he was going to climb the container. The first step, second step and a light third step gave enough air to grab the edge of the container. Sure that the sound he made during his climb would alert the guard, Vasu pulled himself with all of his might and rolled up standing swinging open the baton. Continuing with the rolling motion, Vasu used his momentum and turned anti- clockwise hitting the guard on his cheek with the edge of the baton. The guard fell down swinging but not before firing a shot where Vasu would have been. The sound of the gun startled Vasu. But in a split second, he had his baton raised in the anticipation to hit the guard again. Turned out it wasn't necessary. The guard was down. The gunshot was an unwanted result of Vasu's hit. But now, the other guards had their attention towards the watchtower.

Vasu aware of the chance to get his revenge on the light swung them around and smashed them with all of his might. The guards were rushing towards him. But their momentum was halted at the shock of seeing a pair of red eyes disappearing into the darkness. Consumed by fear, the guards moved towards the watchtower with

caution. Vasu was alert for any momentum. Dogs or men, he was ready for it all. But staying behind this set of containers like a sitting duck was not the ideal plan. So, in the hope that his attire would provide enough cover, Vasu rushed out of the spot and towards the cranes. The pillars weren't wide enough to provide adequate cover. But the container near the pillars was. By the time he reached them, all of the guards had gathered near the broken light and from what he could make out, there were 12 of them. 12 with automatic guns were a difficulty but if he could split them up, he had a slim chance of knocking them all out. Looking around, Vasu found a few scraps, metal and stones. Gathering them up, he threw them in different directions. One hit near the godown, one hit near the lights and rest in varying other positions. With that, he climbed the container to watch the now confused guards scrambling to find the source of the noise. Vasu had them where he wanted. They split up in sets of 4, with each group taking the task of a particular area. One group was heading towards him, the second other towards the godown, and the third stood at the watch station. 4 people with automatic guns were walking in his directions.

Vasu waited on top of the containers to get close to the arriving group.

Reaching as near as possible, Vasu lept from the container and swung the baton right to left in the hopes of catching two of the guards at once. No luck this time. Only one was hit. Rolling over to break his fall, Vasu was now in the middle of the remaining three and dangerously close to getting hit by a bullet. So, he stepped back swung the guard to his right by stepping in the same direction. Using the falling man as a guard, before a shot could be fired, Vasu stepped right again and swung two hits on the next guard. First at the knee and the next on his head. Realizing that this position was now exposing him to the muzzle of the last standing guard, he stepped left to confuse him, barely missing the fired bullet and swapped the baton to his left hand. First, he hit the right hand, controlling the trigger. It led to the guard pointing the gun down. Then he used the momentum of his swing to pass the baton to his right hand and with adept footwork, positioned himself for a

perfect attack. On the top of the neck, his attack did just the thing he wanted and dropped the guard like a sack of potatoes. Without another thought, he ran towards the nearest container and climbed. Rather than standing or sitting down crouched, Vasu slept on his back, only listening to the activities. Catching the breath and lowering his heartbeat, he could hear the voices of the other teams. One of the team was near the site of the incident. Which one could be here he thought? The obvious answer would be the nearest team. The one going towards the godown. But the intelligent thing would have been for the team at the watchtower to rush here. This was also a possibility given their traps set for him.

Turning his glasses off, he turned on his chest and crawled at the edge of the container, there was a team here, 2 were checking on the knocked-out guards and the rest sweeping the perimeter. He crawled back into the cover and lifted his body like a push-up and looked for the teams. Both of them were missing. So now he had 8 guards in the area. All of them alerted to his presence. There was no hope of even jumping on another container. So patience was required. He knew that. But while laying down and clamping down his instincts, a sentence alerted him and brought back the adrenaline. "Check on top of the containers." That was the line uttered by one of the guards. But still controlling his instincts, Vasu restrained himself from standing up like a pole and instead got back up on his knees crawling like an infant. He could see 2 of the guards huddled near the container next to the knocked out guards. This was alarming. At this distance, he could not take all of them out and avoid bullets. So, still in the same position, he crawled back away from the gathered gang and climbed down at a safe point. There was still hope of him not getting caught if he hid behind the containers. And now that one team was busy with getting one of their member on the top of the container, the other team sweeping the perimeter could be taken out easily. So he prepared himself for attack and hide. Turning around the corner of the container, he was met by a muzzle and a surprised guard. Advantage Vasu. He took the opportunity and knocked the guard out by holding his gun with his left hand and hitting thrice, knees, shoulder and head to knock out the guard. One down, three to go. Rushing towards the other container, he could see two of them in a back-to-back position. They were prepared for the attack on both fronts. At least that's what they thought. With the darkness on his side, Vasu rushed towards them still near the container to hide himself. He knocked both of them out before they could react. With a fluid motion, first swing away from his body and the next towards his body, Vasu was surprised at how easy this was with a weapon. Then there was one. Now, Vasu was thinking of the other team already. How could he rush them? Looking towards the container they were guarding, the guards standing below had taken a triangular position. With one forward and the two with their backs at their container. The fourth guard was already on top and scanning the perimeter. Now there was no way he could take out their guard and take them down. But before they could call the other team, Vasu ran towards the remaining guard. He waited for the last man to turn away from him, locking his baton back into a short stick, he ran and stuck the edge of the stick on the guard's neck. Mistaking it for a gun, the man dropped his guard and slowly raised his hands. Vasu swiftly took away the automatic gun, dropped it down and grabbed the guard by his shoulder. He took the stick away from him stepping back and instructed him.

"Call out for them." Confused, the guard tried to look back with a questioning look but Vasu stopped him from doing so by repeating the question with high ferocity, "Call out for them to help you." The guard did. With that, Vasu opened up the stick and knocked him unconscious. His plan had worked, the team, splitting in two, came to aid the others. A big mistake. As soon as the guards appeared, Vasu took them out but with some effort. The guards fought back a little rather than shooting him. For every two hits Vasu dished out, there one of theirs that landed. The plan was still a success because now there were only two left. He now could scare the remaining into submission. But at this distance risking it was not a choice. So

slowly, he made his way towards the container where the rest stood guard. By the time Vasu got near their container hidden, both the guards were down from the container, making it easy for him. Like shooting fish in a barrel. And it was, with a simple opportunity, Vasu took out both of them like he did the rest. Relieved from the prospect of getting shot, Vasu made his way first towards the godown. As he put his hands on the door, Vasu hesitated. "What if there is a guard here just like at the lighthouse?" He thought to himself. With a deep breath, Vasu stepped aside from the door, and yelled to the potential guard inside, "All your friends are dead. Come out and I will let you go." There was no response. But a couple of seconds later, a shower of bullets unleashed, penetrating holes in the metal door. Praying that a stray bullet doesn't leave, Vasu prepared to enter the building as soon as the bullet storm would end. There was silence, almost deafening. This was the chance. And Vasu took it. With his glasses on, Vasu pulled open the doors of the godown and entered. Noticing the guard looking at him desperately trying to reload the gun, Vasu swiftly made his way. Swinging open the baton, there was just a split second between the baton opening and the guard lifting his gun. However, he was late. Before anything could be done, the guard's face was met with a hollow but strong and fast approaching titanium rod. Down he went, like titanic, slowly but surely.

Leading the kids towards the safe point, Vasu realized that in all of this, he hadn't given a thought to Arjun's safety. The guards were near him. Despite all of their efforts, Arjun was again in danger exposed without a defence. Nervousness grew in Vasu's mind with every step he took towards the safe point. He knew for a fact that the guards didn't go inside the place, but the thoughts of Arjun in danger were weighing down, crushing all logic and reasoning. The answer was just a corner ahead. There he was. Sitting in a running van with his head down. Vasu called out for Arjun, to which he lifted his head and drove the Van out on the road. Loading the kids in the back, Vasu climbed on the front seat and took off his mask.

Without saying a word to each other, they shared a smile and drove off.

CHAPTER FOUR

INTEGRITY &
CANDOUR

The weather was undeniably cold today, even for Sector 7. The breeze and the dew brought about a silence that Khan was unfamiliar with at this sector. It had all gone quiet, no doubt about it but still, there wasn't any peace. But in the stillness of the dawn, the city seemed beautiful. In that moment, there was no distraction, no suffering, not even the slightest of discomfort. There was just stillness and silence. That was the gift of today. And Khan decided to take it in as much as he can. He liked taking all the good things that he could. Rare was a day when there was even the smallest form of comfort or pleasure he couldn't take. Now this comfort was only added to by the sight of Rishabh. He carried with him the breakfast of champions, Hot, spiced tea. It was the apogee of beverages. Like a ritual of a cult, all of the cops had to drink it. No matter the Sector. Handing Khan one of the glass, Rishabh joined him sipping his mind opener. The tea was the only break Khan got from the paperwork and reading. Ashfaq hadn't returned and now Khan owed him a full day. "No worries", he thought. There will be many more opportunities. But right now, the case of the black mask had occupied him. There was a list of suspects he had to draw. And eliminate them with great scrutiny. Investigating was unlike the films that people saw. There was not much drama or action to write about. Just people talking, reading, and talking again at the core of it. If there was any action, it was only experienced at the end of the case, once there were a couple of suspects left. If the movies portrayed the actual investigating procedures of detectives and cops, all you would be left with was some people having a conversation for

90% of the film and then a few slaps and punches. "The whole night was wasted." Out of nowhere, Rishabh passed the statement. Khan felt it was unwarranted. He was aware that the night was uneventful for a cop, but no so much to be called waste. "What? Why did you think that?" Wanting to know why his subordinate felt such way, Khan asked.

"No. I meant for the others. We at least did some paperwork." He replied realizing that without context the line might have seemed like a rude comment toward his senior.

"Oh!" Khan exclaimed with the relief that he hadn't bored his colleague. But still not clear why it would have been for the entire sector's force, he continued. "I still don't get it. Please explain."

"I was radioed a message. While they were here waiting for the Black Mask, he did his job in Sector 9. HQ's info was wrong." Rishabh explained hoping that this would satisfy his senior. Khan felt bad for the boys. Not many times would that have felt unsatisfactory. He understood that most of the barricades were just for precaution and wouldn't yield much, but when set up with an objective, it was achievable. So, having wasted all of that energy and resources in the night would have felt demotivating. Khan sympathized with them. Having been outsmarted on multiple occasions, Khan knew exactly how much and where it would hurt. But there was not much that could be done other than putting your head down and working your ass off. Hoping that his day would reap better results than his colleagues' time did, Khan prepared himself to visit as many of the victims' family and friends for information as he could. Any link would help crack the case and find a definitive suspect. He had lined them up in the most convenient way possible with room for any unscheduled visits. Now he waited for the morning team to arrive. He also had to line up a lie that would explain the leave with complete satisfaction and no room for error. Woman. That was easy to understand for everyone and would restrict any intrusive questioning. Khan knew that his colleagues cared for him. And the prospect Khan settling down would get approval from the entire department. Feeling guilty at the prospect of lying to the department, he already had planned a dinner and drinks night as a form of apology. That would expel any feeling of betrayal. And no one would turn down free drinks. Win- Win. It had been almost an hour before the new team arrived and a few minutes later so did the night team. It took HQ long enough to give out relieving orders. But that was the norm. Every sector head, like Khan, would often fight HQ order by questing, deviating, and outright denying as much as they could. That was also the most effective form of bonding exercise that no HR would have thought of. Collective Dissension.

Ashfaq with him brought the opportunity to get more info on the black mask case. Even if it was negative news, Khan thought of it as an addition to the case. Giving him enough time to relax and have a tea, Khan went into Ashfaq's cabin. Knocking on the door twice, he opened it to find his tired officer leaning back completely on his chair, his face looking up with a wet towel covering it. The glass on his table was filled with steaming hot tea.

"That bad?" Khan startled a drowsy Ashfaq. He hadn't been home in 24 hours and sleeping on duty was now a necessity.

"Yes sir, I didn't realize you came in," said Ashfaq shooting up from his chair with half the energy but complete effort.

"It's okay. Sit. Tell me what happened first and then leave for the day." Khan said motion for Ashfaq to sit while he sat as well.

"It was just a waste of time." Ashfaq was echoing Rishabh's words. But the emotions here were of utter disappointment. "HQ, well Panditya & Shah, had all of us block roads at all the major junctions. They were tipped that Sector 7's gang IRA was the target and we could catch them."

"Didn't they join you? And how did they get such a tip?" Now actually curious of their operating style Khan asked hoping this would clarify things.

"They did. For 15 minutes. Then they got bored and left for 'investigation'." Ashfaq felt real detest towards them. Warranted in this case, as both of them felt today. "And the source, I asked them. Where did they find such an accurate piece of information?" With a mocking tone, he continued, "We do not reveal our sources. Just do as you are ordered." With that Ashfaq scoffed and leaned back on his seat.

Khan was at this point chuckling. And looking at Ashfaq's pitiful face he cleared, "You did a great impersonation." With both of their spirits lifted from the ridiculousness of the situation, Khan ordered, "Now get up, get cleaned up, and go report to your wife. If I find you here in 10 minutes, I will suspend you." With that, he went back to his office. Sitting down and worried that his investigation might also yield similar unsatisfactory results, Khan started questioning his drive. The reason to pursue this case with such dedication seemed quite insignificant. Justice. Everybody seeks the same. Why did he want to bring this man to justice with such ardour that he would risk his and other's careers? Was it all justified? Could he be wrong and was just angry at the man being able to work outside the system and bring about significant changes?

Realizing that this feeling was the same he felt in his first case with the army intelligence. He was partnered on a similar case during one of the minor conflicts. The suspect in question was to be investigated for war crimes including but not limited to torture, murder, rape and perfidy. All of these crimes were allegedly committed by a certain well-decorated officer during the 6-month standoff with the neighbours. The trade agreement talks had increased the tensions between the nations and the religious differences had just increased the mounting fallout. These types of situations caused a lot of citizens to spew out their hostility on anyone that opposed or even questioned the government's approach. But among these, the men in green were seemingly unphased. At least that is what the collective defence league had the citizens believe. There were anomalies. Sometimes even the soldiers went overboard. They were human after all. A man's resolve and values can only take so much before there is a reaction. And in the case of someone who had trained for 2 years in every form of weather and stood at the wall as the wall for another 3 years, there was an explosion of unmatched proportions. It started from what Khan and his senior partner on the case found out, a village's protest to the army and government's actions. The intrusion that this conflict was causing had a devastating effect on the villages near the border. And one among those decided to voice their concerns. There was a letter at first, stating their suffering to the PMO. Which was then followed by a letter signed by the entire village. That brought media attention that the government couldn't deal with. Soldiers weren't happy with the situation either, after all, they are like the citizens they protect. But while every other troop member dealt with the situation in a peaceful manner, there was one who couldn't. His first act of such violence was raping a woman from the village. The accusations and call for justice that followed were turned down and ignored because even the thought of an army officer committing such atrocities was sacrilege. Then a spy caught trying to sneak in was murdered by the officer when left in charge of his incarceration. This was also dismissed as the injury sustained by the infiltrator were extensive. This was when one of the senior officers had a seed of doubt, and rather than live with it, he wrote of his concerns to the CO. This resulted in the dispatch of intelligence officers under the guise of a survey for safety. During all of this, an enemy squad that was supposed to surrender after being defeated post infiltration was found dead riddled with bullets. According to the report filed, it was stated to be a frantic retort. However, in reality, this was just filed under pressure from the morally corroded officer. During the investigation, or the guise of survey, details and clues were obtained that warranted an official investigation. But before all of that, the procedure was to question fellow officers and finally the accused. The news of questioning had reached that officer before it should have, which resulted in him deserting his unit and attempting to infiltrate the enemy lines for a last-man-standing attack. He was caught, held, and tortured for over 6 months. Due to the extensive training from the army, no secrets were revealed to the enemy. His eventual release came with a diplomatic but unsanctioned exchange of POWs and the officer's eventual Capital Punishment.

Even though during all this Khan had grown to be physically invincible, his ideologies hadn't been shaped. They were like wet clay waiting for the right pressure and hand to shape it into his own. That case influenced him enough to realize that even the most honourable people are capable of the cruellest acts. The thoughts of the officer's action being potentially justified changed when he encountered the people that were affected by his actions. His idea of justice began to take shape at that moment and it became what it is today. The events of that case still act as an anchor for him when Khan feels lost in the sea of an ideological storm. There are many ideas and forms of justifications being thrown around every day. People, without any second thought to the consequence of violence accept it as the only way. There are exceptions, even Khan believed that. But in every odd case, we want a violent outcome. We have grown numb to the suffering of others. Just our personal outrage matters. While swimming in the pool of ideological nonsense, Khan was deep diving without a care for the outside world.

To his surprise, there was a knock on the door. It was Talpade. He was carrying with himself the usual dignity and pride that you'd expect from an officer of the law.

"Ehrm. Good morning sir."

"Oh! Good morning. Come in." Talpade sits down with uncharacteristic swiftness.

"Sir, there is a piece of news that I am not supposed to tell you." He continues. "Yesterday Sector 9 was hit again by Black Mask."

"Again? You mean it was hit once before?"

"Yes. What is even more surprising that there was a witness left alive."

"That is great news. We would find a ton of information there.

But wait, what changed with this gang?"

"That is the thing, sir, according to the witness, the mask didn't kill them first but knocked them out. And later when he got up, all of them were dead."

"So he killed them after knocking out? That's odd." The surprise and confusion were visible on both of their faces.

Talpade went on. "There is more."

"The first time around, the mask didn't kill anyone. According to the witness, there were hostages. He just rescued them."

"Go on."

"A case was registered with the Sector 9 by a caretaker of one of the orphanage. Their kids were taken by the gang that night."

"So he helped them?"

"Yes, that's what has been bugging us all. But Panitya and Shah are fine with it, and want to move along."

"What do you mean?"

"They want this information out in the press." "And turn that psycho into a hero?"

"Exactly."

"What does CG want?"

"There has been no news from her. I think she doesn't even know yet."

"This is serious." Slowing down from his first instinct to call Laxmi, Khan decided to get more information. "Any more info on the mask?"

"Yes. We have a profile from the report. He was dressed in all black by had red eyes."

"Red!? You mean he had contacts?"

"No. He had glowing red eyes." Talpade continued, "There's more. He was also using a baton. And could disappear apparently." Khan signalled Talpade to continue "I think it was a baton because there were signs of attack with a blunt instrument."

"What else? How were they murdered and how many were there?"

"Shot in the head. And there were 14 this time."

This was the largest body count yet. Khan immediately responded, "Fuck! How wasn't the media all over it?"

"Sector 9 sir. Nobody cares. Plus, Shah has a reputation with them. Although they must have received all the info, nobody would print before the all-clear was given."

"Yeah." Khan thought over the incident for a while and then said, "There one question I care about more than all of it. How did you get all of this information? You are one of my officers."

"I-I shouldn't be telling you this but, they offered a bribe and I took it," Talpade said this while looking behind as if he was bribing Khan himself.

"What was it? Money or promotion?" Khan asked curiously. "Promise of promotion. I took it considering the potential ocean of information." Now taking the weight of the chest, Talpade spoke freely, "Where else could I get all this information without paying?" "You are right. Tell you what. Don't risk your cover by coming in here. Text me on my number with this." Khan handed Talpade a black cell phone and continued, "It's a burner. Whatever you write or dial, it erases instantly."

"Thank You."

Talpade nodded and replied, "Sir, please keep me in the loop. I might not be working on it but that doesn't mean I can't help."

"Of course. I'll take your leave."

The case was getting more and more complicated. The motives of the mask were getting elaborate as well, but not in the direction Khan was hoping they would. The action of the man suggests a dual personality. Or in this case there just were two men. Two men who either were misguided or were exceptionally deceptive. Either way, they were too dangerous to be left out without restraints. Maybe a guiding hand but still with restraint. Surprised that Laxmi hadn't updated Khan with the information, he decided to call her. But in the back of his mind was still the alternate situation that she simply didn't know. One of them made her compliant with the narrative and the other naïve of the situation. This was unacceptable to Khan if they were to work together again. The call was disconnected just after two rings. It was uncharacteristic of her. Maybe she was in a meeting. But this early? The thoughts and leading questions had just been developing when the phone in his hand buzzed. It was a text from Laxmi.

"sorry can't talk text me the issue will get back asap" Not thinking much of it, Khan decided that his concern deserved more than the 160 characters of an SMS. So, he replied, "I will call later. Not urgent."

Walking out of the police station, Khan was sure that today was a good day. The information gathered by Sector 9 was of utmost importance and would help at least physically profile the criminal. The claims were a little outrageous but given the situation, everyone, every testimony, and every piece of potential evidence deserved a second look. Now, it was his task to put together the puzzle that was the mask's psychological profile. That would help catch him by predicting his moves. Any insight today would be priceless.

Last night didn't end well for Vasu. Despite that success, his arrival in his house was met by an angry, disappointed parent who knew that she had been fooled. And this was one fight that Vasu could never win. And last night was no different. No matter what he would try and say, his disappearance wasn't justified. The act was wrong, no matter the reason. And for once, Vasu had stated the reason that could have been acceptable. His lies of meeting a girl were met with mixed feelings. While his mother was happy that he had found someone, the act of sneaking out still wasn't justified. And to push the idea of not lying to your mother, there was punishment delivered. No more bike riding. Vasu accepted knowing that this was the easiest way out. He had no bike. The damage had caused some issues with it later, so he had to leave it at the refuge. Hence no worry about breaking the law.

Maybe that was for the best he would always think. Maybe there were things that mom knew that he didn't. But all that rationalization would come hours, sometimes days after the initial fight. His instincts would always get him in a fight and then, his guts wouldn't back him up. They knew better than his brain, don't fight with your mother.

The next morning did not get better for him. His phone rang and there it was. On the other line was Acharya. The instructions were simple. Get down here as soon as you can. And he did, the routine journey felt bleaker, the people seemed more annoyed and the trains seemed faster. He was in trouble and nothing about the surrounding was encouraging. He was practising his excuses all along, how - it was who he was, or the right thing. They were all practised. Vasu was aware that the events of last night were dangerous, but he also knew that anyone would have done the same thing. That was his line of defence. As he reached the refuge, Vasu prepared, tightened his shoulders, gripped his bag, and with a deep breath opened the door. Aware of Acharya's whereabout due to the time of the day, he went straight into his office. There he was sitting at his desk, reading a small but sizable book. The title couldn't be read as the book was placed on the desk. But Acharya's interest in it meant that it was a classic novel, Agatha Christie, Hemmingway, or even Wells. It could have been any of them. But before Vasu to get in a word, Acharya's head raised, looking towards him, he asked the most obvious question.

"What were you thinking?" Acharya was angry more than he was disappointed.

Vasu tried to go along, justifying his actions, "I thoug-"

"Oh right. I forgot. You never do. You always took decisions like it was choosing a flavour of candy. Let's go with this one." He interrupted

"No. I thought it through. I was aware of what I was doing."

"Oh good. I thought you had flipped the coin again." The sarcasm was overwhelming.

"Nooo. I stopped doing that. I have matured you know."

"Yes. That's what I thought. A mature man would have stolen my weapon and goggles, dressed up like a clown, and jumped in the middle of a gang, fighting them on a whim. Hmmm, very mature." It had peaked now.

"I didn-"

Acharya didn't care for Vasu's reasonings anymore, "Don't even think about denying that. Arjun told me everything. How is it that he became more reasonable than you? Where is my gear that you stole?"

"Home. Well hidden. And you are right. I am sorry. I shouldn't have stolen your things or even stolen a car and a van. But I am not going to apologize for saving those kids."

"You think doing what you did was right? Not just morally but personally. Did you really think that there was no other way?"

"What way? Wait for cops to raid the compound while kids are already halfway around the world? I couldn't let that happen."

"Really? Why is that? Some things are beyond your control. Interfering with them would lead to chaos in your life. Do you want that?"

"That is just another one of your illogical spiritual mumbo jumbo. I am not a kid anymore. Those things will not work on me." Vasu had stood up frustrated with Acharya's relentless attack.

"With every line you speak, you are displaying your immaturity. Think about what you have done. And focus on how it will affect you."

Vasu was boiling over with anger as well. "What I did last night was

save those kids. And what it already did for me is to lift my guilt." He was trying his best to be reasonable. "Yes! I made a mistake when I left them there to save the kids of our home. But I did what was right and now my conscience is clear."

"Your actions to rectify one mistake had led you into a cache of other problems." Realizing that the anger would not help either, Acharya calmed down and tried to reason his concerns as peacefully as he could. "Think my child. What if you get caught? What if one of those cops comes here looking for you and blames all of those murders on you. What will you do? No, what will your mother do?"

Vasu had calmed down thinking about it. At least on the surface. But there was still some head deep down. "Nothing will happen to me or my mother. Please do not worry about us, I can take care of her. And if-IF the cops find me, I will tell them the truth and I will be exonerated. You taught us, Truth always prevails."

"Again, with the naïve talk. The truth prevails only when people are standing up for it. Do you see anyone standing up for the truth these days?"

"I am. Arjun is. And I was hoping you would be too. But I guess I was wrong. You abandoned the pursuit of truth like you abandoned whatever you were before."

Acharya didn't like this jab from Vasu, "Speak only of things you know. My path was none of your concern."

"Exactly!"

"So this is where you wish to draw the line? Walk away from us all?"

"If protecting the people I care about with any means necessary is walking away from you, then yes. Gladly."

"Fine then. I cannot stop you. Do as you wish. But always remember, I am here for whenever you feel lost."

This was an unprecedented disaster, thought Vasu. Never before had he been angrier with Acharya. There had been disagreements but never to this extent. No matter, for the first time in his life, Vasu was clear about his purpose. What he did last night gave him a feeling like never before. He was ecstatic and felt like his actions meant, stood for something. And he wished to continue this path. But one of the things that Acharya said made sense. What about mother? There was no way she could be told about this. Moreover, there was a chance that there would be a direct or an indirect attack on her. So, Vasu had to come up with a plan to keep her safe. Staying at the home was a way, but there was no way in hell she would move here. Hoping that the journey back would help with the planning, he decided to make his way back. Shutting the door behind him, Vasu was startled by Arjun. This was unlike him and they hadn't talked about the incident since last night. The expression Arjun carried spoke volumes to Vasu. He had been given a talking to by Acharya as well. So wanting to make his friend feel better, Vasu tried his best to air out the sourness of the situation. But Arjun struck first.

"We shouldn't have done it?" Arjun said shaking his head.

Not sure what his shook friend was trying to say, he asked, "What the hell?"

"Last night will get both of us in trouble. Real trouble."

Vasu was now frustrated. Acharya had pushed him to the edge and now Arjun was just poking by being cryptic. "We helped the kids get out. For fuck's sake talk clearly!"

"All of them are dead." Arjun had genuine fear in his voice.

Vasu heard and processed it as best as he could, "How? I-I just hit them? Fuck!"

"Yeah, I think you shouldn't come here anymore." Arjun had said that to protect the place that he and Vasu loved. A place they called home. Hoping that Vasu would understand the request Arjun was making, he put for the concern.

But Vasu didn't appreciate that remark. He felt that as soon as the work was done, Arjun was kicking him out. He felt betrayed, "What the fuck? I risked my life for this place and you want me to not-Fuck you!!" Vasu's anger had peaked again, he exploded.

Arjun tried his best to explain, "Listen-"

But Vasu was no longer listening. His anger had been freed of its leash and eating at any reasonable thinking. "No, you listen to me fucker. I was in there getting shot at while you stood aside safe in a building. I was willing to give away my life so that the kids would return back to this place. Did you really think I did all that to endanger these kids, this place?"

Arjun didn't want to explain anymore. Just like Vasu, his fear was taking over and he too lost control, "Then what's your plan when the cops arrest you." He paused to listen for Vasu's response. Since there wasn't any he continued. "Exactly. If the cops don't see you here anymore, we could deny then knowledge of your fight or your existence. At least that way this place won't go down with you."

Vasu wasn't expecting that line. At least not from Arjun. Even though he knew they had their differences but Vasu thought that Arjun would understand how he felt about the place. Why he was so attached to it. Vasu now just wanted to retaliate against Arjun's attack. "Alright, I will not come by here. But who will protect you after I'm gone?" He was waiting for Arjun's answer, sarcasm anything that he could use as a weapon. However, there wasn't a reply. Vasu didn't know much of what he wanted to do now, but he knew at least this, "Don't ever call me again. Fuck You!"

Vasu walked away still thinking of the conversations that had him so pissed. But it took him a while to realise the core of both the argument. Shit just got real. Vasu just realized the gravity of the situation. The people he apparently knocked out were dead. But they weren't when he left. Vasu was now not that sure whether he really just knocked them out or he actually killed them. The baton was strong and his swings were hard. But Vasu knew how much to restrain. However, now was not the time and place. Now he had to just get clear and give his mind some space to think. There was too much information delivered among too much drama and there was no getting around the fact that Vasu's life was in danger. There were many conclusions that he could draw but nothing would help him besides solid facts. His only source of information up until now had abandoned him. Now, he had to work towards getting some form himself. But where to begin? Local people won't talk to anyone they don't know. Not even cops. Maybe journalists. That's it. That would work. He could talk as a journalist with the cops and get accurate solid information. Maybe visit a police station or even talk to a police officer that would be friendly. Walking his way towards the station, he gave his alibi a try. What he did, where he was from, what he wanted were all important. He had to have his story straight. Saying that he was a journalist wouldn't work, he needed an id or someone who could vouch for him. He could say he was a student. That would also require id but Vasu remembered he still had his id from college. He could use that to get by. But only if people didn't look too closely. It was risky, but it was better than nothing. The second was the timing. He realized that turning up at a police station before they have released any information would draw suspicion and incriminate him easily. So, he had to wait. Acharya's talk of patience is what came to his mind at the moment. And finally, he also had to make a friend. Someone he could get information from regularly. That might be the most difficult one. Given the media's reputation of asking questions that were too difficult sometimes, getting a cop to feed information regularly would be a massive challenge. Maybe bribing one would help, but that could just get him shot. Not a chance in hell. The train he took gave him enough time to properly formulate a story. All he had to do was wait. Wait for the right opportunity and approach a friendly cop. Someone who would be willing to get him the right information at the right time.

Khan had now reached Sector 5 in pursuit of clues hoping for a breakthrough in this case. Nothing substantial was gained from his previous inquiries and all of them had the usual common link. They didn't talk about their business. The victim's secretive dealings meant that only the other party besides the victim had the right information. That was what Khan found frustrating. All of this was tied up too tightly thought Khan visiting the 4th victim's family. Subodh Mishra was a policy advisor for the current government. His role seemed small but any input from people like Subodh Mishra could change the tide of a bill. Their knowledge was supposed to be impeccable and their opinions, flawless. Khan rarely had sympathy for politicians. His opinion of them being blood- sucking tics on the body that was democracy was never changing. Subodh's job however was deceptively more powerful and important. It warranted far more attention towards the member holding the position than it was given. Even Khan wasn't much aware of it. All he knew was such a position existed and nothing more. Had the position been given enough attention, Subodh's death might not have gone under the radar. His case was curious in the sense that it was just a simple murder. Well, as simple as murder could be. The body was found early in the morning with no assault marks besides the fatal knife wound. According to the accounts of her wife, Subodh had been out with friends after which he never returned. There were calls made, but before an official complaint could be registered, it was too late. There was no next of kin, so Khan had to be careful here. Subodh lived in the eastern district of the sector like every other bureaucrat in the city. That was their society. The majority, or opposition, left, or right, liberal, or authoritarian, all of them lived here. The presence of cops was not appreciated. Lately, there was an increase in personal security by the residents in the hope of reducing police interference in the name of safety. Khan had already successfully used the journalist routine. But here, it was a risky venture. Behind the gated community lived several people Khan had pissed off personally. And politicians remember even if you don't. His well-pressed blue shirt, black trousers, and a well-set hairstyle said office manager rather than a journalist. But that was still a better look than the usually buttoned-down, creased white shirt and khaki pants; the certified look of a policeman. As he approached the two-storey bungalow of the policy advisor, he got more of a successful businessman atmosphere rather than a government servant. Nonetheless, he rang the bell and waited patiently. There was an answer. It was Subodh Mishra's wife, Kajal. Her dark circles were proof that her struggle wasn't over. She was wearing a washed-out green saree that matched her mournful face.

Khan realizing that this wouldn't be as easy as he dreamt, dropped all of his reservations and grew sympathy that he never thought he would feel for a politician.

"Hello"

"Hi, how can I help you?" she asked softly.

"I am an independent journalist working on a report of unsolved tragic deaths. I was hoping I could talk to you for a few minutes." Khan said with as much professionalism and politeness as he could. "I see. But why after all this time? Don't you have everything you need in papers?" It was a valid question from her. Details of the case were published by the hounds to the horror of the widow.

"Those are established newspapers; I am an independent journalist. I like to personally check the details to make sure there isn't any false information. I hope you understand." This was the part that Khan always had doubts about. He never managed to like this part of his investigation.

"Fine. Show me your id."

"Mam, I don't have an id. Like I said-"

Khan didn't have an ID. He knew that the independent reports had the ID from their collective from but Khan didn't want to copy it. That's where Kajal Mishra had a problem. She asked, "Yes, an independent reporter. But you must have some sort of identification. How am I supposed to trust you?"

"I believe this would help." Khan presented an old counterfeit card. He was given it by an old friend no more. "I no longer work there but I carry this to get into places. You know. It makes things easier."

"Fine, come on in." She led Khan inside. "Why did you leave the paper?"

"We had different ideas of what reporting means." He was expressing a truth covered in a thin layer of a lie. "You remember the TechKom Incident?"

She knew right away, "Yes, that was such a scandal. I am glad you left before that. Good people lost their jobs because of some rotten apples."

"Yes." As they sat down, Khan took out his notebook and continued.

"Shall we begin?"

"Of course."

"What was Mr Mishra like?" Khan asked as compassionately as he could. "Did he ever talk about work? Anyone he could have ticked off?"

She tried to wave off the answer like it was an uncomfortable topic. "He worked for the government. There were tons of people that hated his guts. I mean-"

"Someone that stood out. Someone that got inside his head." Khan interrupted.

"No. I don't think so." Kajal didn't speak much.

Khan wanted to lean further hoping it would open her up. "I was hoping you could provide some insight. I am still unhappy that his murder remains unsolved."

"I know but I have moved on." She stated dismissively. "He is gone and no amount of investigating or punishing or justice could bring him back."

He was not happy with all of it. "I understand. I am sorry I brought up the subject. Maybe, I'll leave. This is more than enough for the article." Khan had tried his best not to poke. He knew the feeling of loss was escalated by the lack of justice. "I understand how you feel. Even though the dead don't care, it's the living that suffers along with the pain. Again, I am really sorry. I will not bother you again." Khan said that and tried to get up to leave.

Kajal stopped him, "Wait. There is something." She was hesitant but still continued, "Subodh was annoyed with a recent policy. It was nothing but I have not seen him bothered by a policy before. Before he was murdered, Subodh mentioned meeting someone to amend it."

This was enough for Khan, "This is good enough. Is there anything else?"

"No, I am sorry."

"It's alright. You have helped plenty. I promise you I will do my best to get these people to justice."

As Khan was leaving, from the edge of his eye he could spot a familiar figure. Not wanting to get recognized, Khan tried to speed walk out of there. Not successful. He was spotted by the figure and was stopped by his loud call.

"Khan!" It was Yashpal Mishra. He continued, "SI Ashraful Khan, right?"

"Mr Yashpal. You have a great memory." Khan was surprised and uncomfortable.

"Yes, I don't forget interesting people." He continued, "So, what brings you here?"

"Just a friendly visit. And yourself?"

"Same. I was visiting Mrs Mishra. I usually check up on her."

"And these two?" Khan said pointing at the armed guards, "They are well-wishers as well?"

"No. Did I say something to piss you off?" Yashpal was not happy with Khan's comments.

"No, it's not you. It's all politicians." He cleared it up.

"You said that last time but I thought I made it clear. I am not a politician. I am here to represent the voice of the people"

"That's what a politician would say."

Yashpal chuckled, "Nice one. I have been wanting to talk to you regarding this black mask guy."

"I am sorry but I cannot-"

"Please, I am not in power. We are just two people talking." "Alright. What do you want to know?"

"Have you found any clues regarding the case? I have a similar feeling to CG on this. No good people kill."

It was odd for Khan to be on the same page as Yashpal. "You have that right. And no, I am sorry but I am no longer on the case. I couldn't talk on the progress of it either."

"Well, we both know you are still investigating it." Yashpal knew of the secret investigation, or did he?" I mean why else would you be here?"

"I can neither confirm nor-"

"Please, I am trying to help. I will support you in prosecuting this criminal if you can catch him before the elections."

"And how would that help you?"

"Well, an upstanding citizen and a police officer standing with me are more than enough. Don't worry. You catch them, I will help you out with the criminal proceedings, judge, and defence."

"I mean-"

"You are concerned with justice, I know. That's why I am offering you the only bribe that I can, my complete confidence and support. Whether you accept it or not is up to you."

This was a dilemma. Here was a politician, a species that Khan hated from his core, offering help to achieve goals that were impossible without bureaucracy. He weighed out his options and arrived at the conclusion that an exception doesn't make a habit. So, with a heavy heart and a stain on his principles, he replied "Okay. But only because of Laxmi."

"That's the spirit. You and I will be a great team."

This was not ideal for Khan. Aligning with a politician was the last thing on his bucket list. But, even Khan knew that support in prosecuting those criminals is not found easily. He had to have an ally in the higher-ups. And Yashpal's popularity meant that his support would help gain traction to an already difficult case. Adhering to Laxmi's advice involuntarily, Khan had agreed to sleep with the enemy. So, the future was secure, sort of. But the present, that had got even more interesting. A policy change that got Mishra killed. What the policy was will help Khan get details that seemed like a gold mine. A lot of digging to find dirt, dust, disease, and eventually unsatisfactory nuggets of justice. But that's how things go. His next destination was Mishra's office but before that CG's office needed a visit. A phone call would have helped but a visit would annoy her more. Forced to accept distasteful things, Khan wanted to pass that flavour over.

Vasu was jumping from one new channel to another like his life depended on it. Luckily, his mother wasn't around. And he was glad for that. Having endured a similar fit of madness, she had told him off aggressively enough to never have to endure again. Most mothers would have smacked him. But on that day, Vasu was glad she wasn't most mothers. The flipping went on long enough for Vasu to be bored as well. He had no choice but to stick to one channel. National Communication Service was a government established news channel. Even though this network was established by a ruling party, the board on this news organization was only answerable to the people. It had elected officials on the board that regulated the content for the duration of 7 years before re-election. Now, this was a sleep inducting boredom that Vasu couldn't tolerate. But the only reason he kept his channel on was due to its signature tune for breaking news. This was played ritually since its inception. This meant that he could leave the channel on, not pay attention to it and only listen in when the music comes on. "This was a great idea", were the first words that came out of Vasu when he heard the music 2 hours later. That's how long he would have had to endure the news. Came on the anchor to announce the breaking news.

"We interrupt your regular broadcast for this breaking news. The black mask has struck again. According to the investigating officers, the gang struck this time was White Dragon. This dangerous gang was suspected to be involved in child trafficking, extortion, and kidnapping among other things in Sector 9. The incident occurred last night around 1 A.M but the details of this incident were hidden to confirm the attacker involved. According to reports a member of White Dragon has survived and provided testimony of the incident to the police. Here is Detective Panditya Suri with the details."

"We were informed of the incident by one of Sector 9's patrolling van. They quickly called in the HQ and we mobilized our troops to examine the crime scene. This was in line with the pattern of previous incidents but due to the enormity of the number of victims, we had to observe precautions."

"What about the witness, what did he confessed to?" asked the reporter on the ground with Panditya.

"Well, he basically shared the details of their organization. It is an organization and not a gang, and about their operations. We found out intricate details that wouldn't have been possible without last night's incident. And in light of the information, a warrant has been issued and arrests are being conducted of the people involved."

"What about the black mask? Any details on his identity? This is the first witness to have contact."

"Yes, there were a few details mentioned. But they were of a supernatural kind." Panditya chuckled at this statement.

The reporter was confused. "Excuse me?"

He straightened up and replied, "Yes, the ahem-the witness is traumatized due to the incident and his testimony about the person is sketchy."

"But what did he say? The people would like to know." The reporter said looking at the camera.

"This is his statement." He cleared his voice again before continuing. "And I quote, 'The thing had red glowing eyes. And he could disappear. He went from places to places killing people. We never saw him coming.' I think this testimony will not stand in court and we would need more than a ghost that can vanish and a red-eye devil to catch the person." The news then shifted back to the dumb-founded anchor.

He already had the lines ready and spewed it as soon as he could, "So, as mentioned by the investigating officers, yesterday was quite a productive day but without any effort put in by the police department. A vigilante was doing the job that the justice system should have done. Additionally, some reporters have dubbed the man in the mask as Phantom Butcher. More on that later."

"This is quite a shameful day for the justice department, getting shown up but a lone man in a mask. I mean, what is next?" said the co-anchor.

"I understand your frustration with the police but not everyone agrees with you. Earlier, while on his regular visits to the victims without justice, Yashpal Vohra was very vocal in support of the police department. If you are unaware, Yashpal Vohra is an independent candidate opposite the incumbent Mayor in the upcoming elections. He is standing for the people. And even his party has quickly grown into the largest in the city. Let's take a look." They again moved but this time to an anchor standing with Yashpal Mishra.

"What do you think of the investigation regarding the black mask?"

Yashpal was stern and confident in his answer. "I think the shameful incapacity of some police officers is tarnishing the image of the entire police department. There are good officers working hard to catch the criminals and I believe people should support those that are working for them, not for the Mayor."

"Why certain members? Doesn't the handling of Subodh Mishra's case raise the doubts of the entire police force's competency?"

"Yes, I agree that there are discrepancies when it comes to investigations. Subodh Mishra was my opposition but I believe justice should be equal. And in his case despite some members being supporters of Subodh's party, he hasn't received justice. And that is sad. I would like to request the police departments to conduct an internal inquiry on why such high profile cases are at a standstill. If there is no concern for someone inside the government, the common and poor people have no hope."

"So, are you also in the stance of defunding and purging the police department?"

"No, this isn't a black and white scenario. There are officers who want the right thing. Serving the people is all they care about. So defunding the entire police department would put the city in shambles. But I am a staunch believer in decreasing regulations. There should be less red tape around the department's capabilities. No politician should be able to blackmail a police officer with a transfer to get his way. If I get elected, this would be one of those rules that I will amend. Less power with the powerful."

"You keep mentioning that there are good officers. The people would love to present their problems to officers like you are describing. Who are they? And how are they still good?"

"SI Khan from Sector 7 would be the first that comes to mind. He-"

"The officer involved in that serial killer case 5 years ago?" "Yes, him."

"But wasn't he suspended for lack of action?"

"There, that statement points out your misrepresentation of the facts. The suspension was said to be due to a lack of action, but you didn't dig enough to get the truth. You just believed what the government said and took it a face value. His suspension was issued because of a government official's involvement in hiding details of the case. Khan wanted all of the truth out but the people in power didn't. And in fact,

Khan and I share the same lack of action from the current series of cases."

"You mean where justice is served rightfully?"

"Is your understanding of justice so limited? Do you have any proof that the people killed by the man were innocent? Did you know that the black mask also killed a 16-year-old killed by that man?" Yashpal was visibly frustrated. "Yes, one the 2nd crime scene, there was a 16-year-old kid who had strayed down the wrong path. At that age, one can easily be swayed. Did you really think that kid who was involved in theft should have been killed on the street like a dog? I urge people to think about what they are supporting. There should be justice, yes. But equally for everyone."

The reporter turned to the camera and continued, "As you can see Yashpal Vohra's passion regarding this case. His clash with the system and its varying injustices have given him a platform and substantial following. For the first time in 15 years, a candidate has divided this city. You may think he is dangerous but others find hope. There will be discussed further regarding this tonight on prim-"

Vasu had just found his answer. This one broadcast had revealed things to him that could have taken him ages to find. One, there was no mention of the kids, so no way it could lead to the refuge at least. Second, if he wanted more information on the case, Khan was the guy to approach. Now that the information was there, he could investigate and figure out the identity of the black mask. But approaching such a policeman still had some risks. Yashpal Vohra's support did help things along but to convince the cop, he had to get a proper story. Any holes and he could be in trouble. So, he took out his old college id and checked if there was anything other than the bare minimum of information there. College Name, Name, Photo, Enrollment id, Batch Year, and Course were the details listed on there. All he had to do was cover the course part and it would be good to go. Luckily the background on the id was white. A piece of plain paper could hide the detail and he could re-laminate over it. Glueing over a thin strip of paper, Vasu made sure by putting the lamination for a test to ensure there were no anomalies. It looked fine to him. After laminating it at the local store, he got on the train to Sector 7. The note he had left for his mother would suffice. The excuse he'd written on the letter wasn't a lie. He was going to sector 7. Just not at his friend's place. At this time of the day, the traffic and movement of people were limited. To get a fast train he had to check the timings at the station. But he was glad that the time of the day meant that catching the fast train would be easy. The journey would be short and getting on it would no longer require the determination of a charging soldier on a battlefield. The journey was mundane. Not much to see, only tall garish buildings that Vasu had grown indifferent towards.

Like many other Police stations, Sector 7 had followed in keeping it near the main railway station. It made sense for infrastructure to be spread around from the centre rather than just flowing away from the city. As he made his way into the station, the familiar wave of nervousness made its way through Vasu's veins. The flashback of his first night's fighting flooded his mind. That didn't go too well and this wasn't confidence building. He put on the id hoping that there would be just a routine check and stepped in. There was a desk manned by two officers right inside the entrance. Bravely, he approached the bench and began the story he'd practised.

"Excuse me." Vasu continued after the officer looked at him. "I am a journalism student here for an interview."

"Interview?" The officer looked over Vasu as he stated in surprise.

"I mean it was an assignment and I am here for an interview… for the assignment." Vasu fumbled his way through the line.

"Are you from NJU College as well?" The officer now looked down unbothered.

"No, I am from Theresa College. Why?"

"There is another student like you here for the interview." The officer continued while pointing away. "Go sit over there and I will check if anybody is available."

"Could you please check if SI Khan is available?"

"Why?"

"I heard his name from Yashpal Vohra on the TV and-"

"Got it got it. Sir is not in yet. If you want his interview, then you will have to wait."

"It's okay. I will wait."

"But there is no guarantee that he will meet you. He is always busy."

"It's okay. I will make an appointment if that will be the case." "Your funeral. If you want to wait. Go take a seat over there."

Vasu made his way to the twin bench that the officer pointed to. Walking over there he could see the room with the officers and another with a small cell. All of this made him very nervous. The last time he was inside a police station, he was 15 years old. That felt like another life. Even that wasn't voluntary. So being here today was a new adventure. And one that Vasu wanted to succeed at. Sitting at the bench, he could smell the sweet scent that filled the area with a sweet aroma. It was odd for a scent to be bombarded with such ghastly visuals. Looking right to the only person sitting there, the scene improved drastically. Vasu presumed this was the other student for the interview. A side glance gave Vasu only a singular detail, the bright yellow top. That also didn't match the atmosphere. It was like a ray of sunshine on a rainy day, Vasu held off looking in that direction as much as he could but he had to surrender to the scent and the yellow. A quick glance in the direction and Vasu was quickly enamoured. He wanted another look. All he had noticed at that moment was her face. Like Vasu, she had a honey-like golden skin tone, with hair tied up in a little bun and a light pink lipstick. The girl was completely occupied by the thick book with her lips moving, mouthing the words on the page. Vasu's nervousness was still there, but for the wrong reasons now. This was the second time in his life a girl had made him this skittish. However, unlike the previous occasion, Vasu was going to make a move. He knew that, the sentence forming in his throat knew that but the universe didn't. So when he opened his mouth and looked at her, a weak, scared goat-like noise came out which was supposed to be, "Hi!". Cursing himself under the breath, he attempted to work his luck again. This time with the ever-charming, "Hello!" After a pause, she looked at Vasu and with a surprise replied, "Hi!"

"Are you here for the interview as well?" A brilliant line he thought. That's what Romeo asked Juliet.

"Yes." She replied with a deep soft voice. "Hi!, Tarita from NJU."

The voice was uncharacteristic but Vasu didn't mind. His attention was on the yellow, "I am Vasu from Theresa College"

"The semester assignment got you huh?"

Vasu didn't realize that the assignment thing was not just an excuse. He tried covering up. "Yes. I was hoping I could just avoid it."

"Really? How early did you get it? We got it just last week." "Oh! I did get it a few days earlier but -" He wasn't sure. So faking it along, he added, "we were told about it at the start." "That's odd. Who's the teacher?"

"Oh! I'd rather not talk about him." "Fine." She didn't like the answer.

Vasu realized that after it came out. So, to rectify the situation, he shifted the topic. "Are you going to wait for SI Khan as well?"

"No, who is that?"

"Oh, he's one of the good ones. I am going to wait for him rather than talk to one of them."

"Really? And how do you know that?"

"Well, he is backed by someone I follow. Politically I mean." "Who?"

"Yashpal Vohra."

She didn't like him apparently. It was evident from her statement. "Oh, the new populist guy."

Vasu understood that and asked, "Yes, and what's wrong with that?"

"Nothing I mean. If you like populism."

"What's wrong with that? Don't you think elites in this city have it easy?"

"I do. But I don't think populism's the answer." "So, communism?"

"No! What are you stupid?" She had snapped at Vasu. But realizing it wasn't appropriate, she came back with, "I am sorry."

"It's okay. I am sorry too. That was uncalled for." Vasu was the one who fired first. So, he apologized. "So what is it?"

"Socialism."

He nodded and replied, "Okay but you have to admit there are things wrong with that as well."

"There are problems in every ideology. But the point is to support one which on paper at least helps everyone."

"And that is socialism?" Vasu genuinely wanted to know. "Do you know of another?"

At that point, an officer walked up to them. "Inspector Talpade is free. You can meet him now." He said to the girl in yellow

"Thank You!" She was almost got up but sat down and asked the officer. "By the way, when will Inspector Khan be free?"

"He is not here yet."

"Then I think I will wait for him if you don't mind."

"Fine. But you might go home disappointed." The officer cleared things up again.

She kept smiling until the officer went away and then looking at Vasu she said, "If the man is not as good as you say, then I will kill you!"

Vasu chuckled and replied, "You know we are in a police station right?"

"I know. Yet here I am, threatening you." She said that without flinching.

He tried to give the girl a B-plan and slid in something for him. "Okay, If the SI is not right or even if we don't get a chance to meet him, I will finish your project."

"And one more." She was grinning at that. Vasu was shocked and exclaimed. "What? No!"

"Not so confident on your dear leader now are you?" Now, this was a jab.

And it hit right where intended, "Okay, I will do two of your projects." He paused and asked, "What is the other one?"

"Mass Communication Studies. I hate that subject." She was shaking her head.

"Me too. But, I will do that for you."

"So, tell me how did you start following the leader?"

"Umm..." Vasu looked down hoping to not delve into the story. "Oh, come on. Tell me." But she wanted to know.

Reluctantly, Vasu replied, "Okay. It was 2 years ago. I was at a college fest when I heard him speak for the first time. He was a social activist back then. His speech was moving, but I had forgotten it by the time I got home. You know how things are. You hear motivating speeches and watch movies that want you to go out and change the world. But then you leave the theatre and remember that other things have far more importance. But when he sought me out and talked to me regarding my father's death, it changed things for me. It gave me the realization, there are people who will go out and work towards the change. Maybe I cannot change the world, but I definitely can support the man willing to."

"That sounds hopeful. But what happened to your father? If you don't mind me asking."

Vasu was hesitant but replied, "He uh- he was shot by a burglar. He owned a uh- a convenience store in a bad neighbourhood and one bad day, he didn't come home. The guy was never found."

"I am sorry. That must have been hard. Growing up with." She was holding Vasu's hand now.

"No. It wasn't. My mom was excellent through all of that."

For the next few minutes, there was silence. She wanted to give time him to absorb back all the feelings that came flooding and waited for him to pick up the conversation. He eventually did. "What's your deal? Why did you get involved with politics?"

"A girl can't have interests?"

"No! I mean yes! um.." Vasu was surprised.

"I'm just kidding. I do love politics. My parents nudged me toward that."

"Are they politicians?"

"God no! They are business people. Pure and simple. They just supported me through some of my issues and somehow we ended up talking politics. I took it from there."

"Oh! Can I ask?" Vasu wanted to know more about the issues. But she wasn't ready. "No! We're not there yet."

"Okay."

"I-" Whatever the sentence that was, it got lost with the interference of the officer from earlier. "Sir is here. He will give you both 10 mins. Go on in his office." He pointed towards the central door in the building. It was on the surface a regular door. But its position in the middle gave it some superficial importance.

"Okay." They made their way with a collective assertion. Opening the door sat a giant executive desk. And manning the desk was a traditionally handsome, with a rough full beard, slick back haired man. His attire however didn't give an authoritarian feel. It wasn't matching his demeanour as well. His command over his subordinates was only matched by the politeness in his voice. "Please, have a seat." He spoke with a smooth low voice.

"Thank You" they both spoke as one sharing a glance and a smile.

"So, you wanted to interview me for an assignment, is that right?"

Vasu waited for Tarita to lead. "Yes. We are journalism students. And as a part of our practical assignments, we had to interview an official and get answers on our topic of choice."

"Okay, that's the first time I've heard of such a thing but, future journalists should always be exposed to interviews. What are your topics?"

"Mine is the case concerning the Black Sunday Killings." "Oh! And mine is the black mask case."

"I think it's 'Phantom Butcher' now. There is a problem with that though. I cannot share details on that particular case because first, it is an ongoing investigation. And second, I am not the investigating officer on that case. But you," pointing to Tarita "I will answer all of the questions as honestly as I can."

So, Tarita took the lead and began with the first question, "While investigating the Black Sunday case, you had trouble finding clues and even finding out the pattern of the victims. What was the reason?"

"The victims didn't have any physical connections that could have been assumed to be a pattern. All that connected the victims was their source of meat. The deli they preferred gave us an opening into a list of suspects, which eventually led to the arrest. I believe that had the family been more open to answering the questions from the police and even the officer that started the investigation had been thorough, we would have saved a lot of the victims."

"But it even took you 2 months and 8 victims to find the killer. Why didn't you find the pattern earlier?"

"I think that would be because of all the attention that had been growing around the case. It made it difficult to get information. I share some fault in that as well. My temperament to work on the cases by myself was what led to my greatest failure. The loss of lives that occurred that day will never leave my conscience." Tarita's interview involved much more technical questions relating to the case. She took up longer than she intended, but Vasu was not phased. All of his attention was dedicated to her. As soon as her questions and interview were done, both Tarita and Khan shifted their attention to Vasu.

Caught off guard, Vasu fumbled his words, "Um.. what about the bla- black mask case did you find different? I mean difficult" he had asked the most generic, basic but more importantly wrong question. "I think you have the wrong questions there. You need a minute?"

"No. I am sorry." Vasu collected himself and asked the right question, "What I wanted to ask was how were all of the victims murdered in the recent port massacre?"

"As I said earlier, I will be unable to comment on the case. If you have any other case in mind, then I will answer questions regarding the same." Vasu suddenly hit with the realization that he didn't think this through, halted his sentences, and decided to not go through with this. Any information that he may dispense could implicate him and put him on the suspect list. This would stop Vasu from helping and instead give free rein to the real criminal. So, instead of this case, Vasu decided to ask of any other. But which one. He wasn't aware of any other of Khan's case. But eventually, a name struck like a lightning. "Subodh Mishra."

"Excuse me?"

"The case of Subodh Mishra. What went wrong there? Could you not find any legitimate suspects?"

"I was not on the case. However, I understand your concern. The case is a priority for us. But from what was found at the crime scene, there were 4 suspects drawn. All of them had valid alibi's. I am sorry that is also one of our failings."

"He was killed.."

"By a knife, a stab wound."

"So, is it related to the black mask killings?"

"No, I mean, there is no evidence to suggest that they are related. The cuts are similar, but not the same. It is not enough to link the case with the black mask killings."

"Oh! How are the wounds in both cases different? Any particular pattern differentiating them?"

"Not much. But the position of the cuts. Rather than a single to the throat, there are multiple to the stomach and chest. It seemed that in this case, the killer wanted the victim to suffer. That would suggest some form of emotional motive." Khan had indirectly given the information Vasu wanted.

"Okay. And any techniques that you would have brought in the case? Or anything different you would have done?"

"Yes, always visit the crime scene multiple times. You never know what a fresh look can bring to the table."

"Um..." Vasu thought it over by pretending to look over the notes, and said, "That's it, I think."

"Great! I know this is just another assignment but I hope both of you end up as a successful journalist. There is potential."

"Thank You!"

"Two things, First, don't ever compromise truth for anything. And second," pointing a Vasu, "keep practising. You need it."

That was it. Tarita and Vasu walked out of the office feeling educated. Having experienced what it was like to talk with a professional and to even get tips from that was an unmatched experience. At least that's how Tarita felt. Vasu was focusing on the last bit of advice. Visiting the crime scene again. Maybe there was something he didn't notice. Maybe, he could find something new that would help him find the black mask. His distracted mind was pulled out by Tarita's snapping fingers. She had been asking him something, but Vasu wasn't paying attention. With a sigh of disappointment, Tarita repeated herself, "Was that all you wanted to ask?"

"Yes, I mean, I guess."

"You guess. Are you planning to skim through the interview and write a lengthy essay?"

"Yeah, I just-I'm sorry but I have something on my mind." "Clearly not the assignment. What are you thinking?"

"Nothing sorry. The assignment," Vasu snapped out and gave his attention to Tarita. "I will get enough to pass."

"And that is fine with you?"

"Of course. The experience was enough. Especially watching you interview that confidently." Vasu said that with a cheeky smile. Tarita wanted to test him. "Oh, okay. What were my questions then?"

Vasu was caught off guard. "You know, about the case" "Name some, name… 5 questions. And I will believe you."

"Ohkay. You asked him why wasn't he able to find evidence." Vasu knew he was caught but still tried his best to fake it. "Why was the case so difficult?" Another one, "How could you have done things differently?" And the final one he could think of was, "How many is that?"

"Three."

"Okay, the evidence-"

"Already done."

"Fine. But all of them were similar. I know that for sure." Vasu tried to sneak out of this dilemma. But Tarita wouldn't let him. "First, you answered 2 out of 3. Secondly, no they weren't similar. You didn't listen." Realizing she wouldn't relent, Vasu did. "Alright. I'll admit I was distracted."

"Really?" Tarita was surprised at the honesty. "But I will do fine with the assignment."

"I am sure. 'A' grades are very easy to come by, right?" "No, I mean, I will get 'C'. I am confident."

"You will get an 'F' and an FO." She chuckled. "Nooo. I will be just fine."

"Alright if you say so. Just remember my words when your teacher tears the assignment apart." Said this and started to leave.

Vasu wanted to continue this. So he frantically thought of something, "Wait, hold on. Maybe you are right. What would it take for you to share your interview notes?"

Tarita stopped, turned and curiously asked, "Now why would I do that?"

"Well, because you are nice and we are-"

"No. I don't think so." She paused and continued, "Okay, I will humour you."

"Yes!" Vasu was visibly happy.

But Tarita tried to control, "Don't get excited. You have to do something for me first."

"Anything. Tell me." "Are you sure?" "Yes!"

"Alright. Your funeral. I want a vinyl disk of a song, 'Time in a bottle'. I don't know the album."

"Okay, who's the artist?"

"Figure that out. I just know the name of the song from the radio."

Vasu used to listen to the radio rarely. But he was surprised that Tarita remembered a song off it. "Wow! How often do you listen in? Maybe you can call the radio station."

"Well, I could, but then why should I share the notes?" "Alright. Give me your number then?"

"Why?"

"How else am I going give you the disk and get the notes? I need to contact you right?"

"Alright. That's a good save. Here." Impressed, she wrote down and handed Vasu the piece of paper. "This is my home phone. Call only after 3. Or else no one will answer."

"Great! I will get this in no time. I have a contact." "Good luck."

Vasu and Tarita parted ways with a smile. What started as a stressful day for Vasu was now no longer sitting on his chest weighing down. He was smiling for once. But here was the dilemma, visiting the crime scene is easy to talk about but the risks of going there were far too high. He had to be cautious. Today, there wasn't the foresight of Arjun or the support of Acharya with him. It was just him. Him and the black mask.

CHAPTER FIVE

First Encounter

Khan had no other obligations for tonight. He and Ashfaq were squared and there were no other problems that could be solved by staying at the station. There was a connection between Subodh Mishra's case and the Phantom case. But the links were not clear. Not yet. He already had an appointment at Subodh's office for tomorrow. There he could check the projects, question the employees, and figure out any discrepancy that the other officers had missed. As for tonight, there was a chance to check out Sector 9's crime scene. Talpade had been handed the security of the scene and he could call in a favour. This would also clear away any doubts about this particular case. What could be more informative than looking at the crime scene rather than at the pictures? Khan knew that even though Panditya or Shah might not have done a great job, other detectives in the force were more than capable of handling the task. Nevertheless, his own eyes had to be there. So, texting Talpade of his intentions, Khan set off. The journey to Sector 9 would be a long one. Although a city, Yaatnāh was so much more than that. The sectorial division of the city had helped the residents reduce unnecessary travel and hence save time. Sector 8, an industrial hub was close to the economical housing and immigration friendly area of sector 7. Sectors 1 & 2 on the other hand were close to each other creating a colony of snobby, rich businessmen that cared more about golf, designer items, and country clubs. It worked in their favour that both the sectors had a great helping of the beautiful coastline associated with the city teeming with the best resorts and restaurants. While Sector 3 was not designated as any particular point of societal gathering, it did become an IT hub with some residential compounds popping up on the northern side. Sector 4 was a major towering spectacle with most of the middle-classes settling in for an unquiet ride. Sector 5 on the other hand was full of liars, cheats, and lazy individuals who more often than not would rob people of Sector 4 to fill their own pockets; the government employees. They had greasy hands, but the people slipping them regularly were also as much if not more responsible. But that's how life went. To get to Sector 9 Khan had to pass through the Animal reserve in Sector 6 and the eastern corridor of Sector 5. The entire trip was about 30 km. In most parts of the countries that distance meant you were travelling to another city. But not here, not in this city. Since this was a long and tedious journey, Khan opted to take the sedan rather than the SUV. Both were standard-issue, but the sedan would prove to be less of a hassle in city traffic and more importantly, would actually drive smoothly. It was rare for Khan to take the sedan as his patrolling car in Sector 7 as it mostly involved bad roads, unfinished city blocks, and just plain old off-roading. So, this was a welcome change.

Most of Sector 7 and the Animal reserve were a breeze as usual. Not much in the way of traffic or stress. But the 5th sector was his main concern. Most of the 5th was as Khan knew, a maze of unwanted turns and signals. And today Khan didn't want to deal with that. So, he decided to take the outer, longer ring road and ease the mental pain. It was supposed to be tedious bringing down the high. But that tediousness would end with the appearance of the 9th corridor. And it did. As he entered the north-eastern section, the traffic had appeared. Here, most of the traffic was constrained to the western bloc. Entering through this part of the Sector, one would see some of the development that the rest of the city enjoyed. You knew that there was an attempt to keep the people happy. But as soon as you delved deeper into the bottom state, you'd realize that the attempt wasn't genuine. It really was just a cosmetic blanket on the bloodstain. No clean-up, not a single attempt to help. Then again, most of the residents didn't care. Those who did were tired of speaking up and the rest had just moved on. Everyone had grown submissive to their sufferings and would simply act unwittingly to any action for or against their collective benefit. The buildings had a real archaic look. There was an architectural style of the brutalist nature imitating the far left-leaning ethos of the by-gone era. They were sold concrete structure with no actual personality, just a living space for the workers. You could not have been able to identify one from the other. At least when they were erected. Now, the patches of algae, dust, rust, and decay became their identifications. The societies or blocs are not named but rather numbered. Khan had disdain for the sector. Not because of the people, but because of the idea that this area stood for. Not moving on. Not changing with the rest of the city. The people had been kept in their homes and boxes by the statesman for pocket change. That's what this place was receiving in infrastructure funding and yet all of it was swallowed down by the representatives. The education funding was sufficient but not exuberant. But the medical funding was non-existent. There was another issue, the industries. All of them moved away. At least all the profitable ones did. However, it also took the most productive and responsible people with them. There was a case for keeping some industries here but the people didn't support the man speaking up for those issues. There were riots and protests but in the end, no matter what the people want, it's the leaders in the government that had the real power.

Reaching the port, Khan recalled the last time he was here. It was his first posting. The port even in those times was a dwindling but a working pillar of the trade and was protected like it should have been. The presence of the military at the port was made mandatory with a reform in the trade agreement. This was not only to do the obvious protection but also to reduce any corruption that had been escalating. It was considered an honour to get such an important first posting. But he wasn't there for long. A simple mistake and he was shipped off to the desolate end on the other side of the country. Whatever time he spent here though was memorable. And with every block, Khan could remember the state they were in on his last visit. His disappointment was immeasurable, and his day was ruined. On his next turn, he could see the gates of the port along with the bright yellow police tape. This shifted the focus. Suddenly, there were no other buildings, ships, duties, officers, or even the dream of a better time. All there was in the moment were gates to a crime scene. A crime scene that would reveal more than any other had done previously. Khan was sure that here, the black mask made a mistake. Here, the mask would slip and reveal the true visceral, ruthless face that would carry the criminal to his incarceration. Khan was confident that there would be revelations.

Vasu, not sure about his ability to lie through tonight, had already devised a plan. Since his mother was already suspicious of his activities, Vasu had already spent the evening talking to Tarita. This was ideal as his mother could eavesdrop on the conversation and Vasu could use Tarita as a scapegoat for his escape. This wasn't ideal for him. There was a chance that she could actually deny letting him out and all of this work would lead to nothing. But the risk had to be taken. The foot was already raised and to justify all of the time he'd invested, Vasu had to take the leap. It worked. The prospects of her son finding the love of his life outweighed the worries, any worries that had made their way into her mind. Her choice today was emotional. But why wouldn't it be? She was a mother after all. Vasu, realizing what he had done, decided to roll with it and take complete advantage of the situation. He stepped out with the promise of returning by midnight. On his way to Sector 9, the memories of the incident, Arjun, Acharya, and the gang all come flooding back. He realized that there was no help there if he would get in trouble. He had no backup to fall on. But he also knew that if he is unable to find a way to save himself, there was a chance that he could be charged for all of those murders, or worse, killed by the actual black mask. The journey to the station was unpleasant. Not physically, but mentally. Every second his train of thought would arrive at a new building of misery and pain. First, it was how was Acharya feeling about the whole situation. Was he still mad? Is he disappointed that his cherished items are now accessories to murder? Second, how could Arjun act like an asshole? Wasn't the risk he took that night enough to get Arjun's confidence? Finally, will he ever be able to visit the home again? Had he lost the last fortress of solitude? All of them worse than the rest. And all of them rotating, rationalizing even the most distressing spectacles. But Vasu needed to get out of the headspace.

So, he looked towards the sunshine. His conversation with Tarita was quite impressive. Even the length was. There was clearly a spark that Vasu felt when talking to her. In a way, this reminded him of Shreya. But there were stark differences, mainly the courage to approach. With Tarita it was present, nay it was emboldened. Vasu's confidence spoke of his attraction more than he ever did to himself. The conversation at first was mundane. There was hesitance from the other end to engage. But with time, both found comfort. Especially in the choice of music. Fleetwood Mac. There was a topic they could talk about for hours. However, the talk wasn't limited to just that. In a very limited time according to Vasu, they had talked on all of the topics that they could find, shared interest or not. Music, books, movies, comedy, and even the odd politics. Their names were thrown around like it was a free-for-all. But sadly, for Vasu, at the end of the day, the conversation was halted at the meet-up. He did muster the courage to ask for a date, but it was denied. The reason, a challenge. The same challenge that Vasu had promised to fulfil earlier. That was chosen as a barter for the date. But it wasn't all disappointing. Tarita also hinted at her interest by indirectly informing Vasu of the album's potential location. All he had to do was figure it out and purchase it. These thoughts were enough to get him to Sector 9. The train journey no longer felt like a pain, but a beautiful movie with a much-anticipated sequel. The journey towards the port would be difficult. There was no vehicle that Vasu could borrow. A taxi would have been fine but the cash Vasu had carried would only be enough to get him to the home. This will be difficult. A walk to the port will cost him 30 minutes but more importantly vital energy that he might need. Vasu had been anticipating trouble, and to counter that, the mask, the glasses, and the baton all were in the backpack that he was carrying. He could borrow, but who at the home would help him. So, in the hope that the taxi ride back would be preferable, he purchased a small water bottle from a nearby medical store and began his hike to the Old Port.

The journey was as expected, boring and tiring. But to ensure that he had enough energy left, Vasu kept taking breaks every 5 minutes. There were parks, benches, and the odd bus station where he could rest his feet and comb through his thoughts. All in all, five breaks were needed to actually complete the journey and reach the factory where Arjun was parked the last time. There was no other way but to scout the place for himself. He knew there were cops, but he wasn't sure where they would be. So carefully, he made his way towards the corner where he could observe the entrance. He could see the yellow tape and the parked police vehicle near the entrance. So just rushing in was no longer the option. He also had to check how many officers were inside. One wouldn't be a problem. He could easily sneak past that officer. However, two or three would be a major issue. And here, he wouldn't even be able to use the baton justifiably. So, the option of winging it was out as well. But one thing from that night was a helpful prospect. The lack of floodlights. That meant, Vasu could hide in the bushes and check out the watch pattern of the officer stationed. He could just as easily climb the building and observe the area with a proper view to gather intel on the officer's movements. So, he walked over quietly to the bushes and waited to observe any movements.

The laid-out markers spoke to Khan like music. There was a pattern he could follow. But it was broken in places. He had to create a perfect flowing narrative to understand the thoughts and intentions of the individual involved. And he was still of the two criminal's theory. He was expecting the evidence here to support that conclusion. So, selecting a marked bodyline, he created an anchor point for his event visualization and decided to move from there. But the entrance area was more revealing than he anticipated. He noticed the broken glass from the floodlight, and realized according to the reports, one of the criminals found dead was on that very container. That meant that the criminal couldn't have entered through the main gates. Or else he would have been filled with a large helping of lead from the man up above. That ruled out one of the breaching points and added to the skillset of the Phantom. But the car found smashed into the wall outside the entrance was one of the major pieces of evidence pointing to the main entrance breach. Khan's mind lit up when he noticed the set of unlit containers on the other side of the port. They were close to the wall and even his trained eyes were not aware of them right away. Khan theorized that the car accident was a distraction caused by the accomplice while the real perpetrator snuck up over the wall. This gave him enough time and space to go over to the container and take out his first victim. Then, he would have moved over to the other container and taken out guards one-by-one. This was followed by him picking up the pieces of information and creating a crime scene. All of it eventually led him to the final set of body lines. They were surrounded by a container. From what Khan could make out, they were standing in a last-stand position. A do or die if you will. All of it was starting to make sense. Khan realized the gravity of the case. The skills of this man were hard to fathom for him. He recognized the gang as being ruthless and unnerving even when facing and running out the previous members of the crime families. To scare such a focused and determined criminal group was no small feat. And Khan now had reason to believe that there were two people with such calibre running around doing as they pleased.

But among all of this, two points stood out. They were glaring errors ignored by the previous team. Allegations that there were kids kidnapped and rescued by such a murderous freak. And second, the blunt force trauma that all of the victims in this incident received. There was no getting around the fact that something was not right. Either Khan was completely wrong about the individual's intentions or it was just a mere coincidence that the kids were freed that very night. Now Khan wasn't a fan of coincidences. To him, they were merely the thin veil covering the truth. And if this was the case here as well, he wanted the truth. No matter what the result. With that intention, Khan decided to investigate the claims that the kids were kept in the godown. He moved towards them and elected to check out the first one for any signs that could provide weight to the claims.

Vasu, from his vantage point, could observe the entrance. The glasses at this point were of great use. His vision was greatly enhanced giving him a clearer field of view. Through the glasses, Vasu noticed the individual that was standing just below the floodlights. The movements of that individual surprised Vasu. He was looking at things observing them and taking notes. An investigation had been conducted, thought Vasu. Then why was this person repeating the process? No matter, he thought, this also cleared his doubts of the number of people present. There was only one. So, as soon as the man moved to the left of Vasu's vision, he stepped out and prepared to rush towards the entrance. However, his instincts stopped him. There was a chance that he could return, realized Vasu. So, he slowly stepped back in and reminded himself; patience. That's what always got to him, or the lack of it. And today was not the day to test it. There was no rush, no kids getting shipped off, and no people out to murder him. He had to hold down himself and wait for the window, rather than smashing in the door. And with that explanation satisfactory to him, Vasu waited patiently, intently. Sure enough, the man came back near the entrance to look at the light again. But he moved on even more quickly this time. Was this the cue? Vasu knew that again; the man could return. But his patience ran out. So, like on his first time around, Vasu rushed towards the entrance and stopped just before the street lights began. He stood there in the anticipation of the man returning. But he never did, so, Vasu snuck towards the container with the floodlights minding the broken glass. The man wasn't visible from here. Hoping that a higher vantage point would help, Vasu climbed on the floodlight container. The watchtower was still there. But now, there was a barely visible white chalk line. The line was outlining what Vasu was dreading to look at. The shadow of a man long gone. And indirectly Vasu was responsible for that. Still not recovered from the poring guilt, Vasu could now see movement from the corner of his eye. It was the officer. He was now standing beside a container. His position meant that Vasu was unable to view him. Before any chance to move to a better position, the officer moved away from the container and started to walk towards the godown.

Vasu, at this point, realized his lack of investigative skills. Unaware of where to begin, he decided to trace back his steps. Looking for any detail that stood out this way around. This led him to the set of unlit containers on the other side of the gate. There, in the darkness, Vasu with his glasses was able to roughly reach the spot that he landed on.

Following along with his memories, he was moving gingerly looking around like his life depended on it. As he came out in the clear, he remembered the distraction that led all of the guards outside and him towards the lighthouse. Now, he had a chance to notice another set of containers to the left of him, nearer to the lighthouse. They were few in numbers but the gap between them could have allowed someone to sit. He first moved towards that spot, carefully. The gap was just enough for a man to stand. Maybe it was the lack of gap that caused him to ignore this place he thought. Examining the place, Vasu couldn't find anything. So, he went towards the lighthouse. It was open from the night before. However, a glaring difference was that there was an outline right before the entrance. This was telling. He knew that the guard was last seen on the top of the lighthouse. This gave him a reason to believe that the incident happened a few minutes after he'd left. Either he came by after they left or he was here all this time. Vasu was relieved to find any proof good enough for him to be vindicated. He still didn't have enough evidence to save him in court. The evidence was proof enough for him and maybe to prove to Acharya or Arjun. The lighthouse examination didn't reveal much to him either. But stepping outside, Vasu could see a light moving inside the godown.

Someone definitely was kidnapped. Khan still didn't have enough to conclude that they were kids. But the food stains, the piss bucket, and the water tubs were evidence enough that someone was kept here against their will. This godown was big enough Khan figured to keep up to 30 adults. So, 40 kids would not have been a big deal. The noise that the kids created would not affect them as the place is very nearly isolated. Like Point Nemo. More importantly, this unmonitored port could have been used as a drop and pick up point for any small boats that could smuggle whatever items they wanted. Circumstantial evidence and testimonies of individuals were all Khan had. Meanwhile, on the upper floor, Khan checked out all the windows. One of the windows had a broken glass but it was not recent. However, there was a dent in the frame. It seemed recent. And what was more surprising for Khan was the fact that it was on the inside. It means someone used the window to escape. Now, why would the Phantom, if it was the Phantom that struck, would try to pry open the window and sneak out? This now added to the mystery that was becoming this case. While on the other side of the window, there was a swift movement between the containers. Khan's peripheral had movement but he concluded that it could be a bat or a shadow or even the glare from the dirty window. But Khan was sure that he saw movement outside, even though the windows were not that clear. So, aware of the danger this situation could possess, Khan carefully placed the torch on the floor and moved towards the window. He made sure that his movements were minimal and his body could not be seen that easily. The torch wasn't just placed down. Khan had rolled it around hoping that the movement would provide enough cover to not draw any suspicion.

Vasu moved carefully, glancing towards the moving light with every other step. He knew that any sudden movement would give away his position and grab the attention of the officer inside. This would draw out an unwanted conflict. Carefully moving around the containers, Vasu walked towards the position where he had knocked out the last set of guards. There were lines around here as well. Curiously, all three weren't in the same position with their head towards the container. So maybe they were awake by the time the real attacker came and killed them. Next, he decided to examine all of them, on-by one. With every line he found, there was something different. While someone was in a different direction than he was supposed to be, another would be in a completely different place. This could be good news thought Vasu. There was a chance that all of them were awake for the attack and the witness could answer critical questions. Vasu had to talk with him. But first and foremost, he had to get out of here. A terrible thought occurred in the middle of all of that. What if he had all of this completely wrong? What if his theory was wrong and all he was doing was getting more and more into trouble? Was there any chance that he could be right? Or was this just speculation? These thoughts of self-doubt made their impact. There was now a huge dent in Vasu's confidence and self-worth. He knew these thoughts were wrong, but for some reason, he couldn't shake them off. He had to clear them if he wanted to escape this trap. With a deep breath, Vasu decided to collect himself and his thoughts. Jumping to conclusions while standing here was not ideal. And what's more, he wasn't even getting anywhere with his 'investigating'. It all seemed pointless, bordering on dangerous. He had no reason to believe that there would be any conclusive evidence sitting there waiting to clear his name and conscience. So, like any other fool, he stumbled into a crime scene like a bumbling idiot and now there was an officer who could possibly shoot him. So rather than wait here and ponder on his self-worth, Vasu moved towards the entrance. Confident that the darkness would protect him, he didn't bother taking the longer, safer route. He instead opted to walk straight through the container. A big mistake.

There was a light metallic squeak. It was odd as the only sound that should have been audible were the waves of the ocean. But this interruption was enough to get Vasu back on his agile feet. He pushed his body towards the container near him. Then he leapt towards the container that sat towards the godown and stuck to it as if his life depended on it. Realizing that the officer could have spotted him, he turned off his glasses and with minute movements, pushed his head out to take a look towards the godown. The torch was still lit. But it wasn't moving. Unknown to Vasu it had been sitting like that for a good 5 minutes. This wasn't ideal, but it wasn't as dangerous either. The officer was alone and there was a higher chance of him sneaking away from one guy than it was from a gang. So, arriving at the conclusion that the top of the container would be the safest spot, he, using all of the strength in his body to mask any sound, climbed aboard and rolled on his back. A deep breath and a second to get his bearings, Vasu worked to reduce his heartbeat and listen in on any footsteps. For what felt like a decade, Vasu couldn't hear any. It was as if he had overreacted. But a glance at the torch showed lack of any movement. And he wasn't going to risk getting caught or worse shot due to a silly mistake. And so, he waited, patiently like he'd never done before. It was difficult, but for the first time, he passed the test. His patience greeted him with the sound of light footsteps coming in from the left. Vasu was thankful for his instincts as that would have been in his blind spot had he stayed on the ground. They were feathered like the person was taking slow steps to avoid detection. Scared to raise his head, Vasu laid there hoping that the officer would not look on top of the roof. For what felt like a lifetime, Vasu had to lay down. At this point all he could hope for was luck. It was on his side. The footsteps moved away from him, towards the godown. Turning his face towards the godown was not possible from his position. So, gathering up the courage, he lifted his body as slowly and quietly as he could and turned towards the godown. Nobody in sight. Scared that he might be behind, Vasu turned to look for the officer. Still, no one to find. He took a deep breath of relief and stepped down from the container.

He still didn't dare to turn on the glasses. Darkness was his friend today. And with its blanket around him, he moved slowly towards the main gate darting around the container and keeping one eye towards the godown. But in his rush to get out of this tricky situation, Vasu had a couple of missteps. On this night, with the quietness that is heard around this place, those missteps were like loud bangs. And someone heard them. "Stop! Or I'll shoot." As soon as Vasu heard those words, he froze. Not on his command, but the mind's won. He was no longer in control. His heart was beating so loudly, there wasn't space for any other noise. Realizing the gravity of the situation, Vasu took deep breaths. With every passing second, he could hear a voice, growing louder. And finally, it was clear, "Raise your hands over your head. This is your final warning." Crap! There was no way out. Any movement and there would be bullets firing at him. And if the cop was remotely talented, it would be his head that would be the target. Patience was key here. So, slowly, he raised his hands. Then stayed right over his head. Now the cop was alert, but after a few seconds, he started talking, whispering really. Vasu thought he was trying to talk to him but listening carefully brought on the realization that he had called someone. Probably back-up. Not ideal, but still there was a window of opportunity to escape. He had to risk it. Maybe the cop was distracted enough to actually let slip. Closing his eyes, Vasu made a run for it. "Stop!" he heard the cop screaming. He had made it right alongside the gate before he heard a bullet being fired. Now sure that staying will be his death, he dashed will all his might. Soon, he was in the darkness. There were no subsequent shots fired, but Vasu didn't want to be distracted with the question, why? He kept on running. No direction as to where, the only destination that mattered now was not here. But he knew that he had to process the location and then come up with an escape plan. However, he turned right, out of instinct. Probably the right choice going on familiar grounds. Arjun's watchtower building was a choice but that was too open and lacking in hiding spots. He had to choose a building with great hiding points. Just as he was formulating that the first block passed and again, he had a choice of turns. Straight along or left. Left. Because there was no good building the other way. Turing left might have been a stupid choice though. Unfamiliar grounds. So, he chose the first building he found good enough. It was the second building on the right. A was a light pink office building 4 storeys high. Vasu had never noticed this before. It was odd for an office building near the docks. Nevertheless, he entered and started looking for a good hiding spot.

Burning chest, sweaty palms, and a heavy handgun. That is what Khan was carrying with him while chasing the 'Phantom'. Four months of mystery and this was his chance to solve it. His chase had brought him to the entrance of an old office building. The entrance to the building was a typical small wall that ran along either side. There was no door, probably taken by scrappers. His gun was still raised as he lit up the torch and entered the building. There was not much on the ground floor. One large room and a set of concrete stairs leading to the upper floors. Checking the empty room, Khan started climbing. The stairs, along with his age were working against him today. Glimpses of a black figure is all that he could spot on reaching each floor. But as soon as he reached the fourth floor, complete silence. This brought the caution and stability back in his step. His slow steps meant that there was nary a sound to distract him or alert his target. As he carefully reached the next set of stairs crossing the doors, he wondered if this was all a ruse to lure him. He could not hear any sound that would indicate somebody's presence. Both the option, climbing on to the roof and staying here, had their problems. He still had no reason to believe that the Phantom had stayed on this floor. So, with a gamble, Khan made his choice. The roof. He decided to be cautious realizing that there was no way out for the Phantom. With every step, Khan was readjusting the grip on his gun. This was to ensure there no sweat and moisture that could dampen his reflex. Reaching the door, he stopped, calmed himself down, and rewound the basic training. Check the front, back, and top. With the ferocity of a fresh cadet, he opened the door, stepped out, and at lightning pace checked his left, right, back, and the upper side roof of the door. Having found no one, Khan swiftly returned his gaze and handgun towards the odd point. There was a section with a short wall right in the middle of the roof. A ventilation section perhaps. Slowly with single steps, he starts moving around the wall. Surprisingly, he saw a hand rising from behind the wall followed by a second. With his gun and attention completely covering those hands he loudly and with an authoritative voice spoke, "Surrender yourself. That's the only chance you have of getting out of here alive." The voice replied with what Khan felt was fear and stress, "Don't shoot. I'm not the bad guy." Khan now uncertain, thought this was something else, decide to still keep his guard up just in case. He replied, "Then why did you run?" The voice on the other side still with the same tone spoke, "I have no evidence for my innocence. You would just blame all of these killings on me." This was unprecedented. Could there be a third guy? He had to know but, he also had to be vigilant in case this man might not be as innocent as he claimed to be. He was taking small, cautious steps with every sentence. Now Khan was almost around the wall. The first step ahead showed a black boot. The second showed the body and a metallic baton. The third and final step revealed those red eyes that were creating such a ruckus. They were staring at him. It was the Phantom just as that witness described. And he spoke, "I have never killed anyone. The other guy did." Khan not believing what he had just heard replied, "Bullshit! You expect me to believe that?" With a sigh, the Phantom lowered his right hand and turned off the red light. Those special night vision glasses were what gave him that distinct look. This amused Khan, realizing how from a distance even he was spooked. The Phantom still keeping one of his arms raised and with another started to remove the mask with the glasses. It was just a man. Even though Khan knew that this revelation was a great relief for him. But the face was memorable. He realized it was the same kid that had interviewed him. Before he to say anything, Khan, with surprised asked, "You?" He wanted to ask if the kid was Phantom but at this point, Khan just knew. There was no way this amateur who chose to run on top of a building rather than attack was the dreaded killer. But he was also surprised that the kid was dressed exactly as described by that criminal witness. So, just to be sure, Khan asked the question he knew the answer to. "You are not the Phantom, right?" The kid shook his head left-right. "You didn't kill any of those gang members?" The reply was again the same motion. "What the hell are you doing here? And where did you get the outfit?" This was the real question. Khan wanted some answers.

After Vasu was done explaining all of the things that mattered, he looked towards Khan with the positive response that he wanted. It was some time before he got that. During his story, Khan had gently but cautiously started to lower his gun. And Vasu with little confidence he had stood up by the end of his story. There was some confusion on Khan's part but there was also some confusion for Vasu. So, in the end, he waited to answer some of Khan's question first. "You still have some questions, please ask."

Khan took a deep breath and asked his first question, "You were here on two separate nights?"

"Yes, yesterday and the day before that."

Surprised that Vasu held his own on two separate occasions, Khan asked "Did you notice anything unusual the second time around?"

Thinking about it again, Vasu couldn't remember anything odd.

So he replied, "No, I don't think so."

The next question from Khan was, "How many kids did you say were kidnapped again?"

"17 from the Home and 23 others. There were in total 40 kids when I first got there."

To confirm his claims of the kidnapping, he needed hard evidence. From Vasu's story, Khan remembered a mention of a complaint, so he asked, "Do you have a copy of the FIR?"

Vasu realizing that a copy might have been given to Acharya, said, "I don't but Acharya, the head of the refuge has."

"Okay." Scratching his head and pacing left and right Khan continued, "I think I have your story straight. Now, why did you come back here?" Khan wanted to know the reason for the third visit. According to Vasu, the kids were safe leaving no reason for him to come back.

"I thought that maybe I could find something I missed. But before I could, you spotted me."

"Yeah! Next time don't move so frequently. That makes you easy to spot." Khan was now comfortable in the knowledge that this was just a kid. Someone who didn't realize what he got himself into. He with a chuckle asked, "Are you a journalist student, or was that a lie?"

Vasu also getting comfortable, replied, "No, that was so I could ask you about the case. But I was scared you might arrest me if I poked too hard."

"Probably true. And the girl?"

"Oh, she's genuine. I just ran into her at the station." There was a hint of defence in Vasu's statement.

Even though Khan was sure this kid was safe, he still wanted to confirm the claims. "Okay, give me your id. Any id."

Taken aback by the sudden command. Vasu asked, "What? Why?"

"Just give me. I will keep it until I verify your story." Khan replied waving off any of Vasu's concerns.

"Okay, but I also need something from you." He said hoping to get some leverage and get some answers.

"You are in no position to ask. But go on, humour me." Kahn said with half a smile and a ton of confidence.

Now, Vasu was sure he could get some details but he went for the big one. He requested, "I want all the details of this case."

Surprised, Khan asked, "Why do you care?"

"I want to clear my name. I don't want to be arrested for crimes I haven't committed." Vasu replied with a legit concern.

"And why do you think someone will arrest you?" Khan was aware of the potential arrest, but he wanted to make sure they were on the same page.

"The story, didn't you hear? Anyone investigating the case will come searching back to the refuge. And from there to me." Vasu replied hoping to get what he wanted.

Khan, now sure of the kids' inexperience waved off the concern and replied, "No they won't. They don't believe that there were any kids. You are in the clear. So, go home. Stay safe."

"But-"

Not wanting to deal with him anymore, Khan decided to get the kid out of this black and back to safety. He ordered, "Get out of here before I arrest you."

Khan wanted to solve this case and Vasu would just be a distraction, a liability. He decided to send him back for his safety as well. What most people didn't realize was that cases like these never came with a happy ending. And Khan was fine with that. He had seen enough rough scenarios to understand the weight that these instances brought with them. However, someone as inexperienced as Vasu would be distraught and scarred for life. No one should have to suffer from such trauma. So, three people, he thought. That's what this case has come to. Not only there were two ruthless criminals, but there was also a kid unsure of his actions. And Khan was now in the middle of this. He had no reason to believe otherwise, but as was his nature, he just wanted to be sure. He decided to take the journey and ask the person that will probably verify Vasu's story.

Vasu on the other hand was disappointed. Walking down the stairs, he wasn't sure why he still didn't get closure. Maybe just the assurance itself was not enough. Maybe bringing the criminal to justice would give him that feeling. But Vasu also had realized today that this was beyond his league. He was caught up and cornered by a single cop. He even doubted his abilities from the nights before. Maybe they were incompetent rather than him being skilful. All of the feelings that had left him before reaching here, came flooding back. And he had to travel back home with the weight of his possible incapability. This was going to be a difficult journey. The street was there, the road was laid out but the journey was long and difficult. It was his choice whether to walk or not. But he also realized that there were people he could talk to. Maybe not as directly as he would have with Acharya, but indirectly. Unaware of what he had done, he looked at this phone that had already dialled Tarita's number. Even as he brought the phone towards his ears, he was unsure about the content of his upcoming conversation. But he was also sure that he wanted to have one.

Khan's destination wasn't far away. Since the time of night was late and the Sector wasn't as populous, it took him all of 10 minutes to reach the place in question. The building would have looked just as abandoned as some that were on the way had there not been a dim light glowing in one of the windows. The left one from the entrance had a light so dim, it could have very well been a table lamp. The knock on the door was followed by silence. There was no answer for a few seconds, so Khan knocked again. This time the door was opened in a slow, soft motion. An old man stood a step higher than Khan. He had a full head of hair and all of them were almost greyed out. Oddly enough there was a band-aid on the top right of his forehead. His attire was deep red and what Khan recognized to be some form of religious garb. His face was wrinkled and clean-shaven. There was an expression of surprise and concern. Before there were any questions, Khan raised his identification and brought it closer to the old man's face. He explained, "I am sorry for being here this late, but I am Senior Inspector A.G Khan. I wanted to ask you about the FIR you had filed. Can we please talk for a few minutes?" There was a brief pause as the old man examined the identification and thought over the idea of inviting a stranger inside. But a few minutes later, Khan was not only sitting with Acharya in his office sipping Tea, but he had also been informed of the incident that took place in the corridor that he came through. This had cleared up two things for him. One, Vasu wasn't lying. There really was an abduction and he was just helping. The other, he still hadn't progressed with the case. Both of them were bleak news for Khan. With concern for Vasu's actions, he decided to bring the topic up but treading carefully. "I ran into one of your kids today, Vasu."

"Oh! He isn't a kid of this place. He is just someone who cares about this place. I know him through his parents."

"Well, he was the one who told me about the incident." "Really?" Acharya was surprised that Vasu talked to someone rather than take action himself.

"Yes, but the circumstances weren't ideal." Khan was downplaying the situation earlier for Acharya's benefit.

Hoping this was just a small issue, he said, "I hope they weren't as bad as I am imagining them to be."

Khan said giving Acharya a guiding thread, "No, but I want to be sure we are talking about the same thing."

"By that, if you mean him running around dressed like a criminal fighting dangerous people then yes, we are talking about the same thing." Acharya was aware of the ridiculousness of Vasu's actions.

"Why would he take that step?" Even he was baffled at the choice.

"As I said, he cares about this place. And like any kid here, he did everything he could to protect this place. I hope he hasn't caused you any trouble." Acharya's fears came true. Vasu got involved in a troublesome situation.

"No, nothing that serious." Khan tried to assure Acharya. "He was trying to solve this case to clear his name. If you get in contact with him, could you please tell him that I will not go after him? Maybe he would believe you more than me." He said with concern. "Sure. Anything I can to help the police. But I have to tell you. He will interfere again. The Vasu I have known all these years, will not quit until he has found the answers, the truth. He is just as stubborn as his father." Acharya had a small chuckle at the end remembering Vasu's father.

"Then why not call his father. Maybe he can talk some sense into the kid." Khan wanted Vasu as far away from the case as possible. And for that, he was willing to even break some old codes.

"That is not an option. He passed away. And I have no way of contacting his mother either." Acharya said with a concerned face.

"Oh, I am sorry. What happened?" He was taken aback at the revelation.

With a heavy heart, Acharya replied, "What happens to anyone around here. Trouble came looking for him. In his case, it was a drugged-up robber who couldn't hold his finger on the gun. It was all over before anyone could do anything."

This wasn't something Khan wanted to hear. He had experience with childhood trauma and he felt Vasu's pain. "That's awful. Must have been difficult to get over that trauma."

"It was. We tried to help as much as we can but there's only so much you can do to help. Sometimes I think he still isn't over all that." There was concern in Acharya's voice.

Khan, now happy with the information got up and politely said, "Well, thank you for the tea. I'll take your leave." The tea reminded him of the northern flavours. It felt calming.

"Thank you for coming. It is nice to know that people like you care. Please, feel free to drop by for tea anytime."

"Thank you for the offer. And please if you can talk to him.

Maybe you can convince him to not get involved."

Khan, stepping out of the place felt relieved and peaceful. Acharya had given him clarity on Vasu's situation and brought his focus back to the real criminal out there. But there was also the question of Vasu's involvement. Today's incident was an insight into what the kid was like and the talk with the old man just increased his understanding. He knew that Vasu would come back and get involved, just not when he would. The reason for such a thought was the similarity in their behaviour. The upbringing with trauma and the desire to help people. That's what got Khan involved with the justice department. And Vasu got involved too, just indirectly. At the end of the day, Khan just wanted to keep everybody safe. Even if they didn't know how to themselves. That was the reason why he took risks daily and why he will keep taking them till his last breath.

CHAPTER SIX

ALLIANCES

The morning didn't come easy for Vasu. Even though his mind was at rest, there wasn't any peace. Lying in bed, pacing around, drinking warm milk, neither of the solutions helped him sleep. Again, he was in a situation where he was lost. Didn't know what he was doing. The night did provide him with perspective or at least what he wanted right now. The case. Vasu wasn't sure why, but he was sure that he wanted to get involved. But there was also the question of convincing Khan. He wouldn't let Vasu help given his inexperience. So, he had to provide Khan with an acceptable answer. Something that would convince him. Blank. That's what his mind came up with. But he decided to visit Khan later on and get him to work with him somehow. With that aside, Vasu moved on with the day. It was early morning. Early enough that his mother wouldn't have woken up. Aware of the hard work that his mother puts to run the house, Vasu had this chance to put in some of his efforts. He knew she would love it. Maybe a great breakfast, he thought. There were few items that Vasu knew how to cook. So, in the hope that the right ingredients were available, he got to work. First, he started on the main dish, a combination of veggies and flat rice. With some on-the-go modifications, they were ready. Next came the tea. A regular cup was easy. But Vasu liked to prepare his special, spiced version. The timing of his breakfast was just right. His mother came out of her room to the smell of hot tea. She was just as surprised as Vasu was proud. He had poured all the love and hard work into it. Her first question to Vasu was, "What brought this on? Anything special today?".

She knew something was wrong. But Vasu couldn't tell her. "No, I just wanted to do it."

"It all looks really good but how? When did you wake up?" "Early. Stop thinking about it. Come over and enjoy it." Vasu just wanted to enjoy the meal with her.

Vasu had impressed her mother. She had taught Vasu how to cook but the way he went about and produced the result was quite something. The aroma and the eventual taste had woken her up to a delightful morning. Good breakfast could change her mood for the rest of the day and this one had already set the bar high. Both of them still were aware of the elephant in the corner though. It had to be addressed.

"Okay, now tell me the truth." She spoke gently but firmly. "About what?" Vasu had little room for escape and he wanted to use it as much as he could.

"Why did you get up so early did all this?" She knew, mother always knows.

"No reason, I swear." Not wanting to indulge in a disappointing conversation, Vasu still dodged the topic.

Without a second thought, she said, "I don't believe you." "Trust me. I am fine. Everything is fine." He was assuring both of them.

"Fine. Tell me when you feel like it." She gave up in the hope that he would tell when the time was right,

Vasu knew there was no getting around this. Her mother had a sense, like an intuition regarding these things. There was no point in hiding. But Vasu just couldn't tell her everything. He had to find a way around. Blanket the other items and tell her just the core points. "Okay," he took a deep breath and continued, "there is this assignment." And there it was.

"What about it?"

He knew the lie had to be believable and her mother would believe any college-related problems. "Well, it's complicated. I want to take part in this assignment but the teacher won't let me."

She was surprised. "The teacher won't let you do an assignment? What kind of teacher is that? What kind of college is that?"

That sounded better in his head. As soon as the words came out, Vasu knew they were wrong. But now he had to work around it. "No, I mean." Thinking this through first he continued, "It's an extra-curricular thing. I don't have to do it. But I want to."

"Okay, and why wouldn't the teacher let you do it? Did she give you a reason?" She asked curiously.

"Well, she told me that I wasn't ready for it. It was out of my league and it could hurt my regular work." That wasn't a lie.

"Hmmm," She thought for a while. Vasu had put forth a dilemma and maybe she had the answer. After a few seconds, she asked the tough question. "Do you really want to do this assignment? I mean the teacher might be right. You could just end up wasting your time."

Somehow Vasu didn't have to think this through. He had the answer earlier than he had anticipated. "Yes, I do want to. And I promise it won't waste my time. This assignment will help me in future."

"Really? How? I mean if it was important wouldn't it be mandatory."

"No-" Vasu's time as a liar wasn't going well. But today the lie wasn't all of that. There was some truth to it and maybe that's what was helping Vasu get around this line of questioning. "It is an off- the-course thing but it is very informative and I really want to do it."

The solution was simple for her. "Okay. Fine. Then tell your teacher about it."

"I tried but he's a strict one." That was the biggest issue for Vasu. "So what? You should show her your passion. Tell her how much you want it. And promise that this will not affect your regular work." She had experience in this. Maybe not to Vasu's knowledge but she still provided the solution that she had used.

Surprised that the answer was that simple, "You really think that would work?"

With confidence, she replied, "Yes, no matter how strict the teacher is. A student's dedication will melt their stubbornness. And while you are on it. You have to show me the assignment and promise me that this won't affect your regular course either."

"I promise you ma it won't" Maybe that was the answer. For all he knew, his dedication was all that Khan was looking for. Training can help him physically but maybe the commitment came first. So, he decided to take up his mother's advice. "I will tell her how much I want the assignment. I mean, what's worse that could happen?"

"He could suspend you."

"What?" Shocked at the statement, Vasu still didn't realize that this wasn't a professor he was talking about. The suspension wasn't an issue.

Letting out a chuckle, she assured Vasu, "No! I'm just kidding. Nothing will happen. Trust me. And more importantly, trust yourself."

"Thank You." Vasu felt relieved due to her confidence.

"Okay, I will now get ready. I don't want to be late." Ganga's job in the hospital meant that shift timings had to be followed strictly. But she also was aware of the support that her son needed. "You can talk to me about anything you know, right?"

"Yes." That's all Vasu needed to say.

There was nothing else that they had to say. Ganga had to get ready for her work. The timings were murderous but they journey, that's what would kill people. Getting on those trains every day and evening like clockwork was not ideal for a healthy life. But there was no escape from it for most people. While the train was full of average office workers, there were aspiring artists, writer, and even the odd inventor. All of them were hard hit by life but had something of their own. A light that was dying of decay but not for the lack of effort. Vasu too used to be one of them. But today he was going to live on his terms and protect the light with his life.

Vasu had left for college for the first time since that fateful night. Although he wasn't prepared. His mind wasn't at rest and all that went around in that place was the case. How on that night, his lack of talent against Khan was clearly distinguishable. How could he rectify that anomaly? He could train with Khan but it was too early. He might not find Khan there. Even though Vasu left at midnight from the port, he knew Khan might have left even late. What's more, Khan was a Sector 7 cop. There was no way that he could have reached that late and come in the station early in the morning. So, Vasu had time to kill and no intention to actually go to college. Searching for that album might help. The store that Tarita had recommended was in Sector 4 itself but on the western side. Vasu had never been to that place. However, there was a station leading to the area he wanted to go to, but he might also have to hike further. No worries. It was the first time Khan was in a lawmaker's office. He had been in courts but this was the office where a potential law could be drafted. It was bizarre. All that hatred of politicians and bureaucrats and here he was sitting in one's office staring at the people working. They were no different from the rest; the cops, the office workers, the factory workers, any other person trying to earn a living and make an impact in the world. Maybe that's why he thought they were corruptible. Because it was just a job for them. Subodh's position hadn't been filled yet despite it being due for a while. The documents were all in the same place probably. This was a good opportunity for Khan. The first time a government's worker being helpful despite not doing any actual work. It was ironic at the least. The building was a stellar example of the infrastructural development of the city. Never had any government building looked this clean and crisp. The white marble exterior was reminiscent of the exuberant personal choices of dictators rather than a democracy. The designs in each of the buildings were handcrafted and were certainly noteworthy. It looked as good as any culturally significant building might have. The budget would have been knocked out of the park thought Khan the first time he laid eyes on the building. It was flashy but not ghastly. The interior was more subtle. The warm glow of the lights was similar to the exotic hotels. The carpets and the furniture would put most castles to shame. It was a mystery as to why this building was erected as well as it was. Maybe because most of the money peddlers had to work out of this building. That may explain the lush choices. But what was even more baffling was that this design was deviating from any other government building in the city. Why go to all that trouble and show the people that their money was of no concern to them? It didn't make sense. Maybe it was their over-confidence that had brought on such abhorrent display of power and corruption.

Khan was led to the office of Subodh Mishra. It was in the eastern wing, on the ground floor along with his colleagues' offices. The office was quite adequate. Not small or tiny but not as large as Khan was expecting. In fact, it was closer in size to Khan's own office. It was just the right size. The desks and the furniture followed the design cues from the rest of the building. The dark brown lacquered surface was quite the match with the deep shades of the leather sofas. Even the chairs were in such dark hues. The carpet on the other hand was quite the opposite. Its taupe colour and the self-design surface felt out of place with the rest of the furniture. It didn't even match the rest of the building's carpets. As he sat on the sofa, the assistant leading him informed Khan that the requested documents would be delivered in a few minutes. So, he waited. At least at first. After a few seconds, his restlessness grew and he started wandering around the office looking at the various knick-knacks. Subodh's desk was clean. There was just bare essential stationery, In-Out boxes for documents, and a desk lamp as there would be. Nothing out of the ordinary. Behind his desk, on the right was a small bookshelf. It had the usual books on law, economics, and the constitution but among them was a fiction book. A hard-bound copy of '1984'. It was a grim read even for someone in Subodh's position. Khan hadn't read the book but was familiar with the story. His feelings were mixed regarding the position it had among the literary ranks. But in his humble opinion, it felt too dark and gloomy for a layman to get through. Even if there was something to learn from it, most of the people would not have read that story long enough to get to the core of it.

On the other side were some plants and a small bonsai tree. After a few minutes, Khan sat down with the opinion that it would take longer than anticipated to get those documents. He rested his feet near the wooden coffee table along with the sofa. It was empty and clean besides a glass ashtray. Khan with a deep breath relaxed and put his head back trying to clear his mind. The knock was what broke his concentration. He had a good stasis going on before he was disturbed. But it was for a good reason. The documents. There was a large stack of them. The assistant had brought them in. All in all, there were 8 files. Each about 100 pages of technical sheets and planning data. Figures that Khan had no familiarity with. The files were now on the coffee table and he requested around an hour to go through all of them.

All of the projects were around Sector 5, 4 & 3. Most of them concerning the 5th. The data files contained concerning data from budget, tenders, permit documents, and forms pertaining to them. While most of these Khan wasn't familiar with, he did possess the basic idea of what the documents should contain. He was looking for any anomalies, especially with the budget. The figures in that could reveal more than a man ever could. However, on this occasion, the numbers didn't reveal anything. There was a small hope of ray with the project in Sector 4 but it turned out to be just another typo. He had almost spent 45 minutes on these files and there was nothing to show for. So he started to put those documents back into their respective files and began stacking them back up. That's the least he could have done. The tower, however small, was unstable and with little warning came down like bricks and steel beams. It had also given up on its integrity and dispersed all of the documents around the couches.

Khan let out an audible sigh. It was warranted in this case. Now he had to put those files back together. But more importantly, he had to now find the documents from under the table and not damage them. First, he collected those that were laying down on the floor and put them on the coffee table. He then moved the coffee table away from the sofas to ease the manoeuvring. It helped. It became quite a simple task to find other documents and retrieve them. A couple of them however were further away under the sofa. This had led to Khan down on all fours and looking for them. Khan was near the large sofa when something odd caught his eye, or rather his hand. The floor had a dip in it. Khan felt the drop along with the metallic base that sat underneath. This was an odd arrangement. So, against his better judgment, he pulled the carpet away from the sofas bringing it near to the coffee table and the office desk. And there it was. A safe on the floor. The door hiding it was open but the safe was closed. It wasn't a fancy multi- lock or the digit-input style. It was just an old-school, rugged iron safe that opened with a key. Its greenish paint was fading away gradiating into the iron's black. The handle was a simple aluminium pull lever. This was a revelation. Khan knew there might be nothing of importance in here. His widow might have emptied it and left it open unknowingly, but he had to look. Even if there was a minute chance that there was something that could help him in this case, he had to look. So, he locked the office door restricting any interruptions and then got to looking for any keys. First, he looked in the drawers of the office table. There was a bundle in the bottom drawer. Khan patiently tried every one that would fit. No luck. Not one of those keys worked.

It was time to look around the room. He would give it 10 minutes. If Khan couldn't find the key by then, he would abandon the idea completely. If it would still bother him then he could resort to asking Subodh's widow regarding the safe. That would yield some results. It was sheer luck that Khan found this safe, however, there was not much left to help him find the key. The desk as assumed was clear. Its stationary cup was nothing ordinary and contained the usual pencil pen and other office supplies. Then as he turned towards the bookshelf, it hit him like a freight train. The answer was staring right at him. How could he have missed it? It was as obvious as the carpet. '1984'. Khan was beside himself when he picked up the book and opened it. The key was put in there in a similar fashion to what they did in the films. Grooved and slid in the middle of the meat of the pages. There were approximately 40 of the first pages that were left untouched. Probably to not make it obvious. The feeling that came in flooding after the realization that his prediction yielded wanted results was akin to smugness mixed with pride. It was like an ideological cocktail that only left a bad aftertaste for the room. The key was a black iron weight, no longer than his index finger. The loop at the end was as small as his thumb but the front comb was large. Probably too large. At least for the size of the key. The pipe was hollow as well indicating another security requisite. As he lifted the key, its weight reminded Khan was how guns felt. Looking at them one would assume lightweight. But the actual stress that such an object puts out is far more significant. Something to do with the density of iron. This time Khan didn't have to check. It was the right key.

The safe lock had three turns necessary to open the safe. When Khan turned key the first time, the handle wouldn't budge. He repeated the process until it did. The handle turned with a mechanical grind that could be heard and felt. With that Khan pulled the safe open. The door of the safe was heavy. That wasn't a surprise given the security measures that Khan had experienced already. The door had 4 layers of iron, each smaller in size yet thicker and denser. The rest of the safe followed a similar pattern. The contents of the safe were evidence and Khan didn't have a pair of gloves to handle them. He checked his pockets for the usual handkerchief. It was in the left-back pocket of his trousers, a habit that was parted to him by his elder brother. He lifted the contents one at a time. The first was the standout golden pieces of nuggets. 100 grams each. There were 4 of them. Then were the bond papers. A small statue of what looked like Buddha. Khan was surprised at this. The final thing that he took out was the file. Red cover, just as large as the others he had been catching up on if not more. Now Khan needed time to read this file. And there was no way he'd get some here. So, He had to sneak the contents of the entire safe out without anyone asking too much about it. The file he could ask for, maybe that won't be the issue. But the rest of it? That would be hard to get out of here. Maybe call for backup. Someone from the nearby station could help him. But he had no contacts here that could help him. Talpade. He must know someone. And so, he dialled.

Khan was open about what he wanted from Talpade. He'd even provided him with the plan. All he wanted was someone trustworthy coming in with a bag and Khan would take care of the rest. And he needed someone to come in quickly. Talpade complied. Promised Khan that in 10 minutes someone would be present at the door with discretion. Relieved that there was someone Khan could trust in the force, he got back to getting things in their place. First, he closed the safe. And put the carpet and the keys back in their place. He also made sure to wipe his prints from the handle and the keys. It was to protect himself and ensure deniability. Now he got back to putting the items he'd found on the table. He arranged them, putting the statue and the nuggets on top of the papers. While sorting the dispersed papers, Khan gave a thorough thought to the items that he had found. The file was of use possibly. But the bonds, the gold, and the statue were not significant. He could call in the investigating officer but that would mean Khan's involvement would be filed as well. More importantly, the items would be shifted into evidence and deny the required assistance that those items would provide to the grieving widow. He could look the other way and give all of the items directly to Mrs Mishra. That would be the right thing.

Khan had just opened the red file and relaxed. Suddenly there was a knock on the door. At first, Khan had stood up alerted. He was expecting the assistant to show up looking to get those files back. So preparing for that he shifted the contents of the safe in the top drawer of the table and opened the door. It was a young woman in her early twenties, wearing a hybrid attire of western and traditional style carrying a shoulder bag made out of some sort of fabric. She was an unfamiliar face, so Khan knew who it was.

Or rather who sent her. Without a word Khan quickly went to the drawer and took out the file, the bond papers, and the statue. He handed those over and instructed her to wait outside the building. Khan shut the door and then took out the nuggets. He placed them in his trouser pockets carefully hiding them with his wallet on top. He then proceeded to hand over the remaining files to the assistant and hurried out of the building. Khan found the young woman waiting near the parking area and approached. Khan requested that she travel with him and would drop her at her desired location. Sitting in the car the woman opened the bag to give away the items she helped smuggle out, but Khan was not ready to take them here. He had to first get away from the building. They had passed at least a kilometre before Khan asked for the items. He then dropped the woman off at her desired location and thanked her. This was a huge favour for Khan and he assured that there would be similar help offered if required in the future. Khan then texted Talpade regarding the success of the small operation.

The album wasn't a hard find as it turned out. The employee at the store, Siddharth, was very helpful. Even though he wasn't particularly aware of the genre, he did provide Vasu with a helping hand that got him the album. The album was not as cheap as he thought. It didn't matter. This was the ticket. And he quickly placed the call to cash in. The first ring and he realized it wasn't time enough for anyone to answer. Maybe it would wise to wait till 3. But as soon as the phone moved away from his ear, there was an answer.

"Hello!" There was a low but sweet voice on the other end. "Oh! Hi! Its Vasu." He said nervously but enthusiastically.

"Hey! Hi! Did you listen to Van Halen?" This was referring to the conversation Vasu had with Tarita last night. The talk had veered off to their preferred music and Tartia recommended a few of her favourites.

"I-I didn't actually. I did however find the album." Vasu swiftly shifted the conversation to the important topic.

"You mean 'the' album? They had it?" She sounded surprised even though the shop was recommended by her.

"Well, it wasn't as easy to find, but I did it." Vasu played down the lack of effort on his part. It had been easy but she wouldn't have been impressed by that. So he played up his part in the discovery of the album

"Hmmm…So, what's the album called?" Tarita asked curiously.

Vasu had to look on the backside of the cover for the information. "You don't mess with Jim, 1972."

"And the artist?"

It was right there, but Vasu had difficulty pronouncing the artist's name. He persevered though. "Jim Croce. You should listen to other songs by him. They are just as good."

"Really? Well, you have to give me the album fast then." There was a hurrying tone in her voice. She sounded just as excited as Vasu now.

"Sure. When can we meet?" He asked. "When do you want to meet?"

There was enough tension in the conversation and neither of them knew what to say." Well, how about tomorrow?" He said it with a thin veneer of confidence hiding the massive wall of nervousness.

"Okay, tomorrow's fine. What time?" She was still as excited and nervous.

That was a relief for Vasu. He had been waiting to meet here ever since that first day. He didn't want to put this off any further but Vasu also knew of the other task in hand. So he relented today and replied. "I'll meet you after college. We can go out for coffee."

"Coffee?" There was a hint of surprise mixed in her voice now. "Yes, coffee. What? You don't like coffee?" The veneer was getting thinner.

"I do it's just that. Nevermind. Do you want me to bring the assignment?"

Vasu knew the end of Tarita's sentence and dreaded asking more about that. So he focused on the second sentence. "The assign- Oh! Yeah, there's no need for that?"

Surprised, she asked, "Really? Why?"

"I'll explain when we meet." He had to sweep this under the rug. So he left this line of inquiry for tomorrow. Anyways it would mean more time to talk then.

"Okay, see you tomorrow then?" "Okay, it's a date then."

"Bye!"

Vasu decided to end the call before the awkwardness grew further. It might not have been a good move but he had to make a choice. So, with a giddy smile, Vasu started his hike towards the station. His happiness knew no bounds. The confidence level had shot up enough that for the first time he had asked someone out on a date. It would remain so. Asking Khan with this confidence, Vasu could not have wished for more. There was no more reason to wait. Even if he had to sit at the station waiting for Khan to arrive, it was alright with Vasu. No more holding off on the tough situations.

The long journey to Sector 7 wasn't as tedious today as it had been the day before. There were pictures and imaginary scenarios playing in Vasu's head regarding his first date. Where to take her, what to talk about. Vasu knew this won't be the first time he will be talking to Tarita, but the context was different. It was foreign and he was nervous. Even he knew this type of nervousness was nice. And that it stood for something good. Getting off the train, his hands reached for his phone. For a second, Vasu wasn't aware of his actions, but as soon as the phone appeared, confusion followed. Why? Texting his mother regarding the delay. Even though it was just 4 p.m. Chances were, by the time he reached home, it would have been 8. I felt outrageous while typing, but the math had some sense. Even if there is a chance that Khan would be there at the station. It would take Vasu some time to convince the guy. And that required time. He had been prepared, but his mother wasn't aware of the commitment. Informing her was a wise choice. Texting done; Vasu focused his mind. The only path he saw was to catch the criminal. Even though the reason he was doing wasn't clear, his intentions were what mattered. And Vasu, with his mother's advice in his mind, wanted to make his intentions clear to Khan.

For him, the intent reigned superior. Vasu was hoping at this point that someone like Khan would understand and welcome him and his skills. With a deep breath, he stepped back into the station. His nervousness was clear even to him. Vasu had to hide it. So, he pictured his mother walking behind him. This helped. The support of his mother helped Vasu in these types of situations. Approaching the officer, he asked for a meeting with Khan. The next question baffled him though. The reason. Vasu had no reply, at first. Quick on his feet, he mentioned their interview the other day and stated that it was a follow-up visit.

Vasu had been waiting for the past hour. It was almost a quarter past five and Khan hadn't yet arrived. He was running out of patience. But this wasn't the place to do so. These weren't the folks to mess with, not in their house. So, realizing his helplessness, he tucked in his tail and sat down again. The floor tile wasn't as interesting as Vasu's gaze was making out it to be, but the walls and the people were far less interesting or interested. Khan's first thought entering the station wasn't the walls, the floor, the officers, or the case. It was, why. And he led with that question.

"You?"

"Oh! H-Hi! I don't know if you remember me but,-" He wanted to explain himself.

"What do you want?" No chance. Right to the point.

"Yes, I wanted to talk more regarding our last encounter." Vasu was trying to be sly about the last night's meeting.

"I didn't think there was more to talk about. In fact, I was very clear about that." Khan had no patience for Vasu. He had to go through the finer points in the file to find any more connections.

"Please, just listen to me first. I will walk out if you don't like my idea." This was Vasu's Hail Mary

"Alright, I don't like your idea. Goodbye!" Khan didn't bite.

"Si-Sir, please. This case, this interview is very important to me.

Please!" He poured all the emotions into this.

Entering his office at this point, Khan looked at Vasu and replied. "I don't think so. You already have all that you need. Now you are just being interruptive."

"Please, just listen once. Just once." He was adamant.

Khan had to relent. There must be something in his mind to be this persuasive. So, he replied, "Fine. Close the door. You have 5 minutes."

That's all Vasu needed. A chance. "Alright. I know why you don't want to work with me. I am inexperienced."

Khan agreed, in fact, this was the first time something Vasu said had made sense to him. "That is just the surface." He knew what the real problem was.

"You also believe that I am naive. That will endanger your life along with mine." Vasu wanted to outline what he thought Khan had an issue with.

"My thoughts exactly." And Khan agreed so far.

"But, what you seem to forget that I took out an entire gang of criminals all by myself. With absolutely no experience. Do you know how?" Now he had started to defend his actions.

"Luck!" This really was what Khan had felt. Watching the kid take such stupid decisions during their encounter, Khan was sure that Vasu had nothing but luck on his side.

"Not just that. It was also my skills, my dedication to helping others and my willingness. Because I cared for the people involved. I wanted to help them. And now that I realized that this case goes beyond what I could have imagined, I want to help other people as well." He was emotional about this point. Vasu's caring nature was driving him to this point.

Khan related to all of the emotions but he also wanted to look at the facts. "Last night you told me that you wanted to clear your name. And now this? What do you really want?"

Khan's question was on point. But Vasu had anticipated this line of inquiry. And he had come prepared. "I want to just help. All my life, I just wanted to help people find justice. Every time I see someone denied it, my blood boils. It- It reminds me of my father. And how it broke my mother. I don't want anyone else to go through all that. If could help one person avoid facing injustice, I will do it. And if today, I back out, and I don't help them, I will never be able to face my mother. Please just let me help."

A sympathetic Khan said, "I understand where you are coming from. But you have to also understand that what I do, what every other officer in the world does every day, is risk their life. Because we took an oath. An oath to protect the people no matter what. No matter if it is our life that is the cost. And the person we are dealing with has skills that are beyond any other gang. I have seen what he leaves behind and it is not pretty. There have been more deaths by that individual in the past few months than the rest of the city could manage."

Vasu wasn't denying the danger. He replied, "I get it. You believe that I am throwing away my life. But maybe this is what my purpose is. Maybe I came here to help people. And if that is the case, I have a duty just like you. What would you have done if you were in my place? Tell me."

Khan and Vasu both knew the answer. But Khan wanted the focus on Vasu and not on himself. "It doesn't matter what I would have done. We are different people."

"How? I mean we have the same intentions. We both want to help people. How are we different?" Vasu truly had come to believe that Khan was the good guy. His interaction with the man had warmed him.

"Intent is not always the answer. There are other things." Vasu's sympathetic attitude towards his friends had opened Khan up. Never had he explained himself and his ideas to this point. And there was more.

Vasu did want to understand. "Like what? You mean that you are trained and I am not?"

It was training first and foremost. So, "Yes. And that is what could kill you."

"Maybe. But weren't you an unskilled man once? Would that have stopped you from helping others?" He knew there was merit in his arguments but his confidence was dropping by the minute.

Khan stumbled but came back with, "I told you we aren't the same. I understand your passion. I completely understand where you are coming from but I cannot let you risk your life on my watch. I have seen enough people die around me and I am not about to let you either. You are just a kid. Grow-up then we will talk."

Vasu was losing confidence but gaining his emotions, and oddly, rationality. "So that's it? You are afraid that if I die, it will be on you? Don't you think that I have a say in what I do? Don't you think that every man is free-willed? Then why would my actions and their consequences be a burden for you?"

Khan was tired but he was also understanding of Vasu's ideology. "You just don't get it. You don't understand what it's like when someone you have worked with, shared moments with dies while you stand there helpless. Unable to save them."

"I know what it is like. And that's why I want to help people, so no one ever has to feel that way. If I die doing that, I will be proud. My mother, my father, every god-damn person I know will be proud." Vasu did understand. Not to the extent, Khan might have but enough to drive him to take such action.

Khan was losing this argument. He didn't want the kid working with him. It was dangerous. But he couldn't even refute his willingness to work with him. Maybe Khan could have just told him off and played the authority card, but he didn't want to. Not today. Today Khan had a glimpse of his past self and for the first time, he had a chance to shape someone's life. Especially someone that could be a significant force of change in the future. But he also liked the kid. It was duty and desire calling him. And he had to decide whether to answer or not. And he made his decision.

"Alright. But if you want to work with me, there are conditions, rules you must follow."

"Name them. I agree with them all." Vasu replied with a suddenness

Not so fast Khan thought. "Listen first. You do what I say when I say. You cannot argue with me. My order will be final."

That was easy enough. "Agreed."

Khan went on. "You don't keep any distractions around. No side jobs, no activities, no friends when you are working on the case."

This would prove to be more complicated but it was still doable. All he had to do was not pick up his phone while he was with Khan. "Agreed."

Khan thought he had to clarify. Clear up any doubts that may arise in the future. "That means, if I call you, drop everything you have. Everything."

Vasu had no choice but to agree. "I understand."

"And finally, you cannot tell anyone about this. No one, not your mother, not your friend, girl-friend, anyone." This was the most important aspect. Secrecy.

This would be the most difficult. Finding excuses. Even though he had been making them for a few years, this felt somehow different. But Vasu had to agree, so he said, "Okay."

"Good. Now let's begin working." Khan was happy he had cleared things up.

It surprised Vasu that he had to work immediately. "Right now?" "Yes, right now. Are you-"

He knew what might be at the end of the sentence so he interrupted with what Khan wanted to hear. "Alright. Where do we begin?"

The first order of business, "The records on Yashpal Vohra. We need to go through them." Khan had found Yashpal's name while he took a glance on the way here. Khan had stopped in the Animal reserve to look that the file without any interruptions. He had to be sure that it was necessary and not a red herring that could deviate him from the case. Khan couldn't wait to dig into the file, hence the early read in the middle of the road.

"Why? Why him?" Vasu was surprised at the mention of him. "Because Subodh Mishra's last meeting was supposed to be with him. I found a file in his secret safe." Khan shows the red file to Vasu.

"According to this, Subodh and Yashpal were working on a project, or possibly Yashpal was pushing Subodh to work on it. Anyway, the deal went south and Subodh rejected the project." He showed Vasu the note rejecting the project at the bottom of the final page. "I think Subodh hid this file because Yashpal might have something incriminating on him. But that is just speculation at this point."

Vasu had trouble believing Khan. "I think you are wrong. That man is working to help the people. It must be someone else."

"Maybe I am wrong but evidence right now points at him. So, we will look into him. Are we going to have a problem with that?" Khan asked.

"No, I just wanted to let you know what I think." Vasu had to relent. He had agreed to follow Khan's orders.

"Good. You can think whatever you want as long as it doesn't affect our work." Khan was aware that people had personal beliefs and were fine with that if they didn't interfere.

"It won't. I promise." Vasu knew that this was a personal dilemma. But if he had to choose between this and his loyalty, he would choose the job. And so, he asked, "So, where should we begin?"

Khan was glad that Vasu was on board. He would require Vasu's help. "His records, he was arrested once. They must have some information about his life. We will go through them. Come on."

Khan took Vasu on a drive to Sector 5. He also instructed Vasu to read the file out loud to him while they drive. There were forms and financial details on paper that Khan wanted to go through. This way he could have helped Vasu understand some of the technical details and he could reconfirm what he had glanced at. Vasu was also glad to learn something new. This was beyond his speciality but he was dedicated to learning and if Khan knew something, Vasu wanted to as well. His first rule now had become to learn what Khan knows, no matter how much he didn't like it. He was hoping that this would help him become a better detective. The file didn't contain more than what Khan knew, so when they had gone through it, the conversation shifted.

"Alright, how am I going to help now?" Asked Vasu hoping that Khan would reveal his plan.

"We are going to comb through his records. You are helping me do this thing quickly." It was as simple as he had said.

Vasu was surprised that it was all that had to be done. "Alright. I just thought that-"

"Investigation won't be as boring, right?" Khan knew what the kid was thinking. He had been in his shoes once.

"Yeah" Vasu relented.

Khan wanted Vasu to understand the importance of the investigation, rather than jumping into the situation headfirst. "Trust me. This part is what really matters. The fight and the arrest are just the climaxes. You need to go through all of this stuff. And most of an investigator's life is most of this stuff."

"I understand. It's hard work." Vasu had a grip on the subject matter.

Khan hoping to find out more about his new partner decided to ask something that had been in the back of his mind. "Tell me something. Where did you learn to fight?"

The answer was simple. "Acharya. He taught me when I was living there."

"The old man? I am not surprised." Khan replied. Surprised at that, Vasu asked. "Why not?"

"The way he carried himself, it screamed authority. Like military." From one disciplined man to another.

This Vasu knew about, even though it was just the basic detail. "Yeah! We assumed. But he never talks about it."

"No many do. It's not exactly something you want to remember daily." Khan replied.

Vasu wanted to know about it, so he asked. "But, isn't serving your country something to be proud of?"

To which Khan said, "It is, don't get me wrong. But it changes you. War and to some extent fighting introduces you to some of the aspects of humanity you'd rather not look at."

So, Vasu asked the obvious question, "You are ex-military as well, right?"

"Yes."

"Can I ask you something?" "Sure."

"Why'd you join?" A tough question for many.

"Honestly, money." Khan didn't want to lie to the kid. Not about something like this.

Surprised, Vasu asked. "Money? I thought you wanted to serve the country."

Khan knew many who said such things but he was honest. "Yeah, that's what people want to say. Most of us there just wanted a paycheck."

"How long were you in the military?"

"10 years."

"Wow! That long?" It was over the required 3-year mandate.

Khan was 7 years over that time.

"Yes, it didn't feel that long though." "What do you mean?"

"Nothing." Khan didn't want to continue down this alley. He had a few unwanted liabilities that wanted to keep covered.

"So, why did you leave?"

This is also something people lie about, even Khan. But today was not one of those days. He replied, "I… I was tired of the blood." He had flashes of the front line duty while he continued the conversation. It was painful to even recall. "I couldn't wake up every day and just look at the blood. It was the war. That was a very difficult time and I just didn't want to stay there when it was over." Khan had just opened up an old wound for someone he barely knew. So, he wanted that trust in return. "Tell me the truth about you."

"What truth?"

"All of it. Where are you from, the college, your family, everything." Khan wanted to know from the kid who he was.

"Um… Okay. I grew up in Sector 9 with my family and the Home. Acharya taught me a great deal. After my father-. After he passed away, Acharya helped my mother and me a lot. But she couldn't live in the neighbourhood anymore. So, we moved to Sector 4 and I now attend college there. It is nice now. Moving away really helped both of us. But I guess you always have a connection with people you grew up with. So, sometimes I visit the places, the people. It just my way I guess of… you know." Vasu began this like any other introduction he had given throughout schools and colleges but it ended in a different way.

"Now I understand why you helped the kids. Why you took that risk. But I still don't understand how you got in."

"You mean the first or the second time?" Vasu asked jokingly. "Both." Khan was serious. In that, he wanted to know from Vasu. "Well, the first time, I just walked through the front gate. There were just a few gang members that night. But the second time, it was impossible. So, we decided to ram a car near the front gate while I climbed the walls." Vasu explained it as simply as he could. But it wasn't that simple. Khan had questions. "Okay, what? First, who's we? And climb that 10 feet wall? How?"

Vasu cleared, "Arjun. He helped me rescue the kids both times.

And I was on the roof of the car. It gave me a boost."

"Bold. And stupid. You could've got killed. Both of you." He realized the risks that Vasu had taken previously and Khan wasn't impressed.

"But I didn't." Even Vasu knew that wasn't a wise answer.

Khan continued this line of questioning. "And how'd you escape?"

"Van. Both times. The first time, I used my bike to run away but they caught and destroyed it. The second time they were all knocked out." He replied.

"Impressive." Khan felt the bravery was at least warranting some praise.

"Thank You"

This went on for the rest of the journey. Sometimes Khan would ask the questions, other times Vasu would. They both shared a piece of each other's life. Both were familiar with the pain of the other. Maybe that's what brought them together. It was no like they would talk about it. In fact, they talked about everything other than that. Khan opened up about his childhood, his dreams of becoming an actor before joining the military, and his father. He had committed suicide. Inability to pay off debtors. That had become an unwanted way out for the farmers. It still is now. Not many of them have the ability to pay off the debt. So, they either sell their land or just give away their lives. Vasu on the other hand talked about Acharya, how he helped him in his darkest moments. For him Acharya was family. It was sad that he couldn't visit any longer but maybe it was for the best. There was also a mutual love for bikes. This conversation was sparked when Vasu again mentioned the loss of his bike. Khan sympathized and mentioned his intention to restore his old café racer. It was a scrap buy thought to be a write-off but not if Khan had a say. He wanted to ride it and push it to the limit but only if he ever could get around to repairing it. Nicknamed the Widowmaker by critics, it was supposedly an experiment that turned out to be uncontrollable, dangerous and the bikes were pulled out of the market after lawsuits. But it was still a classic and one that Khan loved. There were only a few around and none were in working condition. They discussed the bike at length. Khan explained its history, its V-twin engine, its ridiculous torque, the carburettor, the wet clutch, and they even had an argument on the brakes. Khan liked the feel of the authentic drums, while Vasu preferred the performance of the disk. This went on all the way till Sector 5. It might have gone further had the subject not just turned grim.

Khan and Vasu were now entering the HQ compound. The idea was to visit the records room and find the file on Yashpal. It might not have been wise to bring a civilian along but Khan had to take the risk. He couldn't bring out the file to train the prodigy however, he could bring the prodigy to the file. It was necessary for Vasu's training and there was no getting around it. So, Khan decided to make Vasu his partner. There would not have been a badge to prove it but if that would be brought up, Khan was prepared for that as well.

"We're here. Follow me and act like you belong."

"What do you mean?" Vasu was taken aback by such an odd request.

"You are a visitor and I am taking you into a classified room. Act like you are a cop, like my partner." Khan had relayed enough information to Vasu.

"Alright." Not wanting to push this further, Vasu agreed.

Khan went straight for the records building. As he entered, he could see Parthi standing with her sling bag, her coat, and disapproval. This emotion was targeted towards the arrival of Khan. Parthi was aware that she had to accompany Khan somewhere possibly and would probably be late for getting home.

"What do you want now?" There were exhaustion and irritation reflected in Parthi's speech.

"Personnel files. I want to look at someone's records." Khan was as usual on point.

"Name." So was Parthi. "Not here."

"Write it." Parthi was aware of the protocol. If there was someone beyond reproach, someone who was important enough to create a public outcry, they would write the names down rather than speak them out loud. And this was one of those. Khan had written the name to which Parthi replied, "Okay."

"Thank You. I promise you I will only be a few minutes." Khan said reassuring Parthi that he would not create discomfort any further.

"The kid can stay here. Follow me." Parthi said pointing towards Vasu.

"No, he's not a kid. I mean he's not just a kid." This was the moment. Khan had to stand up for Vasu and establish him as his partner. "A prodigy. He is assigned as my partner. So I thought I would bring him here and teach him a few things."

"I'll need his ID." Parthi wanted some proof of Khan's explanation.

"He hasn't got one." Khan was blunt. "What do you mean?"

"Special Privileges, Section 15A. He just has to be accompanied by a-"

"I know the rules. I wrote few of them." Parthi was offended at the idea that someone like Khan, a flagrant violator of ruled would actually point them out to her. She was right in a way. There were a few sections that she helped amended and write a couple that was in circulation. So, she hurried along with the conversation, "Fine. But you need to record this in the register."

"Okay." Khan had no choice but to agree.

Aware that only Vasu's entry was required, he filled in the details on the register at the reception desk. and omitted out the superior's section hoping that Parthi wouldn't notice.

"Follow me," She said as Khan closed the register.

Khan was aware of the procedure. They walked down into the underground section past the guards and into the records room that Khan had visited. But there is another door past that room leading into the classified room guarded by a heady door with vault-like security measures. There was a digital passcode panel that kept the room secured while a 24/7 monitoring system ensured that no one unwanted could leave if he ever managed to enter. This was state- of-the-art and Khan knew it right away. This is how banks guard money these days.

"This is the personnel files room. They are arranged in alphabetical order." The files were stacked and coded in alphabetical order. It was similar to the other records room, only smaller. This section was filled with personnel files belonging to important members of the government and other people of interest. "You have 8 minutes after which the guards upstairs will evict you, whether you are done or not."

"Alright. Thanks."

Vasu was taken aback by the facilities to store some documents. It was baffling to see such a secure and secretive set-up for what he thought was not that important. For Khan, however, it all made sense. This room could be the most important in all of the city. The files in here could contain secrets and information that could make or break a government. It had to be kept safe. Now they had a chance to find out what this room could give them. Khan and Vasu made their way towards the appropriate alphabet to look for the file. There was a whole drawer dedicated to the letter, so they combed through it to find the one they were looking for. Vohra, Yashpal. It was there, just as Khan had anticipated. Any arrest you get your own file. Maybe not in a secure room like this one but it exists somewhere on the police database. The file was quite thin as Vasu pointed that out. Even Khan was surprised. There might have been no more than 12 pages in that small white file. Opening it up, the reason became obvious.

"No records before 4 years." Khan was baffled at the development.

"Yeah, so?" Vasu didn't understand it yet.

"When they arrest you, Police go through your complete life. Everything, your ID, your job, the town you grew up in, all of it is recorded and verified. In his file, there are some details but none of it is verified."

"So? Someone must have forgotten." Vasu thought of it to be an average mistake.

"That is not possible. This shouldn't happen." But for Khan, it wasn't.

"Who filed it? Maybe we can ask him."

"Good idea." Khan was impressed and quickly returned to the page to find the investigator's name. "L. Vijay. Shit!" It wasn't good and Khan's face said so.

"What?"

"He died. Last year, he committed suicide." Khan remembered the event like it was yesterday. That was a shocking affair to find one of his colleagues had taken such a drastic measure.

"What happened?"

"Money trouble. But…" Khan stopped to think it through. "Come on, say it." But Vasu wanted to hear it.

"This may sound crazy but, I think this is one more proof against Yashpal." Khan was adamant at this point that Yashpal was somehow involved and guilty.

"You are wrong. His records are unverified. That doesn't mean he is guilty." Vasu on the other hand thought that Khan was just antagonizing his character.

Khan however had an explanation for his suspicion. "Then explain to me why isn't any of his details verified. Not the town was born, his mother, father, next of kin, school, college, none of it has been verified. Why?"

"I don't' know. But that doesn't make him a murderer." It didn't make sense to Vasu.

"Think this through Vasu. He was having a problem with Subodh Mishra. Subodh was killed in the same way as the gang members. And Yashpal, a clean-cut guy who is running for mayor has none of his details verified. Doesn't it sound just wrong?" Khan had a point and he could see the gears turning in Vasu.

"Maybe. I don-"

Vasu and Khan's conversation was interrupted by a knock on the door. It was the guards and they wanted the partners to leave. There was no doubt that they were going to but how, was up to them. Khan knew there was no point in staying here any longer. There was no information that they could find here to help them. The file was empty so whatever details that they wanted, they had to collect. So, they make their way upstairs and out of the building.

"What do you want to do next?" Vasu asked in the hope that the answer isn't what he's anticipating to be.

"Follow him." That was the only way left for him.

"What? All-day?" Vasu wasn't on board yet but that didn't mean he wasn't willing to help.

"No, just at night." "For how long?"

"Just until we find something. Anything that tells us that he is or isn't the guy we are looking for."

"I have a better idea. Just ask him."

"Okay. What if you are wrong and he is the murderer?" Khan wanted to clear this once and for all for Vasu. "You just warned him about a cop and a mask-wearing vigilante that are on to him. How long before he kills both of us?" Khan paused to listen to Vasu's reply. But there wasn't one. So he continued. "We will follow him for a few days."

"I can't at night. My mom won't let me."

"I told you before. I call, you come. Make some excuse. Tell her you are out with your friends, a girl, anything."

"Alright. But I don't like lying."

"Nobody does. Not until it gets you what you want."

Khan had a point and Vasu knew it. If there was even a minute chance that Yashpal was involved, he had to check it. Even if it was just looking the other way. For Vasu, this was a sour thought. Investigating the man who had been nice to him and helped him. What would his mother have thought? Luckily, this wasn't her burden. It never should be. She had enough of those and could use a day off from it. With a heavy heart, Vasu agreed to get on board. Maybe this was a test and he had to show loyalty. Maybe not. This investigation, no matter how hard or inconvenient to his life it got, Vasu wanted to complete it. Even if it meant going against his beliefs. But now, another question had to be answered. How would he get out? Regularly? Maybe a late-night job would convince her mother? But at the end of that, he had to produce an income. And even that would be stretching as Vasu knew her mother was strictly against night jobs. Never understood the reason. He had to think of one and fast. In a few hours. For a second a terrible thought entered his mind. Tell her the truth! The truth? And then what? Expect cooperation? No. There will be just disdain, derision, and grounding. No access to the outside world. But suddenly, the answer was there, floating, right in front of his face and thoughts. Partial truth was the answer. Vasu knew that the name Yashpal Vohra will get him freedom. Maybe use that name to get just that. Partial truth. So he dialled. Khan had been patient with Vasu. He knew that new recruits even with the most disciplined mind, find trouble with following orders. Especially ones that are hit on a personal level. But the kid's dedication and his willingness to work around his personal opinions had impressed Khan. Politicians have a certain hold over their followers' minds. Even the 'good ones' use similar tactics to keep their sheep following. That tactic keeps everyone loyal and defends that leader's belief without a thought. Khan had experience in the position. And no matter how ridiculous the belief or position, there will be defenders. Left or Right, Liberal or Conservative, Authoritarian or Anarchist, all of them were at their core the same. Manipulative. Sometimes that was necessary for the good cause, but how does one decide? It's just an opinion, even if you think it is about saving lives. Khan's experience during the immigration riots, the student uprising, the farmers banding, or the unemployment scare, all of those protests boiled down to one calling the other wrong. And all of those sides had passionate, intellectual, blinded citizens who just wanted to get their way. No compromise. What baffles Khan, even more, was that people never changed alliances. No one had a change of heart and would at least sympathized with the sufferings of their fellow man. Not even the established celebrity would speak for it. They would support the power but not until the money was involved. Then you work and speak for even the worst of human acts. Vasu's willingness to work on the case had given Khan hope. Now all he had to work on was Vasu's skills and he would have a perfect partner. There might be some rough edges to Vasu's morality but they were if nothing, workable.

He was now relieved that Vasu was calling someone. His mother perhaps. It was just right. As much as Khan wanted to be disinterested in the conversation, the proximity and the recent bonding conversation had him eavesdropping. It was one-sided but Khan could easily have guessed what the other person spoke. It began with usual greetings and had dinner conversation. It stayed so until Vasu brought up the important conversation.

"I will be late tonight." He paused with his best poker face. "Because I-I am working. It's important." Now it was gone. "No it's not a night shift job it's something else." Now he was frustrated and nervous. "Do you remember Yashpal Vohra?" There was a glimpse of hope on Vasu's face. "Yes. I am working for him." And the hope grew. "I'll tell you about it later." Now it was confidence and irritation. "Alright. I am working with him on his campaign." The irritation had grown. "Yes I know but the real work is done at night." The nervousness crept back in. "You know planning, the posters, and the PR." It was prominent now. "Yeah, it's his house we'll be at." Vasu was tired at this point. "No, I cannot do that. I'll be working." His head was down. Any lower and it would have been in his lap. "Alright, I'll try but I cannot guarantee anything." There was nodding down below. "Okay, I will. And you take care as well. Good Night." And with that, his head came back up. That was self-explanatory but Khan still wanted to poke out more information so, "What did you tell her?"

"I lied that I was working for him." "So, your mom's a fan too."

"Of course."

"Then that is quite a great lie. How often you do that?"

"Recently it's been a lot. I should stop."

"Not as easy to quit. But it works for now."

Khan related to the sentiment. Lying was not a nice habit, especially when you do it to people close to you. But it was necessary. And Vasu had to learn to live with it if he wanted to continue doing this job. Now the job demanded their commitment through the night. They had to watch Yashpal, so, Khan started his car. It was in Sector 3 oddly. For someone claiming to be a man of the people, Yashpal was living in one of the riches sectors of the city. But that wasn't the concern today. Just what he got up to the night. And it was going to be a long night. So, Khan decided to get some Wakers just in case. Coffee wasn't that strong but that energy drink could wake up a dead man. And that is how the drink was advertised. Khan had bought a 6 pack to prepare them for the stakeout.

CHAPTER SEVEN

Misplaced Judgement

It had been 3 Wakers, 2 cups of coffee, and 3 A.M. Both Vasu and Khan were tired, nay exhausted at the lack of any noteworthy event. Vasu was particularly bored as he hadn't done such a seemingly mundane task ever. Khan didn't show it but had it in him to just walk away. It had been a while for him. However, the potential ramification of such an action was keeping his butt right where it was. He had the ability to endure and it was not to be let down today, not in this case.

With a fleeting yawn, Vasu asked, "How long do we stay here before you admit defeat? I mean-"

"As long as I am satisfied." Replied Khan.

"Or you find any detail to implicate Yashpal. I understand." Vasu said, unwavering in his confidence of Yashpal's innocence.

"You still don't believe what you saw?"

"What? You mean the vague reference to him," said Vasu lifting the file they had brought along. "or you mean the lack of information at that records place?"

"Both." Khan didn't want to say anything hoping to move away from this pointless discussion. But he also wanted to know about Vasu's dedicated defence of the man. So he said with a hint of sarcasm. "I guess now I know who you'll be voting for this time." Vasu took a pause and gave a look as if there was nothing he had to say. But Khan wanted to push in this direction. So, he asked "And what policy of his do you like the most?" with a tone of condescension.

"All of them!" replied Vasu with confidence snapping at Khan's condescension.

"Name some. I would like to know." Khan glance at Vasu and there it was. As expected a face of derision. But he continued, "If it turns out he is innocent, I might vote for him."

"Vasu thought it over. It might be a genuine interest that Khan could be displaying. "I mean, he wants to work for the people. He meets and helps them however he can. That's what makes him special." Replied Vasu with wavering confidence.

"Alright, but what policy will he bring about, what law that will help the people? He must have said something." Khan was now pushing Vasu's buttons. He'd heard all the arguments but Khan still wanted to hear them from his new partner.

Vasu had little to answer. But his confidence was still there and it answered, "He did, but, I might have not listened. Tell you what, listen to one of his speeches, you will find out all he is about."

"I did, closely." Khan was sceptical.

"What do you mean?" Vasu was surprised that a man so hell- bent on prosecuting his idol had listened to his speech.

With his complete attention towards Vasu, Khan said with a straight face, "When he came for a rally in the 7th, the entire precinct was there to his aid. I heard his speech that day."

Vasu was impressed and felt like he had an in, "Good. So you know all that you need to know."

Khan though didn't even give an inch of consideration. "No, he never mentioned any policy that he was going to implement. I thought since you were a fan, maybe you know something that I don't."

Vasu was now sure that Khan was just playing with him. There was no curiosity nor open-mindedness on his side and he didn't want to continue the argument. "I do, but you don't seem genuinely interested."

"Oh come on, you have an undecided voter sitting here asking for more details on your candidate. Tell me why I should vote for him." Khan was ready and thought that he could still push Vasu to a point that he could look at it himself.

What Khan said made sense to Vasu. Why would he not speak about Yashpal, how he had appealed to him in the first place and how he genuinely felt that there was a wave of good times on the horizon. He wanted Khan to know where the passion was coming from. So, he took the opportunity despite his scepticism of Khan's intention and began, "Alright, first, he is a great guy. I don't think you need any more reason than that-" Khan raised his eyebrows to state his doubt but Vasu continued, "but, I think there is more to him that will convince you. If you had paid any attention to his speeches, you would understand that he fighting against dynasty politics. He is fighting for the people. Aren't you tired of the rich dynasty folk telling you how you should live life and adjust to the shortcomings of society? He is the first man to say no. That's why he is going to win and there will be a renaissance. There will be a new day. Trust me, it's his time. It's our time. If there are some people who are not happy with the changes, it is because they have become complacent. It's our duty to…" Without realising it, Vasu was quoting from Yashpal's speech. It hadn't occurred to him in his passionate rant that Khan's mind had wandered off.

Khan had started to look ahead towards Yashpal's residence. It was a walled community that he was living in but there were no gates. So, Khan's car had roughly a clear view of Yashpal's house and the living room. His house was the first one in the community and all of the movements that occurred were in that room. Since there was no other way out of that society, Khan didn't have to worry about covering other spots. It was at this hour when he was least expecting there to be something, he could see movements in Yashpal's house. A dim light followed by two, maybe three shadows. "Shhh!!" Khan interrupted Vasu's reverence of the dear leader and drew his attention to far more important matters. "Look, there is movement," Khan said pointing towards Yashpal's house.

Vasu turned to look. "Oh! I see it yeah!" There was a movement in the house but since there had been no lights, it was hard to make out who, how many, or why. "Why hide in the shadows?"

"I don't know," Khan replied, intrigued by the development. It then occurred to him, "Use those glasses of yours." They would be very handy right now.

Vasu realized, "Yeah!" He could have used them earlier. Those were his glasses but it didn't occur to him to use them. He was distracted. Fortunately, he had the foresight to bring those along. Or rather, the insight to not leave them at home risking the chance of his mother finding out. He took them out of his bag and set them to visibility green.

"What do you see?" Khan asked after a few seconds.

Vasu paused. He was looking for someone. His head went left, right, up, down looking for someone, though with minimal visible movements. "I can't see anyone now. Shit! We missed it." Vasu was appalled with his distracted nature. There it was, something ground breaking going around in this silent night, but he didn't have the patience or the concentration enough to spot it. While he was engaging in self-reproach, further events were unfolding.

Khan having spotted a figure moving out of the house, warned Vasu. "Hide your glasses, there's someone coming." They both ducked or rather slunk back below the dashboard hoping the night would cover the rest.

There was silence for a moment, while the man disappeared. Only the crickets and their breathing was audible. A few seconds later though, a figure in black leather vests and pants was leaving on his bike. Vasu recognized the bike's make and model. He wanted to comment but refrained due to the serious nature of the moment. It was a bike from a well-known Japanese company. He was surprised that there was no sound from this massive superbike. The bike didn't have its headlights on but the man had no trouble with visibility. He drove off with slow, quiet momentum.

As soon as the man turned away from the parked car, Vasu asked. "What do we do?" He was surprised at the lack of action or reaction from Khan.

Khan apparently waiting for the right moment replied. "Let's follow him."

The car started and that's when Vasu realized the delay. The noise in the quiet of the night would have alerted the probable suspect. He was glad to have joined Khan today. Just one evening was enlightening to Vasu on many levels. The knowledge that the smallest of things bring about the most significant changes was quite the revelation. Khan even had the foresight to start the car without his headlights. He started following the bike at a distance The roads were quiet at this time, at least here in this neighbourhood. They were a single lane each way. Unlit roads were the norm in 9th and some places in 4th but here, there wasn't a single lamp powerless. The first turn was the opportunity Khan was looking for. He turned on the light and continued following. It was all residential areas, apartments, societies, gated communities, and the occasional small commercial sections passing by. Vasu had heard that wealth was all west but it was odd for him to see the painter, well-maintained appearances of the community. Even the signals here were functional. Fortunately, all of them were open at this hour. With every passing society, every yellow, closed signal, and every lit street lamp Vasu realized that they were heading out of the sector. But he was still unsure of the direction. So, he asked. "Which way are we going?"

Khan was sure of the direction but unsure of the eventual destination. But he replied with confidence, "West. At the moment at least."

Their stake-out in the southeast of the 3rd meant that any further and Sector 2 would be incoming. Khan had been following closely for a while now, so he decided to fall back a few meters to ensure the safeguarding of any obscurity.

"What are you doing? You'll lose him." A startled Vasu asked Khan. He was stating his concern and fear of losing the one solid lead in this case.

"Don't worry. It's so he won't spot us." Replied a calm and collected Khan.

Their difference in behaviour under pressure was quite visible. Khan on one hand was as cool as a man can be. Calculative, thoughtful of other's behaviour, and on his feet with ideas. Vasu on the other hand was displaying his lack of control. His nervous yet excited attitude stated how much he cared for this, however, he was also displaying a lack of thoughtful process. His instincts to jump in were at the forefront and his inability to control such a distracted concoction of emotions was evident. The now partners on duty had diligently followed the individual for quite some time. The clock on the dash suggested 20 minutes. They had passed all of Sector 3, entered Sector 2, and were now heading southwest. The change in scenery wasn't evident to Vasu at first. The residential areas were persistent at first and they still had a modern, over-the-top look. But suddenly there was a change of scenery. The beautiful, well- formed, bright painted buildings and bungalows were replaced with white and grey painted small buildings. There was no form, just function to their architecture. It was quite drab and monotonous bordering on being thoughtless. The contrast in the current the former scenery was so sudden that Vasu's eyes took time to adjust and it took his brain even longer. There wasn't that much vehicle movement on the road if you discount the trucks and lorries passing them by every other minute. He turned to Khan for some assurance and grounding arguments. But one look at him and Vasu could observe Khan's focus and determination. He might have noticed the changes in scenery but there was nothing that could take his eye off the target.

Hoping that he might get answers, Vasu asked. "Where are we? Is this-"

"Sector 2, yes." Khan interrupted by confirming his knowledge of the surroundings. He continued, "He seems to be going towards the port. Be ready-" Just as he was saying that, a lorry ahead of them tried a manoeuvre to get in the overtaking lane. Khan was caught by surprise. He slammed the middle pedal suddenly locking his brakes up and generating a significant amount of smoke. The lorry on the other hand tried to dodge the car it might have missed and tried to pull away again with its horns blaring. On any other day, this might have been a lucky escape even for someone driving as regularly as Khan. Today was not that day. This incident created a chain of events starting with the rider spotting the dodge catastrophe. He suspected the car following him and slowed down to confirm. In a few seconds, the rider was right on Khan's bonnet and looking at him. The eye contact spooked him and opened up the taps to the superbike. Khan's patrol car was not a match for this performance even at its best. This however was a hard-used, old service car driven around like a slug machine. It had no chance in hell. But for Vasu, it was amusing to see the bike pull away as it did. The noise was there now. It was undeniably a straight engine but his understanding that this was similar to that of a typical sedan, he did not expect it to have such an impressive soundtrack. The sound it generated was a typical four-pot bike sound but it was quite something to hear live The thumping base first and foremost was not present on the races Vasu watched on TV. Then there was the sheer sense of speed. For a few unmistakable moments, Vasu got the feeling that they were at a standstill. He watched the bike disappear into the distance like it was an animated object. To confirm that all if it wasn't an illusion, he had to look at the car's speedometer. They were doing 70 km/h. Now, Vasu had ridden the bike all the way to a sweet 100 but this, this was not that. This might have been more than 200. He was far more impressed than he was disappointed or irritated by the turn of events. Riding a bike at that speed was impressive in and of itself but to do that around vehicles, with death roaming on the horizon just created a new level of admiration for Vasu. He thought of his bike and how it could have helped at this point, not in chasing down the rider but in keeping up, without letting the ruse down.

At this point, it was inevitable that they had to turn around. They probably should have gone back to Yashpal's house in the anticipation that the biker might return. But Khan wanted to be sure before they returned. He thought that going all the way into the port might actually be helpful. He turned around as soon as he realized that his conclusions might be far-fetched. Maybe the rider wasn't heading that way, that it was just his speculation and nothing more. There were far too many destinations around the area that the rider could be just as easily visiting. Vasu wasn't surprised by the U-turn as much as he was surprised at the time it took Khan to do so. But to each his own he thought. The journey back was quiet and slow. It felt like ages before they reached back to their new burrow. There was no conversation required now. Both Khan and Vasu knew nothing they could say would change the fact they lost the lead and came crashing down back to where they began. Vasu slunk back into the seat now sure that there won't be any exciting action coming his way tonight. Khan on the other hand stared right at Yashpal's house as if he was burning a hole right through it with his eyes. The expression on him hadn't changed but the air around him sure did. It was no longer calm.

Sweetness, earthy scents, and a strong cardamom flavour were running through Vasu's mind. It was unwarranted. Here he was sitting, looking at Tarita and the coffee in his hand, but it didn't smell like coffee. It was smelling different, somehow wrong. He tried his best to ignore the smell and continue his conversation with Tarita but a sudden shaking woke Vasu right up. His eyes didn't open properly but now he was sure of the smell, not so much of the place. His eyes opened to a calmer Khan offering tea to him. It was not how he imagined his morning to be like but there was no amount of complaining that would change it now. By the time he picked up the tea and confirmed the smell, all of the details of his dreams were lost. All that he could now recall was the smell of tea in his sleep. He put the paper cup on the dashboard as carefully as he could and rubbed his eyes to help them open up. It was closer to dawn outside. The light wasn't there yet but the blue tint of the sky indicated it wasn't far away. Vasu moved his forcefully opened eyes to the clock and found out it was a quarter after five. He had been sleeping for an odd hour before Khan had woken up. They still had to talk about the events of last night but that warranted a large swig of morning brew. Both enjoyed their hot aromatic cups in silence, looking at the sky imagining things going differently. It was peaceful, could have even been serene for that moment before Vasu realized that his Tea was nearly empty and Khan had already been through his. He took the last sip of his tea but didn't enjoy it. It tasted bitter somehow. And then it began.

"I am sorry about losing the lead last night." Khan was serious about the comment but he was staring straight at Yashpal's house.

Vasu was surprised. He was expecting him to be blamed for distracting him. There was also a defensive argument prepared. "It's okay." That's all he could say. But Khan's honesty reflected his lack of self-responsibility. Vasu with all of his courage continued, "I am sorry as well. I distracted you."

Both were quiet for a second. Each of them knew they weren't at fault but this conversation had proven to be liberating. Khan knew there wasn't much they could do sitting around here.

"Let's get out of here. You go home, get some sleep and we will talk about this later." Khan's thinking was that the night's watch and the incident might have taken a toll on their minds. It could be difficult to make the right choices with potentially impaired judgment. A night's rest might help.

"Really? Is that it? You want to quit?" Vasu on the other hand believed that they needed to correct the mistake. And going back home without doing so was a mistake, a gesture of them giving up. He didn't want that, but neither did Khan.

"No, this isn't quitting." Khan wanted to explain how he thought resting might help them both. But instead of taking the conversation that way and getting into an inevitable argument with Vasu, he divulged in the plan that he thought of. It could be a potential breakthrough. "The man we saw yesterday left on a bike without a number plate. But I don't think there would be more than a few of those expensive bikes around. -"

"It was a black Sokudo M10." Vasu had noticed the bike and he wanted Khan to know that he was paying attention. "You won't find much of those imports, yes." He agreed that not many people had the money and the desirability of that bike. There were alternatives available and this strictly was for the passionate and informed riders who wanted no compromise.

"Yes, so I will look into that and find about Yashpal's staff. Maybe there is something there." Khan had already planned it all to look into. He suspected that the rider was a member of Yashpal's staff that was engaging and helping him with the other side of things.

Vasu thought that there was still not much he was given to do. He had the intention of helping but no opportunity. So, he addressed that elephant. "And what would I do?"

"You get some rest and practice. I will call you when I have all the data. You can then help me sort it." Khan wanted Vasu to not get exposed. Their partnership was still a well-kept secret and letting it out would jeopardize both of their goals and lives.

"Alright then." Even though he didn't like it, Vasu agreed. He had grown to understand the working style of his partner and didn't want to question it at this point. Not because he likes it, but because he knew he'd lose the argument.

"I'll drop you off at your house," Khan said while starting up the car.

Vasu agrees by nodding his head. He still had a ringing, unfading voice that kept reaping the same sentence. It didn't make sense to him at first. What would be the point? Won't it just give away that fact that we are onto him? It then hit him.

Just as Khan had started to pull the car out of the parallel space, Vasu said, "Let's meet him."

Khan was quite in shock at this suggestion. "Why?! He'll know that we are onto him."

Vasu was ready with an explanation, "That's just it. If it is him, he would be quite confident that no one had figured it out. No one is looking out for him. But as soon as he finds out that we have our doubts-"

"He'll do something stupid." Vasu nodded in agreement as Khan practically finished his sentence. "If he doesn't commit a mistake, maybe the guy from last night will. That's a good plan." Khan was impressed with Vasu's idea. It was a risky trick, especially with such a dangerous man, but there was nothing more they could have done than biding time. This way, the eventual happening would occur far sooner than either of those could have anticipated.

So, he put the car right back in the same spot and decided to wait a few hours. They had hoped to find any movement in Yashpal's house before they could approach. It was nearly 7 before Vasu spotted any movement. Yashpal was getting ready and having a conversation with a female. So, Khan strode on towards the society with a refreshed, reinstated confidence. Vasu followed practically giddy. But as soon as they entered the society, it hit him. What if this isn't the guy? Won't this antagonize him for Yashpal? What if Yashpal recognizes him? Won't that change his opinion and discourage similar activities for the foreseeable future? Vasu knew this train of thought was wrong; he had to get off and focus on the job at hand, but there's not much he could do to control it. He had always done his. Doubt himself. But Vasu had little time for dismantling his self-confidence. They were already near Yashpal's residence Khan was approaching the door. Once the bell was rung there was no turning back. Vasu wanted with all of his might to stop this from happening. He didn't want things to change. But something was stopping him from doing so. Something in the back of his mind now had taken control and wanted to go through this. With the first press of the bell, there was a sweet yet high-pitched chime they could hear. It was muffled but he could clearly make out the fact that it was a single tone. But within the second he could hear a loud base thumping. It was loud enough to vibrate his inner ear and make his body warm and sweaty. Vasu was confused at first for soon enough realized that it was his heartbeat. The rate was high enough that even Khan could have heard. Vasu looked at Khan only to find him saying something. He had to calm down to listen.

Khan said, "Wait in the car." Vasu was confused, he looked at the car still not having processed Khan's sentence. He repeated, "Go wait in the car."

Vasu was relieved hearing that line. He wanted to walk away but was curious to know the reason. "Sure, but why?"

"No one should know about my partner, especially-" Khan didn't have to complete the sentence. Vasu was happy to comply. He took the car's keys from Khan and walked back towards the car not looking back at Khan even once. Khan was baffled at Vasu's easy agreement but he had to focus on the job at hand. He rang the bell once, no answer. After a few seconds of silence, he pressed the button again. Curiously, there still was no answer. The third time was different though as soon as he pressed the button, the door opened and Khan was standing eye-to-eye with a stranger.

"Hi, can I help you?" The woman was dressed in a formal, office worker-type attire. She was decked out in a grey skirt, black heels, grey jacket covering the white buttoned-up shirt. Her voice was high-pitched but not enough to be annoying. Her voice and tone were polite yet the words that came out were of authority. She knew of the power in her hand.

The question was pointed towards Khan. "Hi, I am sorry but I wanted to talk with Mr Yashpal Vohra."

"What's so urgent and more importantly who are you?" The woman was stern with her question. And the early hour seemed to bother her.

"Oh yes, I am sorry. My name is Ashraful. I am a friend of Mr Yashpal… professionally and I was hoping to talk to him regarding something urgent." Khan replied as politely as he could.

This softened the lady. "Alright. But what is this about?"

Khan didn't want to go down this road. He knew that explaining to her the entire situation would just be a chore. So, he tried to work around it. "Well, it is kind of a sensitive matter. If you don't mind I would rather not discuss it outside."

"Okay alright. Come in." The woman was understanding. She was familiar with the type of information Yashpal, or any other politician might have to deal with. That's what led her to bring the pair inside. He stepped into the living room and the woman turned towards them to ask, "So, what's this about?"

Khan didn't want to explain this to her. Not because it was sensitive information or anything, but the toll of the night was still on his head. "I think it's better if you call him"

The woman however wasn't budging. "That's not how this works. You have to first tell me and then I will decide if it's worth his time."

"Don't worry it-" Just as Khan was explaining, he was interrupted.

"Khan! What a pleasant surprise!" A voice came from behind. It was Yashpal. His interruption was a blessing.

Khan was ironically happy to see the man. "Hi! Can we talk in private?"

"Sure." Yashpal obliged and excused his assistant out of the room. "Julie, could you please excuse us for a second?"

Khan waited for Julie to leave before he began, "Alright. Do you remember Subodh Mishra?"

"Subodh? Yes of course. What about him?"

"Well, I found a link related to his case." Khan wanted to check Yashpal's response, any face twitches or micro emotion that he may let out. He was vigilant in observing the details.

"That great news. Especially for Mrs Mishra."

There was a sense of excitement in Yashpal's voice. But there was also something at the back. Something Khan couldn't put his finger on. He replied, "I think we should refrain from telling her until we are satisfied that the lead is genuine."

"Sure. You know better. But that still doesn't answer the question, why are you here?"

Yashpal's excitement went down. And now Khan was ready. What he was about to say would be permanently etched in Yashpal's memory, for better or for worse, like writing on stone. "Well, the link is you." He watched carefully, looking out for any nervousness, any tense twitch that his face might display. Even his body could have been giving out the hints and Khan was anticipating that. In fact, he was counting on it.

"Pardon?"

Yashpal's face and body movement were just dripping out confusion. No matter how hard Khan looked, there wasn't a hint of nervousness, just confusion. He repeated his accusation but with succinct absoluteness, "You." Khan had now etched this in stone and slathered on a coat of varnish for good measure. He was aware of the dangers of accusing a potential Mayor, how it might just end his career. But he was willing to take the risk. Khan wanted this case for redemption perhaps. He had never cared about the public opinion of him, but his self-worth had been damaged when he was kicked off the other case. So, to get that back, he would do whatever possible. He clarified his position and hinted at the potential, "I visited Subodh's office the other day." Khan noticed a twitch, but it was not of nervousness, anger probably. "There were some files I needed to look over, but unfortunately there was nothing in there." The face of Yashpal remained the same, unmoving like a mountain in a blizzard. "But interviewing the staff revealed that you were working on a project with him." Yashpal sat down and leaned back on his sofa. He was looking straight ahead, thinking for a while before his confidence returned.

"I think they are mistaken. I have never met Subodh regarding any project whatsoever. All of our meetings were strictly social."

Khan although wasn't satisfied, refrained from pushing too hard. He was suspicious of the man but didn't want to make it obvious. "I understand but I needed to verify. I hope you understand."

"It's alright. But why at this hour? You could have come in later in the day."

Khan had anticipated the question. He knew the timing of approach wasn't right either way and that's why he had pursued this inquiry at the early hour of the day. "It's better to get this stuff done discreetly." Khan was right about this. The fewer people that know about the investigation, the better. "This way it is better for both of us."

Khan paused for a second deciding on how to approach the next matter. He wanted a casual conversation without alerting him so, he said. "I saw a bike here last night, in the area I mean." He had delivered a googly. Yashpal was careful about the discreet and secretive nature of the bike and the rider. It was supposed to have been well hidden. Hearing about the bike from Khan drew Yashpal's complete attention to him.

"What bike?"

Khan replied, "Oh! It was a black M10 I guess. I couldn't see it properly." Khan had an urge to push more. Maybe mention the missing number plate but it was too risky right now. He awaited a response from Yashpal who was thinking.

"M10? Is it a good bike? I am not that familiar with them, sorry."

He answered Yashpal's question, "Yes, it's a good fast sports bike."

"Do you know anyone who's got one? I just wanted to ask where they bought it. You know, I want one so…"

"No, sorry. I will ask a friend if you like." Yashpal said looking at Khan. "Anything else?"

Khan was worried at the relative awkwardness of the conversation. Maybe the line of inquiry had created it so. But this wasn't the place to analyse. So, stepping back to return he said, "No, I think that's it. Thank-"

"How's the other case coming along? Any progress?"

Khan wasn't anticipating the question from Yashpal. He had to snap back and reply, "Nothing big. But trust me if I ever find anything on that case, you'll be the first one to find out." That was a snide remark at Yashpal and one that Khan wasn't proud of. But it was out and unlike a defective car, he couldn't recall it for repairs.

Khan awkwardly left after that tense and weird conversation. Still, Khan felt he owed Vasu a clarification on sending him back. He also wanted to inform Vasu of their conversation. Khan opened the car door and before sitting down, Vasu asked Khan about the conversation with Yashpal. He wanted to clarify the whole returning to the car issue but this was far more important. Khan divulged into the conversation. He mentioned all of the questions and tried to phrase Yashpal's answers as best as he could. Vasu was captured in the conversation imagining what he would have done. There were also doubts regards some of the things Khan had said, so he waited for Khan to finish and then started with the questions, or rather his doubts.

He began with the one that baffled him the most, "The staff interview? Why did you lie?"

Khan wanted to poke rather than stab. "I didn't want to reveal it all yet. I just wanted to find out his tell."

"What difference would it make?" Vasu wasn't sure how it would be different. Khan had hinted rather than tell it outright. Either way, Yashpal knew.

Khan assured Vasu this was the right thing. "Well, now he's not sure whether we know everything or not. He'll be racking his brain up thinking about it all day." He wanted Yashpal to think about his actions. This way, Khan thought he would make a few mistakes in the future.

Vasu was satisfied with the answer. So he moved on to the next line of inquiry. "Alright. I get that. What about the tell?" Vasu had heard the term in a movie. It was related to gambling, about how a player can find out if there was bluffing from one's expressions.

Khan wasn't sure what he read was right. The man's confidence had misguided his radar. He thought he was reading too much into it. "I didn't find any. It was like he was telling the truth. Even I almost believed him."

"But you think he is lying, right?" Vasu asked this to ensure they were on the same page.

"Yes," Khan assured.

"Good, me too." Vasu had just arrived at that conclusion after that conversation.

"Really? What changed?" Khan noticed the confidence and wanted to find out about the moment that changed it for Vasu.

"The bike thing." Khan was surprised. Vasu knew something that Khan didn't. "He was talking about his favourite bike in an interview."

Khan realized where the man stumbled. Lying is all about good memory and unless you have a database like a supercomputer, you didn't have enough memory of everything you speak of. And at that point, someone like Vasu would catch the error. "And let me guess. It was an M10." Khan was glad Vasu was with him. It provided him with an important hint he never would have found.

"Yes," Vasu confirmed.

"Well, I am glad you understand the person we are dealing with now."

"So, we stick to your earlier plan?" Vasu was now hoping to be actively involved. Even though he wasn't satisfied with the amount of work, he was looking forward to the work that night.

"Yes, and I will try to put an eye on this guy." Khan wasn't sure that was possible but he had to try. They drove off from the ominous place with the hope that this day would yield better fruit than the night.

Vasu reached home just as her mother had left. That was evident with the freshness and the warmth of the breakfast. It had been a tough night, exhausting, yet Vasu didn't feel hungry. Or rather the confrontations and events had hampered his appetite. The delicious food he saw on the table was no longer appealing. Hoping that he'd eat some when he woke up, Vasu put all of it in the fridge after finding some space in the cabinets and the racks. He fell down on the bed like a massive rock. It wasn't long before he fell asleep. Khan on the other hand was still driving back to his station. The bed wasn't appealing to him but the conversation he had with Yashpal today was insightful. It was curious how the man reminded him of an old army tale. Their behaviour and their movements were similar to that of the individual in the story. But he thought that it was just the exhaustion that was rustling his brain up. So, to switch things up, Khan started thinking of plans to find out the individual behind the mask and avoid another stake-out.

The drive back to the station was mundane but it gave an idea to him that could work. It was a long shot and his memory wasn't as sharp as before but maybe Vasu could help him. It was early in the morning so Khan wasn't sure whether it was Ashfaq or Talpade at the helm. From the past few days' events though, Khan knew he had reliable people around him. It didn't bother him anymore that he had to work with other people. Stepping back into his station, his home ground, Khan was optimistic about today's ventures. He was looking forward to working on this case. But the exhaustion hadn't loosened its grip. It was still lurking in the back of his mind. Khan quickly orders one of his subordinates to call in either Ashfaq or Talpade, whoever was present in his office. He sat down on his chair and leaned back to a comfortable position. His desk didn't have a footrest, that would have made a considerable difference. He thought maybe taking off his shoes might help. His leather boots were sturdy standard-issue uniform brown. Although they severed their purpose, one wouldn't have called them comfortable. Especially after a 20-hour wearing spree. Taking them off freed the toes and gave out the feeling of lightness. It was warranted in this case as leather boots were quite heavy with thick soles.

Khan had just shut his eye, or rather they had grown heavy enough for him to not keep open when he was sprung awoke by the knocking sound. He said, "Come in."

It was Talpade. He was at the station early having anticipated Khan's arrival to be the same. Talpade wanted to discuss the events of the past day but as soon as he walked in, he knew there was more than that he would find out. "Good Morning sir, you called me?"

"Yes, come in. Sit." Talpade drew the chair opposite Khan and sat down. Khan with a deep breath proceeded to explain, "I need another favour. I know I have been asking too much of you but I cannot trust other people."

Talpade wanted to stop Khan, it was embarrassing for him. But the discipline of a policeman was stopping him. "Please sir, you are a superior and a mentor. It's a learning experience watching you work. Tell me. How can I help?"

"You know the favour I asked off you yesterday," Khan waited for Talpade to realized which he did in a second. "I had found an important lead in the Phantom case. A file I found, that you helped me sneak out has provided me with a potential suspect. I cannot say who that is without getting you in trouble." Khan had all the gratitude for Talpade and he wanted to express it. For the entire duration of this case, it was nothing but help from his subordinate that was consistently given.

Talpade understood the situation, the importance of this case and wanted to help, get on board. "I understand sir, but I would like to know more about this case and help you more actively if I can."

Khan was appreciative of the offer but he didn't want Talpade to be in the same mess as him. So he said, "Trust me, having you working with me will be bad for your career. Especially in this case. I am glad you offered me such assistance and believe me that would have been splendid. But this case needs more discretion than usual." Khan wanted to mention the danger of the case as well but refrained knowing that Talpade wouldn't have cared. "And I also have someone working with me. He is a work in progress but I believe by the end of this all, he will be ready to work full time."

"Who is the partner? Or is that something I shouldn't know?" He was disappointed, knowing that someone else has a chance to work with Khan, and tried his best to hide it, but couldn't.

"If I tell you, then you might get in trouble with the dynamic duo." Khan was referring to Panditya & Shah. "Believe me, you have been more than helpful working for me like this, and I would like you to help me again."

"Of course, tell me." Talpade was ready for the orders.

"I need the complete staff list of the Yashpal Mishra's campaign." Khan knew the weight of this request.

Even Talpade recognized that. There were a lot of eyes on Yashpal and any action or intent for that same would not be welcomed by those supporting him. And the list of those was far longer than people knew about. Then there was the question of public opinion. That was all in his favour. Hence the difficulty in access. "That might be difficult without turning heads."

"I know. I can provide you with a reason to get that." Khan had a plan to get around that dilemma. He wanted to show Yashpal in danger so the ruse to help him would provide access to the data. "You can file an official FIR with this." Khan takes out a blank sheet of A4 size paper starts writing in large blocky letters, 'I WILL KILL IF HE WINS. STOP ME IF YOU CAN!' Khan tried his best to write differently than his own handwriting. He did that by changing how he held his pen. Now, here was a letter threatening the safety of a candidate running for office and the police force has to do whatever necessary to protect him. Khan slid the paper to Talpade and watched as his lips widened into a smile. He continued, "Get a complete list of the staff and their details to ensure there is no leak in the security."

"I believe I can work with this. And where was that this was discovered?"

"This morning at that politician's doorstep. A senior inspector was visiting to casually meet that politician and he discovered this note. He gave it to you as an assignment to work on." Khan replied. "Maybe we can get two of our own people, trustworthy people to follow him around. You know, for his safety." The message was sent, and the plan was explained. He knew he could count on Talpade for the right course of this plan.

"This is a high-priority case. I will get on this right away." "Thank You."

Khan was back in his resting position, leaning looking at the fan. He was trying to get as comfortable as possible. It wasn't as easy but somehow he managed and fell asleep.

It was a clear, cool evening. The breeze was just right, there was an earthy scent in the air as Vasu was riding his bike. Only it wasn't his bike. It looked like a café racer and was way more powerful than his own wreck. That's when Vasu realized the heavy yet high- pitched scream of a superbike coming from behind him. The bike was an all-black M10 ridden by Yashpal. It was odd Vasu thought, he had never thought about running into the man so soon. Yashpal overtook him, turned around, and pointed a gun at him. Vasu froze in the moment, neither his hands nor his feet were moving. He wanted to stop or drive off but none of those options seemed to be on the table. He took his eyes off Yashpal and looked at his arms and feet. All of his limbs were holding tightly at the bike, making sure he wouldn't fall off. But as it turns out, that wasn't a priority concern. He looked up to check on Yashpal and his metal instrument. It was still there pointing at him.

Suddenly, there was a loud bang followed by a bright white light. Vasu was on his arms and knees, panting and sweating from the nightmare that just occurred. What terrified him to the core was that this was in its entirety a possibility. He sat down, trying to control his breathing and ground himself into reality. It took him a while before he felt relaxed and secure enough to get up.

Vasu walked out in the kitchen and opened up the fridge, reaching out for the big, cold bottle of water. He opened it and started chugging it as if he had just returned from the Dakar. The water helped with the dry mouth that had started to develop, while the temperate was helping with the sweat and the uneasy feeling. It took only a few seconds before the bottle was empty. The usual brushless bitter teeth that bothered him and discouraged consumption of anything edible, were not a concern now. He was now happy to take a deep breath and appreciate the surrounding. It wasn't much, but he was home. He was someplace he could recognize and feel safe. The nightmare was fuzzy now, except for the single haunting image, Yashpal firing a gun at him. He tried to distract himself, looked at the clock, and panicked again. It was half- past four. He had plans to meet Tarita after her college. Vasu slept through the afternoon and missed his date by an hour and a half. He was disappointed, but probably not as much as Tarita would be. Vasu rushed towards his phone. In his panic, he had completely forgotten where he had put it. It took him some time, a lot of effort, and some nervousness looking around to finally find the phone. It was on his bed. The time it took to dial Tarita's number could have been counted in single-digit seconds or less. The ring gave him a hint as to why he was calling. What excuse could he have given her?

Not many came to mind and now it was too late to continue and try out any of those that occurred. The call was received at the other end.

"Hello!" Vasu was nervous, almost shaking.

"Hi, it's me." He waited for a response from the other side. There wasn't any, so he continued. "I know I stood you up. That was really shitty of me. I am very sorry." Again he waited only for silence to follow. "Please Tarita I am really sorry. Trust me I was looking forward to this date. I had the album in my bag all day. Please."

"Alright, I'll humour you." Tarita replied with a flat tone and asked the obvious question, "Why?"

"I-" Vasu was tempted to tell the truth but stopped himself and instead gave a derivative answer. "I was out all night, working."

"You got a job?" A hint of surprise had entered Tarita's flat tone. "Not exactly. It's a project, an unofficial one." Vasu tried to explain as best as he could without revealing anything. "What's it on?" But Tarita wanted to know more.

He thought about it and gave the simplest explanation he could. "Election-related. I can't say more."

This sparked interest in Tarita. She continued the line of inquiry. "Late night?"

"Yes, that's when we are able to work." Vasu was now mimicking the answer he had given to his mother.

"I don't believe you. Why can't you tell me more?" Her patience was running out. She wanted answers and Vasu wasn't providing them. It was frustrating for her.

Vasu had to wait a while to think about it. How could he dodge this persistent question? The answer was obvious. "Because you know strict rules. It's election Tarita. You know how the government is."

It hit her suddenly, "Oh! You are working with that idol of yours." Vasu had mentioned who he admired.

He almost chuckled at Tarita's response. "Not exactly."

"What do you mean?" She was again confused and put into a blind alley.

"I am sorry Tarita but I can't say more." Vasu didn't want to give away details. At least not until he knew he was safe to do so.

Tarita thought about it and something had softened her up enough to say, "I'll meet you again, for the album. Nothing more. We can go out and talk later when you tell me all about your project. Till then, no more of my company." She was stern in her assertion.

"Alright. I will take you out to breakfast and give you the album. And I promise you I will tell you about my project as soon as everything works out. Promise." Vasu agreed and accepted that this was the best possible outcome from his mistake.

"Okay. What time?"

"What is your college timing?" Vasu asked, hoping to meet her early if there was a chance.

"I am not going tomorrow." She replied.

"Why?" It was surprising for Vasu to find out about this.

"I can't tell you that." She had got him. It was the 'gotcha' moment Tarita was waiting for.

"Alright, fair enough." Half a smile had made its way on Vasu's face. "How about 9?"

"I guess it could work. I might be late a little. I am not a morning person." She said truthfully.

Vasu didn't mind. He had no other choice anyway. "Not an issue.

Take all the time you want. I will see you tomorrow."

"Hope so. Bye!" Another snide remark at Vasu and she was happy with where the conversation went.

"Bye!" And so was Vasu.

Vasu had just dodged a bullet. He almost missed out on one of the good things in his life. He was sure that Tarita and he could work out but the task Vasu had taken upon was a major interference. He had to complete it fast so that there could be a chance for a more serene life.

In Sector 7, Khan had been awake for a while now. He was going through a meal having missed two in a row. The files were being delivered in a few minutes. It was already late in the afternoon but Khan was sure he had time to read through some of the details and prepare himself. The phone call however carried different news. It was from Talpade. He had called in to inform Khan that detailed information of the staff members could not be accessed without a proper court order. All he could deliver was the basic details like name, contact, and pictures. He also had an update on the tail Khan asked for. It wasn't happening either. Khan was a bit disappointed but he knew all information was valuable. He completed his meal and waited for a few minutes for the file to arrive. Meanwhile, he had called Vasu and told him to be ready for another night. The file came in a few minutes after the call. Rather than sit there and read the file at his desk, Khan decided that he could sit at the stake-out and read there. It would be a multi-tasking opportunity. He left the station with the unmarked sedan again. The sky had turned towards dusk by the time he had reached to pick up Vasu. As he got in the car, Khan handed over the file to him and said.

"This is a list of Yashpal's campaign staff. Look through it and tell me if you find anyone suspicious." Khan wanted to check Vasu's attention to detail.

"How did you get it?" Vasu asked.

Khan smiled and replied, "Perks of being a police officer."

Vasu opened up the file and looked through a few staff members' information. He was surprised at the lack of detailed data and asked Khan, "There is only basic information here. How would I be able to judge someone from that?" Vasu had a point. You would at least need some insight into the person's character to get a feel of what they are like.

"Well read through them at least. You might find someone of interest." Khan was disappointed with Vasu's lack of interest in the file. He anticipated some insight that might suggest Vasu could read other people. To Khan, this was a necessary part of the job.

"Okay." Vasu obliged. Although he did go through the file, he didn't read into any of them. Just a glance over to reassure Khan. "71 people are working on his campaign. How do they pay these people?"

"Well you know there are donations to the campaign." Khan was familiar with election campaigns. He was involved professionally with a candidate probably a decade ago or so it felt. That had allowed him to observe the inside functioning of a campaign.

Vasu wasn't satisfied with the reply. "But still, think about it. 71 people. That's probably as big as a mid-size company. You need a working income to pay that many people." Vasu wasn't sure Khan understood the scale of the operation. He had to outline it to get his point through.

Khan however was familiar with the number. It was larger than usual but so was the campaign. "The donations cover all of that. Think about it, you get a tax cut for doing a favour for a politician, why wouldn't you spend money on that?"

It did make some sense. But the scale or rather the amount seemed ridiculous to Vasu. "But how much could he receive."

"Alright, don't tell anyone" Khan divulged Vasu in an undercover failed mission that he was involved in. "we were tracking the paper trail of a businessman who had committed fraud. Guess how much would he have donated to a political campaign."

Vasu was quick to reply, though the question was still under review in his mind. "That depends, how much does he earn?"

"Let's say he is the CEO of any major company. Like 'Credence', that telecom company." Khan said this to give Vasu a scale of the party involved. Credence was a multi-national home-grown company still run by the same family. It had its reach overseas will multiple business ventures.

"Alright, I guess 10-20 Lakhs." Vasu thought that this was a significant amount for even a well-settled executive to cough up. Even if it was for his benefit.

Khan anticipated a low number and was ready for his bomb of a reply. "He had donated 2.6 crores."

It landed with a bang. "Holy Shit!"

"It was embezzled money of course but still, why donate right?" Khan paused to look at Vasu nodding in agreement. "There could be a potential gold mine Yashpal is sitting on while spending peanuts."

He then moved the story to the present day and adjusted it to the climate Khan and Vasu were fighting.

Vasu was taken aback by the information. "Who knew? I should have become a politician." He joked.

"You can lie good enough. Maybe you should." Khan punched back. But a moment later he dropped the joke and continued. "You know, maybe you should. Work with me, learn the functioning of the government inside and out. You'll meet people this way, they'll know your name and what you are willing to do for them." Khan had a serious tone which brought Vasu's complete attention to his words.

He thought about it. What would he do, how, and why? All of the questions got brought out the sentence, "I don't know how I'll hold under pressure."

Khan was surprised by the line. "What? You can take down an entire gang but this scares you?" It was baffling to him that a person would go through physical torture but not get involved in one of the most important aspects of life. This especially hit him when Vasu said it.

Vasu on the other hand had thought about all the torture and embarrassing moments, the humiliation, or even the loss that would follow pursuing that path. And when thinking about something scared him, he was definitely not going to do it. He tried to explain it to Khan as best as he could. "Both of these are different. With this job I get to go home worry-free."

"That's because this is your first assignment." That was true. Khan knew of the burden this job carried and soon Vasu would find out.

The first assignments are tough, yes, but from Khan's understanding, it was always the second one that hurt more. Knowing of the pain you are going to go through again and still doing it required heart and bravery. Vasu was going to need it. But tonight was not the time to indulge Vasu in such a heavy talk. Maybe later thought Khan and dropped the subject.

It was dark by the time they reached the society from last night. Unfortunately, the same parking spot was not available today. Khan had to park his car further back which led to a difficult situation. How to keep an eye now? Regardless, they walked over to the parked SUV. Vasu and Khan had to find a way to get back to their spot. So Khan inspected the porcelain license plate and pulled them as hard as he could. It chipped away a section of the license place. As soon as Vasu saw what Khan was doing, he stood near him to cover him up. Due to a good fitment, it didn't budge any further. So Khan found a big sharp stone and started hitting it to break it. It took a few seconds to break the plate but it was worth it. He then proceeded to do the same with the front number plate. He made sure not to damage the car, not leave any marks on the paint job. Khan was clever this way. He knew that reporting a suspicious car without a license would get it seized for a minimum of 24 hours. Maybe the owner would get in trouble but Khan couldn't worry about that right now. The spot mattered. And Khan did what he knew to be wrong but justified. They waited near the car while a tow truck arrived. Khan noticed that the house was empty. There was absolutely no movement there and it was completely dark. They had a chance. He alerted Vasu to the same.

"Look. Empty." Khan said pointing at the house

"So?" Vasu was confused as to what Khan wanted to convey. "Let's go in. Look around." It was the obvious thing for Khan to do.

But not for Vasu. He was sceptical. "Are you sure? Won't that get you in trouble?"

"Who cares, this is a golden opportunity and I am not missing on it." He said as they moved towards the entrance of the compound.

"Alright but if we get caught I am ratting on you," Vasu said jokingly. "I don't want to go to jail." There was some genuine fear behind that line.

They walk as calmly and discreetly they can towards the house. Approaching the door, Khan bends down and starts to work on the lock. He knew the basic lock picking, hence the trouble here. Vasu was doing the same thing he did with the license place. He stood watch covering Khan. It was almost 10 seconds and Vasu had grown out of patience.

"How much longer?" Vasu asked with a tone that would suggest that he wanted to relieve himself.

"It is harder than it looks. Just keep watch." Khan said with frustration.

As it turned out Vasu didn't have to keep watch. Both of them heard some footsteps, like a boot on wood. It was audible but barely. Khan and Vasu both peeked in to find a middle-aged individual walking down Yashpal's stairs. They both panicked and rushed towards the parked car outside the society. The timing and speed were impeccable. Neither of them looked back fearing that might just waste time. The car was parked further but as soon as they passed the SUV, they knew they were in the clear. Both slowed down, took a breather, and entered their car.

"You said no one would be in there." He said panting.

"I didn't spot anyone. How should I have known?" Khan defended his actions and judgment.

"Do you think he saw us?" Vasu asked genuinely worried.

"I don't know," Khan said shaking his head, closing his eye, and leaning back.

"Who was it?" Vasu asked looking at Khan. "It definitely wasn't Yashpal" He was sure of it.

"No." So was Khan. Then it occurred to him. "Maybe the rider from last night?" He didn't get a proper look but the glimpse was enough to arrive at the conclusion. He suggested, "One way to find out"

"You want to go back?" Vasu asked with a shaking head. "Yes, but with a reason." Khan wanted to clear things. "What?"

"To talk to Yashpal. We don't know he isn't here." Khan explained.

Vasu knew that this might work. But he still was scared from the incident. What they were doing was a crime and the fact that his bag contained the evidence wasn't providing him with a good state of mind. "Alright. Just give me a moment." He said, hoping to delay the inevitable.

Khan said to hurry up Vasu. "He might be gone."

Just as Khan said that the same rider from last night drove out of the society and headed in the same direction. Khan didn't start the car immediately though.

"What are you doing? We'll miss him." Vasu asked concerned that the man who wanted to go inside the house a couple of seconds ago, sat there still when a suspect is running away.

"We won't," Khan said trying to reassure Vasu. Khan counted to 5 before starting and pursuing the rider, following him at a safe distance. With every passing street, Khan got closer and closer until he was just as close as the last night. There were cars, traffic at this time though. But that was helpful, better camouflage for the pair. They followed past the same route again. All of last night's landmarks were appearing again like clockwork. And then came the route for the docks. The road had suddenly expanded. From a six-lane highway, it became a 10 lane road. The lanes were wider to provide better manoeuvrability to the loading trucks. Vasu was smitten by the looks of it. He started imagining it empty. How he could have tested his bike to its limits. Even though it was just a 125cc blow pot, there was some grunt to it. Enough to get it to 100. He was picturing the view at that speed, the wind, the noise, and even the vibration. He was in bliss. After a few seconds though he came back and put his mind back at the task. Vasu had visited the old port but never the new one. It would be a new adventure. He was also worried about Khan. He was following the rider a bit too closely. He wanted to say something but last night when he did say something, it all went to the shits. Not risking it tonight thought Vasu.

When they reached near the port gates, they had to get in line, for inspection. It was a mandatory procedure to ensure the safety of an important military point as well. Unlike the other ports of the country, there wasn't just the Port Authority here. I mean they were in charge but the real security was provided by the military. There were the uniformed as well as the casually dressed men. The casually dressed members of the military branch were from the special forces unit trained to infiltrate. Their object was simple, keep an eye on anyone or anything suspicious. They would formulate a plan and ensure proper execution in case of any potential threats. This would seem unnecessary to an outsider but 2 potential terror attacks were avoided due to the presence of the special forces. On the outside, this port seemed like just another shipping lot, but really it was a militarized fortress where civilians were allowed to visit. While waiting in line, Khan explained all of this to Vasu while he listened with complete attention. How the security and the chain of command functioned. He also mentioned that if you are former military, the id card can get you a visit anytime but you have to be accompanied by a uniformed officer. Vasu was impressed with the amount of security at the compound and oddly he felt even more unsafe now, uncomfortable. For him, the security wasn't representing the preparedness or the willingness towards safety but rather the severity of the threat or the potential threat. But the chances of such a threat occurring on the same night they were visiting were ridiculous. He had seen danger, lived through it and he somehow felt that this was the type of threat he could tackle, especially given the number of good guys around. There wasn't confidence in the thought process, just hope, and wilful thinking.

They had been moving at a steady pace. The rider was 2 vehicles ahead of them in the line. Khan was able to spot him past the van and the low-slung sports car. Such expensive cars or bikes were not common but not unheard of either at the port. Chances were that they were either being imported or exported. No one working in here had an expensive mode of transport. Well, except someone who owned the trucks. They were almost as expensive as an executive sedan car. Most people working here were the blue- collar honest folk that wanted to add just a little butter to their toast. And if that butter came from a rich kid's bread, the toast tasted sweet without the cup of tea. It was 20 minutes, maybe less before the rider got his turn inside. The sports car was next. It took only about a minute for the rider to be cleared. They couldn't see inside, the entrance on their left and they were parallel to the door. They guessed so because the car went in next. Their field of view diminished as soon the rider took the left turn inside the gates. It took longer for the car to be cleared almost 6 minutes. They knew there was no way they could escape this. Waiting is all they could do. Vasu started looking around sitting upright in his seat. He wanted to get a look inside. But there was no way. The gates were designed so that no one had a clear view of the inside without standing opposite the gates. Khan, Vasu, and the car weren't.

He had started tapping the door pockets and handles. His body was representative of his mind. Khan on the other hand had rested his head on his knuckles, resting on the armbar attached to the door. It had made its way after about 5 minutes and stayed there without adjustment. The only time Khan moved was to look at Vasu when he began tapping. Then van went in next. Khan was aware that the van would take longer to get through the checks but Vasu hadn't caught on to the pattern. He had his eye on the clock, tapping away at the dashboard now. After 5 minutes his control was let loose.

"What's taking so long?" Vasu asked, nearly screamed with impatience.

"They are checking cars, thoroughly," Khan said calmly.

"How long does it take to check a car." Vasu wasn't impressed with the slow working of the security. He thought this was like any other government workspace slow and inconvenient.

"6 minutes from what I have noticed," Khan said glancing at the car clock.

Vasu looked at Khan's demeanour and was taken aback by his uncaring attitude. "You are calm for someone who is about to lose a major suspect."

"What else can you do?" He asked looking at Vasu. "You want me to start tapping at the steering wheel?" A snide remark that he hoped would shut the kid up. And it did.

Vasu didn't reply to that remark. He knew that Khan was messing with him and Vasu didn't want to give more ammunition. The van had cleared at the 8-minute mark apparently because the guard standing at the gate waved them in. They entered through the gates where they were approached by a guard and surrounding their car were 4 other armed officers. It wasn't much just your usual sub-machine gun.

"Good Evening. Your IDs please." Said the camouflaged man approaching the window. He had a submachine gun on his shoulder and was leaning down to take a look at the passengers of the car. There were a few feet of distance thought between him and the car. Precaution probably.

"Good Evening." Replied Khan waiting for the next question. "What is your business here?" Asked the army officer.

"My name is Ashraful Khan. I am a Senior Inspector with the Sector 7 police. This is my partner Vasu. We followed in a suspect here and we're hoping you wouldn't mind letting us look around to find him." Khan said that calmly and clearly. He was ex-military and knew that lies would not get him anywhere. The truth however was appreciated even where it was inconvenient.

"I would have to get this cleared with my superior first though." Said the office straightening up and taking out his walkie-talkie.

Khan pulled out a card from his top pocket. He had kept it there when left his house today. "That's quite alright go ahead with it. But as you do, please consider this card as well." He handed over the card to the officer.

The officer examined the card carefully and leaned down again to look at the card, verifying the picture. He stood back straight up and walked away from the car talking to his superior. The other officers still stood near the car waiting for their orders. The officer came back in a minute and approached the window again

"What are your plans. Would you arrest the suspect I mean?" He asked expecting a clear answer.

Khan obliged. "No actually, we just wanted to observe him. He's a potential murder suspect and we wanted to check if there is any chance or clue that he could lead us to."

The officer paused for a second and replied. "Okay sir, you can go in. Just a small piece of advice from our superior, don't start a fight. You won't be treated differently." There was a sense of rigid warning given to Khan.

He appreciated the gesture and said, "I understand. Thank You." The officer remarked, "I hope you find what you are looking for." "I will if you can point the direction in which a rider went. He was 2 cars ahead of us." He knew the officer would answer honestly. "That would be there." He said pointing towards the right-hand side at a road lane of the port. It was the storage section of the port. The road would lead them to a series of godowns.

"Thank You again for being so helpful," Khan said gratefully.

The officers order his subordinates to back down and waved the partners clear. Khan started the car and moved gently forward.

"What was that all about? The second card and everything?" Vasu asked completely ignorant towards the situation. His attention was completely taken by the four armed men covering their car. He had even taken a look at the watchtower and the sand wall with a rifleman standing guard at it.

Khan replied, "Well kid, you cannot start investigating inside the port without a proper permit. You need a court order. My second ID was military. He rallied the information to his superiors who considered the ID and let me conduct my business."

Vasu was impressed at Khan's pull. He had to confirm, "So he recognized you."

Khan wasn't sure so he said, "Well, if it was Captain Siraj Hassan, then yes, he recognized me. Or else it was someone considerate."

That wasn't the answer Vasu was expecting. So he phrased it differently. "Are you that well known?"

"Not to that many people, no. Just a few." Khan replied. "Like who." Vasu wanted to know more.

"Can we focus?" But Khan wasn't going to distract himself with this line of questioning. They had to focus.

Vasu agreed and dropped the subject. "Alright."

They were heading in the direction that the officer pointed at hoping to find the bike or the rider. They wouldn't be able to recognize the face but the attire, that would stand out. Especially among the orange of the sea shanty singers. Khan was driving slowly so that they could each look in their respective directors and look for the suspect. They had to cross a few godowns, and multiple stacks of shipping containers before Vasu spotted the bike among such a stack. It was just sitting there parked, waiting for its owner. Khan pulled in a few meters ahead to avoid any unwanted exposure and they got out to look for the owner of the vehicle. There was a number plate, so like any other cop, Khan noted down the number to cross-check the owner later. They couldn't find the rider nearby though. But there was a godown a few meters behind. They formulated the plan. Walking in there would risk their cover and drive away from the rider. The goal here was to find out the reason for the rider's visit. It could open a link to Yashpal and eventually to his killing spree. Vasu suggested standing on the steps to look inside the godowns like he had done during his encounter with the gang.

"No, that won't provide enough visibility. The godown too large and we are finding an individual." Khan said looking up at the windows.

"It helped me that night." Vasu was sure that this was the best way based on his experience.

Khan had his doubts and made it known. "That's because you knew what you were looking for and it was empty."

Vasu looked at Khan for a better plan and asked. "So, what then? Go in and risk getting spotted."

Not sure if that was that bad an idea he replied, "Yes, that might be the only way."

Khan had a point. If they wanted to look for the rider, they had to risk this. So they entered the godown. It was unmanned unlike the other ones and open too. The interior was completely different from what Vasu had seen on the other port. There were sections dividing the godown creating a sort of storage room with a smaller capacity. And this godown had a solid roof. This meant that the steps' windows would have provided only the half picture. Khan and Vasu had to investigate the sections separately. Vasu took the roof while Khan had decided to stay down. Khan also informed Vasu that if anyone with authority approached with any scrutiny, he could tell them that he was in the wrong godown. That was to be their excuse out. The roof could be accessed with two large staircases. One was a regular metal stair about eight feet wide while the other was a flat metal plate. Vasu didn't understand at first, but as he walked upstairs it made sense to him, to bring the cargo down easily.

Khan carefully walked towards the end of the godown. He was slow, peaking at every section or divider and then examining the contents. All of the sections seemed to contain the same branding, ChalCham. This was an unfamiliar company, and the writings on the boxes didn't seem to be local either. The script was northern but the language was completely different. Maybe from the east thought Khan. The boxes or rather the printing on them had two different colours, pink and blue. He looked around, making sure that no one was around to catch him, and opened one of the pink boxes with his car keys. Inside there were 10 pink packages of ready-to-make cookie dough. This was odd. Why would there be such a large quantity? He realized that Yashpal often flaunted his generosity. And one of those was his giveaway of food. Yashpal regularly donated food. That's what it could have been. He chucked inside because he anticipated these to be filled with smuggled-in items like drugs or gold. As he walked away the blue boxes were staring back at him. Calling him to open them. It was his instincts actually. Even though Khan knew that there was nothing wrong here, he had to take a look. So, again with his keys, he tore open a box, a blue on this time. There were similar 10 blue packages of ready-to-make cookie dough. Khan was kicking himself. He was so sure that there would be something inside these boxes, so sure that there was a bigger ploy at work but alas, nothing but a good deed. He thought even the worst people in the world sometimes do good.

Vasu on the upper side walked up nearly getting caught by two individuals talking. He quickly got inside one of the sections to hide himself. The sections on the upper floor had a different layout. Instead of having a passageway in the middle of the room, there were two passageways near both of the walls. The individuals talking were closers to the passageway touching the stairs. Vasu wanted to move in closer but the lights and the structure would make him as visible as the sun in the sky. He also wanted to be closer to the exit in case of any exposure. He hid behind the large pile of boxes in the first section ready to move. The conversation was loud enough for him to hear but the structure of the godown meant there was an exorbitant amount of echo. Vasu had trouble making out anything from their talk. It took him a while before he could decipher things back to an intelligible language. There were keywords that he noted in his mind to put together a sentence. With the help of a little concentration he heard and put together the first sentence – 'I am happy with the boxes and product's condition.' The next sentence he heard was, 'The blue ones will be moved tomorrow. The pink day after.' He had to remember these things as well. As soon as he listened in on the third sentence, Vasu was started by the sound of the door slamming. An inordinate amount of thoughts and scenarios shot through his mind. Was Khan caught? Did he slam the door by mistake? How would Vasu get out? What if he gets caught? The was between the time the door was slammed a figure walking up the stairs. Their loud footsteps were alarming the two people talking, halting their conversation. The appearance of the new individual was not welcomed by the rest. The conversation they had was tense and with every word, the rider seemed to be getting angry by the second. Vasu heard the conversation and memorized every word said. As soon as there seemed to be a concluding tone appearing in the talk, he slowly and carefully made his way down.

Khan had moved towards the door was looking at the stairs for Vasu when he was coming down. Vasu hinted at Khan to leave and he obliged. They rushed out to their car and sat down for a breather.

As they gave looks at the weirdly covert mission being successful, the godown's door slammed again. It didn't sound as loud with the ambient noise but it was clearly from the godown. They were anticipating a loud noise coming from a smaller capacity engine. Unmistakably it did a few seconds later. The sound was loud and faded out fast. That was the cue for Khan to pull out of their hiding spot and follow. They could see the rider going towards the exit of the port. So they followed suit.

"So, what did you find?" Khan asked realizing that Vasu might have just discovered a stash of evidence.

Vasu was excited to share the intel he gathered. "I overheard the conversation. Two of them and I think I may have something for us."

"Go on, tell me." Khan couldn't wait. He was driving at the optimum pace to keep the car out of view.

"Okay, so, our dear rider was here to audit the contents of this godown. He approved of their condition and gave out dates for their shipment. Blue boxes tomorrow and pink boxes the day after."

"Did you hear where he was taking them?" Khan asked, hoping that there was even more information at hand.

But Vasu didn't have much. "No, because that's when the third guy walked in."

Khan chuckled when he heard Vasu mention the third guy "Yeah, I almost got caught by him." Khan was downstairs right in the view of the godown when the guy entered. Lucky for him he was close enough to the section to hide. He wanted to continue the conversation rather than interrupt with his own story. He asked, "So, what did he talk about?"

"As soon as he appeared our rider, started to lose his cool. The third guy told the rider that this was his area and if he wanted to conduct business, he had to pay him and his gang off."

Khan was surprised at the gall of the interrupting man. Even though he was unaware of who he was dealing with, this was a dangerous line that he had thrown out. "Extorting money from a killer, not a good idea."

"The rider said, do you know who I am?" Khan looked over to Vasu expecting the golden egg. "I thought he was going to confess but he didn't." But his dreams were squashed. "They argued about what and how. But all the third guy cared about was getting money from the rider. He also mentioned that the first shipment was free."

"So, this is the second shipment." It raised Khan's eyebrows. "Yeah, and he knew there were three more were on their way."

Vasu was now calming down and analysing the ongoing situation and the development they were presented with. "It pissed off our rider and that's when I thought this conversation was over and I came down."

Khan was impressed and happy with Vasu's work. He had successfully completed a difficult surveillance task all by himself. "Good job kid. This was quite an amazing thing. Now we know who to look out for."

"What do you mean?" Vasu asked not realizing what Khan had just said.

"I'll explain. First tell me, what gang did that guy say he belonged to?" Khan asked for the final question before explaining it to Vasu.

He answered, "Blue Buzzards or something."

"Great. If our rider is the killer, we know what gang is going to be hit. We have a chance to catch him. You said he was pissed off right?" Khan had just explained and asked the question that would decide the fate of the case.

Vasu realized what his action meant, but only after Khan explained to him. He was happy to help and replied to Khan's question, "Yes, I thought he would have killed him in there."

"Good, I will put out an anonymous tip on this information and we will follow the rider to the crime scene," Khan said while picking up his phone to dial a number. "I am impressed, great job!" Khan's call was answered. It was Talpade and Khan tipped him off about tonight's attack. He also explained that the tip had to be anonymous. Talpade assured Khan that he would pass off the information to the investigating officer and ensure that the criminal is caught.

"What about you, what did you find?" Vasu asked Khan as soon as his call was over.

"Nothing. Just some cookie dough?" Khan said with a disappointment.

"Cookie dough?" Vasu was surprised.

"Yeah, that's what was inside the boxes," Khan confirmed. "Then why move them separately?" The mystery bugged Vasu.

And knowing what was inside didn't help much either.

Khan didn't want to focus on the new mystery so he drew Vasu's attention back to the case at hand. "I don't know. That's not our concern right now. Let's focus on nailing the bastard."

Khan for the first time in a while was happy, from the core. This complicated case that had been eating away at him could finally be solved. All he had to do was to hope that human behaviour and emotion would persist and they will have a solid lead in the case. Khan and Vasu followed the rider back to Yashpal's house down the same route at the same speed. It went like a mundane drive to work. The rider disappeared though as soon as he entered the compound of Yashpal's society. The pair took their spot that was now empty and sat back in anticipation of the action that would unfold soon.

CHAPTER EIGHT

THE ANTI-CLIMAX

It was 10 p.m when Talpade arrived at the scene. They had been waiting for him, he had brought the pair some dinner. Vasu was sceptical of being introduced to another officer at first. He had always held a negative impression of the professionals that worked in that department. His reservations were squashed when Khan mentioned how Talpade had been an asset to the investigation. Vasu was impressed. He had thought that it was Khan alone who was doing all the work. But to find that another individual from the department was just as dedicated and competent enough to perform his duties had won him over. Khan had trusted Vasu that night, there was no reason for Vasu not to trust Talpade. A leap of faith if nothing else he thought.

Talpade arrived in his patrol car. Since no other parking space was available he had to find one a few blocks down. It took him a while but he made it back in a few minutes. He sat in the back seat of the car occupying the middle seat at first to get a better look at both the occupants. Khan introduced Talpade to Vasu.

"Vasu meet Senior Inspector Mahesh Talpade." Said Khan while moving his hand from the former to the latter not taking his eyes off the house. "Mahesh meet Vasu, my partner on this case." He repeated the gesture, only in reverse. Vasu had heard those words for the first time. He had been working with Khan diligently but never gave it a thought. This line gave him the realization that he was a partner, a detective, an investigator.

Talpade looked at the kid sitting in the front seat with Khan. He glanced at him said "Hi!" and moved his attention back towards Khan. "So, what are we looking at here?"

Khan still staring at Yashpal's house, pointed at it, and said, "See that house? That's our target. We are waiting for any movement in there." He paused for a while, waiting for Talpade to respond with any detail or input. Since nothing came through, he moved on to another topic. The anonymous tip that Khan passed on through Talpade. "Did you pass on the tip to the dynamic duo?" He said that referring to the pair of Panditya & Shah.

Talpade sighed like he didn't want to talk about that particular topic but he replied. "Yes, but I don't think they are going to take it seriously." There was disappointment in his voice followed by a hint of disgust.

Khan was surprised at the reply. Who could ignore such an important piece of information? Details that could help them with the case were presented to them. All they had to do was act on it. Why would they not do it? Khan was confused, so to confirm it, he asked, "What do you mean?"

There was a pause from Talpade before the reply. He knew where the conversation was headed and it wasn't a desirable place. "When I approached them with the information they asked more unnecessary questions than usual. I think they want to catch the guy without anyone's help." That was the core stupidity that Khan hated. Especially when it came to cases like these. Some officers he knew were so encapsulated by potential fame that they would ignore even the most important shreds of evidence presented by a fellow officer just to avoid sharing their limelight.

Khan slammed his fist on the steering wheel and replied. "Damn it. I should have known. Those idiots." He stepped out with his phone already calling a number. Vasu noticed the frustration and realized that even at the highest of working, there was still incompetency, jealousy, and unwillingness to work together. It was no different he thought than what people did during their college projects. Some people will never change he thought.

Talpade was now alone in the car with Vasu. There was undeniable thick air moving between them. Vasu wasn't sure what it was but neither was Talpade. At least not at first. So to release some of that air out of the car he asked Vasu, "Shouldn't we be over there rather than here?" He was of course referring to the gang and the place that they might get attacked at.

Vasu had to take a moment to realize what Talpade was talking about. At first, he thought the officer was referring to the residence there were currently watching. But before he replied, it dawned on him and rectified his answer accordingly. "Well, apparently there is a slight chance that the incident might not go as planned. So, to be sure we are sitting at the source." He said to confirm their doubts at the potential of the rider's action. There was definitely a burst of anger shown by the rider which according to Khan indicated that there might be retaliation, but they also weren't sure that the anger would be unleashed today.

There were surprise and confusion spilling out with Talpade's reply. "If you know who the killer is then let's just arrest them." He thought why would they sit out here waiting for an incident when they have a reasonable doubt on the suspected killer. Surely, detaining the suspect and questioning would be a better way to get the confession rather than hoping that they catch him red-handed. But that's when he realized it wasn't an official investigation. Detaining someone without proof will get them in trouble and free a potential suspect. They require proof and there wasn't any. He stepped back on his last remark by asking to confirm. "Oh wait, no proof?"

Vasu replied, "Nothing solid. That's why we sit here waiting for the suspect." He wasn't sure why the officer would ask such a silly question. If there was any proof, then they would have arrested the suspect. Why would they be sitting out here waiting for any shred of evidence?

Talpade noticed the last remark from Vasu and what it meant. Even the tone was quite obvious to him. He wanted to avoid that path, so he asked Vasu, "How do you know him?" Talpade wanted to know how the two came about to working together. Was Vasu a young, talented, prodigal detective with some quirkiness, or was he someone Khan knew of? There could be millions of possibilities and Talpade wanted to find the answer to the mystery of the young man sitting in his idol's car working with him.

This created a dilemma for Vasu. He wasn't sure if Khan had told Talpade regarding their meeting. If he hadn't said anything, then spilling the beans would get Vasu in trouble along with Khan. He had to be on the same page with his partner on this. So, trusting his better judgment on people, Vasu replied, "I think it's better if you hear it from him" hoping that would be the best way.

Khan had just opened the door when Vasu was saying that to Talpade. Khan wanted to join the conversation having completed one with Laxmi. "Hear what?"

Glad to see Khan step in, he replied. "About me." Vasu was hoping that it was enough to hint Khan into the conversation and get him to take over the story.

It didn't hit Khan what was bothering Vasu or what was stopping him from saying it our right. "Why? You can tell him."

Vasu realized that Khan didn't think it was that big of a deal. But he wanted to be sure that it wasn't and for him getting Khan to say the story would be better. "I think you can explain it better. It might sound unreal if I say it."

Khan relented to Vasu's request and replied, "Fine." He turned his body towards the house again but kept an eye on Talpade's expression through his rear-view mirror. "He was a suspect for the case." Vasu didn't look back. He didn't want a view of anything while Khan started with the worst piece of information on his story. Talpade had to confirm it. He didn't understand how Khan could take the suspect of such a dangerous case and make him his partner.

"This case?" His voice was louder than he had expected.

Khan continued his explanation to the relief of Vasu. "Yes. Do you remember the incident in the 9th? There were blunt instrument injuries?" He was hoping to walk Talpade slowly along with the story, getting him to the point carefully for their benefit.

 He knew the case, so he replied. "Yes."

Khan continues, "It was him." He paused for a while, scaring both Vasu and Talpade. Unknown to him, both of them wanted Khan to continue with the story for different reasons. Realizing what he had done by pausing, he continued to calm both of them down. "He didn't kill them, just knocked them out. Apparently, the gang over there had taken some kids and he rescued them wearing a mask."

Talpade now confused about the whole incident, asked to clarify, "But weren't they all dead?"

Running out of patience for Khan's poor storytelling skills, Vasu took over, "I could have said it better" He said while looking at Khan. Vasu then turned towards Talpade and explained it as best he could, "I just rescued them, the real killer must have been tracking me and killed them to frame me."

Talpade now piecing the story together realized that Khan had accepted an unknown, unproven young man as his partner. The weight of Khan's decision and the impact it was about to make was clear from Talpade's question addressing the elephant in the room, "And he just accepted you as a partner?"

Vasu not recognizing what was about to go down, naively replied to Talpade's question. "Pretty much I guess." His attitude was a bit dismissive towards the whole issue. He wanted to get over this uncomfortable line of questions and focus on the case at hand.

Talpade meanwhile had trouble accepting the fact that this kid basically sitting in the front seat of the car had walked into a great chance just because he was stupid enough to wear a mask and fight some criminals. His frustration was visible and could no longer hold his emotion or control his words. "You know I have worked hard, sincerely for 6 years to get here. I have idolized this man" he was pointing at Khan and then at Vasu as he continued, "and you, a kid became a partner after a night of beating up gang members?" The thoughts had racked up his mind, but speaking the sentence out loud really send a wave of pain through his being.

It just dawned on Vasu why there was an uncomfortable atmosphere before. He also realized with Talpade's sentence what kind of opportunity he had slid in while stepping on this man's shoes to get it probably. He wanted to assure Talpade that the situation was different, the motives were different. He wanted to say something that made sense to them and would quench Talpade's frustration. "I know-"

Khan interrupted with similar feelings to Vasu. "The circumstances with him were different. He was in the perfect situation where I could have used him and not get it pinned down on me." Although he had just realized the gravity of bringing Talpade on board while not accepting him as a partner before. Khan knew of Talpade's admiration but always wanted him to be his own man. But instead of explaining that, Khan resorted to a well-put- together, circumstantial lie that might work.

Talpade saw through the deceit, "I don't believe you." He didn't believe in the explanation any more than Khan did.

Hoping to alleviate the atmosphere, Vasu used his disbelief as an attempt in commentating humour,

"Count me in on that."

Talpade meanwhile didn't appreciate the remark. He wanted to assert his feeling regarding the topic and was speaking against Khan for the first time. "No, I really don't. You are not the type of person who would put others in danger." He was aware of Khan's nature and the explanation didn't fit his personality. It was easy for him to spot the deviation and lie.

It was not the right thing. Khan knew that, so to rectify the entire situation, to put back the confidence Talpade had in him, Khan did the one thing that might help. He admitted, "I am sorry, I didn't want to disappoint you, Mahesh. I promise this won't happen again." Khan had always known that accepting one's mistake was one of the most difficult things in life. He didn't want to be the man that makes mistakes as much as he wanted to be a man that is aware and accepting of his shortcomings.

Even though he was happy hearing that admittance from Khan, there was still some bitterness that remained regarding the whole situation. So, Talpade said, "What's done is done." He had accepted the fact that no matter what he did or how he felt, the action had been taken, he had missed the boat to no fault of his own.

Vasu still wanting to lift the room tried his best by saying, "If it makes any difference, he is really a boring company." This line of humour he thought would be well received by Talpade hoping that he was aware of Khan's serious attitude. "You were saved from two nights of silence and brooding stares." He added to the remark. Vasu looked back at Talpade with the hope of validation and some form of relief on his face or any positive emotion.

Talpade wasn't impressed with Vasu's lame attempt at a joke. He wasn't happy with the timing of it either. He made his position clear, "No, it doesn't help."

"Do you want to leave?" Khan asked with a vague emotion.

Vasu wasn't sure whether Khan was joining him in joking around the situation or he mistook his joke as a serious remark. He had to confirm. "No, why?" There was no reply from Khan. Vasu dropped the topic and the three sat there soaking in the discomfort of the room. After a few seconds, Vasu was unable to handle the discomfort and asked a question to divert everyone else's mind. "Can I ask you something?" He addressed this to Talpade by looking at him.

Talpade was looking out of the window. He replied without looking towards Vasu, "What?" The tone was bland, uninterested, which

Talpade at this point definitely was. Even Vasu knew.

"How are you a Senior Inspector like him? I thought he was your senior" He asked. Khan addressed himself as an SI. But he also introduced Talpade as SI. This confused him as to what decided the superior and the subordinate.

"My official designation is Deputy Senior Inspector," Talpade replied to Vasu's query. He was aware of the confusion people would have. "We just omit it sometimes." This was his answer every time this question had come along.

Vasu wanted more details, "Do you work alone or are there more of you?"

"Yes, there are always at least two in any station. In my case, we both cover 12-hour shifts. I work during the day, my colleague during the night." Talpade obliged.

" So, when does he work?" asked Vasu pointing at Khan.

Talpade although a bit annoyed at the incessant questions replied, "He has a standard timetable. Sometimes we call him in to get some advice on a case."

Khan chimed in, "I could have told you that if you had just asked."

Vasu was quick to respond. "Given that I had just found out about it, I think this was the right time."

Khan wasn't happy with Vasu's tone. "Whatever, let's just concentrate on the case." But not wanting to further disturb the atmosphere, he restrained the topic.

The wave of tension brought on by the partner dilemma was not going to be lifted any time soon. Even though Talpade didn't like Khan's decision to not choose him as a partner, it was oddly Vasu he felt resentment towards. It had been growing long before they had met. But now that Talpade was introduced to Vasu, it had just grown another layer. The fact that an untrained, young, vigilante was given a chance sooner than someone like him had really chipped away at him and his confidence in Khan. The idolizing had faltered after Khan's such misstep and Talpade was just plain disappointed with him. The only reason he was sitting in this car was that it was his duty and no longer because Khan had asked him to do so.

Vasu felt a little awkward now. His confidence that Khan had agreed to work with him because of his passion to help was sitting low. Even he had started to wonder about the reason for Khan's decision. He awaited a chance now to ask him about it, but there was none on the horizon given that there was Mahesh sitting in the back seat. He sat there on the seat squished between awkwardness and doubts. It was quite a mishmash of emotions and that really faltered his concentration. The three sat there for the next few hours in silence. The clock moved its arms, once around, twice, thrice, and even the fourth time. Still, there wasn't any activity. Vasu wash now leaning back and slunk down in an awkward yet comfortable position. Talpade sat behind Vasu but not looking at Khan. His attention was on the road, however, empty it stayed. Khan meanwhile had forgotten all about the argument earlier and had his eye fixed on Yashpal's house.

A stretch came calling for Khan with his partner the yawn. He looked at the clock and it was almost half-past two. That's when he spotted movement. He looked at Vasu hoping to get him to put on his glasses, but he was half asleep. He shook the kid and without explanation went, "The glasses?"

"What?" said Vasu recovering from a fade-out.

He was not ready to oblige so Khan had to repeat again, "Glasses, put on your damn glasses." He panicked and started to look around. With every passing second Khan could see the moment, the event escaping. Vasu fumbled a little before putting on the glasses.

He watched the house concentrating on the living room. "Yashpal and the rider are arguing." Vasu was startled as he saw Yashpal point at the car, at him. He almost yelled out, "Fuck! He pointed at us."

Khan was taken aback at this remark. He knew that this wasn't an ideal spot to be staying at for long but they had to, He asked the redundant question just out of sheer surprise at the turn of events. "What?"

"This was a bad idea." Vasu didn't want to continue looking at the targets to know they were aware of the surveillance.

"Keep looking," Khan said. He wanted to make sure if they were in danger. Vasu had to look to find out.

Another glance at the behest of Khan thought Vasu. As he looked in the direction again, the living room was empty. "They are gone." He said in disbelief.

"Damn it," Khan said in frustration, he had no more information regarding the potential outcome of their exposure.

The rider drove out of the society with blistering speed. The sound was audible. In fact, at this time of the night, it was so loud that it could have been heard from the moon. It was base(y), crackling splutters followed by a high tenor line from the I-4. It was as if Zeus was gargling with lightning and thunder. Khan, Vasu, and Talpade, all three of them readied themselves for the anticipated confrontation. Khan pulled out the car as fast as he could, or rather the car could. Compared to the rider, the car was down on power, high on weight, and zero in manoeuvrability. Even the car and the bike had a similar amount of power, there was little chance that it would have been able to keep up. By the time the trio had crossed the first junction, the rider was out of sight. Lucky for them, Talpade had already details on the potential location of the Buzzards. They were supposed to be in an industrial estate in sector 2 loading some goods. No points for guessing what that was. This was supposedly the first step in expansion after the gang in 9th was nearly wiped out. And they were in for a surprise tonight.

Khan had to drive to the limit if they were to make it to the destination in time but as it turned out, he was not a fast driver. This was evident from the fact that he could only keep the car at around 60 in the city.

Vasu looked at the speedometer and knew exactly that they would be late. He glanced towards Talpade who had a similar nervous expression plastered all over him. He was hesitant to speak out because of the command chain and the respect he had to give. Vasu thought to step in ask Khan."May-"

He was interrupted by Khan who acknowledged his shortcomings and decided to step aside. "We won't make it at this speed. I think you should drive Mahesh."

Vasu knew this was the better choice. But the time loss worried him the most. He asked Khan hoping that there will be a good explanation for the switch. "Won't that waste more time?"

Khan replied pointing at Talpade, confident in his abilities, "He'll have to make up."

Khan pulled over to the side and switched seats quickly. Talpade didn't waste time adjusting the seat while idle. He did that on the go along with all the three rear-view mirrors. Vasu sat impressed at the skills of his new colleague. He weaved through the traffic at 80, 90, even on occasions over a 100. Even though Vasu enjoyed the speed, his sphincter was tight. You couldn't even pass air through it which was a good thing. He didn't mind going at those speeds when he was in control. But it was a whole different story when it came to being a passenger. His constant looking at the speedometer and the road had taken up all of his concentration. He had almost forgotten that he was about to engage in a fistfight with a deadly assassin.

The route the trio was going on was the same as before. They passed the residential sectors quickly after which the traffic subsided. It became easier for Talpade to hit the top speed. It was around 140 when the car became noisy, wavering to the wind. That's when Talpade stepped off and brought it back to 120.

Khan asked Talpade, "What was the place you said?" Khan in the head of the chase had forgotten the name of the location Talpade had mentioned in their phone call earlier. He wanted to put things into perspective by knowing the exact location of their destination.

"FreezeOne," Talpade replied. He added, "It is supposed to be a cold storage facility for fish."

Khan wasn't aware of the company. He wanted to find out more, especially how the building looked like. "Alright, what's the layout of the place? Did you take a look at it?"

Talpade was not ready to answer that question. He didn't look up for a building layout. All he had checked were the names associated and the financials. "No, I am sorry but that didn't occur to me." He knew that this wasn't standard procedure, yet he was disappointed that Khan thought of it but he didn't

Vasu was confused as to why Khan needed to know such information. "Layout?" he asked.

Khan replied swiftly, "So that we don't go in blind." It was a remark at Vasu's blind, head-in attempt in which luck played as much of an important role as did his skills. Vasu looked at Khan understanding what he had said. Khan continued looking at Talpade. "Okay, if it's anything like I assume, there will be three maybe four entrances. One of which will be for transport. That's where they all might be." Khan was familiar with the general blueprints. He had investigated enough of those. But he was also prepared for any anomalies that may be presented tonight.

"What about the rider?" Talpade asked not sure what to expect. "He'll be going in blind too. So, with any luck, he might be surveying the place until we get there." Khan predicted that by putting himself in the rider's shoes. He would have taken a good look at the place, the covers, and the exits before engaging in battle.

Vasu wanted more details so he asked, "So, what's the plan? Just go in and arrest him?"

Khan understood the concern so he decided to formulate a plan that will be safe for all of them and inform them of the dangers involved. "Okay so, we don't know which one prefers the knife and which one likes the bullet. We need to be prepared for both." That's his first concern. Khan was aware that there might be either of them present.

In any case, both were dangerous. Their skill level was presented at all the other crime scenes, so three of them knew how dangerous it might be. Talpade was alerted on finding out the fact that there might be two of them but accepted it quickly. Khan continued, "There are vests inside luckily and we both are carrying our firearms." He had noted the inventory of the cars before he took them out. The undercover vehicle they were in had limited instruments but enough for tonight hoped Khan. "If he just carrying a knife then it will be easier. Or else…" He dropped the sentence knowing that he didn't need to say it out loud. The knife-wielder was easy to handle. They could exploit the fact that he might be a close-quarters combatant and use the guns as insurance. Khan also was aware of the possibility that the rider might be just as good at throwing the knives, so he thought cover at the location might be enough to protect them

Vasu added to Khan's plan with what he thought might be the right thing to do. "We each take an entrance and hit them from multiple sides right?"

"Yeah, look you both know the risks but I still want you to be careful. In case something goes wrong, leave. Go to the CG and no one else and tell her everything." Khan had it all planned out. Even though he hadn't told Laxmi about Vasu or Talpade's involvement, he was aware that she would help out nonetheless. It might not in the same path they expect but it will be helpful nonetheless.

"She knows about our plan?" Talpade didn't realize that CG was involved in the investigation.

"Not exactly" replied Khan hinting to Talpade that she wasn't aware of everything. But just to be sure he added, "I'll explain later." They drove towards the destination. It was a series of compounds that Khan didn't recognize. He awaited Talpade's cue pointing towards the destination. Talpade looked for the building he had seen in the pictures on the file. A couple of minutes later, he spotted the site and alerted others. "That's it. The blue one."

Khan spoke out as soon as they got close to the building. "Gunshots."

The compound was unlit, there was constant screaming of orders and panic they could hear. The only thing that overshadowed both of them were the gunshots. They were frequent with occasional bursts of probably the entire magazine. Khan, Vasu, and Talpade knew who they were facing. They also were now preparing their hearts for the maximum possible danger. Khan recognizing the essence of time said to both of his partners, "Hurry." They park the car as close as they could to a cover. It was near the entrance, next to a parked truck.

Both Talpade and Khan head towards the back of the car to retrieve the vests and other equipment. There was just one flashlight though. That might prove to be difficult. As for vests, there were four of them luckily. Three of them had protected at least most of their vital organs with their equipment. Khan and Talpade had guns while Vasu had a metal rod and a pair of night vision glasses. It was enough to take down the pyscho they thought. The gunshots and the screaming had stopped. It was now silent as the night should have been. Oddly, they were far more alert now than they were around the sounds of the gunshot. Ready to move in, Khan pulled Vasu by his arm and said. "This does not make you bulletproof." He wanted to alert Vasu, make him realize the gravity of the situation they were about to walk in. For him, Vasu was still just a civilian, someone he swore to protect. But he also knew the bond he had developed. It was buried deep but he knew about it.

Startled at the serious warning for Khan he thought to respond. "But I thoug-"

Khan interrupted, "You can get shot here," He was pointing at Vasu's head, "here," then his arms and feet, "or here. So don't just go charging in." He warned Vasu as good as he could. The precaution was always what Khan preferred to work on. Vasu was supposed to be prepared for the dangers going in and Khan just wanted them to be imprinted right in the front so that he doesn't forget when he goes charging in.

"Hold on." Vasu stopped them. "There are no lights, it will be dangerous for you." He had a point. They would be walking in an unknown location, literally blind. They had flashlights but the visibility through them is limited. "I will go in with these." He said pointing to his glasses and continued, "Relight the area and give you a clear way in."

Khan disagreed. His opinion was that if Vasu went in alone, he would have no one to watch his back. And the night vision won't give him eyes on the back of his head either. "It's too dangerous for a lone man. Especially for one without a weapon." Khan said hinting at his baton.

"I have this," Vasu replied by lifting his baton.

"That's a steel rod." Added Talpade. "That won't stop a bullet. Unless you swing fast." He said while making a swinging motion with his hands

"First of all, this is Titanium." Vasu was annoyed at the remark and dismissive attitude of Talpade. He said this opening up the baton. He shifted his attention to Khan and said. "And second, I can take care of myself."

Khan was quick to respond, "No you can't." Vasu was further annoyed but refrained from interrupting. He knew Khan had a point. Khan continued, "I have a better plan. We will distract him, draw fire towards us. You can sneak up behind him and take him out." It was better for all of them. They knew the rider will only be able to focus in one direction. And Vasu had the resources and the skills to sneak from behind and take down the target easily.

"I-Alright." He wanted to amend the plan, but there wasn't much he could add to it. So, he complied.

Khan asked looking at his partners, "Are you ready?"

Khan and Talpade raised their arms and pointed their guns along with their flashlight. Khan took the lead and found themselves a proper cover. Near the entrance were two square metal tanks on one end while the other end had a stack of crates. The metal tanks were eight feet high whereas the crates were about three feet but stacked three-fold high filled to the brim. This pattern followed for three rows, further down being replaced by other items. The content of the crates wasn't visible in the darkness. Even though it was risky to stay behind a single point, Khan decided that wooden crates won't be the right choice given that bullet cuts through it like a knife on butter. They flashed their torches around, Khan stood up while Talpade sat down. Khan's light fell on a figure walking towards them but it vanished in a second. It was the rider. In just a second, a shot was fired at the tank. Khan and Talpade retaliated in tandem. The rider was not visible, creating difficulty in tracing his location. Khan hoped that it would be soon taken care of by their third, agile partner.

The rider screamed in his tenor voice, "I should have killed you that night." He was referring to the night he spotted Khan and Vasu tailing.

"Then you would have been fighting another officer that's all," Khan responded. He knew that killing an officer would rumble up the entire force and get them to hunt down the killer. No one wanted their own to die.

The rider responded with, "When I kill you tonight, no one will dare to repeat your mistakes." He said this and started firing his gun again.

Khan wasn't impressed with his threats. He replied, "I am ready to die. Are you?" He wanted the rider to realize that this was not going to go as easy as he was anticipating it to be.

The rider with even more confidence than before responded, "Wish all you want. You won't even be able to lay your hands on me."

Talpade who was now annoyed at the rider said out loud almost screaming. "I will shove my boot up yours and then lay it on your ass." They continued firing.

Vasu stood at the side door, red lights on. He went in around as discussed. This would provide the needed blow leading to the arrest of this nuisance. Vasu moved around carefully not making any sound, looking vigilantly for the rider. His baton in his hand would have been wet with sweat had he not worn gloves. The place was like a godown, but there were crates and storage units that the masked man could have hidden behind. On top of that Vasu wasn't sure about the location of the rider. The shower of bullets wasn't helping. As he moved ahead, the sparks at the opposite end of the wall gave away the location of the electric panel. Chances were that the rider came in and shot the panel first to create a blanket for him to work in silently. Vasu was wondering about the visibility and how the rider would manage to get around it. One step at a time, the flashbacks of the night's events and the emotions that played out were breaking through. His heartbeat grew louder and louder. He had to stop and calm down before moving ahead.

Meanwhile, Khan and Talpade were on their final magazines. There were more bullets in the car but that would leave all of them vulnerable. Hoping that the rider would run out of his bullets soon, they continued firing. Khan wanted to scream the location to Vasu but he was not sure. The darkness followed by sudden bright light and the deafening sound wasn't helping. Had there been a better vantage point, he could have spotted and then shot the rider.

Vasu was now looking right at the rider. He had found him standing, covering himself behind the last of the metal containers. The distraction had worked. Now all he needed to do was to hit the man on his head and end this firefight. He checked around to see if any rouge item would interfere and alert the rider of Vasu's presence. He was taller so Vasu even had to compensate the angle for the blow. Just as Vasu was ready to hit and had swung his arm back with power, the rider ducked down to load his magazine. Vasu was spotted. He let go of his sprung arm to hit the rider but it was stopped. The grip Vasu felt on his hand was tight, like a python would have before eating his prey. Vasu couldn't move the arm, so he recruited his other arm to try and hit the rider but it was too late. There was already a fist headed his way. It landed right on Vasu's cheek chipping the left lens of the glasses. The power or rather the force of the punch was strong enough to knock Vasu clean on his feet. He hadn't felt that force, that sense of pain since his childhood. It was as if the pain was spreading up to his mind. Vasu was hit with a headache and it was about to become permanent. Unbeknownst to him, the rider had already loaded the gun and was now sitting on him pointing it right in Vasu's face. He could smell the oil and almost taste the metal. He snapped out of the punch's pain and used his hand to move the gun away from him just in time. The shot was fired right next to his ear. They were ringing and hurting him. The feeling in his ears had left temporarily and at that moment Vasu thought he had gone deaf. He could hear nothing but the ringing. Fortunately, or out of instinct, he was still holding the rider's gun hand. They were now struggling to get control of the aim. Vasu used all of his strength to keep the gun away from his face while the rider was using his to point it back at him.

In the struggle, Vasu didn't pay attention to the trigger. The rider had his finger on it. He squeezed it, hard. The sound that followed was unbelievably even louder. The ringing in his ears was overshadowed by the sound of the gun. He didn't have time to look how close it was though. An inch maybe. The floor debris had hit him leading to pieces of small shrapnel lodging in the left side of his face. Blood was dripping down from them now. But Vasu didn't have time to notice all that. His entire concentration was fixed on the gun and his strength in keeping it away. The finger was squeezing the trigger again. As he was looking at the rider, he could spot him looking to his right. Before Vasu could look at what was coming, it appeared right before his eyes. A brown leather boot squishing the rider's face and pushing it away. Unbeknownst to either of them, Khan had reached close enough to observe the struggle and aimed a proper kick to the rider's face. Even though he was feeling light and free, Vasu didn't let go of the gun. His hand was gripping it tightly. As soon as the impact and force of the kick got the rider off of him, he got up as fast as he could, holding the hand, and put all of his body weight on it. Khan in tandem started to hit the rider. Now Vasu was feeling the pain. All of his limbs were hurting but more than that his head and his face were killing him. Vasu tried his best to keep his hand away from his face and on the target. As much as he wanted to hold the wounds and address them, he knew this was far important. Not wanting to give up his chances, the rider fired the bullet hoping to startle Vasu and free his hand. The first one did loosen up Vasu's grip. He wasn't anticipating the sound or the vibration. The rider was free and with that, he aimed the gun at Khan who was hitting him. Khan stepped back hoping to avoid the bullet. But it was too late. The rider pulled the trigger with all his strength.

The sound that came out of the gun was similar to that of a small spoon hitting the floor. He tried again, nothing. He kept on doing so until he realized the obvious. In all of the struggle, the rider forgot to count his bullets. Apparently, the shot he fired to get Vasu off his hands was his last. The four men stood there for a second baffled at the development. All of them were in shock at the turn of events. The rider snapped out of it first and threw the gun at Khan. He was ready to fight his way out confident that it wasn't going to be difficult. Khan put his arms up blocking the gun and took his stance as well. Talpade followed suit. Vasu meanwhile struggled. His legs were buckling and the pain was making it difficult to concentrate, but he persevered and took his fighting stance still a little groggy. All three of them were waiting for the other to attack.

They moved about adjusting the position of attack. Talpade went in first hoping to get past the rider's guard. He used the right arm jab only to be dodged and get hit with an uppercut. The rider had stepped aside and used his right arm to hit Talpade exposing his back to Khan. He used that moment's disadvantage and hit the rider from the side. Instead of laying it on his face, Khan went for the safer and effective blow to the abdomen. He punched on the side facing him, landing in a powerful blow. However, Khan was taken back by a retaliating elbow to his face. He stumbled and fell. Vasu during all of this was looking for the baton. He had found and turned around to use it only to find a boot approaching in his face. It was a roundhouse kick. Talpade meanwhile straightened up and prepared to do all of it again, rushed to land a punch on the rider. It didn't work. The rider's kick had turned his body towards Talpade along with his attention. He started to dodge the series of jabs and body punches from Talpade without laying hands on him. Talpade was trained, but only in the basic fighting techniques of the police force. His footing especially wasn't good. At least not as good as it could have been. The rider was analysing Talpade's attacks and realized the struggle of his footing. Talpade wasn't stable. He then proceeded to take a blow from him and get in close to grab Talpade, lift him, and throw him down on his back. He had used Talpade's torso to grab him and lift him to throw. Once on his back, Talpade was hit or rather punted by the rider to incapacitate him for a few moments.

Talpade and Vasu's struggle with the rider had given Khan enough time to get back on his feet. He was ready and in his stance. The rider noticed Khan's movements and got in closer. They were two feet away from the other and waiting for the moment to attack.

The rider confidently claimed, "I am going to end this now." He raised his arms to attack and approached Khan with ferocity.

Khan was silent. He knew the rider would attack now and prepared himself mentally for the defence. Talking out loud about his intentions had given Khan a look into the rider's strategy. His arrogance had provided Khan with an advantage. As the night's silence was consuming both of them, the rider moved in with a punch. Khan shoved it aside and closed in to hit the rider with an uppercut elbow. The rider stumbled back and was now holding his jaw in utter shock. The attack had rattled him and he was pissed. It was visible to the delight of Khan. He was ready for the next wave. The rider was fast with his attacks. Khan blocked each of them but didn't have the time nor the space to move in to attack. For every three blows of the rider, Khan dodge two and took in third. He knew this strategy wasn't going to help him in the long run. But he also knew that the rider would lose some stamina as well. He was waiting for a window, something that could give him a chance to hit back and get out of the back foot. But there wasn't any. Khan had to think of something quickly, his body was in pain from the blows. He decided to step aside hoping to throw the momentum off of the rider and plant a punch to his distracted face. In the next wave, he did just that. Khan stepped left. Still holding his guard up, even though he was ready to hit. The rider's intensity and concentration in the attack were so high, he didn't anticipate the move. Khan swung a blow to the rider's face while simultaneously getting hit on his abdomen. Both men stepped back and stumbled from the blow. All of this gave Vasu a chance to get up and compose himself. His contribution to this fight until now was just staying alive. He had to change that and look for his baton. That might be the only option left to hold down the rider. It was closer to one of the metallic containers. He looked towards Talpade who himself was getting up to attack. Vasu raised his baton to indicate his intentions. The message was received by Talpade who obliged by moving towards the fighting men and joining them to keep the rider distracted. This was the best chance Vasu was going to get. All of the three men were trading blows, not giving up any of their positions. Vasu swiftly and quietly moved around to the back of the rider. He was ready, the baton was extended and the aim locked. Swung to down hard, hoping that his arms would have enough force after his struggle to knock the man out. It landed hard, giving Vasu vibrations throughout his arm. The rider fell down like a heavy bag and started to bleed from his head. As soon as Vasu saw the blood he panicked fearing that he might have killed the man. Vasu was dreading the moment and dropped the baton to use both of his arms to hold his head. Khan and Talpade, now free of the assault kneeled down for a second to catch their breath. It had been an exhausting night for them. But the blood created a panic for them as well. Khan approached the rider by crawling on his knees to examine the wound. He checked thoroughly and placed the handcuffs on him before talking to Vasu who was now sitting on the floor out of breath and seemingly out of his senses.

Khan said to a terrified Vasu, "He will be fine." He didn't respond so Khan tried calling out to him. "Vasu." No response again. Now Khan was yelling, hoping the loud voice would be enough to get his attention. "Vasu!" Vasu looked at Khan. He was in shock but now he was ready to listen. "He will be fine. It's just a small cut. You didn't crack his skull."

Vasu responded with a wavering voice, "I thought-"

Khan was quick to interrupt. He knew where this was going and it was not the right time. "You thought wrong. He will be fine, probably will have a concussion." He approached Vasu and placed his hand on his shoulder, "Are you okay?"

The gesture itself was enough for him to relax. He responded, "I need a minute" and looked at Khan

Khan gave him an assuring look and proceeded to check up on Talpade, "Mahesh? Everything okay?" he asked.

Talpade hoping to lighten Vasu's mood responded pointing at him, "Same as him."

Vasu took a deep breath and stood up. He asked Khan not sure what came next, "So, what to do with him?"

"Arrest him," responded Khan. "file a case and get to Yashpal." That was the straight route they were hoping to go on

Vasu was happy to hear that. This had been a tough week for him and knowing that it will be all soon over was elevating. He looked at the rider and noticed a detail. His hands were tied but his feet were free. Khan hadn't considered the possibility that he would use his body however he can to get free. So, he suggested. "You'll need to tie the feet."

Talpade found it quite odd. So he asked, "What? Why?"

"He'll attack as soon as he wakes up. I don't want to fight him again. Especially in the car." Vasu wanted to be safe, that's all.

Khan agreed, "I'll check the car for another pair."

Talpade was rested, he got up and moved towards Vasu. He was curious about Vasu's intentions, so asked, "What will you do now?"

Vasu didn't understand, "What do you mean?"

Talpade clarified, "Well, we are arresting him." He said pointing at the rider. "Soon, we will have Yashpal. What will you do after that? Join the force?" This was a genuine curiosity for Talpade.

"I don't know. I haven't thought about it." Vasu hadn't given it a lasting thought and wanted to take things as they came. "One thing at a time."

Khan came back with another set of handcuffs. He locked the feet of the rider just as tightly as he had done for the hands. Khan then proceeds to take his handkerchief out and tie it tightly around the rider's head to stop the bleeding. Khan noticed the rider's appearance and made a note of it. The skin was wheatish, suggesting a native birth. His height was a few inches of six. That coupled with the lean body helped him with the speed. Khan was sure that this was a well-trained man from the skills. He had also noticed the scar on his neck just below the ear. There was a slight but noticeable chip in the jaw near the scar as well. He predicted a gunshot wound. This was important to understand and remember to search for the rider's records. Khan pointed it out to both Vasu and Talpade. They were just as curious about the origins of the scar as Khan. Vasu and Talpade then proceeded to lift the lying man and place him in the car. Talpade suggested placing the rider behind the driver's seat. This would help put two guns on him for safety. One in the hands of the front seat passenger, and one in the back. This was a great suggestion. Khan decided to drive the car with Vasu as a front-seat passenger. Talpade meanwhile sat on the back seat pointing the gun at the rider.

As they drove off Vasu asked the important question. "Where are we taking him?"

It was obvious for Talpade, "To the police station."

Vasu wasn't sure, since they picked up the rider in the 2nd. "Which one?"

Talpade and Khan both were silent and thinking on the subject. They had this dilemma before but usually, the answer is wherever the investigating officer desires. It is ultimately his case. But in this scenario, there wasn't an investigation officer on board. There were just two rogue cops and a vigilante who came along for help. Khan was unsure of the jurisdiction issue. So he called the only person that could have cleared it up without a bias, Laxmi. The ring was longer than usual. But it was to be. After all, the time was not her usual working hour.

As soon as the call was received, Khan went in with the meat of the question. "We have the prime suspect." There was a pause, Khan listened to the inquiry on the other line and answered, "No, I arrested him in the 2nd. He had information connecting a major name to the crimes." He paused again and then responded. "Yes. And I was hoping-" He was interrupted mid-sentence. After a brief wait, he asked, "How would the case be affected?" He was in disbelief of what was being said on the other line. He responded with scrutiny, "No judge is going to question that." With every passing second of silence Khan's face was relaxing. As if the things being said were exactly what he expected. "You have my back, right?" He asked. The answer brought a little smile to his face. He responded. "Yeah." He was listening again. Probably a question. "I'll tell you when he tells me." Both Talpade and Vasu realized what the question was and how big of a lie this was.

Vasu looked at Khan hoping he would say something. But there was nothing. After a few seconds, he had to ask, "So?"

"7th" Khan replied.

Vasu sat there thinking about the long journey ahead now relaxed. They had to go across the town, literally. He knew it would be a tedious ride ahead but he wasn't sure how long it would last.

Then it was the case of returning home with his injuries. First came the visible ones like the shrapnel wounds on his face, the mark left by the kick, and others he hadn't even noticed yet. However, it was the internal injuries that could lead to Vasu falling down right in front of his mother and drive her into a panic. He didn't want that. But he also knew rest was required to heal the injuries. He would be able to rest in the police station. That wasn't a pretty image for him, uncomfortable, but there was no other way. Vasu also needed to think ahead. After the case is done, what would he do? Continue along with this was on the table but not desirable right now. The toll that this one case had taken, the scars it was going to leave were not something Vasu was fond of. It was more than he expected. But he thought one thing at a time. The case isn't done yet. The rider might not comply; they might need another way out.

Khan was doubtful that the rider would answer their questions easily. He was already planning to get him to a safe house and use various interrogation techniques to get their answers. He was glancing behind hoping to keep an eye on the rider as well. But he was slumped in the corner with his head against the window. The rider opened his eyes slowly and turned his head towards the man pointing a gun at him.

"He's awake," Talpade said, warning the others. Vasu slumped down and put his mask and glasses back on.

The rider looked around, hoping to catch a glimpse of the people that had got better of him. Looking at the man in the mask, he said. "I will kill you first asshole."

Talpade familiar with such threats joked at Vasu, "It's your lucky day."

The rider not appreciating the humour turned to look at Talpade and told him, "You'll be next."

"Okay," Talpade replied, not bothered by the threats. He looked at his gun and then at the rider and responded, "but can you outrun a bullet?"

Khan was now able to look at the rider's face from the mirror.

He asked, "Why did you do it?"

The rider was unimpressed. He responded, "Is that it? Is that how you are going to interrogate me?" He made a face showing his disgust at the tactics of the trio.

Vasu didn't like the behaviour but wanted to assert the fact that they weren't interrogating. At least not yet. "He's just asking a question."

Now looking straight at Vasu, the rider responded, "Okay, here's my answer. Fuck You. Fuck all of you" he said giving a glance to all of them.

Talpade with a blob of sarcasm replied, "Such an original answer.

Thank you for that brilliant insight into your mind."

Vasu didn't care for that. He waited for a second and then said, "We know it's Yashpal."

The rider was smiling at this point, with confidence, and said, "Really? Then go arrest him as well."

Quickly Talpade responded with, "Oh he's next." He paused and continued, "The question now is who'll talk first. You or him."

The rider burst out laughing. It was loud and irritating all three of them. Pacing himself down he said, "You really think it's that easy?" He looked around, "You have no idea then. You're just a bunch of lucky amateurs." He paused, looked at his cuffs, and said, "I challenge you to keep me like this for more than an hour."

This was not the first time Talpade had heard such a comment. His experience with overprotected, entitled rich kids had helped him create a perfect bomb to destroy that attitude, "Is your daddy coming to rescue you?" He said with disingenuous concern.

There was silence, no laughter or chuckle or even a smile anymore. The rider looked at Talpade with an angry expression and said, "You just moved up on the list."

Talpade smiled, looked at Vasu, and said, "Sorry man, but I think I am far more dangerous than you."

Rider responded quickly, "Annoying." He paused for a smiling Talpade to look and him and continued, "I will split that jaw wide open. Then we'll find out how much you can talk."

Khan was ready to jump in. He said, "I think you are afraid."

The rider replied, "What?" But he knew.

Khan added to his last remark. "You know deep down that Yashpal won't come for you."

The rider was dismissive of that sentence and asked, "And why would I think that?"

"The fight," Khan replied. "You had an argument tonight. I am guessing regarding the gang you just murdered. He warned you not to do it. But you didn't listen and got yourself arrested." He paused to look at the rider whose confidence was now slowly disappearing. Khan continued, "Now he's about to become the Mayor of the city. Why would he put his reputation on the line for a man who doesn't follow his orders?" Vasu listened to the entire conversation, he realized what was at play and was quite impressed. Between the two of them, Khan and Talpade were messing with the rider's emotion hoping that an outburst would get him to talk. This was an interrogation now.

The rider replied. "You don't know what you're talking about." "I think-"

He interrupted, "You don't." There was anger but there was also a lack of confidence in his voice. "We have been through hell together. This, this is nothing for him." He said this and looked away Khan dismissed the rider's claims, "I think you are exaggerating." He was shifting his focus between the nearly empty road and the rider. "Anyone in his position would not associate with you. You have become a liability by getting yourself arrested. Why would he help you?"

The question irked him. In fact, he was speechless. He tried to respond, "Bec-"

Khan interrupted quickly not wanting to let the iron cool down. "See. You don't have an answer."

He did not appreciate the interruption, "He's my friend" replied the rider.

Talpade chimed in, "Really? Then how come none of us know you. Not even your name."

The rider didn't like Talpade's interruption and with an irritated voice replied. "Because you are not supposed to."

Vasu now sure about the end goal, felt confident to step in as well. "It's because he wants to keep his hands clean. And what better way than to turn you in and claim victory."

Talpade was impressed with Vasu's remark. He glanced at Vasu in approval before adding to the point he raised, "That's a good plan. I mean who knows him. He could be anyone. He could be a hired gun or a foreign spy. If I were in Yashpal's place, I would just abandon him. Claim that I had never met him."

"He wouldn't do that. Because-"

"He's your friend. Yeah, we know." Talpade interrupted to the dismay of the rider.

Khan was now ready to chime in. He knew the type of people that the rider was and spoke from that experience, "How many people did you betray to get where you are? What's one more for him?"

Now just adding fuel to the fire, Talpade asked, "Do you have a lawyer? I think you might need a lawyer you know, to cut a deal with us. Phantom knows a good lawyer right?"

Vasu was happy to work with Talpade, "Yeah, he's my cousin. I promise you he's good."

Rider screamed out in frustration, "Shut up. All of you."

There was silence for a while before Khan continued the mental torture, "You are right. I don't think you need to know what's about to happen. The torture and pain you will have to go through so we can get information out of you. Meanwhile, he is sleeping comfortably in his house."

Talpade as usual was ready to annoy, "It's a nice house by the way.

Do you live there? Or do you live somewhere in a small apartment, cold and lonely?" Again the fake concern made its return.

Vasu wanted a piece of Talpade's sweet pie, he joined in, "What about the cars he's driven in? Do you have one of those?"

Talpade looked at Vasu and asked, "The convoy cars?" Vasu nodded and Talpade continued. "Oh, they are so comfortable." He looked at the rider, "I sat in one of those a few months back. I have never liked any other car since." Talpade was hitting the limit. "My bed felt harder than those seats."

Khan realizing not to push too hard too early said, "I think that's enough. Our rider here has a lot to think about. Leave him be."

Talpade took the cue and quieted down, "Okay." He also knew what was supposed to come in next. He took out the bottle of water from the door pocket and asked the rider, "Water?"

"Rudra." He said looking out of the window with a flat tone. "What?" Talpade had to ask to make sure they were on the same page.

He repeated, "My name is Rudra."

Talpade with a tone of sympathy replied, "Hi Rudra, I am Mahesh." He tried to continue the conversation, "Where are you from?"

"Not here." He replied quickly.

Talpade realized that they might have pushed hard to he backed off a little. "It's okay. We are just talking."

After a brief pause, Rudra replied, "North. That's all I'll say." "It's okay," Talpade said in an assuring tone.

Rudra looked ahead at the centre console and requested, "Could you lower the a/c? I fell a little chilly."

Talpade gestured to Vasu who obliged. He continued as he looked at Rudra, "My aunt doesn't like it either. Says that people from 'Sand Dunes' hate it."

"Really? She's from-" "Rannthar, yes."

Now in a soft voice, he said, "I am from there as well. We get cold easily."

Talpade was now lowering his gun, he continued the conversation, "Oh, then the temperature here would be killer for you. Especially in the 3rd."

"It's okay." He replied appreciating the concern.

As genuine as he could appear to be, Talpade asked, "You know what, this case aside, you seem like a nice man. Why would you get involved with Yashpal and his dirty politics?"

"He's a friend," Rudra replied with confidence. "And when a friend needs help; you do whatever you can."

Talpade could recognize the truth in that sentence, "That's what I mean. You are nice enough to risk your life." Talpade paused, waiting for a reply from the rider who was looking out of the window curiously.

Rudra now aware of his surroundings asked, "Where are you taking me?"

Noticing the panic in his voice, Khan replied. "7th. That's where we will process you."

"That's wrong." Rudra was losing the calm again. "You cannot do that. It's illegal."

Still trying to be genuine Talpade replied, "Oh come on Rudra.

You know that's not true."

Rudra was now upset, "But it is. You cannot just transfer me from 2nd to the 7th without papers."

"That's only valid when we have filed an FIR. Not before that." Khan was quick to dismiss that claim.

Rudra was now visibly frustrated, nervous even. Information provided by Khan had an impact that no other remark before had. He was looking vulnerable by the minute. Talpade sitting in the back seat had his eye on the man. His delight was knowing that now it would be easy to break him. Khan's tactic had worked and as soon as there was a chip in the armour, they could split open the whole thing. His frustration earlier with Khan was gone. There was still some bitterness with Vasu but nothing they couldn't just resolve later he thought.

Khan decided to go easy on the driving. All of them were exhausted. And putting them in the mental strain of a fast drive wasn't advisable. He was slower than usual in fact. The injury to his abdomen had limited his access to a full steering lock. His legs were hurting from the knee down reducing the feel of the pedals.

While the swelling on his face from the punches was causing visual problems. He could have asked any of the others to drive but he was worried that in his state he might not be able to keep a proper eye on their suspect.

Vasu on the other hand was struggling to look through the now chipped glasses. His face wasn't happy with the mask either and the pain in his arm was unbearable while holding the heavy metal- laden gun. The only sliver of joy was knowing that all of this was close to getting finished. He wanted a minute free to think about himself and his priorities. Maybe the meeting with Tarita would provide that refresher. Vasu was now focusing half on the arrested prisoner, and the other time on the road passing. The highway was relatively empty. There were the occasional cars going past but it wasn't much to keep his attention up. The cycle went on for him for a while. Again Vasu's attention was drawn towards the light approaching them. It was approaching too fast. More curiously, it was a bike. A streak of dread had just brushed Vasu's spine. He was no longer tired, just alert to what was approaching. He wanted to alert others but wasn't sure what to say to convince them of the possible threat. He was juggling between telling and keeping quiet. But before he could say anything, a small hole had formed in the middle of it surrounded by multiple cracks. He looked at others to find Talpade ducking along with Rudra and Khan leaning down as well. Realizing what had just happened, Vasu turned around and faced the road. He looked up hoping to check if he was low enough to cover his entire head. The first thing that caught attention was a hole in the rear-view mirror.

There was a sudden surge of speed in the car. Khan had his foot bolted to the ground throwing caution to the wind. He wanted to get away as soon as possible. He looked around possibly for an exit off the road. Vasu now had no idea regarding the position of the incoming threat. He was sure neither did the others. He looked around to take a look at Rudra out of curiosity. He was in a panic as well, confused more than anything though. Vasu felt a little bad for the man. But there was no time to ponder on the morality of things. Danger just had closed in on them. This was evident by the shower of bullets shattering the front and the back windows. Khan and Vasu had ducked enough to save themselves from the bullets that had hit the headrest of their seats. There was silence again. However, Vasu could hear the sound of the approaching danger thanks to the now half-open car. The wind had brought along the sound of an I-4. Vasu was sure it was Rudra's bike. But that wasn't possible. The bike was back in Sector 2 unless it was retrieved by what Vasu thought was Yashpal. The sound was getting louder by the second. Khan tried to move left and right in the hope that they could ram the rider down and make their escape. But it was fruitless. Khan's reduced visibility was causing gaps in his judgment. He didn't have enough information to aim the car around. For Vasu, the bike's sound was all that he focused on. It was so loud that he could have been standing right next to it. The sound that followed was louder and more frightening. It was the sound of a gun firing. Only this time it didn't stop. What brought out the dread even more was the fact was that there was debris flying around the car with the holes. Suddenly, there was a loud explosion that led to Khan losing control of the car. It started wavering about. He ordered everyone, even Rudra to jump out of the car. Vasu opened the door and the road's speed gave him some hesitation. But he knew staying in there was death. So, he jumped, took a leap of faith. The impact was hard. In a matter of seconds, he could feel pain in his shoulder, hips, knees and suddenly there was nothing. Blackout. Vasu woke up and immediately took off the glasses and rolled down the mask. They were too much to handle now. It took a while for him to adjust to the yellow, reddish light hitting his eyes. The warmth and the colour for a moment gave him the impression that he was in his bed woken up by the light of the sun. But the hard, gritty tarmac was proof otherwise. He snapped out remembering that he had just fallen out of a car and tried to stand up. But the sight in front of him took away the courage and the will. It was the car he was in moments ago, flipped upside down and burning. There was debris lying around. The pain was returning as well. There was also a sensation of burning on his wounds curiously. He checked them out and looked around for his partners. There was no one to his left, just the divider that seemed distant a minute ago. On his right a little ahead though stood Khan, leaning down to hold his knee. Vasu tried to call out but the voice refused to leave his mouth. There was no one else around to Vasu's dismay.

Khan had just noticed Vasu woken up. He was sitting upright and staring aimlessly at the burning car. He knew how the kid felt. But he also knew that it was no time to grieve on the loss. He had already called for backup and realized it would be a while for them to get to the location. Khan approached Vasu in the hope that a conversation might help both of them. "Are you okay?"

Vasu was unresponsive at first, captured by the flame and the thoughts of its potential. He snapped realizing that Khan had just asked a question. Before he could repeat it, Vasu replied. "Yes, Did-" Khan interrupted knowing the question that was about to be raised. The wounds were fresh enough not to be spoken of. He replied, "No, it's just us."

Vasu had no choice but to accept and process the fact. He took a deep breath and closed his eyes. Then a moment later he asked, "Who was it? Did you see?"

"I didn't need to," Khan replied.

The bike. Vasu recognized the sound of the bike. So, he said, "But the bike-"

Khan responded, "I don't know about that either." He looked behind to check for any incoming traffic and continued. "Backup is on the way." Shifting his attention towards Vasu Khan said, "Give those to me" pointing at the glasses and the mask.

Vasu handed them over and was hit by the realization that they had landed exactly where they were before. He looked towards Khan for answers, "What are we going to do?"

But he didn't have any. "I don't know." At least not now. "Right now, we need to get you back to your home."

"No" Vasu wanted to stay, help somehow.

"It's not a request. I am ordering you." But Khan knew what the toll of tonight would be and Vasu was crossing this path for the first time.

Vasu looked at Khan and almost panting he said, "I will not follow. He killed Mahesh. I-"

Khan interrupted knowing full well how Vasu felt, "I know. He will pay for it. But you cannot risk your life anymore." Khan wasn't comfortable with the idea of risking his life anymore. He wanted safety for now.

Vasu wasn't convinced, "Why? He risked his life. You risk it.

Why not me?"

"Because you deserve a better life. Go back home and work for that better life." Khan had thought about it every day since that fateful night. He knew how much Vasu wanted to help but he also knew the kind of man he was; the kind of man he will grow up to be. He hit Vasu right where it mattered. "Think of your mother. What would I tell her if something happens to you?"

"That I died trying to protect others." He wasn't backing off. Not yet.

"What about her? What will happen to her after you die?" Khan could see the emotions churning. He could see the confusion and fear spooling in Vasu. "Exactly. Go home and hug your mother while you can. I promise you Mahesh's death won't go in vain." He assured Vasu.

Khan and Vasu sat there looking at the havoc wreaked upon them. The cruel nature of humanity was on display. Both of them were surprised at the extreme that someone could go to just to stay in power. For Khan, this wasn't new. But to see such behaviour in the middle of civilization, by the very people he swore to protect was hurting him. He knew there was more than this to people, but he also knew that this was a naive thought. For him, the threshold had been crossed.

The ambulance was first to arrive. Khan and Vasu weren't sure how much the time had passed but the flames on the car were dim. The medics took both around and sat them at the back of the ambulance checking them for all injuries. Khan's were substantial compared to Vasu's. The toll of going toe-to-toe, exchanging blows with Rudra was a couple of broken ribs, black eyes, swollen knuckles and eyes, and a cracked finger. Vasu on the other hand had minor injuries on his face, a damaged eardrum, chipped arm, and bruised coccyx. The fire brigade arrived just as the paramedics were examining them. Most of their job was done by that time. All they had to do now was put out a minor fire. The rest would be handled by the forensics team. Khan got up just as the fire was put out. He walked towards the car to find that the traffic on the other side of the road was slowing down just to take a look at the car and its ashes. Khan was hoping that he could treat it like just another case. It wouldn't get to him that this was his colleague, a man that had helped him on numerous occasions, a man that admired him to no end, a friend even. He reached as close as he could to the dripping car It was still hot even though the flames were out. He bent down to look in at the back seat. What he saw was difficult to explain, even for him. There were half burnt-half charred remains of what used to be two human beings slumped over the roof of now a flipped car. Despite all his training, his experience, and his will, Khan couldn't help but think that one of those - things a minute ago was a happy, confident, hard-working man that had put his life on the line only a single request. At the moment, Khan was feeling just as responsible as the man who put Mahesh here. He turned around to find a group of police cars along with some uniformed and some plain-clothed officers stepping out to assist in any way they can. A couple of them had even approached Vasu to question him. But from what Khan saw, he didn't even utter a word. His hand immediately reached to his pockets, checking for the mask and glasses. This was the time he had suddenly realized that they had forgotten the baton. Vasu and Khan didn't realize that there was a baton probably in that wreck of a car. Khan had to retrieve it before some here would. He moved back towards the car, ignoring the remains as much as he could to find the baton. It became difficult to find it in the black flaky remains of the car. There was nothing in the front seat except the endless blackness of the burned-out remains of what used to be an acceptable car. So, sure that it wasn't on this end, Khan moved towards the other side of the car hoping that he could find a silver object in the blackness of death.

Moving on to the other side, there was a shine, even though it was dull, something was visible in the brightness of the half- moon light. Hoping that it could be the baton he moved towards the object. It was lying a good 10 feet away from the wreck of what used to be a car. He moved towards the shining object as it lost its light and started to fade away into darkness. Khan picked it up not knowing when he would have the chance to give it back to Vasu. He wasn't sure if Vasu even remembered the baton. The shock and trauma might have been too much for him. Khan hid it like a gun in his pants at the back. He was waiting for an opportunity as he moved back towards the ambulance.

An unmarked car approached what had now become a police envoy. Khan noticed the black colour and thought it could have been a local politician. He realized he was wrong as soon as he could see Laxmi stepping out of the back of the car. He was nervous, not sure why. Khan had never felt that way at the arrival of his old partner. He wasn't ready to handle the emotions. As soon as Khan approached Laxmi, she indicated they talk in a bit of privacy away from the crowding crime scene.

"What happened?" She asked calm, composed, and unaffected by the scene in front of her.

"We were taking the suspect back like I told you and were hit by a lone rider." Khan said looking back at the car, rubbing his forehead "SMG." He was disappointed, but whom he didn't know. "He hit the car's tire and the gas tank." Khan was looking at the disaster as it happened.

Laxmi asked, "Who was it? Did you get a look?"

"No, but I have an idea," Khan said that with controlled anger.

Anger that he had been holding back from Vasu.

She saw that anger in him. She knew that it was different from any other case. "Go on," she said wanting to hear the answer.

"You won't like it" warned Khan.

She paused looked at Khan, and with unnerving authority replied, "That's for me to decide."

"Yashpal Vohra."

Laxmi closed her eyes, took her time to process this information, and agreed, "Yeah, I don't like it." She continued, "Do you have any proof or is it one of those instincts."

"The man we had arrested, he was about to testify against him. We had a case befor-" Khan said holding back his feelings, "before this happened."

"So, no proofs." Laxmi stood there hoping that there was more to it than this. Khan's face said quite the opposite. "I am sorry; we cannot move on him unless you have solid proof." Khan knew that. But at this moment Laxmi felt that she had to clear it up. "Let me know if there is anything else on the case." She looked towards Vasu, realized that she didn't recognize him. And knowing Khan there definitely was a reason behind his presence. She asked, "Who is the kid?"

"Oh, he's-" Khan didn't feel like explaining. "It's a long story for some other day."

She didn't push further. "Get him home then." "Yeah"

Khan had lost all the will and desire to do anything right now. All he cared about was getting the culprit, Yashpal. For him, there was no other goal, no other motive more important in the moment. He knew there was no way he could rest before putting this to bed. But Khan was experienced enough to realize that the emotions flowing through him right now were not supposed to be making decisions for him. Not now, not ever. All he needed to do at the moment was to flush everything negative and clear his mind, his path, and his emotions. So, as an opportunity to get that time, he decided to drop Vasu off at this house and think his plan through before executing it.

CHAPTER NINE

FINALITY OF DEFEAT

Vasu was woken up by his mother. She had a day off, or so he thought. It was entirely possible that she could have skipped work that day to look after Vasu's injuries. Khan knew that this might be entirely possible. That Vasu's mother could discover his injuries and impede him from leaving the house. In fact, Khan was counting on it. They hadn't talked about the incident all night. The entire ride to Vasu's home Khan was silent. Vasu didn't mind that. He was comfortable with the silence. The impact of the night had a toll so high that Vasu wasn't sure he would want to go and help Khan that day. He needed the day off. But the day off at home didn't go as planned. Vasu's was woken up and greeted by anger and disappointment from his mother. She wanted to know why her son had returned bruised and beaten as if he came from war. He wasn't ready for the conversation to explain to her what went wrong, how his night was much like a battle. A battle they had lost. But she wouldn't understand and give Vasu much-needed space. She was on it from the moment Vasu had his eyes open. It was as if she hadn't moved from his room since the morning, waiting for the inevitable. "Where were you last night?" She asked, angrily. Vasu didn't respond. His brain wasn't ready to lie just yet. He yawned and stretched his arms to disguise the fact. "Did you fall off the bike?" She tried to be more specific hoping it would generate a response. But there wasn't any. After much frustrating silence, she resorted to the general line of questioning, "What were you doing?" The frustration was audible.

Vasu was already annoyed at her mother. Partially because still wasn't sure of the lie he'd want to present. On top of that, the realization dawned on him that he had missed the breakfast with Tarita as he'd planned. It was an important promise he had failed to keep. Hoping to call her he searched around for the phone, spotting it in her mother's hand he stretched out his hand gesturing at the phone, and tried to ask, "Can I-"

She interrupted now even angrier. She swatted away Vasu's hand and sternly said, "Not until you tell me what happened to you."

He wanted to get past that question. The desperation, the annoyance, and the fear were now melting to create a monster of anger in his brain. He tried to control it and shrug off the topic, "It was nothing, I fell off the bike."

She didn't believe that "Really? Where is the bike." It was the inevitable question. Vasu had somehow skipped having this conversation with his mother. The state of the bike was unknown to her and the response from Vasu had not really been acceptable.

Vasu, on the other hand, slipped his leash on the beast and with sudden anger replied, "Under a god damn truck. Give me the phone." He knew what just happened. He got back control of the anger but it was too late.

"Don't talk to me in that tone." It was rare for Vasu to speak to her that way. And that was uncalled for she thought. The sentence especially was hurting because that was one of the fears she had for Vasu, "Tell me the truth or you are never leaving the apartment." She said hoping to corner him into answering.

Vasu had control on the anger but his annoyance had returned at the persistence of the question. He thought logic might sway it away, "Does it matter?"

It didn't sway anything, "Yes, it matters. I need to know how you got those injuries. Look at your face!" She said pointing at the scratched, scarred section of Vasu's face from the dirt shrapnel.

Vasu now was hoping to slip out of this as fast as he could. He tried his best to give a reasonable excuse, "I swear, I fell off the bike." His mother wasn't believing it at all. So to make it more believable he added, "I was on the highway on my way to get-"

She interrupted, "I don't care where you were going. Tell me who hit you?" If she was to believe Vasu's story, there must have been a guilty party and she wanted to know the truth.

"Nobody hit me. I was distracted by the lights and crashed into a car." He replied, as reasonably as he could. There was no truth to the story but there was believability.

The words highway and car brought up the news she had watched last night. KNC broadcasted the incident Vasu was involved in as a fatal accident. She had recalled the image and immediately asked Vasu, "Was it the car that flipped? Were you there?" The anger was overshadowed by fear and worry.

He immediately knew what she was talking about. It brought a wave of fear and nervousness over his mind but controlling them as best as he could he replied, "No, God no. I was on…" But he couldn't complete the sentence, or rather the lie.

"Where?" She asked snapping Vasu back to the conversation.

"I was on that highway, but that was not the car that hit me. I promise." He tried to be more believable and give the response that she wanted.

But it wasn't. "That's it then. You are done with the job. Tell them you quit right now." She said sitting down on the bed next to Vasu and handing over the phone.

Vasu took the phone from her and responded, "No, I am not going to do that."

She didn't understand why Vasu was ready to risk his life for a job. She wanted to know. "Why not? You got injured doing-"

He interrupted, "It wasn't their fault. They helped me in fact." Vasu was referring to Khan at this point and he realized that sentence might not work with the lie he had concocted.

"How?" it didn't.

Vasu paused, thought about it for a while, and tried to respond. "They-"

But by then his mother had grown impatient and accidentally interrupted, "Tell me!"

Vasu's frustration was boiling over, "It doesn't matter. What's done is done. Let's just move on and we can fo-"

She knew now that it was an attempt to deviate from something worse, "We are not moving on. Not from this."

"Then what? Are we going to talk about this all day?" He wanted to know the endgame.

"Yes! Or until you promise on my life that you will quit this job." She just laid it all out.

Vasu tried to argue, "Mom! -"

"No! I am not listening to any of your excuses anymore. Swear on my life." She said by taking Vasu's hand and placing it on her head. She was tired, scared for Vasu's life, and wanted assurance, any form of guarantee that he would stay safe.

Vasu felt uncomfortable with that, not sure why "I am not doing that."

"Why not?" She wanted to know.

"Because…" Vasu was unable to complete the sentence. "Why?"

"Because I will go back to that job." This was the line they both dreaded to hear. Vasu wasn't sure if it was what he wanted to keep doing but he wasn't ready to quit. Not yet. "I will keep going back to that job. That's the one way …" his sentence trailed off. He knew what was next but didn't want to say it out loud.

"What?"

"That's the only way I could be like father." Vasu had said it. There was no going back. This was a sensitive topic for both of them. The fact that his mother got anxious just by mentioning his father put off Vasu from ever talking about it. But the night and the conversation this morning coupled with the events of the past week had pushed Vasu enough to bring light to this topic.

There was silence in the house now. Neither of them wanted to talk. They were worried about the place this conversation would head. But she knew that there was no way out of it. The way Vasu had been behaving, the way he talked about people to her was too familiar. Her greatest fear had come true, "I don't want you to be like him. That's why I brought you here. Away from all those people." She was referring to their community in Sector 9. Vasu was sad about bringing up this topic. But he also knew that someday they had to address this. Today might have not been ideal. The situation for Vasu was the worst it could possibly have been, but since they were on the topic, he decided to roll with it and clarify his position. "I am sorry to disappoint you, but I want to be like him. I want to help people."

Vasu's behaviour was scaring his mother. She was worried. The accident that brought them here would be repeated and there would be nothing left for her. No one to live for. She wanted to ask Vasu about his priorities. Did she fit in them? "What about me then? Don't you care about me?"

"I do. But…" There was no doubt in his mind that she was meant the world to him. But the fact that he also wanted to be like his father was no longer to be ignored. "I miss him every day. This is the only place where I feel like I am making him proud."

"You don't have to do this for that. He will always be proud of you." She wanted to assure was of how proud she was and how much more he would have been.

That wasn't enough for Vasu though. The feeling still remained. "Maybe. But all I know right now is-"

"You have to do this." She completed his sentence. This was a familiar sight that hadn't left her. Vasu's father was a kind and loving person who gave to the community more than he did to his family. And the fact that Vasu wanted to be like him scared her. She knew the path and destination lay ahead. Now, he would follow too. "I know you won't stop. He never did." The man Ganga feared him most to grow up to be was the one he already was. "But I don't want you to lie to me. But you have to tell me the truth. I will try and accept it." Her concern was not knowing how Vasu was helping others. She thought that maybe if he could tell her, she would work towards understanding it.

"I..." Vasu almost had spoken it out. But he realized the circumstances right now. The timing wasn't right. And her knowing the secret just might risk her life more. "I promise you this will be over soon. And then I will tell you the truth." He wanted to tell her now more than ever. "I promise." He paused, hugged his mother to assure her that it was alright. They sat there in each other's arms with the realization that they were each other's support. Vasu then had spare time to focus on another person that mattered. "I have to meet someone." He got up dialling the number and stumbled the first step. This worried his mother but he gestured to her that he was fine. "Don't' worry I will stay safe. No more injuries." She let him walk out of the room. Vasu called Tarita from the living room but there was no response. The entire call, 20 seconds of ringing indicated that there might not be anyone home. He realized that she might still be waiting at the college, pissed off at this delay. He stepped out of his house grabbing a couple of hundreds from his mother's purse.

Arrival at the train station, catching the train and reaching the designated stop went by for him in bliss. I guess time flies when you have a girl to catch. The walk to Tarita's college wasn't long. Or maybe it was but to Vasu it didn't feel like it. It was at those gates he realized how nervous he was. How much he wanted to run away or throw up, anything far more relaxing would have done it for him. Deep breaths worked for him. And they did here as well. Breath in, breathe out and repeat until the results are what you desire. Or close enough. His mind was clear. He had a chance to think straight. It was stupid he thought for him to come here knowing that she wasn't at the college. Knowing that she had taken the day off and might be at home hurt from the fact he stood her up again. It might have been the last straw thought Vasu. He wasn't even aware of her home address. All of this time that he wasted in this case, he could have spent it with her. With his head down, Vasu started walking back to the station. And this time around he was quite aware of the distance. In fact, he was annoyed at how far away it was. A kilometre didn't sound that long, but to walk the distance was quite a chore.

He stood there on the platform defeated in every which way. On one side he was frustrated at losing everything that mattered. He wasn't good at working for a living, maintaining a relationship, and he had even managed to upset his mother. He knew that all of this was just for a job. And maybe his mother had a point. So, fed up with the events surrounding the work he had taken up, Vasu boarded a train that would lead him to the 7th. He wanted to quit this job but he also wanted to see the case through. Hoping that Khan could provide him with seeing through this dilemma, he headed out in search of the answers.

Khan's morning was no better than Vasu's had been. He hadn't slept the whole night. No amount of painkillers was dulling down the pain. Usually, his insomniac nights were spent thinking about his past life. Something that he rarely talked about seemed to occupy his mind every night. Today was no exception. But the thoughts came in voluntarily unlike the previous times. Khan wanted to remember what he used to be, what caused him to become the man he was; disciplined, strong, and more importantly a man of conscience and virtue. He knew the path left behind and the price everyone else had to pay for him to be here. Most people had skeletons in their closet but not Khan. He had buried his bodies deep. And yet he wandered on the garden that grew as a result of that. The deepest cut to his memory was the events surrounding the assault on the White Plains. It was during the end where they had managed to capture a unit and interrogated them for intel. The interrogation was just a politically correct way to say torture. They had to cut their extremities, burn off their genitals, and in some cases bleed them out dry to get accurate positions of their bunker for further assault. He was leading the torture of one of those prisoners. Khan was adamant like his peers that the torture was essential in their victory over that portion of the land. Their interrogation had resulted in saving the lives of over a thousand soldiers. The assault went along with ease and the enemy forces surrendered. A few weeks later when visiting the captured ground on new orders, Khan discovered the true identity of the tortured soldier. He was a farmer. The only one in his family who participated in the war only after it was knocking on his door. It had been a necessity rather than a choice. But it wasn't for Khan. He had a plethora of tools at his disposal to avoid pushing that man to his fate. He knew that people who went to war had trouble sleeping at night, but he himself had never experienced it. That night he was visited by the haunting images of the tortured soul. He couldn't continue working with the knowledge that he had killed someone innocent, a victim of circumstances. His soul had been scarred up until that point but it had been shot with that discovery. Khan quit, willing to be identified as a deserter and disappeared. Although the tag wasn't an official one, he still considered it so. It took him six years of obscurity to mend his ways and one of the things he had promised himself before starting this new life was that he would not kill anyone. Not until there was a way out. And there always was. That promise had compromised with his job as a police officer but he had managed to work his way up despite this uncompromising dilemma.

The promise he took that day was the one restricting him from taking any action against Yashpal. Khan was sure of his guilt, his crimes and yet had to sit while he worked around the law. It was a very difficult place for Khan to be in especially due to the loss he had faced. What scared him even more was that if Yashpal manages to win the election, the power and his morality would combine to create an untouchable monster that could wreak havoc in anyone's life whenever he desired. Maybe he wouldn't act any different than the other corrupt and downright deplorable that came before him. But Khan had his doubts. If he wanted to work to fill his pockets, he could have risen to power like them as well. But Yashpal had been playing on people's emotions while murdering some of them only to blame it all on another man. He didn't even spare his own friend; what hope do the people of this city have. Khan had already tried to go about it the right way. Now, that path was closed, out of reach, and full of death and despair. He wasn't sure he'd want to take the city let alone Vasu along that path. With one shot, he could spare the city of the years of pain and suffering. By breaking his promise, his vow, he could liberate his own soul and save others'. He had contemplated this path before. But it was foggy and unclear. Now though, the blood spilt and the fires lit had ironically cleared the path for him. It was his destiny, his endgame to salvation. Never had he been more certain of the life he had to take.

Khan had abandoned his cigar, his thoughts, and cleared his mind. He stood up with a renewed purpose and determination. The pain of the wounds was now gone. The restriction that it had laid on his structure was lifted. Over the years, Khan had stored his past but in this case, some of it was literal. He had some of his old gear. Handed over to him by his superior. It was a ceremonial gesture, a decoration not licensed to be used. But that wasn't a concern for him. The was one of the least important laws that he was about to break today. Khan opened up the wardrobe and the box that sat inside it. The gear was still there, just dusty. It was a special issue, blacked-out, light-combat gear for infiltration. The equipment on his person was only the essentials. Gloves were hardback, padded for a repeated offensive attack. The front of the gloves was a softer, gripper material to aid with weapon combat. The vest was clean without slots for additional ammo or equipment, just focusing on the padding for protection from bullets and knives. An equipment belt was issued with a knife slot at the back and additional two ammo slots on either side. And finally, the combat boots were all leather, high-rise fitted with a steel toe for protection in rough terrain.

He put all of the gear in his bag and prepared to leave. Fighting and killing in the broad daylight was a foolish mistake. More importantly, Khan had to be prepared for anything. Yashpal was a resourceful man. Khan could be facing resistance from multiple assailants. He had to be ready, overcome his pain as best as he could and work around it. But the mere thought of the pain had brought it back stumbling down the priority stairs, right at Khan's feet, his shoulders, and most importantly, his ribs. There might have been a solution for it from the Quartermaster during his term as the intelligence officer but now, here in the civilian world, no such cocktail existed. All he remembered was that Adrenaline could provide him with a temporary boost, especially to the motor functions. But the pain was something he would have to manage. The painkillers had helped but they didn't make any impact with movement. He knew the perfect way to get them both. The hospital that most of the officers visited might have a sympathetic doctor. Sector 8 had been home to the hospital that was highly recommended among the officers. Some for the discounts and the treatments that they and their family members had been given but some for the recreational access to materials. Khan decided to head out for the place first. He wasn't sure of the exact location but had a name. As he headed down the stairs, Khan had to step back in for the keys and the piece of paper he had left on the desk. He gave both of those items to the building's guard as he drove off with the junior waiting for him.

Vasu had reached the station just after lunchtime. The officers had scattered around and the desks were unmanned. He waited outside hoping to talk to someone that might let him go through but nobody came by. So, he walked past all of the offices, some had men on duty having their meals while others were just as empty as the desks he left behind. He reached Khan's office, took a deep breath, and knocked on the door twice. It was a light tap with the back of his fingers enough to be audible. Vasu heard a voice call out,

"Come in." It was not Khan's voice. This was clearly a woman. He hesitated for a while but thought just going in won't kill him. Opening the door confirmed his guess. It was a woman, probably in her forties sitting on Khan's desk. Her black tied-up hair, well- ironed uniform, and the ribbons on her badge screamed of someone of authority. Vasu realized that it must have been someone senior but refrained from asking. He wanted to leave now sure that Khan wasn't here. There was no point sitting there. So, Vasu said to the woman, "I was looking for Khan-Inspector Khan. I can-" He had said that pointing towards the door hoping that it would help him leave.

"Sit." She said pointing at the chair. Vasu was familiar with this chair but today it didn't feel right.

"What did you want to meet Khan for?"

"I can't tell you that." Vasu looked away from her afraid.

"You are working with him on the case right?" she asked wanting to know the kid's involvement. It was one of the reasons she was sitting in Khan's office.

Vasu knew he couldn't just tell her everything despite her authority. "No, I just helped him once. He's done the rest."

"So, what are you here for?"

It was a good question. Had Vasu told her the extent of his involvement, the question would invariably have the obvious answer. But now, after the lie, it was sketchy. Yet he tried to add some truth to his answer. "To check up on him and tell him that-"

"You can't get involved anymore." She completes Vasu's sentence aware of the toll this job can take on people. "Great choice. You shouldn't have in the first place." Her disapproval was clear to Vasu but this brought it out in a new light.

"I thought it was a good thing to do." Vasu tried to justify it to her. But not sure why he had to.

"For you or him?" "Both." He replied.

After a brief pause, she asked, "Why did he choose you?" She was just as curious as Talpade was. The question as to why Vasu was given the opportunity that more qualified men were denied was baffling to her.

The answer was clear to Vasu though. "He didn't. I approached." He tried his best to bury the memory of his conversation with Talpade.

"And he just accepted the help?" Not to Laxmi, it wasn't.

"Not at first." He said hinting at his persistence that got him the position.

"Why stop now?" The lent forward with curiosity, "It is too dangerous. Especially with my mom."

"I have a daughter, a husband but I still work to help people. Don't you think your mother would want you to do something good for the people?" She asked hoping to hear a particular answer.

"No, she's scared that I might…" He didn't have to complete that sentence.

"I understand."

"Can I ask you something?"

After a brief pause, she said, "Sure."

"How do you justify it to yourself? Risking your life for others rather than living for yourself." Vasu had asked this question after hearing from her the justification of working for others. He wanted to know more so that he could find the answer for himself.

"I don't have to. What I learned throughout life is that all of these people are my family. So, why wouldn't I help them?"

It seemed like the right answer, except for one thing. "But there are some horrible people in the world. Why would you want to work for them?" There is no reason for a person to risk his life for people who might hurt others.

"Think about it. Is everyone in your family good?" She paused to let Vasu process that question and then continued. "You will always have the negative but that doesn't take anything away from the positive."

It made sense. No matter how others behave, he had to help the good ones and focus on them. But now came another question, "Does it ever get difficult for you. To put everything on the line every day?"

"It does. But when I return home, I know what I did that day might be the reason someone else had a chance to go home. Hug their family like I do."

This might be the right answer but it didn't feel like so to Vasu. He continued that line of inquiry. "If you retire, the world will not stop, right? There will be someone else that will take your place."

"You never know. There is no guarantee that someone is coming to take your place. Would you rather leave that to chance?" She paused again waiting for the realization on Vasu's face. It had dawned on him that she was probably right. The conversation was over according to Laxmi and hinted at Vasu, "I don't think he will be coming today. Go home. I will tell him you were here."

"Would you tell him what I came for?"

"No, that is your choice. You have to tell him."

Vasu realized that she was right, if not anything about the part that he had to speak to Khan face-to-face. But sitting here in the police station wasting time won't help. Maybe he would turn up eventually but there was no surety of that. Vasu was also aware that staying here might bring up more questions about his involvement and give away unwanted details. He took the officer's advice, stood up, and walked away. Getting out of the police station felt like a relief to Vasu. He wanted to go home but not to his mother yet. He wasn't ready to discuss the truth with her either. But maybe someone could help him think through. The only person right now that could have helped him was Acharya. Not only was he against Vasu's choice to fight, but he had also been a guiding light in his time of darkness. This might not have been that simple but it did cause Vasu some confusion. Having a clear, new perspective on the situation might help him see things in a new light. Vasu still wasn't sure whether he could talk with Acharya because of the tension that had strained everything the last time. But he had fewer and fewer choices left. The desperation of the current situation was enough for him to let go of his ego and board the series of trains that would lead him to the home.

The pills were hard to swallow for Khan without water. Maybe there wasn't enough liquid present to ease down the white solid tablets. There were two of them reaching his stomach. One more than prescribed but Khan felt that it was warranted in this case. He had convinced the doctor to prescribe a stronger painkiller by opening up one of the stitches and bleeding out in the waiting room. And as luck would have it, he had been left unattended in the check- up room while the doctor on call attended an emergency outside. The medical cart was open and Khan had a chance to sneak out a syringe and a vial of adrenaline. He had used it before to get himself out of situations and was prepared to do so again if required. His assumption was that Yashpal might not go down easy. Even if he was not as tough as his partner, there was a chance he would have to go through some of his protectors. And fighting multiple guards in his damaged and bruised situation would require serious advantage if it meant finding through dishonest means. The hospital was on the outskirts of Sector 8, closer to the rest of the city. It was a medium-sized hospital with mismanagement that had created a wave for such practices. Khan despised the fact that such a hospital with sub-par care existed. Today though, he was thankful for the advantage that it had just provided him. Getting out of the 8th was easy. There wasn't much traffic yet heading out. Even though it was well into the evening, the real rush heading out of this portion of the city would begin after 8. That too mostly for Sector 7.

His journey to Yashpal's house was a blur. All the ways he had been planning to kill Yashpal were playing out in his mind. The gun, the knives, or even his bare hands, all of it were on the table. And none of it was extreme. Khan had thought it all through, how Yashpal would retaliate, the storm of bullets he might face and even the way he was walking into death or lifetime of incarceration, all of it was just going to be in the way to his goal. The only thing that was worrying him was the fact that Vasu wasn't aware of the plan and what he would have thought of it. Even though he was just a kid unaware of the extremes that were residing on the plane of existence, Khan had hope that someday Vasu might understand his decision. Even though he may not agree with him, Vasu would eventually acknowledge the situation that had brought on the conclusion. Khan was also hoping that Vasu would have enough time to sharpen his skill and hone in his instincts becoming an excellent investigator. He wanted to talk with Vasu, give him a clarification on why he took the decision but that would only create a rift and cause an argument. Something Khan didn't want to go through as of now.

Khan had reached the destination among all of these thoughts. Now was the chance to push them back and concentrate. He parked the car a few spots away from his usual. Walking out of it, he went around the back and started to put his gear on. There was a certain familiarity, a certain state of mind that came with all of the items. He not only knew the position and the purpose of each of the items, but he had also remembered how all of them felt. The weight, the texture, and the manoeuvrability came hand-in-hand with the combat gear. The gun was in its holster, the knives were in their sheaths and the rest of the gear was fit, ready for some action. He had not taken any weapon out yet. It was a residential area and a man in combat gear holding a weapon would a cause for premature alarm. Walking to the house Khan noticed the covered windows. It was curious. This alerted him to the fact that Yashpal was ready for a fight and so was Khan. He reached the door and gripped the handle lightly testing it for locks. It was open. Khan could feel the lightness as if the door was held in its place by the man's grip. Khan was ready to push or rather burst in shooting. But his training as an officer had dulled down that instinct and covered it with 'never fire until fired upon'. He had his gun out, gripped and loaded with the first round without safety.

With a push hard enough to open the door, Khan stepped inside and gripped the gun with his second hand as a support for aiming. There wasn't anyone inside. It was all dark but the room was clear. Khan wasn't sure whether this was a trap or just a mistake but he had to check. Maybe Yashpal wasn't home and this had just provided Khan with a perfect setup to kill him. He had to check though, for traps or hidden cameras. The living room was carpeted completely but Khan could hear the dull sound of wooden flooring. The furniture was basic and brown, something he hadn't noticed earlier. Khan's attention was however drawn by the door under the stairs. Opening up Khan could only find a small closet, just enough size for a man to stand. But curiously, the floor was open. The stairs leading down were dark. Using the torch, Khan lit up the underground enough to find anything that could potentially harm him. Standing up there was nothing that he could see but maybe there was something or someone he could spot while leaning down.

That was a stupid idea though. It would expose the only non-protected, important part of the body to potential knives and bullets. There was another way Khan could check. He looked around the room and found a decorative vase. Khan picked up the small but heavy vase and released it down the hole. Any potential attacker might be startled and would probably attack soon. There was no sound after the crash of the vase. This was a green signal for Khan. Not to go down, but to risk taking a look. As he leaned down, Khan could see a small room filled with metal racks and a small table at the end. He could not spot the contents on the table. Before stepping down the ladder, Khan checked again for anything out of the ordinary. Anything he could have missed out. After looking around and satisfying his inner anxiety, Khan stepped down the metal ladder minding his steps and making sure no sound is emitted from the action. The metal stairs were not aiding but the fact that it was polished to be slipper rather than provide grip was creating more issue. It was curious to find such a design that could well be a deliberate choice to catch an unwanted visitor off-guard On his first step Khan would have slipped down hitting each step with his face rather than his feet if not for the fact that his other leg was planted firmly on the concrete floor. Stepping down the stairs Khan was pondering on the fact that this place wasn't well hidden. He concluded it to be either the sign of an overconfident man or a devious miscreant wanting to lure his target in. Either way, Khan was stepping down. After climbing about five steps down Khan could see the room properly it wasn't well lit but there was a source of incandescent light from somewhere in the room. Probably the desk he thought. And that's when he turned around. This smelled too much like a trap and Khan had an inkling. He knew walking in what it could turn out to be but there was a flawed motivation, reasoning that had pushed him into it. And now he was standing face-to-face with a block of clay, a circuit board, and a small blinking red LED light. Khan knew what it was, but he didn't have a clue as to how much time he had. He turned around and climbed the stairs with the speed his body hadn't known for a while. Khan was slipping but not falling down the steps. He was fast but not making enough progress. In his moment of weakness, Khan was looking at certain death which would now follow him at over 1500 m/s2 if he didn't collect himself enough to get out of this dilemma. The climb up the stairs felt like a lifetime. It was as if he was in purgatory, climbing those stairs again and again. The door to freedom was just as light as he had felt before but more importantly, so was the air. The cool breeze that greeted him as he walked out of the house had been a welcome that Khan didn't want to end. He kept on running until he had reached the gates of the society. Khan stood him with his hands on his knees wondering about what just happened. The explosive was probably timed but if it was up to him, he would have a pressure trigger to ensure proper execution. Maybe Yashpal wasn't smart enough to think of that. Relieved that the threat was not imminent, he looked for his walkie-talkie. It wasn't on his person, maybe he left it in his car. So, wanting to keep an eye on the house, Khan called his station to call in a bomb squad.

The third ring is when Khan felt the push that flung him at the wall of the society. The impact was hard but not as hard as what had hit him in the head. The next thing Khan saw was a small metal room with a silver finish and instruments that were found usually in a hospital. But the room was odd. He tried to sit up and get a clear look but the pain in his head had forced him back down. Managing the weight of the pain, Khan slowly sat up to discover that he was in an ambulance. There was another person sitting at the base of it with a few of the men in uniform standing outside. Khan didn't have to deduce what had happened. It was a plastic explosive rigged with a timer. But the delay in blast gave him the impression that it was to scare rather than to kill. The pain had returned duller than before thanks to the dose of painkiller he had taken earlier. This also meant that the impact of the shockwave and the possible debris hitting him flew at speeds that caused significant damage. Khan excuse himself out of the ambulance only to be stopped by the officers at its exit. He gestured to them that he was fine and wanted to visit ground zero. The cube was big enough to contain approximately 5-7 kg of any plastic explosive but the most likely candidate was Semtex or C-4. This was the point when he realized that his gear was no longer on him. He was relieved of his vest, his gloves and equipment belt along with all of his weapons. The thought that he was found near an explosive site with combat gear was an alarming one. And as he walked towards the explosion site it became clear as to how big the explosion was. The blast had reduced the house to a mound of rubble and debris. Even the house next to it had been damaged enough to sink half of it down on the rest. That would explain the people sitting at the door of the ambulance.

"Lucky!" A voice came from behind him. It was Laxmi approaching Khan from the impact site.

"What?" Khan wasn't sure what Laxmi was referring to with that remark.

"That's how I would describe this entire case for you."

He knew she was right, but feigned ignorance to the fact. "I guess."

"Follow me!" She said leading him away from the crime scene. "Where's your car?"

He replied pointing towards his unmarked sedan, "There."

As soon as they got closer to it, Laxmi almost yelled out, "What the fuck were you doing?" She had the god of wrath possessing her at this point. Aware of Khan's behaviour she continued, "Don't you dare lie to me. I know what that gear meant." Khan's face reflected what he felt at this point. He was busted. He was no longer looking at Laxmi but dodging her. "Have you lost your mind?"

After a moment's pause, Khan looked at her and replied sternly, "It's the only way."

"Yes would be the answer then." She said considering it as an answer to her question. Laxmi continued, "And then what? Come back to work?"

Khan said with his hand over his head. "No, I knew the consequences."

"I don't think you did." She was no longer showing restraint. "You know until now, I just wanted an explanation. Maybe you were tired of it all and thought this was your way out. But now, I just don't give a damn."

Khan wasn't sure what the last line meant. He knew Laxmi cared for him but the line had been blurred now. "What do you mean?"

"Today is your last day in the city." She paused to look at the change in Khan's expression. He went from confused to startled. "I am issuing a transfer order and you will be shipped off to any place but here." She said throwing her hands in the air.

Khan couldn't believe it. He blurted out, "What about the case?" "Fuck the case!" It was immediate.

This was not acceptable to Khan, "I will not leave the city until it's done."

Laxmi didn't care though, "Then I will arrest you. Put you in a hole."

"And I will escape, you know that." He was referring to something Laxmi knew of.

"All I know is that you are no longer the man I knew. You are not even the man that trained me. You are just a coward who is running away from a fight."

Khan was surprised at what Laxmi had branded him as. But he didn't care anymore. He realized that rather than arguing and defending his point, walking away was the easiest way to get out of this conversation and get back to work. "You are right. I will leave." He turned around to walk away.

"One more thing, the kid. How much was he involved?" Laxmi stopped to confirm her doubts. To check whether the story lined up.

Aware of the trouble he might bestow upon Vasu, Khan plainly stated, "He's a nobody."

"I hope it stays that way."

Khan walked away from Laxmi unable to justify his actions. This was the first time she had spoken against his decision, his choice. He was more upset with the fact that even though she knew the dangers and knew what Yashpal was capable of, it was Khan's actions that were unjustifiable to her. On his way back, Khan had started to doubt the decision he had arrived at. Maybe it was not justifiable to kill Yashpal. Maybe there were means, clues that could bring him to justice. But Khan was unable to find them. Laxmi was scared for her career, Vasu was untrained to understand the intricacies and the rest of the force were disinterested in arresting the criminal. All that mattered to them was less work for the rest. He had grown weary of the lack of action from people. How they were complicit in the crimes due to their inaction, but Khan wasn't going to be one of those drones. He had nothing much to lose. He had no attachments that could drive him towards pacifism. The home and the sleep came sooner than expected for Khan. Maybe it was the impact of the pills but he was not interested in staying awake, finding out what the rest of the day entailed.

Khan's deep slumber was disturbed by his phone. His desire to just lie down had been so strong that he hadn't bothered to take out the items in his pocket. His phone was one of those things. It wasn't the sound but the jolt of vibration that had woken him up. As he pulled out the phone from his pants the pain returned to him. The impact of the shockwave was far too hard on him that he had felt earlier. Even though he knew the drugs weren't out of his system yet, their effects had subsided. The hurt was back. As he picked up the phone, the voice on the other end took away the pain far more effectively than any pills had managed to. It was Yashpal. The voice was undeniably his and Khan didn't want to hear it any more than he had to.

Yashpal spoke first. "This is not how I wanted everything to go." There was genuine emotion behind that line. Khan knew that he would be unable to identify Yashpal's lie but this was the toughest one yet. "You have left me no choice."

That was bullshit and Khan thought so too. He countered, "You always had a choice."

"Unlike you, I don't quit." There was determination.

"I am still here," Khan stated to confirm that he wasn't leaving until the case was over.

But that's now what Yashpal was referring to, "You broke the rules, came by to kill me, didn't you?" He was referring to Khan's withdrawal from his principles. "I had my eyes on you. Maybe I was wrong." Khan knew that he was being watched and entered the house with that knowledge, "I thought you could understand."

Khan wasn't sure what that meant, "Understand what?"

"It's too late for that," Yashpal replied quickly and moved on. "Are you a good driver?" He paused to hear from Khan, but there wasn't any answer so he continued. "You have 20 minutes to save the kids from getting shot."

Khan didn't realize whom Yashpal was referring to. "What kids?"

"From your precious home." It was obvious to him now. "Don't come as the Phantom, I need to look into your eyes when I kill all of them."

Yashpal had disconnected the call before Khan could say anything else. He was aware of the situation he was in, but this was truly dangerous. Less for him and more for the kids that Yashpal was planning to kidnap. It was an open challenge to him. But on the bright side, Yashpal had formed the opinion that Khan was the Phantom. He wasn't aware of Vasu's existence. This was an advantage they were provided with. For a moment Khan's ears were ringing with Laxmi's line; Lucky. That's what was his day was feeling like in hindsight. Khan quickly grabbed the mask, the glasses, and the baton. He dialled

Vasu's number hoping that he could join in and give Khan the edge that he so desired. The phone rang, nine times in fact, but there was no answer. He tried again but now the phone was unreachable. Khan wasn't sure what went wrong. But maybe he thought that yesterday had taken its toll on his willpower. Maybe he didn't want to live the life that Khan had. Khan was hoping that at least Vasu had talked this over, but no time for concern right now. Now certain that there was no advantage, that he was walking into a straight-up fistfight, he prepared for the inevitable. Vasu's gear was still in his hands in the hope that he might turn up and need it. He also checked his pockets. They were here, the pills and the vial. Maybe the paramedics didn't bother checking beyond the gear. Lucky indeed.

Khan drove over to the 9th with speeds that only Mahesh had matched before. Midnight was arriving when he passed the reserve. This increased the possibility of reaching on time. Khan knew he still had 8 minutes, maybe the roads would be clear and he could make it just. They weren't. By the time Khan had reached the home, he was well over 10 minutes late. Worried that he was responsible for the deaths of the kids, he went in, bursting through the door unchecked, not minding the corners. This led to him falling to the ground, knocked out. Black-out.

Khan woke up tied to a chair with his mouth taped up tight around his head. His hands were taped as well. Still groggy from the hit, Khan wasn't able to feel his bound feet at all. Not at the moment. The feeling came in slowly along with the realization that they were in the port on Sector 9. It was the godown that he visited a week earlier. He could now see the men that were about to torture him. They were the robbers, fighters, and assassins of the gangs that the black mask had almost cleared out. These 8 men were presumed dead according to the files and now they were standing intently above 12 kids and Vasu. Khan thought he was hallucinating at first but no, there he was sitting down alongside those kids looking straight at Khan. There was a faint smile growing on Vasu. It was concerning Khan at first to watch as his friend with a sinister smile but soon he realized the meaning of it. He was about to engage and would require Khan to assist. That's what the smile meant. Khan nodded lightly looking at Vasu to acknowledge his message. But just as he tightened his fists and started stretching his legs, one of the guards approached Khan with a phone pointed towards him.

"I am sorry for being late. You know how these fundraisers can be." It was Yashpal. "I understand that you are concerned about the kids, I assure you they will be released once justice is served." He was to be killed and so were the kids probably. "I would have made it quick had you not…" Khan wasn't sure what Yashpal meant. But there was no time either. "Chira"

The guard took the phone back to the other one and they started to discuss something. Khan wasn't able to hear much but he was able to figure out the gist of it as Vasu's expression went from a smug smile to a concerning scowl. He knew it was torture and Vasu would have difficulty handling all of them at once. Khan was aware that he had Vasu's baton and it might have been taken by those guards but he was unaware where. Hoping that Vasu knew, Khan looked at him and nodded to assure him that the plan was on. Three men approached Khan and opened up his right arm. Two of them held him while the other started to stick the tape on uncomfortably tight. Khan was familiar with this tactic, it was to reduce the flow of blood to the arm easing the pain and increasing the chances of survival. The point of all of this of course was to cut off his hand. But the weapon they had settled on wasn't a knife, but a butcher's cleaver. During all of this Khan was using up all of his energy to try and get away causing two more of the guards to hold him down and distract the rest of them. This was a cue for Vasu to get to work.

Vasu was taken along with the kids for fighting back. They wanted to take him but the fact that he had interfered with their business had irked them and wanted to torture him as soon as their task was over. Aware of the danger he was getting into he had interfered in the hope that he could overcome all of them but soon he had realized his limits. The gang that he had previously dealt with seemed like amateurs against this lot. He had difficulty making an impact with his punches. He was knocked out easily and brought here. Vasu was awake by the time the guards had brought in Khan and observed the placement of the baton, the mask, and the glasses. While the glasses and the mask were on the table place near the kids, the baton was held by one of the men pointing a gun at them. Khan's resistance had grabbed all of their attention and had given Vasu the opportunity to get clear and save Khan. The struggle meant that all of the men had given all of their attention to Khan even if they didn't want to. The guard had the baton placed on the back of his jeans, just like one would place a gun. Vasu got up slowly not stealing Khan's spotlight and with a swift motion took the baton from him. By the time the guards had turned around to look at the incident, Vasu had already taken his gear and moved into the shadows at the edge of the godown. He was using it as a cover to move about and create a sense of fear. As two of the guards used all of their body weight to keep Khan's hand in its place, the rest were dedicating their attention to the amateur again. One of them started to fire his handgun near the shadows. His thinking was that the glow of the shot would work as a light while the bullet itself would exterminate any nuisance that plagued them. It was useless. The entire magazine wasted not revealing anyone standing in the shadows. This had intrigued even the men holding Khan's hand. They had their bodies at that place but their eyes were fixated on finding the kid that got away. Vasu unknown to them was behind Khan near the gates as they started a search. He had broken the lens off the chipped side of the glasses and was intending to use it to free Khan. He had managed to sneak towards Khan with utter silence and free up his legs enough for mobility.

This development was not welcomed by the guards who pounced at the visible Vasu. They had him pinned down and were kicking him without remorse. Khan meanwhile had managed to use his working hand and freed the other as well. Using the chair as a weapon. Khan had managed to produce enough adrenaline to lift it with one arm and smash it on one of the guards dropping him to the floor like a sack of potatoes. The attention was on Khan again. He stepped back to bring his hand back to life and stood for attack knowing full well that one of his arms was inoperational. He did have a solution for it. The question was who would step up to get experimented on. Each of the men had three guards on them as they took positions to fight.

Khan to be used. Khan pushed the guard ahead to throw Chira off and managed to punch him hard enough to get him on defence. Khan then threw a series of punches at both of them managing to push them back. This gave the third guard an opening to attack Khan who remained unprepared for the attack. As he took a kick and a couple of punches, Khan had gained enough space to launch his own attack. A body punch followed by a series of hooks and a finishing uppercut. The uppercut was followed by a tackle but not by Khan. It was Chira who had managed to free himself and took Khan down. He sat on Khan preparing for the imminent offence. The punches that came in were hard to defend and even worse to take. Khan had to think of a way out. But there wasn't any. He was in a vulnerable position and bleeding from every wound, old or fresh. After the tenth punch, Khan threw his arms out and took two right to his face. The last one was hard enough to knock his lights out. Chira was happy with the outcome and stood up to take down Vasu. Unfortunately for him, the third step he took towards Vasu was followed by a sharp pain that had managed to bring him down on his knees. All he felt like was to hold his groin so that the pain would go away. It was Khan who had managed to fake his blackout and get free only to kick Chira right in the bollocks.

Khan had to deal with the guard that the phone along with two of his partners while Vasu handled the rest. He knew that complete offence against three wasn't a plausible strategy. So Khan decided to mix it up. He would fight on the back foot saving his deepest wound from a direct attack. The phone guy, 'Chira' took the lead. He stepped first with a right swing at Khan. He leaned back and moved left to attack the middle guard standing there unprepared. He threw three punches of which two landed. One on the face and the other on the abdomen. The guard stepped back to collect himself. Khan knew there would be retaliation from the back but which one would it be, he didn't know. There was a chance that Chira would take the lead and he did. Khan had no option to step back. With each step, the ferocity of the attack grew and so did the danger of getting centred in without defence. Khan dodged a punch, prepared to take the next and glanced back at the guard he had attacked. He was up and vulnerable enough for Vasu meanwhile was overwhelmed with the direct fight with the guards. Even with his baton, he had managed to take down two guards while taking damage that had opened up his wounds. He had also managed to open some new ones. Like Khan, he was bleeding from his cheeks, his temple, one of his eye was swelling up, and his body ached, screaming to be let down for a rest. Vasu refused. The task at hand was important. Even with a quarter of his vision gone Vasu was defending himself from the attacker who had now managed to take Vasu's baton and get control of it. Unknown to him Khan was now free and heading for him. As he started to attack, Vasu dodged as best as he could but it wasn't enough. With two of the hits landing on him, he was on his knees. However, as he looked up it was Khan staring at him, not the guard. He was holding his arm out to help Vasu up. As they stood victorious in another battle together, they shared a laugh at the situation that led to the circumstances.

"How did you get here?"

Vasu explained briefly, "I was there when they came for the kids.

They picked me up to torture because I fought."

Khan placed his hand on Vasu's shoulder and said, "It worked out for the best." He was happy with the situation and soon shifted his attention to the elephant that wasn't in the room. "Was the prick ever here?"

"No. Just passed off his job to the goons."

Khan threw his hands in the air and with utter disappointment said, "Great! Another coward."

"He will come by though." Vasu was referring to the conversation he had eavesdropped on earlier.

"When?"

"I don't know. He said later."

Khan took a deep breath, looked at the kids, and said to Vasu, "Alright. Get these kids home. I will wait here for him."

Vasu wasn't having it. "No, I will wait here with you." "That's not an option." He said sternly.

"Why?" Vasu wanted to know why Khan wanted to face Yashpal alone. They had been on the case together until now.

Khan looked down, sighed, and stated without saying it. "You shouldn't be a witness."

It took Vasu a moment. But as soon as he realized, he asked startled at Khan's endgame, "You're killing him?"

"That's the only way." He tried to justify it. "I don't want to risk him getting away." He was imagining the consequences of his inaction right now. Khan ordered Vasu, "Now, go home."

He looked at Khan and brought out the primary concern, "But you are hurt like me." Another glance and he added, "Worse actually."

"I have this," Khan said while taking the vial of yellow liquid and the syringe from the table.

"What's that?" Vasu wasn't sure.

"Adrenaline." That statement cleared it up and gave Vasu more information than he expected.

He still wasn't' sure about leaving Khan, "But-"

"Vasu, you have done enough." He interrupted assuring Vasu. His hand was on Vasu's shoulder again. "You have done great in fact." He knew this wasn't the nicest thing but it was the right thing. "Go home to your mother." And to add to the convincing argument he said, "I will come and pick you up tomorrow for training. You have a lot to learn."

Reluctantly. Vasu walked away with the kids. Khan thought that maybe Vasu might have realized the lie, but he also knew that mention his mother would weaken his will to stay. It was for the best. Khan put the vial of adrenaline in his pocket hoping that he wouldn't require it. He stepped back at the beaten-up men and took out the guns they had. Khan now equipped with two guns took two of his painkillers, ready to kill Yashpal and end the fight before it even begins.

Vasu took the kids away from the godown and towards the exit. His broken body was responding enough to jog, but he wasn't sure how he would get them home. He had to come up with a plan. Not only for that but to save Khan and take out Yashpal. Khan was in worse shape than him and despite what he had said about the adrenaline, Vasu wasn't sure it would help. As he reached the gates of the port with the kids, a familiar van approached. He gathered the kids and went towards it just to be sure, but he didn't have to. The figure stepping out of the van had relaxed him enough to almost fall down with joy. It was Arjun. He came to the same spot with the same van to rescue the kids.

Vasu was surprised. After their last conversation, he was the last person Vasu expect to show up. "Hey, when-"

Arjun interrupted and said enough, "I heard from the old man.

And…"

Vasu was happy that Arjun showed up and delightfully said. "Alright, get them back home." He kept a smile on while he added. "Come back to pick me up after that." Vasu knew this would upset Khan, Acharya, and even Arjun. But he also knew that this was the right thing to do.

"Why?" Arjun tried to get an answer.

"I'll explain later." He said looking back at the port. "Park away from here." Vasu pointed at the building that Arjun had previously sheltered at, "Take that same spot." He then started to rush towards the set of containers.

"Hey-" Arjun tried to stop him but he knew better now. So, he added enough. "stay safe."

Vasu, with his glasses still on, had managed to walk across the container and hide in anticipation of Yashpal's arrival. He sat down as soon as the van's engine sound faded into the night. He had to rest. The fight with Yashpal was imminent. It was hard for Vasu to stay awake because of the exhaustion. All he wanted to think of right now was his bed and how much more comfortable it would be. He was expecting this to be over tonight and was hoping for a much needed six-month break from it all. Khan would like it, but Vasu was sure he wouldn't be able to stay away from it that long either. Vasu was falling asleep tired from even keeping his eyelids up when the sound in the distance had woken him up. It was a bike at full tap rushing at them probably. It was Yashpal. The sound of the bike had brought back the life in his feet, his grip on the baton had strengthened and he was ready for the showdown. For the first time, Vasu wasn't scared of the upcoming problem. And that fact was concreted with the arrival of Yashpal. He had slowed down as soon as he entered the port and parked the bike next to the godown. Khan's eyes were awake, his brain was at full capacity when a man dressed in a white shirt and black trousers entered the godown.

It was Yashpal. Khan had pointed both the guns at him aiming at his heart and his head.

"It expected this. Where's your mask?"

Khan replied slowly, ready to fire. "I don't need it."

"So what? You are going to kill me?" Yashpal didn't show any sign of fear even when he stood a few feet away from two guns pointing at him.

Khan, reinforcing his intentions replied, "If you don't confess, then yes."

Yashpal nodded and with a determined face replied. "Then you will have to kill me."

Yashpal moved towards the right prompting Khan to shoot at him. Even with bullets firing though, Yashpal was still the fastest one around. He moved through the gunfire faster than Khan could aim and shoot. It was like he was chasing his after image. By the fifth round, Yashpal was close to Khan, holding his guns and raising it towards the roof. Khan couldn't believe what he had witnessed. He had forgotten for the moment that he was supposed to attack or at least defend against Yashpal. The image or rather the lack of it was still haunting him. And in this moment of weakness, Yashpal had managed to seize the opening and went in with a body punch. He then proceeded to attack Khan turning him towards the door and pushing him out with every punch. The cheeks, the jaw, the chest, and even the abdomen were attacked by Yashpal without ever providing the opportunity to retaliate. The final kick to the chest sent Khan out flying outside the godown and into the view of Vasu.

The sound of the gunshot had Vasu convinced that it was over. He was expecting Khan to walk out victorious. But Khan didn't walk out. In fact, he came out on his back falling through the open door. Yashpal had been standing over Khan looking at him intently.

This was Vasu's opening. He rushed towards his target minding the sound even though his heart was pounding out of his chest. Despite all his precautions, Yashpal heard Vasu running at him and turned around to face him. Vasu didn't hesitate to engage first. His baton was aimed at Yashpal's head. He swung with intent to at least knock him out. But the fact that he was aware of Vasu's attack was in and of itself a defeat. He stopped the titanium rod coming down to strike him with one hand. He then proceeded to use the elbow to uppercut Vasu causing him to hit the floor. Both Khan and Vasu lay on the floor stumped, stunned by the skills of a seemingly harmless man. He wasn't harmless in his actions, but every interaction they had never gave a hint to what physical harm he was capable of. Yashpal leaned down towards Vasu and looked at him carefully. The broken lens and the open eye was intriguing him as if he was solving the mystery of Vasu's identity.

"This is an interesting development." There was half a smile on Yashpal's face. "So…" He looked at Khan and then back at Vasu. "Fuck!" He said swinging his head down in disappointment. "You are not the Phantom." The smile turned to anger as he stated, "I guess that's why Rudra got arrested."

Khan takes this opportunity to get up and engage Yashpal again. This time the offence was strong and it had managed to push him away from Vasu. None of the attacks were landing. All of them were either deflected or dodged. But the fact that Khan had him defending himself had brought back the confidence he'd lost inside. After a few attacks, fourteen to be precise, Khan's attack was not only blocked but was retaliated against. Yashpal's defence was working along with his offence and soon they had switched sides. It was as if he was defending to understand Khan's technique. Once he had studied that, Khan was no longer in control of the fight. In fact, the first few attacks were hard but defendable the next series of punches and kicks were once again overwhelming. A jab, a punch in the abdomen, an elbow to the bicep, and a knee again in the abdomen dropping Khan was on his knees. The power in Yashpal's attacks was unbelievable. He knew this fight might be over now.

Vasu looking at Yashpal's fight against Khan was stumped at how badly he knew they would be defeated. If Khan didn't stand a chance, a man who went toe-to-toe with Rudra, Vasu wasn't even playing the same game. Despite the fact that this man was completely undefeatable, Vasu picked up his baton and charged at Yashpal with the intention to kill. Even Vasu was surprised at how much ferocity he was displaying. Yashpal was easily avoiding Vasu's swing to the head, shoulders, legs, and even a wild swing at his abdomen. Once Vasu was through and tired, Yashpal started his attacks. The punches felt like a bullet. But the shooting didn't stop. Each of Vasu's body parts, each section of his body storing a vital organ was hit by Yashpal and to finish it off he pulled out a knife from his back and sliced Vasu's thigh bringing him down hard on his butt. Khan hadn't seen the knife before, not until it was red with blood. It was a combat knife similar to what he'd used but larger. The grip was black and the blade seemed to be Damascus steel. But blood was covering it up. There was anger in Yashpal's attacks on Vasu. What he was doing to Khan was just game but to Vasu it was different, there was intent. Khan had picked up on that and figured that Phantom's hands were sullied with Rudra's blood. This was revenge. Khan got up and walked towards Yashpal. Instead of attacking him, he checked up on Vasu. The wound wasn't deep but the pain would feel the same. Khan knew there was no way Vasu was getting up. He had to end this fight alone.

"See, his punishment for helping you," Yashpal said, first pointing at Vasu. And then pointing to Khan added, "Now, your turn."

Khan got up and position himself four feet away from Yashpal calming his mind to attack. He knew the weakness in his body, the difference in skill, and of the lack of weapon but he didn't care. All that mattered to him was this fight had to end. Khan attacked but didn't manage to lay his fist down. In fact, he couldn't get past two punches before Yashpal came in with the knife. He started with the big one. One slice across the chest. This pushed back Khan but didn't deter him away from the fight. The next to be attacked were his arms. Yashpal had abandoned his defence to grab Khan's arm and slice it down. Despite Khan's punches to the face or abdomen, he couldn't push Yashpal away. The only way his hand managed to get free was when there were seven slices across his entire arm. That hand was now useless, with limited mobility and zero attacking capability. Yashpal then proceeded to do the same with Khan's other arm, now with kicks hitting him. It was done. There would be no punches coming his way. Eight slices were made on the other arm. Yashpal wasn't done. He then proceeded to slice down and across his abdomen. There was nothing but red visible now on Khan's upper body. This didn't bring down Khan to the delight of Yashpal who got close and simply slit Khan's throat.

Vasu watched as Yashpal went through his partner, his mentor, and friend. There was nothing he was able to do. Vasu knew the moment attacks began, it was over. But the realization hadn't washed him over until Khan's motionless body fell revealing nothing but crimson on his entire upper body. Vasu had to drag himself towards Khan. He didn't want to leave him but more importantly, he didn't want Khan to leave him either. As he approached Khan, the wetness and the stickiness of the blood were churning his stomach. It didn't matter. He knew it was over. As he rested Khan's head on his feet Vasu didn't even mind the pain. All that mattered was saving Khan. He put his hand over the wound on his neck. He tried to imitate the things he had learned in a movie but it wasn't working. He was frustrated. Khan however was looking at Vasu and raised his arm to say something. Vasu took his friend's arm and gripped it as tightly as he could. It was cold. Vasu looked at Khan and brought his head closer to him in the hope that he could hear his last words. But there was nothing. There was nothing but the weight of Khan's hand. It grew more and more. His eyes had begun to glaze. Vasu was now in tears scared at what was next. Unknown to him he was now holding the lifeless body of his friend. It took him a moment to realize after which he got as close as he could to Khan and dropped a few tears in silence. Vasu was angry. Not only at Yashpal but at his inability to save his friend.

"I will kill you." Vasu was saying that in a low yet determined voice. He had gripped Khan's hand tightly.

"You will do nothing of the sort." Yashpal was now relaxed. He knew the fight was over and anything the Phantom would say was no longer of concern to him. "In fact, you will return back to your life with the knowledge that you will always lose."

Vasu tried his best to deny it. "I won't-"

But Yashpal wasn't listening. He stated his determination, "You will. Or I will do this to your loved one right in front of your eyes. I will stab them while you sit and scream. But you know what I will do first, I will frame you for his murder." He said pointing at Vasu, "Yes, the Phantom killed Inspector Khan." He continued gesturing his hands to imitate the shape of the headline bar on news. "That will be the headlines tomorrow." Yashpal paused to look at the Phantom, get close to Khan's body, and lent down to match the eye level. He said, "Don't put on the mask again, or getting shot will be the best thing to happen to you." Yashpal was now just showing off his confidence. He didn't have to know the identity of the Phantom. It didn't matter who was behind the mask, he was ready to destroy him. He stood up and hit a few keys on his phone stating to Phantom "You have 7 minutes to escape."

"Why?" Yashpal looked at thinking the question was referring to his previous statement. But the next question cleared it up. "Why would to kill him, any of them?"

He didn't want to have the conversation, but after a brief thought, Yashpal sat down near Khan keeping his distance from Vasu, and replied, "Because all of them are guilty." He continued, "Everyone." Yashpal said while pointing at Khan, "He wanted to kill me without thinking about the law." He then pointed at godown hinting at the gang members, "Those filthy criminals wanted to just exploit everyone for money." And finally pointing at Vasu he said, "You are guilty of helping him try and kill me. You are a partner in the conspiracy to murder." Yashpal gestured to Vasu's injuries and continued. "That is your punishment."

Vasu thought about it. For a weak second, Yashpal's justification seemed right. But he quickly realized the hypocrisy, "So are you, killing them all."

"That I am. Go on then, try to kill me." Yashpal said getting up and opening his arms to embrace his fate. He then straightened up and continued, "It's my destiny to change this city, the people. That's why I never fail. I will never fail." He said the last like pointing at him. "And everyone who has tried to stop me, look." His finger was now pointing at Khan.

Vasu didn't have anything to say. He had his head down but then the thought of Khan and Talpade brought back the missing character, "And was Rudra trying to stop you?"

Yashpal paused briefly before replying, "He was the only friend.

I did what he had asked me to do. What a brother would do."

Vasu didn't understand what type of person would justify killing his friend. He stated his disgust, "You are sick, a psycho."

"And you are an amateur." Yashpal snapped back. "Two minutes."

Vasu had to think of his escape. Arjun was probably waiting for him but he had to make his way towards the van. He could call Arjun and get him to bring the Van around but that would be just plain stupid and dangerous. He tried to get up but the pain had managed to bring him down before his feet were flat. The adrenaline he thought. Maybe it wouldn't work just as well as Khan had described but it would help him overcome the pain and get to the escape point. Vasu checked Khan's pockets and found the vial with the syringe. It was no time to be afraid of it. He filled it as best as he could. He wasn't sure what amount was safe but right now he just eye-balled it. Ready to stab himself with the hypodermic needle he held the syringe as tightly as he could like a knife in a stabbing position and buried it in the thigh of the healthy leg pushing down the liquid. It was far more painful than he had imagined. But in terms of management, it was like a paper cut compared to the knife wound.

There was nothing for a few seconds but suddenly he felt the pain in his body fade away. Vasu suddenly had the strength to get up and run. He didn't risk running but he did start walking away. Vasu was afraid that going through the front gate was a trap. He might just end up walking straight into the media and the police. And the fact that he had Khan's blood on his person wouldn't help his innocence. As he passed the gate, Vasu turned around to look at Yashpal who was staring at him waiting for him to make a move. He knew that going to attack him would lead to defeat and death. Not only would that be pointless but Khan's death, Talpade's death both will go down in vain. He had to make it worth it. He had to avenge them. Swallowing his pride down, Vasu resumed waking towards the container on the other side. He was familiar with the route and knew that it would provide enough cover for escape. Vasu's guess was right. Just as he was going through the container in the shadows, the noise of the police cars and the ambulances were in the air. He got on the container struggling to keep his wounded leg in check. There was no other way but to jump over the wall. As he got on and sat up, he could see the flashes of red and blue causing him to remove his mask and glasses. This would help him in case he was seen by any of the arriving cavalries. They drove out to the front gate of the port clearing Vasu a window of opportunity. He jumped and barely caught on the wall. He was struggling to pull his body but managed to do it enough to get his leg over. This action gave him relief but he had accidentally relaxed his body leading to falling down the 20-foot wall. Even the adrenaline was refusing to help here. He laid there for a second before realizing the situation and got up to walk. His movements were now as slow as they had been before the adrenaline but to his luck, Arjun had pulled out of their designated spot and got his van near Vasu to let him in. At this point, the blood from his wounds had collected itself enough to dampen his right trouser leg and he had lost all feeling from it. He limped near the van door and with struggle managed to get on and sit down, passing out immediately.

Vasu woke up in a familiar place. It was the sleeping quarters of the home. He had trouble moving his body, but the feeling in his leg was returning. The pain was there but it was no longer as harsh. It felt the same as it had with the adrenaline. Vasu could feel the weight on both of his arms. Both were stuck with I.V. As he looked around for their contents, he saw a bag of blood for his right arm and some clear liquid connected to his left. At the foot of his bed was Chirag. He was reading his novel, not aware of Vasu gaining consciousness. It was difficult for Vasu to speak so he managed to make a noise quickly shifting Chirag's attention to him. He got up smiled and stepped out of the room. In just a few seconds, Chirag came back with Acharya and Arjun. Both of them were relieved but still worried. There was a faint smile that arrived with great difficulty. As best he could, Vasu managed to squeeze a word out, "K-Kids-"

Acharya stated with an assuring tone, "They are safe." And sat down by Vasu's bed.

"How-"

Acharya realized the question and answered swiftly, "Arjun brought you here and we called a doctor to save you."

Arjun added to Acharya's reply, "You had bled too much and required immediate attention. Luckily he knows a few people." He said pointing at the old man.

"Those are just good people who want to help." Acharya was looking at Vasu. He realized what Khan's death meant to him. What the events tonight would eventually lead to. He wanted to check whether Vasu was ready to process his anger and sorrow. "What happened? Are feeling okay to talk about it?"

"L-Lo-Lost." That was the only word he could utter about the situation. That was enough. He closed his eyes remembering the events leading to the arrival of the police and ambulance and realized the horde of reporters that would have been there as well, "TV-TV"

Acharya knew that would not help now. "Rest for now. You can watch it later."

But Vasu wanted to know. He wanted to find out the extent of the defeat. "Now"

Acharya looked towards Chirag and stated. "Bring the small one here."

Chirag stepped out of the room and after a minute came back with a small antenna TV. He connected the wire to the nearest plug and Turned it on. After a few seconds, he had found the signal to the news channel and it played.

"-a difficult day for all of us. Earlier today Yashpal Vohra, the candidate for Mayor was brutally attacked by the assailant known as the Phantom. Yashpal along with CI Ashraful Khan were working together to catch the criminal looking for clues at the port on Sector 9. That's when they were ambushed by the Phantom who fatally wounded Khan and wounded Yashpal. The attacker was deterred by the arrival of the police. CI Ashraful Khan died saving Yashpal Vohra. Let's hear from Mr Vohra himself again."

Yashpal was standing with a bloodied shirt. There were stitches on his arm that Vasu was surprised with. "We had been working together on the case for quite a while. I had extended my support to Khan aware of his reputation as an incorruptible man. During the course of the investigation, we had managed to discover multiple clues that led us to Sector 9 where we were ambushed, and I... I lost my friend. We had warned the investigating officers earlier about another attack but they refused to do anything. Working for a corrupt government, all they cared about was the money their master threw at them. But Khan, he was the only man in the entire police force working selflessly. And that criminal, he murdered him. I promise everyone, even if I don't win the election, I will bring the Phantom to justice."

"Mr Vohra was attending a fund-raiser just a few hours ago. According to the guests, he left early after a worrying phone call. There were also speculations that the earlier terror attack on Mr Vohra's house was from the Phantom. This would very much solidify that assumption and turn the masked criminal into a terrorist. The statement received from the office of CG has declared that there is no conclusive proof connecting the Phantom to the bombings, only the accounts of eyewitnesses. They are exploring the angle with appropriate scrutiny and will solve the case soon. We will be back with the debate on what punishment should the Phantom receive for his crimes. Stay tuned for that exclusive debate."

Vasu closed his eyes and took deep breaths to control his anger and anxiety. The scale of his defeat had just hit him and it was clear, there was no turning back from it all. He was a terrorist in the eyes of the public, Yashpal was a victim and Khan's sacrifice might go down in vain. He had to make peace with it all. He had to move on

What's next?

How would Vasu deal with this loss? Will he ever be able to get out of Khan's shadow and bring Yashpal to justice? Will he ever be able clear his name and remove the tag of a terrorist? Or will Yashpal win the elections and take over the entire city? Will Yashpal leave Vasu alone? Or was it all a ruse to get him into more trouble? What was the purpose of the cookie dough?

All of the above question will be answered in the second book of the Renaissance series. Megalomania will explore the impact that Khan had on Vasu and the choice he made as a result of his exposure to the events of this book.